Truth Seeker

Amy Denson

Chapter One

A guttural moan sliced through the darkness of the truck's cab, causing Rhett to jump.

"Come on, man! Make your free throws!"

Rhett glared at Jake. "Are you trying to give me a heart attack?"

"It's not my fault no one on the team can make a free throw." Jake was clearly unmoved by their current situation. "What time was this guy supposed to show, anyway? We're going to miss the whole second half."

"He said ten sharp. Let's give him another five minutes, then we'll leave."

"Are you sure someone isn't messing with you? He's already fifteen minutes late. This whole thing seems like a set-up to me." Jake surveyed his mirrors.

Rhett scrolled through his text messages, again, to verify the details. The bright screen in the dark parking garage was blinding. "Five more minutes." He turned back to his cameraman questioningly. "We're losing by twenty. Do you really want to see the second half?"

"Well, if they had made their free throws, we would only be down by fourteen. But, to answer your question, yes. I would much rather be sitting on my favorite stool with beer and a basket of wings." Jake grumbled as he refreshed his phone. "Tell me again why we couldn't meet on the top level, where I actually had service? This guy has watched too many movies. Meeting in the bottom of a parking garage? Who does that?"

"Apparently, we do." Rhett shrugged.

The minutes dragged on as Jake griped about the game and Rhett tried to decipher info about their secret informant.

Suddenly, Rhett nudged Jake, "Look, lights."

The mood in the truck quickly changed. Jake grabbed his camera and focused it on the column near the elevator bank. "Remember, try to get him over there. That's my best chance to get anything clear. Make sure your phone is recording too. Do a sound check as you're walking."

"I've done this before, Mom. You just worry about not being seen." Rhett took a deep breath and climbed out of Jake's Big Horn. "All right, *Deep Throat*, let's see what's so important that we had to meet incognito."

A vehicle pulled in slowly under the low beams of the garage. The driver deliberately stayed close to the shadows, carefully avoiding the brightest parts of the chosen location. Rhett approached cautiously as the driver parked in an unlit corner.

"Of course he found the absolute worst spot. The one place you said not to stand." Rhett mumbled. Jake cursed in the earpiece.

A tall, slender man climbed out of the silver sedan. Hugging the front corner of his rental car, he situated himself directly behind a column. The man's face remained hidden in the shadows. The hair on the back of Rhett's neck stood on edge at this point. Something was off. He could feel it.

Rhett was used to meeting sources in strange locations at all hours, but not since becoming lead anchor at WBN. People were weird and wanted to hide behind anonymity, but this guy literally hid behind a column in the shadows. Mentally, Rhett replayed the cryptic phone call he received that morning. The informant worked for a high-ranking politician and had CIA ties. Something about having evidence of corruption on a jump drive. That he couldn't stay silent anymore, blah, blah, blah. He had Rhett at the mention of hard evidence and exclusive story rights.

Based on their location, Rhett worried Jake wouldn't get this guy on film, but hoped they could find something useful. Rhett guardedly walked toward the man, leaving enough space for a quick getaway. "Any way I can get you to come out from behind that column?"

The man's face was shrouded in shadows. "You want this? You have to come for it."

Rhett sucked in his breath and walked to his informant, knowing Jake would be listening for any sign in Rhett's voice to pounce on the guy.

Incognito Man leaned in closer to Rhett. His eyes darted back and forth to scan the area.

Rhett began, "Good evening. I hope this clandestine meeting is worth all the hype. I'm Rhett Paulson from World Broadcasting Network, but you already know that. Can I finally get your name?"

This man was on edge and fidgety. "Are you sure you weren't followed?"

Rhett's annoyance level rose. "Well, I've been waiting here for thirty minutes and yours are the only headlights I've seen, so I'm guessing we're safe."

"Don't be so sure. You have no idea how many people want to keep this quiet. The information I have for you can take down the entire government and more."

"So you said earlier. Look, I appreciate all the suspense, but I need something more than this film noir plot we've got going on here. If you have evidence, I need it, and I need to know where and how you got it. If it was illegally obtained, I need to know that too." Rhett leveled the man with a gaze. This guy looked like every other bureaucrat in Washington.

A sardonic chuckle escaped the man's throat. "You may call me Nathan Hale. I assure you, I have obtained everything legally. You can use all of it under the Whistleblower Act. Most of these documents are public and easily found, if you know where to look. The key is knowing *how* they all connect and *why* those connections are so important. Washington is great at hiding evidence in plain sight. This jump drive connects all the dots. I just hope you have the guts to expose it. I know who you are, and I don't trust you one bit. But, my handler told me you used to be credible at one time, and he trusts you, so here I am."

That bristled Rhett. He shook it off, as usual. "I'm not sure if that's an insult or a compliment, but I am intrigued by all of this. I can assume I'm not to know the name of this 'handler' either?" Rhett studied the man, trying to place him. "Nathan Hale? Your alias is the first spy hanged in the Revolutionary War? I take it you're not a superstitious man."

"On the contrary. I know my fate. I'm just trying to get as much information out there as I can before they find me."

"They? Who are 'they' and *what* don't they want getting out?" Rhett was growing tired of this guy's cloak-and-dagger-clichés.

He watched in slow motion as the man's face changed. Tires squealed in the periphery, filling the silence. The man's arm moved so quickly, Rhett barely caught the motion. "I hope your friend can still catch as well as he did in college."

Shocked by the personal reference, Rhett's glare pierced the night. Venom dripped with every word from his mouth. "What did you just say?"

"Welcome to the revolution, Mr. Paulson." The man raised his arms up over his head, obviously surrendering to whoever was coming. Then he crumpled to the ground.

Searing pain racked Rhett's left shoulder. The ringing in his ear muffled everything but its own incessant throbbing. Adrenaline, clearly running in overdrive, pumped blood to his already fast beating heart. His body lurched, riddled with a mixture of shaking and hyperawareness. Thoughts of "How did I get here?" played on repeat in Rhett's over-educated brain.

He couldn't even remember where the gunfire came from, only that it hit his informant right between the eyes. Rhett had covered war zones, but he had never been this close to the front line of a firefight until tonight.

Today had started like every other day. He woke up. Ate scrambled eggs. Drank a protein shake. Worked out in his gym for an hour. Showered. Reviewed show notes while his driver fought through city traffic on the way to WBN headquarters. It was a good day. Until he got a phone call from Nathan Hale.

Voices surrounded him. Jake's face blurred in Rhett's line of sight. He watched Jake's lips move, but he couldn't hear anything but ringing. He felt cold and wet, sticky wet. Everything faded to black.

Chapter Two

The busyness outside of the plastic curtain, along with the continuous beeping of machines, was irritating. Shuffling feet and whispered conversations floated around every corner. The sounds of a hospital were unmistakable and downright unnerving.

Madison Lyn breathed deeply as her doctor carefully tugged, pulled, and snipped. She studied a small green stain on the wall. Anything to keep herself from getting dizzy again. Madison was grateful she didn't have to wait long, but definitely itching to get out of this place.

"There you go, Ms. Lyn. Beautiful. You should barely notice any scarring on that gorgeous face of yours. It's some of my best work." The plastic surgeon beamed with pride. His overconfident grin made her more nauseous than the pain medicine had earlier.

Madison inwardly rolled her eyes at the man's arrogance, but was grateful that he came in on a Friday night to stitch up the gash on her head. "Thank you, Dr. Werner. I really appreciate it."

"Well, Cashe *cashed* in his favor." Dr. Werner laughed at his own joke. "See what I did there? Cashe? Cashed?"

Madison worked hard to offer a fake laugh. "I got it. That's a good one. Funny."

"Becky will be back in to clean you up and give you care instructions. It was really great meeting you, Ms. Lyn." Dr. Werner patted her hand. As he turned to saunter out of the room, he paused. "On second thought, I can take a break and come back with coffee if you're up for some company?"

Ugh, no! "Thank you so much, but I think I'll pass on the coffee. Not feeling very social right now. Head wound and all." Madison offered a conciliatory smile and pointed to her wound.

Undeterred, Dr. Werner winked with the entire right side of his face. "Becky will give you my number if you need anything. Or change your mind about the coffee."

Madison gave him a half smile. "Thank you, doctor."

He winked again, but this time added a finger gun in her direction. Madison cringed. As Dr. Werner turned the corner, she groaned and shook off the ick from his inflated charisma. The smell of antiseptic permeated the air. The sterile space was small and packed with equipment. A repetitive beeping became deafening. Madison's ears rang and her head throbbed.

"Wow, that guy was a real tool."

Madison looked at the curtain next to her bed where the sound came from, not sure if she was hearing things. "Is someone there?"

The pale green curtain opened. A guy wearing a backward baseball cap and a shoulder sling sat on the bed parallel to hers. "The doctor. I'm assuming that's who was gushing over his own handiwork."

Madison bristled. "Dr. Werner is an excellent plastic surgeon. He has earned the right to gush over his own work. Now, if you will excuse me." She gestured to the curtain and hoped the mystery guy would close it. He didn't.

"Ouch, that looks like a nasty cut. They loaded you up with stitches."

Madison's hand instinctively covered her forehead. She spared a glance in his direction. "You don't look so great yourself."

The man laughed. "Yeah, this won't be easy to explain on air."

That caught Madison's attention. She looked over at the man's face as he grinned. She uttered a small curse to herself. "Great, you guys will seriously do anything for a little dirt."

His face contorted in confusion. "I'm sorry, what?"

"You're Rhett Paulson, right?"

The baseball hat guy nodded in response.

"Do you want some type of statement as to why I'm here in the ER with twelve stitches in my head? Because you're not getting one." Madison lifted her phone and started frantically texting.

Madison: WHERE ARE YOU???? Tell Rich the press is here.

"Well, I was just trying to make small talk. I've been in this curtain cocoon waiting on my discharge for hours. I was just bored and being polite, but now I'm very curious. Is there a reason the twelve stitches in *your* head are newsworthy enough that someone would fake a trauma center visit to get *the dirt?*"

"Do you not know who I am?" Madison cringed at herself. "Good grief, that sounded so obnoxious," Embarrassment covered her face as she closed her eyes. "This day just keeps getting better."

"I don't. And now, I'm a little afraid to ask. I certainly don't want to be one of 'those people' you obviously don't like." Rhett laughed. He clearly enjoyed this.

Madison steeled herself for this conversation. She gently sat up in her hospital bed, attempting some form of professionalism. A campaign smile firmly in place now. "Allow me to start over. Hi, my name is Madison Lyn. I am the Presidential Campaign Manager for Senator Jackson Cashe."

Rhett tilted his head to study Madison. "So you are."

"So I am." Madison bobbed her head in response, waiting for him to stay more.

"I see it now. You'll have to excuse me. My investigative journalism skills are a little hindered today." Rhett pointed to his shoulder. "Gun-shot wound, concussion, pain meds. Pretty girl sitting in front of me." He shrugged at Madison with a cocky grin.

"Gunshot wound, wow. Unhappy fan?" Madison deadpanned, trying to deflect the cheap compliment.

"Ah, yes. I definitely see it now. The political expert, not injured enough to let down her guard, has successfully changed the subject and rebounded the question back to me. Impressive, even with twelve stitches." Rhett flashed his own impressive smile at her.

Madison tried hard, but unsuccessfully, to prevent a chuckle from escaping her lips. "Guilty as charged. Sorry. Most of my dealings with the press these days aren't usually positive. The press is Rich's department."

"Ah, yes. Rich Miller, PR spin master extraordinaire."

"I definitely won't tell him you said that. It will go straight to his head, and he'll be even more insufferable than he already is." Madison immediately covered her mouth as soon as the words slipped out. Rich drove her crazy every day, but she loved him like a brother and didn't want her words twisted into something she didn't mean. "Please don't repeat that. Rich is a great guy and a dear friend. I meant it to be funny."

Rhett held up his good hand in a truce, "Hey, as far as I'm concerned, we're just two people trying to get out of the hospital after having really bad days."

Madison allowed herself to relax a little. "Thank you." The following lull in conversation became filled with more beeping and shuffling in the hallway. Madison wasn't sure which was worse.

"A normal person would ask how you ended up here, but I'd hate to upset the balance of veiled secrecy we have between us." Rhett nodded toward the bandages on his shoulder.

Madison tried hard not to notice the dimples highlighting his cheeks. "Does your line of work usually result in trauma visits, or was this a personal matter?"

He laughed, which caused the dimples to deepen. "No. I rarely get shot at while working. In fact, this is my first gunshot wound, believe it or not. I'd elaborate, but the FBI sweetly insisted I keep this to myself for now."

"Wow, first you call me pretty, then you namedrop the FBI. You really are a typical news jock." Madison was enjoying this conversation.

A hard laugh ripped through Rhett's chest as he tried to hold his arm into place with a wince. "I can honestly say that I have never been called a news jock before, and I'm not sure if I'm offended or amused."

"I guess you need to work that out for yourself." Madison smiled more flirtatiously than she had intended.

"So, how does a presidential campaign manager get a nasty cut on her head? Or is that also under FBI protection?"

Madison stared at him, deciding whether she wanted to share the information. He looked right back at her. She decided the truth was better than speculation.

"I currently live on a campaign bus with two guys. There was an incident with the refrigerator door, a frozen bag of strawberries, and a blender. I ducked in the wrong direction." Madison shrugged.

"That sounds interesting. I hope the drink was worth it."

"I'll have to ask Rich." Madison smiled as she lifted her phone to read a text message that came in.

Jackson: SS wants me to stay in lockdown on the bus. Rich is on his way to pick you up. He should be there soon. Ask the nurse to switch your bed away from the press. Are you okay?

Madison: I'm fine. False alarm with press. Tell Rich Dr. Werner moved me to a private wing in the ER.

Madison dropped her phone into her lap, then looked back at Mr. Dimples. "Sorry about that. Jackson was checking on me. My ride is on the way."

Rhett's expression made Madison uncomfortable. She glanced away as he blurted out, "So are you two a thing? Off the record, of course."

This caught Madison off guard. She shook her head, adamantly getting her point across. "Nooooo. Jackson, Rich, and I are best friends. We were roommates in college. Nothing more." She wasn't sure why she felt nervous suddenly. Madison had nerves of steel. That's what made her so good at her job.

"*Are* you seeing anyone? I sure hope you're not seeing Dr. Tool, who was flirting with you earlier."

Madison chuckled again. This guy made her laugh, that's for sure. "Not much time for dating when you're running a presidential campaign. We're constantly traveling and working. There's also that 'reporter' angle to worry about." Madison pinned him with a look, daring him to argue. "Besides, I think the only person who Dr. Werner is in love with is Dr. Werner."

"I tend to agree with you about the good doctor, but you didn't really answer my question."

Rhett's smile warmed her to the core. "No, I'm not." Madison shook her head. *Bad idea, Madsi.*

"Well, since I'm single, and you're single. Maybe we can be single together. On a date." There he went with that news jock, cocky look.

"I'm guessing you don't hear 'no' often."

"No, but in my defense, I don't ask nearly as often as one would think. I too am a very busy person. I only ask when the subject interests me."

"Interests you? You should work on your pickup lines, Mr. Paulson."

"Call me Rhett, please. I'm hoping my charm and the wounded dog angle will work in my favor. You didn't say no yet." Rhett looked like a kid waiting for someone to give him an all-day sucker.

Thankfully, two nurses rounded the corner, giving Madison a momentary reprieve to think about the possibility.

"Mr. Paulson, I have your discharge papers. Matt here will chauffer you out of our fine establishment. You are clear to go and your ride is waiting in the fire lane. Ms. Lyn, I will bandage you up and get you on your way." Nurse Becky was all business.

Madison watched Rhett climb into the waiting wheelchair. He attempted to hide the pain that laced his face, but it only made him cuter. *Bad idea Madsi.*

"Well, I'm still waiting for an answer." Rhett looked at her with anticipation and a rotten grin.

"Ugh. Maybe," she groaned.

"Yes! Matt, get me out of here before she changes her mind." Matt turned the wheelchair and started down the hallway. Rhett called over his shoulder, "I'll find you. You won't regret it. I know a great Italian place!"

Madison dropped her head forward, momentarily forgetting about her injury. The throbbing intensified.

"He's a cutie." Nurse Becky smiled at Madison as she opened a packet of gauze and laid her tools along Madison's bed.

"That's the problem. They're always cute. Until they're not." Madison settled her head back onto the pillow and closed her eyes.

"Tell me about it, sweetheart." Becky laughed and went to work.

Chapter Three

Rhett spent the weekend sleeping off the effects of pain meds and trauma. His head hurt, his shoulder ached, and his brain worked overtime, but he had to figure out the dead guy's angle. Rhett felt exhilarated at the prospect of a new investigative piece. It had been a long time since he found his own stories and even longer since he dug up his own research and evidence.

Now, all Rhett had was a bottomless pit of questions and no source. If he only knew the dead guy's name, he could piece together a lead to follow. Rhett focused on the facts, but even those were confusing. Nathan Hale worked for an unknown politician. He had FBI ties, and apparently, he was a Revolutionary War buff. One with a death wish who watched too many detective movies. Once they released the police report, Rhett would at least get a name. He sighed in frustration.

Elevator doors slid open with precision. "Get out of bed, you lazy worm." Jake's voice carried all the way through the penthouse.

Rhett groaned and took another long drink of coffee before he answered, "I'm awake and in the kitchen."

Jake rounded the corner and dropped a stack of newspapers and a casserole dish on the kitchen counter. "I hope you feel as bad as you look."

"Thanks?" Rhett rubbed his temple with his good hand and peered at Jake with one eye opened. "Remind me again why I gave you the elevator code?"

"Because I'm the only person you trust. Because you've known me since we were eight. Because your sorry butt would be lost without me. Shall I go on?" Jake grabbed a handful of grapes from the bowl on the counter.

Rhett finally pried open both eyes. He leaned his head toward the goods Jake delivered. "Please tell me your wife's lasagna is in this container."

"Yes, Alexis made you lasagna. She wants you to know she's furious at you for getting shot and getting me shot at, but she still loves you and is worried about you."

"I thought for sure she would have come over this weekend to yell at me in person." Rhett peeked under the tinfoil. "Mmm, it smells so good."

"She tried, but I assured her the doctors drugged you up so you wouldn't appreciate her fury."

"I can't believe that worked." Rhett laughed at the thought of anything restraining the fierce and persistent Alexis Marchio Baker.

"It didn't. I distracted her with ice cream. You're lucky she's pregnant. You owe me."

Rhett smirked. "Put it on my tab."

"I'm also supposed to make sure you come over for dinner and to watch the game." Jake popped a grape into his mouth. "She misses you."

"Your wife is amazing. She's too good to me."

"I agree. She is amazing, and she is definitely too good to you." Jake laughed at his own joke. He pulled out a stool and sat down before picking up the stack of papers he brought.

"What's up with all that? Need help with your homework, Jakey?" Now Rhett laughed at his own corny joke.

Jake spread the printed news stories across the table. He pointed to each headline. "These are the top news stories for the weekend. Look. Nothing. Nothing today, nothing yesterday. Not one word about what happened to you. Not in print. Not on their websites. Not even on our own station. Nothing. A firefight between the FBI and an at-large-sniper who targeted a political operative. All of which involved a celebrity journalist. An influential man, shot dead in a Washington, D.C. parking garage, and not one word. The only outlet to mention it was Patriot News, and their headline was sketchy at best." Jake flipped through the papers to find the one he needed. "Here it is, 'Beloved Propaganda Spinner for WBN Involved in FBI Raid: No Comment from the Network, Paulson, or the FBI'."

"Aww, they think I'm 'beloved.' That is the nicest thing they have ever said about me. My favorite was when they called me, what was it, 'a slimy buffoon?' My Grammy loved that one." Rhett ignored the papers. Stiffness consumed his achy body as he sipped his coffee.

"Say what you will about them, but they're the only ones who wrote about the incident."

"Jake, come on. I know you like their crazy conspiracy theory crap, but you can't seriously believe the garbage they print."

Jake ignored the slight jab. "Take a step back and think for a minute. Put on your investigator's hat and listen. Don't you think it's weird that there's an FBI raid involving WBN's top anchor injured during a shootout in the middle of D.C., and no one is covering it? Not to mention that the government-employee-yet-to-be-named victim is *still* nameless? Seriously, Rhett, the FBI literally owns a database of fingers and faces, yet they don't know the guy's identity even though they *have* his fingers and face? That's insane."

"No."

"No? That's it? Just no? An informant is taken out by a sniper seconds before the FBI raids our meeting, and you don't even bat an eyelash." Jake shook his head in annoyed defeat. "I don't get you. You've changed."

"Not this again, Jake. I don't know what you want from me. I haven't changed, my hands are tied. This is an active FBI investigation! Of course, there isn't anything in the news. We're not even allowed to talk about it." Rhett pushed himself off the stool and carried his mug to the sink. "Think about it this way. When the story leaks, and it will leak, we'll have the exclusive because we were there when it happened."

Jake shook his head, obviously irritated. "So, are you going to completely ignore a story because the FBI told you to, or will you at least keep the coverup angle in your back pocket?"

Rhett looked at Jake like his friend was crazy. "I never drop a story completely. I'm just going in a different direction unless the sails turn. I always bet on the biggest headline. I want to focus on the guy, not the coverup. Now, let's get moving. I need to figure out who that guy was and what he wanted to share with me that got him killed. I wish that sniper gave me five more minutes."

"Rhett! A man died! *You* almost died!"

"I know. I didn't mean it that way and you know it. It's just, I think he knew he was going to die. I can't explain it. I wish I knew what he was willing to die for before he died. If that makes sense." Rhett rubbed the back of his head, careful to avoid the goose egg where he hit the cement.

Jake pulled out an object from his jacket pocket. It looked like a keychain in the shape of a fishing lure. Jake pried it opened and exposed a jump drive. As he held it up, Rhett could see the words "Ears are everywhere," written on the connector. Jake put it back together before placing the concealed jump drive on the counter.

"While you were in the ER, the FBI showed up at the hospital and grilled me about the meeting. They wanted to know why we were there and who arranged it. They really wanted to know if *Deep Throat* gave you anything because they found nothing on his person."

"They asked me the same questions." Rhett watched Jake closely.

"I told them everything happened so fast and they got there right after he did, so no. It just makes me wonder. If Hale had information the FBI wanted that badly, why didn't they stop him before he made it to the garage? They obviously knew something was going down. And, if they had the garage under surveillance, as they alluded to, how did they miss a sniper? Better yet, how did the sniper miss you? I'm just thinking out loud here, but it seems like that information must be pretty explosive. At the very least, it was worth dying and killing for. Too bad Mr. Hale was shot before he gave it to *you*."

Rhett looked down at the jump drive under Jake's calloused hand. Flashbacks flickered in his memory. *The guy knew us. Knew Jake played catcher. He threw something at Jake before he fell.*

Rhett picked up the jump drive and studied it in his hand. He looked at Jake and nodded. They both knew what they needed to do next. "Those are great questions, Jake, but we have a show to do today, so let's focus on that. If we remember anything, we'll call the FBI." Rhett tucked the keychain into his pocket. He gathered his things, and the two headed toward the elevator doors.

Rhett abruptly stopped, startling Jake. "Wait! I need to put the lasagna in the fridge first." When he returned, he slapped Jake on the shoulder. "Let's go fishing."

Chapter Four

Madison, Jackson, and Rich lived on a bus. It was swanky and high-end, but it was still a tour bus. They traveled the country together, stopping frequently to meet and greet voters along the way. After fifteen states in twelve days, Madison was glad to have a week in her own bed.

Their tour bus served as the major artery of the campaign, but D.C. headquarters was home base. Today, the campaign office buzzed with energy. Interns answered phones and typed furiously on laptops. A group of college volunteers stuck address labels on mailers. Another group unboxed pens and fidget spinners with Jackson's slogan. Madison ran a tight ship.

Jackson led in all the polls. The second debate was quickly approaching. They needed focus in order to knock off more of the competition. Two democratic congressmen dropped out and offered their support to Jackson, hoping for cabinet positions in return. Anything less, and they would support the eighty-year-old senator from California.

Hayman Barnes, Jackson's senior campaign advisor, handled those negotiations. Hayman handled everything. He reminded Madison of those silent film era villains. She pictured him tying damsels in distress to railroad tracks. Madison was no damsel in distress, so Hayman didn't scare her, but she was definitely cautious around the man. Her father taught her to be kind and accommodating to others while keeping a sharp business mind and standing firm on principle. Hayman was anything but kind or accommodating and Madison highly questioned his principles.

Hayman avoided riding on the tour bus. A "friend of the cause" offered him access to a private jet throughout the campaign. Hayman could hop from state to state and stay in the top hotels while Jackson, Rich, and Madison slept on the bus to appeal to middle America. As if middle America drove around in posh tour buses.

After checking on the campaign team's progress, Madison finally made it back to the executive office. They called it the strategy room. Today, it had been all hers. She shimmied off her heels and arched her back in a satisfying stretch. Making a place for herself on the conference table, she settled in for an evening of brainstorming debate questions and potential snafus.

Madison was deep into her spreadsheet when a knock startled her. Ashleigh, Madison's favorite intern, stood in the doorway holding a gorgeous arrangement of flowers.

"Sorry, Ash. Flowers won't raise your salary," Madison chuckled while Ashleigh rolled her eyes.

"Mr. Barnes told us on day one that working for the future president should be payment enough. I'm not holding my breath for a pay raise."

"Your brutal honesty is why you're my favorite, Ashleigh."

"Well, apparently you're someone's favorite something, because these flowers are ah-maze-ing." Ashleigh placed the vase of peonies on the table. Various shades of pink popped against stark green leaves. A sweet fragrance filled the space.

"Are those for me?" Madison was surprised and slightly confused. It wasn't her birthday. Her parents always sent peonies on her birthday.

"They sure are for you." Ashleigh stood back with her arms crossed, obviously waiting to see who sent them.

Madison grinned with a turn of her head. "Thank you, Ashleigh. I'll let you know if I need anything." Madison plucked the card out but wouldn't open it until she was alone.

Ashleigh shrugged in defeat. "Fine. I get it. You don't want to tell me. I'll just be out here if you change your mind."

Madison watched Ashleigh walk away before solving the puzzle. The plain white card had a phone number and the words, "Friendly Neighborhood News Jock." Madison dropped her head and laughed softly to herself. The man was entertaining, that much she would admit. She remained cautious, but he undeniably intrigued her.

Dating anyone right now was flat-out crazy, but dating a member of the press would be absolutely insane. She couldn't even consider this guy, could she? Madison flipped the card over and over in her hand. Surely, she should just ignore this gesture.

Madison placed the card beside her laptop and attempted to study her screen. The words blurred as her eyes drifted to the handwritten card. She needed to focus on work, but those darned flowers kept calling her name. She wasn't sure whether the card or her distracted mind frustrated her more. Madison sighed and picked up her phone. At the very least, basic etiquette demanded a thank you text.

Madison: You took a gamble sending flowers to the campaign office. Sometimes I'm gone for weeks at a time.

She took a deep breath and hit send. It surprised her to see dots pop up so quickly. Madison teetered between regret and anticipation. Her stomach was in knots. She kicked herself for this ridiculous display of nervousness. Madison Lyn did not wait on men's blinking text dots. She was a strong, independent, confident woman.

Rhett: Perks of working in a newsroom. WBN's campaign correspondent came in today and was excited to be home for a week. Plus, your interns love social media. You inadvertently photo bombed one of their #Cashe4Pres posts. I assumed they finally sprung you from the ER. Speaking of how are the twelve stitches?

Madison: You are quite the stickler for details.

Rhett: Occupational hazard. You didn't answer the question.

Madison: Occupational hazard.

Rhett: Touché

Madison: My twelve stitches are healing nicely. Thank you for asking. How is that gunshot wound? Did they find the disgruntled fan who shot you?

Rhett: You should take your comedy act on the road.

Madison: I'm currently enjoying being off the road so I'll pass.

Rhett: There's my opening. Since you're not on the road this week, are you available for drinks? Coffee? Dinner? All of the above?

Madison: Why peonies?

Rhett: Deflect and redirect. Okay. Well, this will either make me seem endearing or creepy stalkerish. I'm hoping for endearing. I may have scanned your social media accounts for hints. Peonies seem to be your favorite. Endearing or stalkerish?

Madison: I reserve the right to with hold judgment.

Rhett: Are you sure you're not the one running for president? You would make a skilled politician. I'm still waiting for my first answer.

Madison: I'll think about it. I have to run, but I wanted to thank you for the flowers. They were unnecessary, but much appreciated. I'll let you know my decision on the date and the stalker vs. endearing question when I decide.

Rhett: I shall wait on pins and needles.

A wide grin engulfed Madison's face. It had been a long time since she found an interesting man to talk to. Experience taught her most men were arrogant and underestimated her, or they were intimidated by her and overcompensated. Or, worse, they felt they could "handle" her, and that really ticked off Madison. The only men who treated her as an equal were Rich, Jackson, and her brothers. Time would tell, but Rhett Paulson seemed like a fun sparring partner.

Reaching across the table for the vase, she breathed in the sweet fragrance of peonies. They reminded Madison of her grandmother. It was sweet that Rhett didn't take the generic route and actually bothered looking for what she liked. She appreciated the extra effort.

A commotion from the front office interrupted Madison's thoughts. Adult women giggled. Twenty-somethings notched up their high-pitched chatter. Madison was sure she heard a swoon or two. Jackson must have returned from picking up dinner. It was a genius level planned photo-op of Jackson being a regular guy, grabbing takeout for his team. Rich stopped to flirt with the giddy volunteers. Hayman entered the room texting and walking, as usual.

Jackson Cashe strode straight for Madison and placed a carryout box in front of her. "Greek salad, extra dressing on the side."

"No baklava? I can't believe you. I thought you knew me." Madison faked offense, but was slightly disappointed. She needed a sugar and honey fix right now.

Jackson laughed and pulled a container from behind his back. "That was too easy. Come on, Madsi. I would never forget your baklava." He handed the box to her. "I'd be afraid of your retaliation."

"I'd argue, but you're right." Madison smiled sweetly, then opened the dessert first to smell it.

"Who sent flowers? Oh no. Madsi, I didn't forget your birthday, did I? No, it's not August." Jackson's face went from alarmed to relaxed to confused in one stream of conscious thought.

"An admirer sent them, if you must know." Madison crossed her arms and leaned back into the chair as Rich entered their strategy domain.

"It's not August. Who sent the flowers?" Rich dropped his bag of takeout on the table and claimed a seat.

"You're late to the party, Rich. It seems our Madsi has an admirer." Jackson crooned.

"Ooohh, who? Is he cute? Does he have a good job? Do we know him?" Rich rested his hands under his chin and batted his eyelashes at Madison. His terrible attempt at being a giggling girlfriend always made her laugh.

Madison chucked a "Cashe 4 Pres" stress ball at Rich's head. He caught it, then laughed and dug into the takeout bag.

"Seriously, Madsi, do we know him?" Jackson took the seat next to Rich and grabbed the bag from him.

Both men, whom Madison loved dearly, were staring expectantly at her. She debated telling them anything at all, but a small part of her wanted them to say she was crazy for even entertaining the thought. An even smaller part hoped they didn't. "I actually met him in the ER. We all know him, but we don't *know*-know him."

Rich and Jackson both stared eagerly at her. Rich waved his hand for her to continue speaking words. They were obviously invested in this conversation.

"The flowers are from Rhett Paulson." Madison watched both of their faces closely.

"A reporter? That's an interesting plot twist. You always warn me to resist muddying the press waters. I didn't realize what a hypocrite you are, Madison Lyn. This is a new side of you," Rich mockingly scolded her.

Jackson punched Rich's arm. "Let's hear her out. Maybe Mr. Paulson is a contender. Madison is very picky with potential suiters. I'm intrigued to see the pro-con list."

"That's right, she always has a pro-con list that never fails to entertain. Is Mr. Paulson too tall? Too short? Too teethy?" Rich took a bite of his gyro while simultaneously ducking from another flying stress ball aimed at his head.

Jackson choked on his laughter. "I forgot about the 'teethy' guy. Remember the bow tie guy? He was a winner."

"Haha. You both are so funny. Not everyone can be as charming and won-derful as the two of you. You have ruined me from dating forever because of your sheer perfection." Madison opened the container and started prepping her dinner. The dressing's tangy aroma reminded her that she was famished.

"I know you're being sarcastic, but I believe there is some truth in what you say. I, for one, am sheer perfection." Rich flashed his flirtiest of grins.

"We're sorry Madsi, you know we love you. Seriously, I've only heard good things about Paulson. He runs in the same circles we do. I just haven't met him in person. You should invite him out with us tonight. Rich rented out the pub down the street, and we've invited the entire staff out as a reward. Hayman thought it was a good idea to take off tonight. Give everyone a morale boost." Jackson's earnestness encouraged her to consider Rhett.

"Yeah, Mads, invite him. I would love to interview your date. Enjoy the flip side for once." Rich beamed up at her with a smirk.

Hayman, who hadn't bothered to speak until now, held out a hand for his food. "Enough chitchat. We're taking the night off to give the appearance that we're not nervous about the debate. Madison is not dating a reporter while we're on the campaign trail, and we definitely aren't inviting a reporter to a staff party at a pub. We have work to do now. Ms. Lyn, if we're finished discussing your love life, I'd like to review the latest poll numbers."

Jackson tried to talk, presumably to defend Madison, but Hayman held up a hand to stop it before it started. Jackson shrugged at Madison, Madison glared at Hayman, and Rich continued eating. Jackson and Rich had encouraged her to consider Rhett, but Hayman's forbiddance sealed the deal.

Madison: I just found out I have tonight off. One drink.

Rhett: I'll take it. I can get out of here by 9:30.

Madison: I'll text you an address and time.

Rhett: Still waiting on pins and needles.

Madison dropped her phone back onto the table, took a bite of salad, and pulled out the latest polling data.

Chapter Five

"Jake, my man. I've still got it. Even with my arm in a sling, I've still got it." Rhett reclined and plopped his feet on his desk. A Cheshire cat grin covered his face.

"What? An STD? Congratulations." Jake tossed a crumpled paper into the garbage can beside Rhett's desk then pumped his fists in the air. "Nothing but net."

"Haha. I'll ignore that since I'm in such a good mood." Rhett rested both hands behind his head. "I have a date tonight with Madison Lyn."

"Should I know her?" Jake pecked away on his phone, not sparing Rhett even a glance.

"You will. If Cashe keeps his momentum going, she'll be his right-hand man. She's the girl from the hospital I told you about."

"I guess that would make her his right-hand *woman*." Jake chuckled to himself. "Alexis says good luck and to wear navy blue. Apparently, It brings out your eyes."

"Good grief, man. Did you just text our entire conversation to your wife? By the way, tell her thank you. I will definitely wear blue. Does it bother you that your wife thinks about my eyes?" Rhett obnoxiously smirked at Jake.

"Nope. She's trying to get you married off so she doesn't have to raise you anymore. And, yes, I text her all day. She's better at conversation than you." Jake raised his eyebrows and considered Rhett for a minute. "You do have nice eyes, by the way. It's important to market your assets."

Rhett rolled the same eyes they were discussing. When Jake and Alexis got married, Rhett feared he'd lose his wingman and best friend. He ended up with an extra wing-woman and homemade lasagna any time he asked. Jake and Alexis were the only family he had left, other than Grammy.

"Earth to Paulson." Jake snapped his fingers at Rhett to get his attention. "You gonna get that?"

Rattled, Rhett looked down at his phone vibrating on the desk beside him. A picture of his mentor holding the Lifetime Achievement Award brightened the screen. Rhett smiled. "Nicholas Branson, to what do I owe the honor? Shouldn't you be sailing a yacht or golfing somewhere in your golden years?"

Nick retired two years ago. His ratings were so high the competition gave up on trying to be first, and resigned themselves to compete for second fiddle. Nick called Rhett into his office one day to tell him the retirement news and was gone two weeks later. After ensuring Nick hadn't lost his mind, Rhett wished his friend good luck and took the time-slot. With Nick's endorsement and guidance, Rhett easily swept the top ratings spot as his own.

"As a matter of fact, I'm on the golf course as we speak. Soaking up the sun and rejoicing that I'm not stuck in an office like you." Nick sounded happy.

"Aw, the life of the retired. I thought you would have died from boredom by now." Rhett grinned into the phone as he rocked back in his chair.

"Speaking of death, I hear you tried to join their ranks. I thought I taught you not to engage with disgruntled fans." Nick's soft laughter brought a smile to Rhett's cheeks. He missed Nick. He missed the comradery and the advice, but mostly he missed Nick's wisdom.

"Is that why you called? Do you miss the game and want your time slot back, old man?"

"Rhett, you know why I called." Nick's voice was serious and direct.

"I'm fine, Nick. Truly. The bullet went straight through and didn't hit anything important. The concussion was the worst part. I'm recovering and back to work today. Jake's here making sure I behave."

"Hey, Nick!" Jake yelled across the desk towards Rhett's hand.

"I'm sure he is, and I'm sure his lovely wife is ready to throttle you both." Nick's fatherly tone couldn't be missed.

"True enough." Rhett shifted in his seat and attempted redirection. "So, how is Miriam? Are you driving her nuts being home all the time?"

"Yes. She's packing as we speak to visit her sister. That's the other reason I'm calling. I have an interview scheduled this week and wanted to grab lunch. I'm taking the train in the morning. Are you available?"

The network paid a fortune for an eight interview series with Nick. He picked the subjects, the settings, and the topics. Subjects begged Nick to cover them. Last month, Nick interviewed the former three presidents together to discuss the divided nation and talk of secession. The ratings came in at a close second to the Super Bowl.

"Only if you tell me the subject of the interview," Rhett laughed, knowing Nick wouldn't crack.

"I'll do one better. I'll take you with me on the next interview. I think you'll enjoy this one."

"You have my attention."

"I thought I might," Nick chuckled. "We'll talk on Friday. I want to try Jacques Boucher's new restaurant. Noon?"

"I look forward to it. Talk to you soon." A feeling of peace washed over Rhett. Hopefully, seeing Nick would help untangle the uneasy feelings Rhett had been wrestling with since the shootout. Nick would know what to do with this jump drive conundrum.

Nick taught Rhett to start from the outside and follow the trails into the center of a story. By the end, there might be a hundred trails to forage, but there was always a seed smack dab in the middle. The seed was the story. The roots were the evidence, and the plant was the headline to draw in the audience. Nick's process had won them both a record number of awards and followers. Rhett would use that same outline to find the actual source of the mysterious jump drive.

"Hey, man. You okay?" Jake watched Rhett with concern.

Rhett shook his head. "Chasing rabbit holes again. Besides, I couldn't be better today. Your wife made me lasagna. I have a date for drinks later. Lunch with Nick on Friday. Either I'm having a great day or people want to make sure I'm not dead." Rhett winced as he stood and closed his laptop. "Let's go, I have an idea."

Jake groaned, "Every time you say that, I end up in jail, in hot water, or in the doghouse with Alexis."

"Come on, I've only gotten us arrested twice." Rhett flashed an enigmatic smile at Jake as he walked out of his office and down the talent corridor of WBN.

"Yeah, but one of those was in Kazakhstan." Jake caught up in two strides.

"We were out in two days. And we got the story, I might add."

The elevator opened as soon as they reached it. Charlotte Harmon sauntered out and fastened her eyes on Rhett. "I'm so glad you're all right, Rhett. I'm here if you need anything at all." Her southern drawl would make sweet iced tea ache. She rubbed his good arm and winked.

"Thanks, Charlotte." Rhett skittered around her and shivered once the doors closed. "I'm not gonna lie, that woman scares me."

Jake agreed. "Me too, but not as much as a Kazakhstan prison, though."

Rhett shrugged. They rode in silence. The ostentatious golden elevator slowly made its way down the shaft. The piped in soft music acted as an odd soundtrack to their already weird week. Jake watched the numbers descend as Rhett hummed along and rocked back and forth on his heels.

"The basement? That's unusual for you. Normally, you send me or Oliver down here into the dregs of the building." Jake studied Rhett.

The door opened, and Rhett walked out with purpose. "You make me sound like the spoiled talent, sending an assistant to do my dirty work."

"You said it," Jake mumbled under his breath, but loud enough for Rhett to hear.

"I'm ignoring that. Ah, here we are." Rhett slowed down and peeked around the cracked door. "Lucas, I need a favor."

Lucas's hair flopped into his face as he looked up at the two men standing in his doorway. Computer parts covered his desk, and a screwdriver hung from between his lips.

"From me?" Lucas looked scared.

"From you." Rhett closed the door behind them.

Chapter Six

The bar sat five blocks over from the campaign office. An antiquated juke-box played music in the corner. Madison purposefully chose this location because the political elite did not frequent it. They herded to the swankier establishments in town for networking and maneuvering. Madison did not need that tonight. She needed low key and discreet.

The battered napkin in her hand had been twisted and folded beyond repair. Madison was not a fidgeter, but her nerves were on edge tonight. The adrena-line from this afternoon had faded, and she was left with second-guessing and apprehension.

The jukebox clicked and screeched as a new CD slid into place. Madison reminisced as the melody floated around her. Her parents loved this band and had played their albums frequently while cooking dinner together. Even now, she could see them dancing in their kitchen. Doctors Daniel and Vivian Lyn were filled with joy and celebrated life. They were also professors who placed great value on education, but it was Madison, not her parents, who applied the pressure to succeed.

Until she met Jackson and Rich, grades and awards had solely measured Madison's life. They brought out her sense of adventure, limited as it may be. Madison took a calming breath, relaxed into her seat, and flattened the battered cocktail napkin back to its original form. Tonight, she would be more like her parents.

Humming along with the chorus, she looked up at just the right time. Rhett Paulson walked through the door and scanned the dark barroom. He locked eyes on Madison and nodded. Nervousness gave way to anticipation. She motioned to the empty seat across from her as he slid into the booth and smiled.

"I'll be honest, part of me thought you might ghost me tonight." His smile was perfected from years of charming America.

"I did manage to spend an evening in the hospital with you. Surely, one drink won't kill me." Madison attempted a flirty smile. She was so bad at this. She needed to channel her inner Rich, only a much lower dose of it. Rich Miller could flirt with a pencil.

Rhett signaled over a waitress who looked annoyed and overworked. This place held a steady stream of business with a small batch of regulars chatting at the bar. A few empty booths and bar stools allowed everyone else room to breathe and be left alone to their own vices. The perfect place to hide a private date.

Madison watched as Rhett charmed the waitress and ordered himself a draft and her a second round.

"I hope I didn't keep you waiting long. I had trouble getting out of the studio after the show." Rhett watched her intently as he lifted her tattered napkin to examine it. "Did this napkin offend you in some way?"

Madison dodged the question about napkin etiquette. "It was a good show tonight. Nice coverage of the European energy crisis. How did you get Chancellor Boudain on your show?"

"A magician never reveals his secrets."

Madison rolled her eyes before pointing her gaze back at Rhett, calling him out on his flippant answer. It worked.

"We called in a few favors. I hope it was worth it. We'll see how the numbers play out this week. And before you ask, no, I can't reveal what favors I called in, but I would like to talk about how you're a fan of the show." Checkmate.

Madison accepted the move and admired his perception. "Don't flatter yourself. It's my job to be informed of what you news jocks say, so occasionally, I do watch your show. I watched specifically tonight in case you turned out to be a dud date and we needed something to talk about." She shrugged in honesty.

Rhett clutched his chest. "Ouch! You wound me. I thought I'd already impressed you with my sparkling wit and conversation."

"The jury is still out, but I'll give you points for entertaining me." Madison flashed her own saucy grin.

Their drinks arrived, giving them both a moment to reset. Rhett raised his out to her, "To entertaining dates." The tinkling of glass hovered in the air as they studied one another over their rims.

"So, how does a campaign manager get a night off the week before a national debate?"

Madison shook her head. "No campaign talk. Anything else is on the table but that. My wildest night in high school. Crazy ex-boyfriend stories. Childhood injuries. I'm an open book, unless the book involves Jackson or Rich." Madison swirled amber liquid in the heavy glass. She watched him with an inviting smile that even surprised herself.

"Duly noted, but now I'm intrigued. I want to hear the answers to all of the above." Rhett shifted in the booth, which squeaked in protest from years of overuse. "I have an idea, if you're up for it?"

Bolstered by some unknown force, Madison grinned. "Try me."

"Think speed dating meets press briefing."

Madison choked out a laugh. "Well, that sounds terrifying. Like Dante's tenth circle of hell. You realize I've spent the last eight years avoiding both of those things, right?"

He laughed at her honesty. "I promise it won't be that bad. We take turns throwing out a topic and then both of us have thirty seconds to respond. For example, I suggest the topic of siblings and then both of us blurt out our answers. I have none." Rhett motioned for Madison to respond.

"Two older brothers. Two younger sisters." Madison countered, "Most embarrassing moment from high school?"

"Wow, you opened hard. All right, I need to think." Rhett rubbed his chin in thought before taking a long drink. "Okay, I know. Freshman year, I asked out the sister of this guy on my team. He found out about it and stole my clothes from the locker room. I had to wear a cheerleading skirt home from practice."

Madison almost choked on her drink, exploding with laughter. "That's awful."

He laughed along with her. "It was! Back then, I had scrawny chicken legs too. I spent the entire summer lifting weights, so if it happened again, I'd at least look good in the skirt."

"Did it happen again?"

"Getting caught in a skirt? I'd like to say no, but pranks abound with teenage boys."

Madison's cheeks were already sore from smiling. The stress of the campaign trail made her forget that not everything was a serious matter. It felt good to sit here with him. Rhett made her laugh.

For the next two hours, Madison let loose in a way that she rarely allowed herself to enjoy. Rhett was unexpectedly different from her circle of acquaintances. Her Ivy League degrees surrounded her with an elite group of friends and opportunities. Sensible ambitiousness painted Madison Lyn even down to her functional wardrobe with designer labels. Tonight, she felt carefree and relaxed. She clocked out of her life for the evening and became a butterfly. The new wings fit perfectly.

Madison didn't want the date to end, but the last swallow of whiskey reminded her that even Cinderella eventually had to leave the ball.

"Okay, so, this is where I test your journalistic skills. We played your game, now we play mine. The person with the most concise recap pays the tab."

Rhett nodded his consent to Madison's wager. "Ladies first," Rhett drawled.

"You grew up on a small farm in West Virginia with your grandparents. Your Grammy makes a mean chili." Madison recalled how he skirted over his mother's death quickly, so she avoided the topic. "You went to college on a baseball scholarship with your best friend, and current cameraman, Jake, who had to untie you from a sorority flagpole freshman year. Jake's wife Alexis sounds amazing. They keep you out of jail and make sure you're fed. You left grad school with a few student loans. I'll pass along your student loan forgiveness plan to Jackson, by the way."

"Thank you. I have more ideas where that came from, if he's interested." Rhett cut in with a laugh.

Madison continued, "Duly noted. You wormed your way into an internship at WBN after hearing *The* Nick Branson as a guest speaker in one of your classes.

Afterwards, you harassed him relentlessly until he agreed to give you feedback on an article you wrote. Much the same way you did to get this date, I might add. Thus began your illustrious career in journalism and the rest is history, as they say. Did I miss anything?"

"That was impressive. Maybe you should work at WBN if your political career doesn't pan out. You've got skills, Miss Lyn." Rhett held up his mug in salute to her presentation of his life.

Madison choked back a laugh. "Let's be clear, it's not *my* political career, it's Jackson's. I'm just along for the ride and the connections. I'll do whatever I can for Jackson, but politics is not my dream field."

"Ah, loyal and driven. Jackson is very lucky." Rhett's voice lowered as he studied her face.

"Yes, he is." Madison smirked, ignoring the question Rhett implied about her relationship with Jackson again. "Your turn."

"Now, how could I top that? Besides, I like to marinate on my interview subjects before providing my expert opinion, so I'll have to get back to you on the recap. This way, I get to chivalristically pick up the tab and ensure a second date. Surely, you want to hear my summary?" Rhett finished the last of his beer and pulled out a worn leather wallet.

"Chivalristically? Are journalists just allowed to make up words now?" Madison couldn't contain her mirth.

"Yes, we can. Most people don't question us. The key is to speak with confidence and with an air of authority." Rhett lowered his voice and looked down at Madison over his brow. Giving her his best authoritative gaze.

"I see. Very academic of you. Is this what you do to your subjects? Wear them down until you get the scoop?"

"Did it work? Do I get a second date?" Rhett's boyish grin had Madison grinning like a schoolgirl. She shook her head.

"Maybe. I'll have to check my schedule. I do travel a lot these days, as evidenced by my office being a tour bus most weeks." Sarcasm oozed from her lips.

"Do you mind if I text you? Off the record, of course." Rhett's grin was hard to resist.

"Somehow, I think everything is on the record with you, but strangely, that doesn't worry me. Yet."

Rhett paid the tab and held out his hand to help Madison out of the booth. She felt tingles when his fingers skimmed her shoulder as he helped her with her jacket. The weight of his hand against the curve of her back was exhilarating. Madison may have imagined it, but the walk to the door felt deliberately slow. The evening air held a slight chill as they exited their cocoon into D.C.'s array of night lights.

"Can I walk you home or get you a cab? I just realized I don't know where you live." Rhett's false bravado almost masked his nervousness. Madison enjoyed making him feel off-kilter. Somehow, it leveled the playing field.

"I'm actually walking a few blocks over to join the staff party. I'm sure they're all sitting around with coffee, playing chess, but just in case, I should probably steer you in the other direction." Madison stood in front of Rhett, his hands gently cupping her elbows.

"Wise of you not to let a fox in the henhouse." Rhett's voice was focused and steady. "I had a great time tonight, Madison Lyn."

"So did I." Her words sounded measured and throaty. She didn't recognize her own voice. A wave of heat and bubbles rose from her belly to her chest.

His eyes asked the question his mouth didn't yet release. Madison answered by leaning into him. It had been a long time since she'd been kissed and even longer since she initiated one. Adrenaline coursed through her body as a thumping grew in her throat. Rhett's lips were soft. The kiss was gentle, yet firm. Strong arms wrapped around her waist as she slid her hands up his broad shoulders for support.

After a long and smoldering first kiss, he leaned back an inch to gaze at her. "You are full of surprises, Miss Lyn."

"As are you, Mr. Paulson. Very unexpected indeed." Madison began untangling herself from his gaze, not trusting herself to stay there much longer.

"I'm going to walk away now." Madison loved and feared the silly grin on her face.

"I'm going to watch you walk away," Rhett shrugged. "If I'm being honest."

Madison laughed and turned to leave. "Goodnight, Rhett."

"Goodnight, Madison. Stay out of ERs."

"You too." She called over her shoulder. She tried her best to saunter away, knowing he was still staring. Madison turned the corner with a smile that reached from her head to her toes. She couldn't help it. Yes, the new butterfly wings fit nicely on her.

Chapter Seven

Rhett rolled his neck back and forth, stretching and cracking it. Tight shoulders and a tense back were job hazards for a reporter deep in a story. Rhett's research team was top-notch, but he wanted to do some preliminary digging before letting them loose on this potential story lead. There was no point wasting their time if the story wouldn't catch the attention of his audience. "Fiery headlines, heat up ratings," was the unofficial network motto.

The phone resting beside him on the desk came to life. A notification popped up, luring him to read a new text.

Private Number: Answer your phone.

"Who is this?" Rhett asked himself. Pulling up the conversation string, Rhett froze. "What the...it can't be."

Rhett startled at the ringing of his office phone. A blinking light indicated the call came through the main receptionist line. Rhett picked up the receiver and tentatively answered, "Yes?"

"Mr. Paulson, a call from a Mr. Austin Roe."

Great, another spy alias. "Put him through." Rhett reached for a pen, then jotted the name on the nearest notepad.

The voice, deep and raspy, obviously filtered through some type of modification app spoke. "Paulson?"

"Imagine my surprise when I receive a text from a dead man's phone alerting me to a call." Rhett pressed the receiver close to his ear. He couldn't miss even a syllable.

"I assure you, Nathan Hale is indeed deceased, and not making phone calls. This burner will be destroyed, but we have others. Don't concern yourself with details. Just be assured we have a unique way of communicating."

"Much like the Culper Spy Ring, Mr. Roe?" Rhett's pen hovered over the notepad, ready for any clues. "Should I be looking for flags hanging from clotheslines on Madison Avenue before heading down to Roe's Tavern?"

Background noise from the news cubes vibrated the glass walls of Rhett's office. Holding onto the receiver for dear life, Rhett stood, stretched, and kicked the door closed with the tip of his sneaker. He ignored the surprised looks from heads popping out over fake office walls. Rhett's door was always open. He started in one of those delusional cubicles and he wanted to always stay grounded to them. Now he was embroiled in some type of spy game and shutting his door, which was highly unusual. The imbalance of it knocked him off-kilter. He needed to focus. To listen.

"Ah, I see Tallmadge was right about you. You know history and you catch on quick. Let's see if you can keep up with us. I'm still not convinced you can be trusted, but others believe in you, so I agreed to a test run. Adam's Ale & Steakhouse, four p.m., go to the bar."

Rhett wrote down the information in his own form of shorthand, which Jake called "Rhett-scribble." It was something between chicken scratch and prehistoric symbols. "And why should I trust you? Last time I answered one of these summonses, I ended up with a hole in my shoulder across from a dead man. Was that a test?"

"That was the price we're willing to pay for freedom. What happened to you was a warning shot, but we weren't the ones who fired. You should find out who did. I'm sure it will surprise you. Make no mistake, you'd be dead if *they* wanted it that way. I'm giving you a story. You can choose to take it or not. I doubt WBN will run it, but I can promise you this information will be useful to you when you open the jump drive."

Icy tingles shot up Rhett's spine. Jake was the only person who knew about the successful handoff of contraband. "What jump drive?"

"Come now, Mr. Paulson, let's not play games. A good man died. Don't insult him or me. Hale had one mission. We know he completed it. I'm giving you a lead. Take it or leave it. Adam's four p.m." The line went dead.

The room stilled while Rhett's head spun. His vision was uber-sensitized, yet his periphery became blurred. The consistent buzz vibrating in his ear set off alarms throughout his system. Adrenaline mixed with fear and something else he couldn't put his finger on. His reporter senses were on high alert. Rhett decided to call the head of IT.

The other line picked up on the second ring. "Go for Stan."

Rhett cringed. "Stan, Rhett Paulson. Hey, I need a trace on the call that was just patched to my office from the main switchboard. I'm also going to need a background check on a cell number. Can you help me out?"

"Not a problem, Paulson. Do I need to notify security?"

"No. They're both for a story I'm following, but I'd appreciate discretion and a quick turnaround." Rhett scratched his head as he reclined in his chair.

"That could be a problem. We have a backlog down here in IT. Backbone of the building, I always say." Stan wasn't budging.

"I'll throw in floor seats for the next fight. You're a Melloni fan, right?" Nick taught Rhett that a good reporter knew everyone's currency. Stan's was flattery and gifts.

Rhett waited patiently during the pause, knowing he had this won. "I'm on it, Paulson. I'll have a report in thirty minutes. Text me the cell number."

"Thanks, Stan. I knew I could count on you." Rhett grunted in annoyance over losing his tickets to Stan. Usually, it didn't irk him this much, but Stan was a creep and arrogant. Rhett dealt with enough of those guys in his life, and hated it when they won. He dreaded breaking the news to Jake about the fight. Hopefully, dinner would soften the blow.

Rhett: Meet me in the lobby at 3:45. Bring tech we used from Czech story.

Jake: That ended in a car chase. What are you getting me into this time?

Rhett: Not sure, but it involves a steak dinner.

Jake: I'm in.

***

Mahogany walls with gaslight sconces wrapped around the dining area. Crisp white linens, leather chairs, and crystal water goblets dressed each table. The crowd was sparse at this time of day.

Rhett and Jake followed a hostess to the bar. As Rhett pulled out a stool, the bartender cleared his throat and nodded to two drinks already waiting on the counter. Their seats had the perfect vantage point for a hallway leading to private dining rooms. Jake looked at Rhett, and the two had a silent conversation as they settled in at the bar.

The bartender approached. "Good evening, gentlemen. Welcome to Adam's."

Rhett stopped him as he launched into the specials. The kid couldn't be more than mid-twenties. "Do you know why we're here?"

"No, sir. A man came in and asked if I had watched your show. Gave me a Benjamin and a drink order. Told me to save you these two seats. Is everything okay?" The kid, obviously polished, had a copy of Atlas Shrugged next to him on the counter.

"No, everything's fine. Thanks?" Rhett coaxed the name from the kid.

"Mike."

"Thanks, Mike."

The kid tapped the bar. "Let me know if you need anything." He walked away and began filling a jar with olives.

"Whoever invited us has a sense of humor. I'll take a microbrew any day over your, what is that anyway, a Shirley Temple?" Jake's laughter was followed by a large smirk.

Rhett grunted, "How do you know the Shirley Temple wasn't for you?"

Jake flashed a "come on, man" look and took a long, satisfying drink of his beer.

Rhett waved over Mike. "I'll have what he's having."

Mike and Jake shared a laugh. "I was wondering if someone was messing with you. I guess I was right." Mike filled a mug from the tap and slid it down to Rhett.

Rhett grumbled to Jake, "Get it out of your system now. We need to figure out what the hell we're doing here."

The two covertly scanned their surroundings. Live piano music infused an ambiance of sophistication. A few patrons enjoyed drinks and soft laughter among themselves. Rhett's stomach rumbled as a plate of crab stuffed mushrooms came out of the kitchen doors. Mike thanked the server before placing the appetizer on the bar. They both looked at the kid questionably.

"I was told to order this when you came in, and make sure you ordered dinner and dessert." Mike held up his hands. "Before you ask, the guy paid in cash and left a large tip for my discretion."

Rhett grunted again as Jake asked for a menu. The rabbit hole was getting deeper and deeper. He and Jake had traveled the world chasing leads and breaking stories. Rhett cut his teeth on investigative journalism and knew this would either end in a massive scoop or as the plot for a violent movie script.

Jake's thick-rimmed glasses were equipped with video and sound recording capabilities. Rhett's lapel pin had the same capabilities but needed a closer range. Rhett twisted the pin, making sure it was straight.

"Don't."

"Don't what?" Rhett looked at Jake.

"Don't get in your head. Let's just follow this like we used to follow old-school tips. You're overthinking it. I see the steam spiraling from your ears. Drink your beer. Eat a steak." Jake took the menu from Mike and started perusing the possibilities.

"Doesn't this bother you at all? We don't do this anymore. We send people out to do the legwork for us now. Why do they keep drawing *me* out? I feel like I'm being played or set up."

"You've gotten comfortable in your new office with your own show, but the old days were fun. Admit it. I'm not saying I want to go back to that. It was dangerous, but it was fun."

"I know. I just can't shake this feeling." Rhett rubbed the back of his neck. The tension and knots increased each day since the first call.

"You got shot, man. That's going to mess with you." Jake clapped a hand on Rhett's good shoulder. "I think this could be good for you. Get your blood pumping again. Back to our roots, you know?"

"Maybe." Rhett opened the leather menu as his treacherous stomach growled. Jake pushed the appetizer plate in front of Rhett. They ordered, ate their mushrooms, and waited.

By the time Mike served their entrees, Rhett had relaxed. Jake had Mike turn the television to a Mountaineer game as they tossed a few barbs around about alma maters and loyalty. For a few minutes, Rhett forgot why they were at Adam's. Then his phone vibrated. He held it up for Jake to see.

Private Number: Heads up.

Both men straightened and went on high alert. Jake flipped the toggle on his glasses to record. Rhett slowly lifted his beer, his eyes scanning the room.

They both turned as voices sounded from the front of the restaurant. The hostess walked the perimeter of the dining area with a short bald man, an older woman with a cane, and Rhett's boss. She led the group down the hallway into a private dining room. Jake looked at Rhett, his mouth opened wide. "Why would the owner of WBN be having a private dinner with the Director of the FDA and the president's chief of staff?"

"I don't know, but we're going to find out." Rhett was invested now.

***

Roe: I hope you know what you're doing.

Tallmadge: Trust me. I know Rhett. He's going to get it. We just need to keep leaving breadcrumbs.

Roe: I just dropped a loaf of bread in his lap. If he doesn't piece it together soon, we need to rethink the plan.

Tallmadge: Agreed, but I have faith in him.
Roe: I don't.
Tallmadge: You've made that clear.

Chapter Eight

Grateful to have a second alone, Madison took a deep breath and murmured to herself, "I can do this." She swiveled around in the chair, bumping her elbow on the conference table edge. "Ouch!"

"Ooh, you're jumpy. What are you hiding?" Rich leaned his torso across the table and plopped both elbows down to hold up his head. "I love it when you get that puzzled look. Tell me everything."

Madison dropped her head and growled, "I thought you left with Jackson for the run through. And I'm not puzzled or jumpy. It startled me, that's all. You just barged in and I wasn't expecting you."

"Uh, Mads, this is a conference room. We've all been in and out of here all week. I call bull crap on you. You *are* hiding something."

"I can't stand you, Rich. You know that, right?"

"You love me and you know it. Just tell me and I'll leave you alone. Scout's honor." Rich held up three fingers and grinned like a kid trying to get a second dessert.

"You weren't a scout, and right now, you look like you're volunteering as tribute in the *Hunger Games*." Madison fingered through a stack of folders, attempting to look busy and *un-puzzled*.

"You don't know that I *wasn't* a scout, and we both know I would never volunteer as tribute." Rich's dark laugh sounded falsely menacing. "Mads, if you just tell me, I'll leave. You being shady makes me want to sit here until you crack, and that would make Hayman very mad. He's already on the warpath because I forgot my charger. They're waiting in the car for me. What's it going to be? Tell me or tell Hayman why I'm late?" Rich crossed his arms and leveled a daring smirk at Madison.

"Argh! You are truly a pain! I'm calling a guy, alright? I'm asking someone on a date. I shouldn't ask him out, right? I should wait for him to ask me? Please don't say a word. Leave me alone in my humiliation and go." Madison shook her head as she lowered it into her palm. Rich's silence unnerved her. Rich was never silent. Ever. She peered up under her fingers. "What? Just say it."

"Madison Mei Lyn, you lift your head and look at me." Rich's voice was thick with conviction.

Madison straightened in her chair and stared directly at her dear, yet pain in the rear, friend. She melted as his face softened.

"You are a strong, confident, highly accomplished woman. If you want to ask out a guy, he should be on his knees thanking you for giving him a chance. If he says no, then he's a loser, and stupid. I don't know much about this guy, but I know you. You don't get flustered and you sure as hell don't get nervous. Whoever he is, he does not deserve you. He should be nervous, not you. Do you hear me?"

Madison nodded her head. Relief, validation, comfort, and gratefulness filled her heart and mind. Rich Miller was a playboy. He was a cocky, outlandish flirt. To the outside world, Rich was all flash and spin. To Jackson and Madison, he was the guy who stayed up all night to help you study for a final. He was the Army brat who knew how to make acquaintances everywhere, but only allowed two people into his inner world. Rich Miller was ride-or-die with Madison and Jackson. She trusted him with her life. "Thank you for reminding me."

Rich nodded. "You are very welcome." He turned and grasped the door handle behind him. Before closing it, he looked at her one last time, "Mads, if things get serious with this guy, don't tell him you like black licorice better than red. That's just weird."

"GO!" Madison laughed at Rich as he closed the glass door and strutted out of the campaign office, winking at volunteers along the way. She picked up her phone and took another deep breath.

The phone rang once, twice, three times. Madison prepared herself to leave a voicemail.

"What a pleasant surprise to hear from you."

Madison grinned in relief. "Either you always answer your phone with a pickup line, or I've made my way onto your contacts list."

"I'm not sure which answer makes me look less like a tool. Can I start over? Hello, Rhett Paulson here. To whom am I speaking?" Rhett's voice even sounded smooth over the phone.

"That was awful." Madison couldn't help but laugh at him.

"I know. I'm tanking, aren't I? I'm usually not this tool-ish. I'll have you know I've been told that I do have game." He laughed as he said it, which made her laugh harder.

"I'm afraid to see what your 'game' looks like, because this is quite entertaining on its own merit."

Madison heard him mumbling something to a voice in the background. "Hey, I'm so sorry. I need to run. I was in a pre-production meeting with my team when this woman I'm trying to get a second date with called me. I stepped out into the hall, but apparently, they need me."

"You're not trying very hard if she's the one doing the calling." Madison pinned him on his own line.

"After the flowers and admitted online stalking, I was going to give it another day. I don't want to scare you off."

Rhett's honesty threw her off guard every time. That was such a rare trait in this city. "I see. Well, I'll let you off the hook and ask you out instead. Turns out I have another free night tomorrow. Are you interested in a late dinner?"

"It's a date! One stipulation?"

"Maybe. What is it?" Madison hadn't felt this much anticipation in years.

"I get to pick the venue this time. Do you trust me?" The hopeful lilt in Rhett's voice touched her.

"That remains to be seen, but I'm game. Where?"

"We have to take the Metro. I'll text you a station and time tomorrow. Does that work?"

"Sounds great."

"I've got to run. Hey, Madison?"

"Yes, Rhett?" Madison nervously twirled a pen in her fingers.

"Thanks for calling."

"You're welcome, Rhett. Goodbye." Madison's smile couldn't get any wider.

"Goodbye, Madison."

Madison closed her eyes and felt like a girl for just a moment.

Chapter Nine

"**G**reat show."

"Loved it."

"You the man!"

Rhett smiled and waved at his crew members as they shouted congratulations on another episode of *Rhett's Take*. Rahemia, his producer, rattled off information as they walked across the set. Rhett tried to keep up with her, but his mind was spinning from the events of the past two days. A dead man's cell phone texted him, which led him to a steakhouse stakeout with Jake. Madison called to ask him out. Then, Rahemia threw him a curve ball with a last-minute guest change during the production meeting. His wounded shoulder ached and his head wasn't far behind.

"Hey, I'm curious why the nutritionist got a spot on the show tonight. Is she related to someone? Have dirt on someone? I mean, she was interesting, and it was an informative interview, but not important enough to bump a senator talking about the new voting bill." Rhett knew he caught Rahemia off guard with his interruption, but something in his gut was twitching.

Rahemia, unflappable as always, continued to talk and walk. "I have no idea, but when the president of the network calls you to make it happen, you make it happen. I'm not sure who she's connected to, but it must be a doozy. Jerry wanted her on tonight. He didn't care who I bumped." She gave Rhett a side glance. "Why? What's your gut telling you this time?"

"This is exactly why we make such a great team." Rhett winked at her. "I'm not sure, but something felt off today. I need to process it."

"Well, we have one more show this week, so either process, marinate, or drop it by this weekend. I need you focused next week. The debate is Tuesday and we need to brainstorm narrative outcomes." Rahemia was back on her tablet, pecking away at her show notes.

"How can we brainstorm the narrative if we don't know the outcomes until the actual debate?"

"You realize that your viewers, especially the female demographic, will believe anything you say about the debate, right? You could tell them Jackson Cashe's hair was purple and they would adjust the color on their display panels."

"Come on, you're exaggerating a little." Rhett attempted to state the obvious.

"Aww, it must be nice to be that cute. How sweet of you to think that, Rhett." Rahemia obnoxiously flashed him a smirk.

"I think I'm offended, Rahemia. Am I nothing more than eye candy to you?" His sarcastic grin canceled his claim of outrage.

Rahemia stopped her screen scrolling and aimed her eyes pointedly at Rhett. "If I had a dime for every one of your admirers, I would own this network. Then, I could do favors for all the 'nutritionists' in my life. I'd start with my personal trainer. I'd like to owe him a favor or two."

Rhett laughed, "Way too much information, Rahemia."

She opened the glass door for Rhett, waving her hand out in front of her. "Beauty before brains, my friend."

The two are intercepted at the edge of the newsroom by Rahemia's production assistant. The poor girl just started last month. She looked like a deer caught in headlights. When she finished speaking to her new boss, Rahemia waved her away flippantly. "Thanks, Kendall. You can head home for the night." The petite girl scurried off quickly.

"Isn't her name Keira?" Rhett questioned his friend.

"Yes, but she needs to be initiated into our world. She's too peppy. I'll break her, then mold her into a powerful machine of efficiency."

Rhett shook his head. "You have an evil streak."

"One day, when she has her own assistant, she'll thank me. Do you want to grab dinner? I'm starving and I was going to review the campaign poll analysis. We can do some early prep work for the debate."

"As tempting and terrifying as that sounds, I promised Jake and Alexis I'd come over tonight. She's still mad at me for getting shot." Rhett shrugged, shed his jacket, and loosened his tie.

"Yikes, that should be fun. I'll send over the reports to your house for you to review." Rahemia went back to her tablet and continued to the elevators. "Later, Rhett."

***

After Rhett had been fed and forgiven by Alexis, she launched her own investigation. "So, I'm dying to hear about the girl." Alexis snuggled into the couch with a bowl of ice cream. She motioned to Jake. "Babe, hand me that blanket. I'm freezing."

"Then why are you eating ice cream?" Rhett watched her shovel a giant spoonful into her mouth.

Alexis glared at Rhett.

"Dude, don't question her about ice cream. That's more dangerous than parking garage shootouts." Jake gently draped a navy and gold plaid blanket onto his wife's lap. She punched him in the arm. "Ouch! See? Don't mess with pregnant Alexis. She's scary."

"Jake!" Alexis scowled between bites. She jabbed the spoon in Rhett's direction. "Spill, Paulson! I want details. Will I like her?"

"It's still early. We've only gone out for drinks. I'm taking her to dinner tomorrow."

"And?" Alexis was a formidable interrogator. She waited for Rhett to add more information.

"And she's a force of nature. She can leap buildings in a single bound. Is that enough intel for you?"

"Rhett, I'm serious." Alexis gave him a warning look.

"Wow, you've already mastered the 'mom look'." Rhett squirmed. "Seriously, Madison is great. I think you'll like her a lot. She's wicked smart, but not snotty.

She's funny, but she doesn't know it. And she thinks I'm funny, which is a bonus."

"So she has questionable taste." Jake wrapped his arm around his wife. Alexis poked him in the ribs before motioning for Rhett to continue.

"Not much more to tell. I'm still getting to know her, but it's definitely promising." Rhett shrugged.

Alexis scrutinized Rhett, which made him feel uncomfortable. "There's something special about this one. I can tell. This girl has a hold on you, Rhett Paulson. It's settled. I need to meet her."

"Slow down, your highness. I don't want to scare her." Rhett ducked as Alexis threw a pillow at him.

"All right, I'm finished with you two. Go do your spy work. Besides, my favorite show is about to start."

Jake kissed Alexis's head as he untangled himself from her. Rhett grabbed his beer and the backpack Lucas had given him earlier. Jake retrieved the plate of chocolate chip cookies from the counter. They headed up to the townhouse's attic office where Jake operated his side business. He was making a name for himself producing ten-minute historical highlight videos. They were a big hit with high schoolers everywhere. Props and history books were stacked in piles on the floor. Jake had other ongoing projects, but history was his passion.

While Jake flipped switches, bringing lights and equipment to life, Rhett unpacked the backpack. "Are you sure this is untraceable?" Jake grabbed a cookie from the plate.

Rhett followed the startup instructions for the military grade laptop. "That's what Lucas said." Rhett pulled out the jump drive and inserted it through the hardshell exterior. "He blocked all Wi-Fi and satellite capabilities. He said something about encryption codes and tracker blocks. Honestly, he lost me after 'here's the device' and handed me the instructions."

"What did Coach always tell you? Good thing you're so pretty?" Jake stuffed a whole cookie in his mouth.

Rhett shook his head and quirked his brow. "You are the second person to tell me that tonight. It never bothered me before, but now I'm getting annoyed. I'm more than just stunning good looks, you know."

"Sure you are, sweetheart." Jake's laughter was uncontrollable now.

Rhett turned slowly in his seat and directly nailed Jake in the arm. "Are you working out without me? That hurt." He shook out his hand.

Jake grabbed another cookie and handed it to Rhett. "Come on. Let's see what almost got us killed."

Rhett took a deep breath, typing in the encryption codes exactly as Lucas taught him. A scrambling of small blocks, files, and numeric codes began flashing across the screen. Finally, the chaos stopped to reveal a list of file folders with cryptic names. "Farmland Monopolies. Fires. Global Food Stations. Water Treatment Facilities. Does that say Cow-Mageddon and Stricken Chickens? Is this a joke?"

Jake answered with a shrug. He pointed to the last folder, "Vitamin Supplement Global Rollout. What's that about?"

"I don't know, but we're about to find out. Let's start at the top, Farmland Monopolies." Rhett clicked the folder and waited for the files to load. "Surely, I didn't get shot for some small-bit agriculture story."

Jake grabbed a pencil and started drawing circles for a massive diagram page. Rhett processed with lists. Jake doodled. Their combined method was chaotic, but artful when they finished. Rhett's Grammy called it their superpower of storytelling.

The spreadsheet went on and on with a massive compilation of addresses. "It's organized by state first and acreage second." Rhett scratched his head.

Jake pulled the first address up on his phone's map app. They both looked at the property. Jake searched the second, then third address. "According to the satellite photos, there's nothing there but empty land." Jake searched the map as Rhett went back to studying the spreadsheet.

"Look. Most are listed as foreclosure or auction." Rhett pointed to the fourth column.

Jake jotted notes on his diagram. "I just watched a documentary about the plight of the American farmer. It was about government regulations and environmentalists bankrupting the farming system. I bet this list checks out based on that."

Rhett scrolled over to the "Deed" column. "According to this, either 'AFP' or 'GAF' own most of the properties. The rest just have "foreign entity" listed. Are the initials people or companies?" Rhett picked up his phone. "You search all leads for GAF. I'll take AFP."

While Jake went down his own rabbit holes, Rhett searched farmland and AFP. Nothing specific came up until the second page of the search list. Rhett grunted, "You have got to be kidding me."

"What?" Jake looked over his shoulder to catch a glimpse of Rhett's phone.

"These are clickbait from crackpot sites. Look, this one is from the Revolution Keepers." Rhett scanned the results, "*Why Doesn't Anyone Care that Entrepreneur Adam Ford Owns the Most Farmland in North America*? And the next is from the Washington Gazette. *Adam Ford, American Farmer or Foe?*"

Jake skimmed the article Rhett had opened. "It's worth looking into." Jake turned to Rhett with a curious expression.

"What? You don't believe that crap, do you?" Rhett was angry and tired. His arm was still healing because of this intel.

"You know what my brother always says, 'it's only a conspiracy theory if it's not true.' At the very least, this list is interesting. It begs the question why Silicon Valley royalty, the guy who created the SurfIn empire, would own this much farmland across one continent."

Rhett rubbed his chin. "I don't know. This whole thing has my senses on high alert. The codenames. Encrypted jump drive. Top secret text messages. Parking garage shootout. All because a tech guru owns land? It's crazy-town, if you ask me. Did you find anything on GAF?"

"Nope. Nothing. Go to the next file." Jake picked up his pencil.

Rhett opened the folder labeled Fire. A spreadsheet with dates and insurance information popped onto the screen. "Three meat-packing plants. Two tree nut farms. An organic food distribution center. Two chicken hatcheries. Fifteen food processing plants, including two for baby food? And this tab has farmer's markets listed by state that have been shut down. This can't be right."

Jake searched the company names. Sure enough, each entry had suffered a catastrophic fire that severely affected, if not ended, their business. "Didn't you interview the Secretary of Agriculture last month about the food shortage predictions? This would explain it."

"Yeah, but he didn't mention any of this. He only talked about weather forecasts, drought conditions, and that weird insect eating its way through Europe." Rhett rubbed his chin. "How did I not know this?"

"Open the next folder. Global Food Stations," Jake urged.

"Food distribution stations designed as aid centers in the event of a global food shortage crisis." Rhett read the description. "There are only ten stations listed across the globe. There are map coordinates, but no websites. No information about their actual locations, only that they're owned by the Global Alliance Foundation. Could that be the GAF from the Farmland Monopolies folder?"

Jake oscillated between filling in his diagram and furiously typing on his laptop. "Global Alliance Foundation doesn't have a website, but I found an article about their food distribution stations. Even that's cryptic." Jake pointed to his screen. "The only name mentioned is Johan Philipsen from the Philipsen Foundation."

"Philipsen? The German philanthropist?"

"The very same."

"A philanthropist with ties to food distribution stations isn't newsworthy, but these other tabs are worth checking. We need to look into the connection between the Global Alliance Foundation, the Philipsen Foundation, and Adam Ford Properties."

"This is a crazy triangle, right?" Jake pointed to his diagram, waiting on Rhett for confirmation as Rhett's phone started vibrating.

"What the..." Rhett's voice trailed off as he stared at the number.

Roe: I see you've opened the puzzle. You'll receive another piece this week.

Rhett and Jake looked at each other before quickly shutting the specialized laptop.

Chapter Ten

The studio felt like a cave with its dark blue, windowless walls. They had worked in a bunker like state for the past two days. Bright lights showcased four podiums on the mock stage. Primaries had whittled away candidates until this point, like sitting ducks waiting to be picked off one by one. The Democratic National Convention loomed before them. This debate was crucial. Everyone felt the weight of each word, glance, and nuance. The cave insulated them, but the heaviness of it was felt by every member of the team.

Madison sat next to Hayman. The long table was littered with notepads, pens, empty coffee cups, and misplaced half-filled water bottles. Madison took notes as Hayman moderated. Rich and two interns played the roles of other candidates. Jackson was a natural politician. He was groomed for this moment. Hayman's title was Campaign Consultant, but everyone knew he ran the entire show. Jackson's father, Jackson Cashe II, was Hayman's college roommate. For decades, the two men had big plans for Jackson. On the campaign trail Hayman barked, Rich deflected, Madison controlled chaos, and Jackson sparkled.

The immigration component of debate prep ended with Hayman slamming his fist on the table. After he made Shelley-the-intern cry, Madison suggested they break for lunch. Hayman huffed off the set with his beeper in hand as the campaign team headed to the conference room for lunch. Madison hated Hayman's beeper. She wanted to ask him why he carried such outdated technology, but they didn't have that kind of relationship. Theirs was that of an oligarch and his minion. Madison shivered. There would be no campaign without Hayman, but the team worked better and harder without his presence.

Two of the interns carried in boxed lunches and drinks. Intern Kelly blushed and giggled at Jackson's heartfelt thank you.

"How is Shelley?" Madison quizzed the women.

"She's fine. She went to the bathroom a minute ago. I'm sure she'll be out soon." Kelly spoke to Madison while ogling Jackson.

Madison rolled her eyes. "Thanks, ladies. Go grab some lunch." Madison popped a grape in her mouth as she unboxed her food.

"Aren't Shelley and Kelly roommates?" Rich watched the interns leave the room.

Madison reached over and hit the back of his head with her palm. "Only you would know that."

"What? I take an interest in our coworkers."

"Mmm-hmm. Well, take more of an interest in the older ones who are out of college, please. We don't need a scandal." Madison's stomach growled as she opened her buffalo chicken wrap.

"Where did Hayman go?" Jackson, ever the mediator, redirected their attention.

"Sir Hayman can't eat with us commoners. I think he said something about a lunch meeting. Which is a good thing, or else we would have to give Shelley hazard pay." Madison arched her brow at Jackson.

"I know. Hayman is an acquired taste, but he knows what he's doing. We just need to trust the plan." Jackson started lunch by eating his brownie first.

"Remember that tonight after your special evening with him. You know how much you love those extended Hayman sessions." Rich laughed as he swapped out his bag of chips for Madison's.

She smiled at their familiarity and their differences. Madison went for protein first. Jackson went for the sweets. Rich went for the salty.

"What?" Rich asked with a chip ready to cross his lips, "These are my favorite and you like pretzels, right?"

Madison nodded with a grin and opened the pretzel bag. "Jackson, we need to polish your responses about the potential secession vote."

"Madsi, there is no way that's going to happen. It's just fodder for extremists. Nothing more than political theater. According to Hayman, they can't even pull it off legally." Jackson waved off Madison's concern.

"Mads is right, and as much as I hate to agree, so is Hayman. The problem is that fodder sells, and we need to be the distributor. Feeding it outrages your voter base. Disputing it outrages your opponents. But worse is ignoring it. We need to craft a message that acknowledges the problems, blames the perpetrators, and makes it look like you, Jackson Cashe, are the answer."

"Isn't that your job?" Jackson deadpanned.

"I gave all my notes to Hayman. He told me he needed to run it by 'the others,' whoever 'they' are, and then he'll provide my team with the uniformed talking points."

"That's helpful, considering we've been working on debate prep all week and we only have two days left. Did he mention any other 'uniformed talking points' we need to change? And who is determining what is uniformed? Who sets the terms?" Madison took a big swig of her water, leveling both men with her questioning stare.

"Those are brilliant questions, Madsi. I'm guessing I'll find out tonight." Jackson deflected.

"Where *are* you going tonight, by the way? Your schedule says personal time, but we know that's not true since Hayman will be there instead of Vanessa," Madison quirked.

"A private donor dinner with a guest list so exclusive, I don't even know the names yet. There's a select number of party VIPs who have yet to decide if they'll support me or Angela Williamson."

"Well, Angela checks all of their boxes, but the masses hate her. You are, hands down, the crowd favorite. Her demographics are the only reason she's still in play right now. She's a complete moron."

Madison choked on her pretzel. "Rich! You can't say that out loud. It's awful."

"I didn't say it out loud. I said it to you two. We all know it's true. That's the problem with choosing attributes instead of people. The voters see right through her. She's an idiot who talks in circles, and not even in rational circles.

I'm not trying to be mean, I'm basing it on the polls. Party leadership won't admit it, but they know it's true. She'll make a great VP option, though. No one will assassinate you."

"Rich!" Madison and Jackson both stopped him.

"Chastise me all you want, but you know I'm right. I couldn't care less about politics. My gift is PR. I can spin anything, anywhere. Even her." Rich nodded in Jackson's direction, "My priority is you, not a bunch of snobs who can afford private dinner parties with presidential candidates. I'm just saying, they aren't the most tuned in group of people. They should pay more attention to the polls and the voters." Rich swiveled in his chair, eating more chips.

"Regardless, this dinner is very important for securing the party nomination." Jackson opened his chicken club sandwich and picked off the tomatoes. "Hayman keeps telling me this group runs the world, and that I'm their favorite."

"Exaggerate much?" Madison groaned under her breath.

Rich chuckled and winked at her. "Well, I'm glad we're not going with you. I need a night off the clock."

"Please don't ask out any of the interns," Madison begged with her eyes.

"Actually, I have other options, thank you very much. I'm having dinner with that girl who moved in next door. I helped her carry a flea market dresser upstairs, so she offered to buy me a pizza."

"Poor girl," Jackson fist bumped Madison.

"Ha-ha," Rich turned his attention to her. "What about you? Do you have plans, or are you spending the evening in sweats, reading a book?"

"Although that sounds wonderful, I actually have a date tonight as well." She grinned at her friends as they showered her with whistles.

"Is it the same guy from last week?" Jackson raised an eyebrow.

Rich followed in a sing-song voice, "The reporter?"

"Yes, and yes. He's taking me on a mystery date."

"Mystery date? Make sure he doesn't have a shovel and rope in his car."

Madison hit Rich in the arm. "Stop it, he's very gentlemanly."

"So was Ted Bundy."

Madison growled at Rich's comment.

"Ooohh, is this getting serious? Is it time for us to meet him?" Jackson crossed his arms in interrogation mode.

"The last time you idiots felt the need to interview one of my dates, he ended up breaking it off later that night. So no, I'd like to keep you two away for as long as possible."

"You're welcome for that one. If I recall, that guy was a real loser." Jackson shrugged.

Rich picked up where Jackson left off, "And he did that weird thing with his hair. Dude, you're not a thirteen-year-old skater boy. Stop flipping your bangs."

"Better yet, get a grownup haircut." Jackson and Rich were in full mode hysterics now.

"Okay, okay. He might not be the best example. Even so, I'm not ready for you to meet Rhett. I don't know if he's my type, but he is providing an unexpected distraction this week." Madison picked at the peanut butter cookie in her box.

The group felt lighter than they had before lunch. "Well, it looks like I'm the only one with a boring night ahead of me. I'd much rather do pizza or a mystery date over a suit and tie donor dinner with Hayman and Janice."

"I hope Janice isn't bringing her dog. That thing's a nuisance," Rich cringed.

"I know. I like dogs, but hers terrifies me," Jackson shivered.

"Well, alert the media. Jackson Cashe is terrified of tiny designer dog breeds. Can you spin that?" Madison asked Rich.

"No way, I'm with him. The whole Barnes family gives me the creeps."

The three of them laughed, but not too hard. Hayman scared them all more than his wife's dog. After a minute of finishing their lunches in silence, Jackson peeked into Madison's box, salivating over her extra peanut butter cookie. "Are you going to finish that?"

She pushed her box toward them as Jackson grabbed the cookie and Rich plucked out the rest of her pretzels. They always managed to find normalcy in the middle of chaos. Madison smiled.

Chapter Eleven

The hottest ticket in town was reservations at Jacques Boucher's newest restaurant. Leave it to Nick Branson to score a table for lunch the same month it debuted. Savourer opened last week to fanfare and a never-ending wait list.

Rhett's overloaded mind spun with jump drive information as his driver weaved in and out of D.C. traffic. He and Jake split up the lists in order to research and verify the different leads they found in the folders. Tying the pieces together was exactly like his mystery source warned, a puzzle. A convoluted five-thousand-piece puzzle shrouded in shades of gray with no picture to guide them. Each folder led them down a new set of rabbit holes.

After lunch with Nick, Rhett would race back for a show production meeting. Switching gears from the jump drive to tonight's guests would be difficult. Never knowing when another cryptic text would come, Rhett now lived in a state of limbo. His attempts to text the informant's number were undeliverable, and the line remained untraceable to WBN's crack IT team.

Rhett's driver stopped in front of the restaurant. A line of hopeful diners waited behind a velvet rope. They readied phones for the next celebrity to enter the restaurant. Rhett smiled, waved, and winked as people shouted his name. As he strutted through the brick walled restaurant, opulence surrounded him. Ironically, the savory aromas reminded him just how much he missed the simplicity of his Grammy's kitchen.

Nick waved around the hostess to get Rhett's attention. Rhett immediately relaxed, filled with comfort and familiarity. Nick always radiated a calming force in their chaotic profession. Rhett needed this lunch more than he realized.

"Rhett, my friend, it is so good to see you in person." Nick stood to hug Rhett. Warmth flooded his senses. Rhett was off-balanced since the shooting. He hadn't grasped how much this clandestine adventure wore him down.

"I would never miss an opportunity to let you buy me lunch," Rhett teased his mentor. "Speaking of, who did you pay off to get a reservation the same month this place opened?"

Nick chuckled. "I interviewed Jacques a few years back. He liked me. I keep telling you, it pays to be nice to your interviewees. You don't always have to entrap them."

"Ah, you're still teaching me, even in your retirement." Rhett gulped down water as he leveled a gaze at his old friend.

"I guess I am." Nick's fatherly smile could not be missed. "How is Jake? I've been following his short film projects. He seems to do very well."

"Great. He's made some inroads into the industry. There are a few upcoming projects he's excited about."

"I heard Alexis is expecting." Nick answered Rhett's confused expression. "Miriam keeps in touch with her."

Rhett nodded. "They've been talking about moving home to be near family. Between the cost of living and crime rates, the balance is shifting in that direction. Plus, Jake can work from anywhere and there are tax breaks for new businesses back home." It was surreal, talking about Jake and Alexis's potential move as if it wouldn't upend his entire world. He looked up at Nick, who weighed Rhett's words.

"I imagine that would be a difficult transition for you. Them leaving."

Rhett shrugged his shoulders in response.

The manager approached their table with a plate of complimentary hors d'oeuvres. "Chef Boucher inquires if you would allow him to offer meal suggestions today." The question was not really a question.

"How could I refuse such a generous gift? Please pass along my deep and humble gratitude." Nick was ever the consummate gentleman. The manager removed their menus and promised to return with a suitable wine pairing.

Nick and Rhett settled into companionable conversation. Words volleyed back and forth, as they do between seasoned friends. Nick had kept busy during retirement. He was active with his grandchildren and traveled "for fun now," as he put it. He and Miriam were looking into buying an RV to travel across the country this fall and winter. They planned to travel north until the weather turned, then change course to cover the southern states. They would make each directional change with the flip of a coin.

Rhett marveled at the peace on Nick's face. This man taught Rhett everything he knew about journalism. Their styles were completely different, but Nick's integrity and ethical pursuit of the truth inspired Rhett in his own career. As they finished their meal and enjoyed dessert, Nick launched into work talk. It felt like old times.

"What are your thoughts on the secession conversation?"

"Come on, Nick. That's just political theater by the far right to shift attention from the election. They don't have a viable presidential candidate, and legally, they don't stand a chance of making a legitimate argument for secession." Rhett leaned back in his chair, stuffed from a seven-course lunch.

"Is it? I hear it's got traction and some powerful backers." Nick countered.

"Do you know something I don't? Based on what network execs are telling us, I think it's dead in the water. Not to mention, the final primary debate is Tuesday and should sway all attention back to center."

Nick studied Rhett with a grin. "For someone who started in this field by asking all the unpopular questions, you seem to tow the company line these days. I thought I taught you better than that."

"All right, Professor Branson, what questions should I be asking?" Rhett grinned as his friend schooled him.

"Well, I'd ask why states are pushing for secession in the first place. Check their poll numbers and agenda points. I'd ask if and why their constituents support the vote, not why the talking heads 'think' they're doing it."

"Talking heads? Really? Weren't you one of us last year?" Rhett smirked, convinced Nick was messing with him.

"I'm serious, Rhett. You cut your teeth investigating corruption leads. This is the biggest story in recent American history, and you're not even curious? If I were you, I'd follow the money. I can guarantee you that every tributary, left and right alike, snakes from the same muddy river. I bet you couldn't find one clean person in the entire city." Nick watched Rhett take in all this information. "I think this vote holds more traction than the experts understand. The people are tired of being pawns. They realized the pigs were running the farm, and filling the barnyard wall with dueling party line propaganda."

Rhett stared open-mouthed across the table. He couldn't believe the words that just spewed from his mentor. Nick, the levelheaded, never-take-a-side and remain impartial newsman, had jumped into the deep end.

"I'm sorry. I thought I was having lunch with my friend Nick, not some doppelgänger from another world. That's a complete one-eighty from your entire career." Rhett couldn't help but wonder about the man who taught him to weigh everything carefully. "What happened to you?"

"Is that really what you want to know?" Tenderness spilled from Nick's voice.

A nagging hurt, because of this man he admired and loved, bubbled inside Rhett. He had wanted to know the *why* for a long time. He watched Nick and decided to finally address the elephant between them.

"Go ahead, Rhett. Ask."

"You want me to ask the why? Why would you leave everything at the top of your career? You could have sat on any board at any network. Created your own content or streaming platform. You were at the top of the game, and you just walked away. I thought we had big plans, but you left. I still don't get it."

"Those are the questions I've been waiting for you to ask for months. I'm surprised it took you so long, but I'm glad you finally voiced them. Before we get too far, there's actually another reason I invited you to lunch today that stems from this conversation." Nick held up his hand to ward off the snarky comment he knew Rhett had waiting in the wings. "Obviously, the main reason was to catch up with a dear friend, but I do have a proposition for you."

"I'm listening," Rhett leveled Nick with suspicious eyes.

"When I began my career, the field of journalism kept the political machine in check because we all had different opinions. We held each other and the establishment accountable. Throughout history, the pen was always mightier than the sword. Pamphlets, newspapers, and scribes were the fighters of truth. The one thing all journalists agreed on was that everyone lied, so they didn't believe anyone. Over the years, the powerful learned how to fight pen with pen instead of sword. Now, all the major media sites are owned by the powerful, not by journalists. They hire people who will present the truth they want presented. Right, left, and even the so-called unbiased sources have tributaries that flow back to that same muddy water I mentioned earlier." Nick stopped to let Rhett process before he continued.

"I retired because the veil was lifted after an interview I did. It doesn't matter who, or what was said, but all of a sudden, I saw clearly. I needed a different perspective, and to do that, I needed distance. I longed to investigate like I used to. Go back to my roots, if you will."

"Did you find the answers you were looking for?" Rhett was confused, and his head spun from this exchange.

"I found a lot more than I intended, and it changed my life. I was baptized last year, and I have committed my life to serving Jesus."

Rhett dropped his head backwards. "Oh no, Nick. Don't you dare. You know my feelings about 'churched people.' They killed my mother and destroyed my life." Rhett shifted uncomfortably in his seat. Anger and sadness came from a sucker punch to the gut by his mentor. "Don't bother trying to evangelize or 'save' me. Keep that garbage to yourself."

"Rhett, may I finish? You asked what changed. I was giving you an honest answer, not trying to preach to you. The rest of the story stems from that starting point. Will you give me the benefit of the doubt and listen to the rest?"

Rhett nodded, annoyance etched on every facial feature.

"This new found faith convicted me to seek the truth and share it. I want to be the journalist I was called to be and shine a light into the darkness. And, I want you to help." Nick again held up his hand to stall Rhett's argument. "I'm not asking you to convert or to push any religious agenda. The opposite, in fact. You are a gifted journalist. I'm asking you to do what you do best. Ask the right questions."

"Go on," Rhett watched Nick carefully.

"My next series of interviews will dissect the potential secession vote. I want to cover the arguments and counterarguments fairly and thoroughly. In order to do that, I need both sides asking questions. You can hold me accountable, as I will you. I would like to end each broadcast with commentary from the two of us summarizing what we've learned. It's unorthodox and risky. I understand if you want to say no, but I hope you seriously consider it."

"What do you hope to gain from these interviews?" Rhett was baffled by Nick's revelations.

"I want to sharpen my pen and fight for the lost art of journalism. I want to teach people to ask questions and not just follow blindly what their favorite celebrity is saying. That includes the two of us. I towed the company line, and covered every one of the 'machine's' talking points. I was a trained monkey and didn't realize it. Now I want to investigate the truth. In order to do that, I need someone to hold me accountable. You are the only person I trust to do that."

"I'm not sure if the trained monkey statement should insult me or not." Rhett took a deep breath and looked around the crowded dining area. The room was packed with connected people able to snag tables, while the rest of America stood outside in line, hoping to get a glimpse. Rhett sighed. He had come so far from the motherless boy playing baseball just to afford college.

"Let me think about it. I'm not promising anything, but I'm not saying no. I have a lead right now that has me running in circles with Jake. I was actually going to run a few things by you today about that, but honestly, I'm fried after this bombshell lunch." Rhett ran a hand through his hair.

"Rhett, regardless of my career status, you know that Miriam and I see you as family. Whatever you decide, I'm always here for you to run stories by or just to talk."

The emotion in Nick's voice moved through Rhett. He was drowning in confusion lately and needed to come up for air soon. Maybe working with Nick again would bring some balance. "Send over your ideas and we'll touch base after the debate. Does that work?"

Nick nodded. "I forgot about the debate. I like that Cashe fellow. There's something about him that seems genuine. What do you think?"

"This may surprise you, but I actually have a date with his campaign manager tonight. We met for drinks earlier this week. I don't know if that makes a difference to your interview series. That could make me appear unbiased."

"Everything is incestuous in Washington. You can't throw a stone down either aisle without it coming back with the same fingerprints. Like I said, muddy waters."

Rhett rubbed his hand down his face. This lunch started peacefully but ended with a load of bricks on his shoulders.

Nick, attempted to recover their lunch, "I know I've put a lot on you and work is busy, but Miriam insists you come stay with us when you can get away for a weekend. Now, no more work talk. Moving onto a lighter and more interesting note, tell me about this date of yours."

"Thanks, I'm taking her to the West End parking lot."

"Wow, big spender," Nick laughed. "Taking her to your favorite spot in the city. I don't think you've ever done that before. It must be getting serious."

"I'm not sure. It could be. Right now, we're still in the getting-to-know-you phase, but I definitely like her."

"Now I'm intrigued."

"You're a newsman, you're always intrigued," Rhett bounced back.

"Truer words were never spoken." Nick smiled.

Chapter Twelve

The electricity grew as they approached their destination. Live music streamed through the night air, filling the space with more anticipation and excitement. Madison could see lights in the distance, reflecting from around the corner. She turned to look at Rhett's excited grin, keeping his secret spot a secret until the last minute.

"Tell me we're not going to a college party. You seriously can't be *that* guy." She had already questioned him when they exited the Metro near campus, but now they were a stone's throw from dormitories.

"No party, but this place will be crawling with college kids." Rhett was obviously enjoying this moment of anticipation.

They rounded the corner and landed in another world. Lights had been strung between tall poles. Picnic tables were scattered all along the parking lot. A live band played in the corner as food trucks lined the outer rim of the blacktop.

Madison took in their surroundings in awe. "This place is amazing. I feel like I'm on a movie set. How did you find it?"

"My buddy Jake and his wife Alexis live nearby. By day it's a community farmer's market they love. They saw a sign advertising the food truck convoy in the evenings. We tried it and ended up coming here every week for years."

"I bet. It has such a unique vibe." Madison gawked at all the students. Some were studying. Some were dancing. "I hope you aren't one of those guys who hits on college girls to inflate his ego," Madison teased.

Rhett leveled a gaze at her. "You know, you do a lot of assuming about me, Miss Lyn. I'm actually on the straight and narrow, but your imagination takes you down twisted paths when it comes to me."

She laughed and held up her hands, "You're right, I'm sorry. I surrender."

"Sadly, the real reason I come here is even more embarrassing," Rhett confessed.

"I'm dying to hear this." Madison stared at him eagerly.

"I'm invisible here. The first few times we came, I realized college students have no idea who I am. The kids with political ambitions are hitting the bars closer to town, trying to network and make connections. Every once in a while, someone will tell me their mom loves me and ask for a picture, but mostly, I'm just some guy who kind of looks familiar to them. It's nice to be just a guy eating at a food truck."

Madison saw a sadness as he shrugged. "Rhett Paulson, you continue to surprise and impress me. I'm in love with this place already."

Rhett's boyish grin warmed her heart and poked at the butterflies that had taken up residence in her stomach since she met him.

"Well, what would you like to eat? I can vouch for the hoagies, the barbecue guy, the taco guy, the salad lady, and the chicken and waffles. I would stay away from the gyros. Jake had a very bad experience there once. I'll save you from the details." Rhett whispered the last part into her ear.

"Thank you for that. Everything looks wonderful, and the smells are killing me. I have no idea what to pick." Madison twirled in a circle, slowly taking in all of her options. "What's your favorite? My father always says to watch the regulars because they know the best options."

"Good advice. My favorite is the Mangia truck. They're two cousins from Philly making hoagies. Their grandparents are Italian immigrants. The bread is soft yet sturdy. The way they stack the meats and cheeses is a pure art form. But their dressing? Oh, the dressing is magical."

Madison was amused by Rhett's impassioned description. "That elaboration was all for a sandwich?"

Rhett, clearly offended, "What? A sandwich? Calling it a sandwich is insulting. Just wait until you taste the artistry of the hoagie. Come on." Rhett gently took Madison's hand in his as he twirled her around once towards an Italian themed food truck in the back corner of the lot.

Sparks sizzled through Madison with his initial touch. Warmth filled her as they walked across the lot. It's like they'd done this a thousand times before. It was more than déjà vu. More than comfortable companionship. It made her feel like home. Madison intensely felt shivers course through her. Was it possible to feel this comfortable and nervous simultaneously?

Rhett asked permission to order Madison's hoagie, and she was glad she agreed. He was correct in his description. Madison had never eaten a sandwich like that in her life. The balance of flavors and textures was perfection. Rhett almost choked when Madison moaned after her first bite. They ate, they laughed, they danced. It was hard to believe their date could get any better, but it did.

Curled up under Rhett's arm, Madison relished the most decadent chocolate-banana milkshake. It was rich and creamy, and so thick she had to battle the straw for every taste.

"Here, try mine." Rhett lowered the straw of his black raspberry shake. "Back home, my mom used to tell me about this restaurant that made her favorite milkshakes. The Canteen. She would go there with her friends in high school. It closed down before I was born, but she loved telling stories about it. I think remembering the innocence of high school made her feel whole again. Grammy tried to recreate the milkshakes for me. Don't get me wrong, I love Grammy's shakes, but the ones from my mom's memories were unattainable. I think she would have loved these." Rhett's voice turned melancholic.

He was far off in thought. He had shared bits and pieces about his mother, but only facts, like a story he was reporting. Madison got the feeling this type of personal slip was a rarity for him, so she savored the intimacy of it. They sat in silence, building their own milkshake memories.

One by one, the trucks closed up shop for the night. The band played their last song, and college students packed up their blankets, books, and backpacks. Rhett stood and held out his hand for Madison. "Ready?"

Her smile twinkled for him. "I am."

They swayed as they walked hand in hand down the street back toward the Metro station. "What does your schedule look like the rest of the weekend?" Rhett leaned closer and nudged her shoulder.

"Debate prep. All day, every day."

"I was actually surprised you had tonight free."

"Jackson had a donor engagement."

"What kind of event with donors doesn't include his campaign manager?"

Madison stiffened a little. Rhett felt it.

"Sorry, I can't help it. Occupational hazard. Grammy says I was born speaking in questions." Rhett shrugged. "I promise I'm not fishing. I'm legitimately trying to get to know you. I hope you know that."

Rhett stopped in the middle of the sidewalk and forced Madison to look at him. "You know that, right?"

Madison's head drooped a little. Did she know that?

Rhett gently lifted her chin with their entwined hands. "Hey, I don't give up the location of my magical hoagie and milkshake place just to get a story."

His chuckle earned a smile. "I know. I'm sorry. I guess this is my occupational hazard. You know, loose lips sink ships, as they say." It was Madison's turn for melancholy, as she tugged at him to keep walking. "Rich and I learned quickly in college that people want to know everything they can about Jackson Cashe of *The* Cashes. We take his privacy personally," Madison offered as an explanation.

"I admire that." Rhett squeezed her hand and smiled over at her. "What if we set ground rules?"

She watched him, unconvinced but charmed. "I'm game. You start."

"For every work question, the other person has to offer up something of equal value. For example, if you want to talk about something annoying from the campaign trail, I have to tell you something internal about WBN. That way, we're both vulnerable." Rhett obviously felt pretty good about his negotiation skills based on his grin.

"What could you possibly tell me that would balance a political nugget of gossip? Makeup tips for prime time?" She straight up teased him now.

"Ouch. No, but what if I told you that someone in makeup was fooling around with two different anchors and neither knows about the other one?" He watched from the corner of his eye as her chin dropped.

"No way, which ones?"

Rhett laughed. "Nope, not until we have an agreement. I can't continue this," he pointed back and forth between them, "unless I know I can trust you."

He teased her now, but it was so cute. Madison was torn between her un-natural code of silence with her roommates and her desire to have an adult relationship with a man not named Jackson or Rich. She was warring with her thoughts as he offered another negotiation term.

"What if I told you something from my past that no one, not even Jake, knows? An admission that could get me talked about, even on my own network. Let's call it collateral. You can keep it in your back pocket."

Curious, she tilted her head to study him. "You would tell me something that scandalous? Why? We barely know each other."

Rhett stopped walking again and took Madison's other hand in his. He studied her face for a minute. She could tell he was making a decision. "In college, my baseball scholarship didn't cover rent. I needed money. I started writing essays, research papers, homework, anything I could write for other people under a pseudonym. Many people owe me for their college degrees. The school paper wrote a series of articles about the 'Silver Tongued Bandit', but no one ever figured out my identity. I made enough to pay for rent, books, and all of grad school. I broke every ethics and code of conduct rule there was and probably owe the IRS some serious change." Rhett watched as she stared at him in shock.

"I'm telling you this because I trust you and I want you to trust me. I know this sounds crazy, but there is something about you I can't figure out Madison. I feel like I've known you forever. Spending time together makes me feel like I'm back home, sitting on Grammy's porch swing. I want more of it."

Home. He felt it, too. Madison closed her eyes and took a deep breath. This cautious, over-prepared, uber-organized, highly skeptical lawyer was about to jump head first down a rabbit hole with the most unlikely potential boyfriend she could imagine.

"I hate Hayman Barnes. He is the most egotistical, misogynistic, narcissistic, elitist snob I have ever met in my entire life." Madison blew out a breath and watched the shock drip from Rhett's face before he replaced it with a relieved smile.

"Tell me how you really feel." They both laughed.

Rhett leaned down and placed a solitary kiss on Madison's lips. The pressure was intense and lingering. His hands cradled her neck and face as his forehead came to rest against hers. "Thank you."

"You're welcome." Madison wrapped her arms tighter around his waist. They stood there, in the middle of the sidewalk, and enjoyed their beautifully vulnerable moment. Neither speaking a word.

She was the one to take his hand as they began to stroll down the sidewalk. "Now tell me more about this 'Silver Tongued Bandit' and how you got away with it."

They talked about everything and nothing as they rode the Metro and Rhett walked her back to the townhouse she shared with Rich and Jackson.

Chapter Thirteen

The room was shrouded in darkness, except for a sliver of moonlight escaping between the heavy blackout curtains. Rhett's head swiveled around to check the red numbers beside his bed. Three in the morning.

Rhett rubbed his eyes and surveyed his surroundings. It wasn't like him to wake up in the middle of the night like this. Something must have startled him. He remembered dreaming, but the visions were already a distant memory. He flipped off the covers and dragged heavy legs out of bed. The pain from his shoulder wound probably woke him. It still burned at times, especially when he tried to roll over at night.

After his date with Madison, Rhett came home to an empty apartment and a cold shower. They talked on her front steps for an hour before he tore himself away from her kisses. He respected that she wanted to take things slowly, but that didn't make it easier to leave. The dim kitchen light guided his feet into the open space.

His penthouse was masculine, with strong lines. Pops of navy blue accented the grays, and whites. At least that's how his decorator described it to him. She said it was clean and industrial. Rhett was still trying to discern how those two words meshed. Gloria Masterson was a regular contributor on WBN's morning program. She hit on him all the time, but Rhett drew the line at cougars. She settled for decorating his new place after the first quarter ratings came in for *Rhett's Take*. Two months later, his penthouse was featured in some interior design magazine with Gloria's face front and center. Rhett appreciated the elegance, but it felt cold and sterile, not homey. This place was nothing like Grammy's house.

Rhett poured himself half a glass of orange juice and leaned against the counter. It was cold and refreshing, just what he needed. The floor to ceiling windows of his corner apartment overlooked the city lights. Sadly, D.C. felt more sinister during the daylight hours than it did at night these days, and that said a lot. Most of his neighbors hired private security guards, so the high crime rates didn't much impact his daily routine.

That's why Jake and Alexis wanted to move. Two stabbings and a drive-by shooting happened in their neighborhood within the past three months. Rhett offered to move them closer to him, but they refused. Jake said he wanted to raise his kid back home, near family. Rhett was family too, but he understood the draw. The thought of them leaving reminded Rhett how alone he was in this town. Surrounded by people, adored by fans, but utterly alone.

He rinsed his glass and started walking back to his bedroom when something on the floor caught his eye. Rhett froze. He looked around for anything out of place. The shadows looked bigger than they did a minute ago. He approached the door leading to the back stairwell and scanned the peephole. The hallway was empty. He bent down to pick up a manila envelope. It was lightweight and blank on the outside.

Rhett walked back into the kitchen and pulled out a stool from under the counter. He felt shaky. Carefully opening the flap, he looked into the envelope, searching for any clues. An engraved invitation slid out onto the countertop. The invitation was for some Global Food Shortage Symposium hosted by the Johan Philipsen Foundation in partnership with the World Finance Organization. Supporters included the SurfIn Collaboration, and the Adam Ford Foundation. He scanned the information and rubbed his chin. An Internet address was handwritten on the back of the invitation.

"For the love. This is crazy. What have I gotten myself into...?" His voice trailed off into the silence of the night. Shivers ran up and down Rhett's spine. This was getting out of control. They were coming to his house now. He walked over to where his phone was charging. He swiped until he located the security system app. Sure enough, at three in the morning, a man from Arrowwood Delivery Services slid the folder under his door from the stairwell. That explained what woke him from sleep. Rhett called down to the doorman.

"Mr. Paulson, sir, is everything all right?"

"Yeah, Jimmy. Hey, did you let a delivery guy upstairs a few minutes ago?" Rhett logged into the building's security feed for residents.

"I did. Just like you asked me to. Did something happen? I can call Arrowwood Delivery if you need me to." Jimmy's voice was riddled with confusion, but not as much as Rhett's mind.

"What do you mean, like I asked you to?"

"Your assistant called right after you came home tonight. Said you wanted to let me know a package was on its way for you and to let them upstairs no matter the time. The ID said it was from WBN, so I assumed it was legit. Was that not from you?" Jimmy was the newest of the doormen, which is why he scored the night shift. He was a good kid, but a little on the flighty side.

"Next time I get a package, have them leave it at the desk. Okay, Jimmy?" Rhett was more annoyed that any attempt of grilling Jimmy would get him nowhere. Rhett could get information out of a turnip, but he wasn't so sure Jimmy would win a game of wits against a turnip.

"You got it, Mr. Paulson. Can I do anything else for you?"

"No, Jimmy, thanks." Rhett gritted his teeth as he hung up and processed his options.

Rhett texted the number of his mystery source. Silence. "Damn it!"

Flipping on lights throughout the apartment, Rhett set up a workspace on the white marble island. His laptop came to life as he plugged in the tactical laptop Lucas gave him for offline activity. Silence broken only by the clicking of the keys as he entered the web address into the empty search bar. He waited as the screen revealed more puzzle pieces.

Flexing his research muscles, Rhett opened over twenty tabs about the symposium, the hosts, and the possibility of a looming food crisis. He shot off an email to Oliver with action points, starting with pulling up any intel they had on the surprise guest nutritionist from his show. He then emailed Rahemia, requesting show coverage for the symposium. Hiding in plain sight was always his favorite investigative tactic.

With no sleep and more leads to follow than he could fathom, Rhett headed for the shower. Later, as he drove into work, the sounds of city life were silenced as his driver navigated the busy streets. The sedan pulled in front of WBN, where a security guard opened the car door. Rhett emerged to a few tourists with cameras. He waved as he dashed into the lobby. Normally, Rhett stopped to ask people where they were from and chatted for a few minutes. He was in no mood today.

Rhett's assistant, Oliver, dutifully waited at the elevator doors with a cup of coffee and a tablet. A few years ago, Rhett and Jake were investigating a lead for a story, and Oliver worked at the diner where they became dependent on the coffee. The kid's wit and sarcasm throughout the weeklong stakeout inspired Rhett to hire him on the spot. Turned out Oliver graduated with a journalism degree from a subpar college and was working two part-time jobs to subsidize his mediocre pay at a local news station. Neither job allowed him to pursue his real passion for writing graphic novels. Rhett, who hadn't found a decent assistant from the pool of brown-nosers at WBN, hired the kid at the end of the week. He saw in Oliver just the right amount of gratitude and irreverence that Rhett needed. Oliver kept Rhett on track and running efficiently, but never let the power get to Rhett's head. Grammy loved Oliver. She sent him Christmas and birthday presents.

"You weren't kidding about not getting any sleep. You look terrible. I'll text makeup and tell them you'll need more time tonight." The elevator started rising to the top.

"All coming from the guy wearing a crumpled band t-shirt from the nineties. Do you even know who they are?" Rhett looked Oliver up and down.

"My parents listened to them all the time. Their first album is a cult classic." Oliver's confidence made Rhett groan.

"Now I feel old *and* tired." Rhett shook his head. "Did you put in the research request for me? I need that information yesterday." They strode out of the elevator and down the corridor with purpose.

"About that. I emailed the request, but I got a response asking for approval from the higher-ups."

Rhett stopped in his tracks. "Have we ever received that before for any other requests?"

"Nada. I was surprised too, so I emailed Rahemia's assistant and asked for clarification, but she hasn't responded yet."

They began walking again. "The other thing you asked for is in motion right now. I sent a network runner to make sure the iced coffee was still cold when it arrived at its destination. Speaking of, why are we sending drinks to Jackson Cashe's campaign office?"

Rhett patted Oliver on the shoulder. "That, my young friend, is how you impress a lady."

Oliver laughed in response. "No offense, but I handle your calendar. I should be giving you dating advice."

"Quantity does not rival quality, young Oliver." Rhett entered his office, picked up the file on his desk, and dropped his laptop bag on his chair. "Now, let's get this party started. Nick Branson is supposed to send over a packet for me to review. We may have a joint project with him. And call Jake. I need him here pronto."

"You got it, boss." Oliver left Rhett's office with a mock salute.

"All right, Adam Ford. What are you up to, and why does it give me the heeby jeebies?" Rhett spoke to the air as he pulled out his notes.

An hour later, Rhett's coffee table looked like a notepad factory had exploded on it. Jake had the tactical laptop on the couch comparing spreadsheets from the jump drive to news stories Oliver pulled from archived shows.

A knock on the opened door caught the attention of all three men. "Knock-knock. You boys look like you're neck deep in some serious research. Anything I should know?" Rahemia assessed the situation before her.

Rhett took a cursory glance around his office, trying to see this from her vantage point. "Not yet. I'm still trying to determine if this is a rabbit hole I want to follow."

"This looks more like a sink hole than a rabbit hole. You sure you don't want to run any ideas by me before you get too far gone?" She came inside, careful to avoid stepping on Oliver's strewn index cards while sneaking a peek. Jake twisted his position on the couch to keep the screen from her view. "Does this have anything to do with your mystery informant and the shooting? Because the FBI warned us against digging too far. Not to mention a direct order from Jerry to drop it completely."

Rhett cocked his head and studied her. "Doesn't that seem weird to you?"

"Rhett," her voice laced with warning, "drop it. I like my job."

Rhett turned on his charm. "Rahemia, trust me. Have I steered you wrong yet? Give me until next week. If I find anything worth following, I'll lay it all out for you. Speaking of follow up, can you get me approval to attend that food crisis simulation symposium thing I emailed you about?" Rhett often found that playing dumb helped him gain intel.

"Yeah, what is that all about? You were annoyed when I booked the nutritionist for the show. Now you want to attend the conference she's headlining?"

"Hmm, that's curious. She's on the panel?"

Rahemia eyed him suspiciously. "Rhett, she talked about food shortages for ten minutes. She works for the Global Alliance Institute for Progress as a food ambassador. Why is this information 'curious' now?"

Jake addressed Rahemia, but his eyes darted to Rhett. "Global Alliance as in GA?"

"Yes, Jake, that generally is how acronyms work. You two are making me nervous. I don't like feeling nervous."

Rhett walked over to Rahemia, resting his arm across her shoulder. He turned her around as he strolled her to the door. "One week, I promise. Get me that approval. I'm becoming increasingly interested in our food ambassador and her institute's seminar."

"For the record, I already submitted a request with Jerry's office. I have Keira making preliminary arrangements for our show to air live from the event. I'm waiting on Jerry to okay it." Rahemia stopped Rhett's forward movement and pinned him with a look. "Paulson, keep me in the loop. You have one day to follow this rabbit hole. One. Day."

"Yes, boss." Rhett flashed his famous smile and closed the door behind her.

Rahemia flung her arms in the air. "You never close your door!"

Rhett smiled, waved, and slowly turned.

Jake crossed his arms. "Well, this just got a lot more interesting."

Chapter Fourteen

R ich's voice carried loudly across the campaign office, "Mads, we're making a coffee order. Do you want something, or is your boyfriend sending a messenger with a special order just for you again?"

"You are hilarious, Rich." She called back to him. "I'll take a large iced caramel macchiato with whole milk, please, and thank you." Madison grunted as she looked to Jackson for support.

"Don't growl at me. I didn't say a word." Jackson kept reading the notes in front of him. "*But*, you do have to admit that sending a network messenger over with a personalized coffee order is an upgrade in the relationship status."

"That was sweet, wasn't it?" Madison wistfully stared off into space before shaking her head in realization that Jackson was now looking directly at her.

"Madsi?"

"What?"

"I've never seen you like this. I think you just swooned a little. Who are you and what have you done with Madison Lyn?"

"Stop." She laughed at herself and him. "I know. I don't know what's come over me. He makes me feel giddy. I make fun of girls who act like this, and now I'm all gaga when I think about him. Ugh. This is crazy."

"What are we talking about?" Rich sauntered back inside the room. He collapsed into his chair and propped his feet on the conference table.

"Madsi just swooned when she thought about her boyfriend."

Madison's head dropped into her hands. "Okay, here we go."

"Mads, I won't pick on you. I think it's sweet. Does he have sisters? Maybe we can triple date. If it goes well, we can have one big wedding and buy houses on the same street." Rich grabbed his notepad to work.

Jackson choked back a laugh. "Leave her alone, Rich. Her boyfriend might come and beat us up after school."

"See? This is exactly why I don't tell you two things." She returned to her laptop screen.

"We're sorry, Madsi. We tease you because we love you." Jackson appeared repentant. His look told Rich to stop the teasing.

"Jackson is right. In all seriousness, the coffee was a nice gesture. Are we ever going to meet the guy?"

She wearily weighed the looks on both of their faces. "Maybe."

Rich swiveled in his chair, watching her. "I think your dad would want us to pre-screen the guy. Or does Daniel Lyn not know about him yet?"

"Don't you dare tell my father." Madison gazed out into the office, then stiffened. "Look busy. Hayman has returned from the gallows and he doesn't look happy."

The air in the room changed. Madison and Rich hardened their postures. Jackson shifted in his chair. Silence filled the room. Coldness followed.

Hayman came in barking orders. "We have a packed itinerary. We need to get moving. Time waits for no man."

Last week, Hayman had requested a change in the debate format. After a visit with a few "friends of the campaign," as he termed them, the party approved the changes. The campaign team had a lot of prep work to do and needed to head back to the mock studio. They would be there all night. The three of them packed up their belongings and headed to the waiting SUVs. As they drove over, Madison took a deep breath and picked up her phone.

Madison: After the debate, we're having a few people over to the townhouse. Are you interested?

She held her breath. Meeting the friends was a status upgrade on her end. It seemed both she and Rhett had made moves in this game of chess dating.

Rhett: Interested? Absolutely! Available? Not until after the after-show is finished. Would that be too late?

Madison: I doubt it. We'll be too wired to sleep.

Rhett: I get to meet the friends. Should I be nervous?

Madison: Only if you insult them during the after-show LOL.

Rhett: Note taken. I've got to go. Show run-through in a minute. Thanks for asking.

Madison: Thanks for the coffee.

Rhett: My pleasure.

The drive to the studio was quick. The team picked up where they left off this morning. Rich and the interns settled at podiums with their talking points. Madison worked with the meta-analysis expert they hired to track audience responses during the debate. Hours flew by in an instant. They were prepared. By now, Jackson could handle any debate curve balls thrown at him.

As the rest of the team took a break, Jackson reviewed notes with Hayman off in a corner. Rich walked over and sat down beside Madison. He wheeled the chair as close as he could get, then leaned into her. "Have you seen the new talking points? There is no way Jackson can say this."

Madison looked down at the paper Rich slid across her keyboard. He backed away a little to scan the room as Madison scanned the document.

"This is the new script Hayman had his assistant place on our podiums. Look at the third and fourth bullet points."

Madison tilted herself toward Rich and covered her mouth with her hand. "Wait, is this for one of you to say acting as another candidate, or Jackson's talking point?"

"All of the above. We've been working from the projected answers my team put together based on what we think the other candidates will say. This is different. This is an actual script. Either Hayman knows something we don't, or all four candidates are randomly doing a one-eighty on the same two platform topics." Rich placed his elbows on his knees and shook his head back and forth. "I don't like this at all. Something isn't adding up."

"How does this line up with the changes to the debate format Hayman requested?"

"Hayman wanted to relegate these two topics to the end of the debate. I assumed it was because they want to hold these topics until after the convention, but now I think it's something else. As time runs out, the moderator will give them each two minutes to cover the last topics. Essentially, if this was coordinated, this will end up becoming an eight-to-ten-minute speech changing the party platform." Rich watched Hayman animatedly speak to Jackson in the distance.

"The viewers will see right through this. How can they flip-flop so blatantly? Jackson won't go for this." Madison shook her head and scooted the paper back to Rich.

"They do it all the time, Mads. Think about it. Filibuster! Four years later, no filibuster. Open borders! Close the borders. Pack the courts! Respect the courts. Political platforms change for the highest bidder each election cycle. Both sides do it. You know this."

"But, that's not Jackson. That's why we're here, right? The party can't force Jackson to change his platform. Can they?"

"I'm telling you Mads, the deeper we get, the muddier the waters." Rich picked up the paper and walked back to the podium to wait for Jackson.

Madison sat forward in her chair and surveyed the room. Everyone scurried about, working hard every day for Jackson's campaign. They canvassed, made calls, stuffed envelopes, and rode in cramped tour buses across the country. What would they all think if Jackson turned on a dime? What would she do?

Chapter Fifteen

City sounds swirled around Rhett. Car horns, loud engines, backup beepers, and people yelling. The city never slept. Rhett had his driver drop him off a block away so he could walk. He needed to clear his head. Rhett's life was becoming disordered, something he worked hard to avoid. Voices swirled around him. Nick, Oliver, Jake, the mysterious texter, and Rahemia, who, for the first time in their relationship, handed him a list of talking points with a "no go" section for his show. Rhett found that very odd.

The debate tonight was surreal. He wasn't sure if it was because of his new relationship with Madison, the uneasy feeling he'd had since the shooting, or if it was something deeper.

Nick messengered over a packet of interviewees, along with extensive bios on each. When Rhett called to discuss the list, Nick strongly suggested he keep the list quiet and told him to stay safe. Normally, that wouldn't phase him, but Nick truly sounded concerned for Rhett's safety. Rhett had covered wars and went undercover with a SEAL team. Why would Nick be concerned now? The shooting had everyone on edge. Rhett rubbed his shoulder. He'd ditched the sling after the first week, but the pain was a constant reminder of his situation.

Rhett attempted to shake the thoughts from his mind as he neared Madison's brownstone. The debate was over. His after-show ratings hit an all-time high. Now he was on his way to see Madison and meet her friends. He needed to put on his game face and focus on his date, not the novelesque ideas floating around his mind like a Noir film from the forties. He was not William Powell, and this was not a detective movie. Rhett breathed deeply and shook his hands out, which he didn't even realize he'd been clenching. Rolling his neck, he picked up his pace and finally made it to Madison's.

After lovely conversations with two separate security checkpoints, Rhett knocked on her door and was rewarded with Madison's brown eyes greeting him.

"Oh no. You look nervous. Did I say something on the after-show to offend someone?" Rhett cocked his head and awaited her response.

Madison tugged on his arm and pulled him inside the doorway. She closed the door and tucked him into a corner, out of eyesight. He leaned down and stole a quick kiss, just in case she changed her mind about him and was about to let him down easy. Her smile as he pulled away gave him hope.

"No, but I wanted to warn you that after we finished the initial debate rehash, the crowd turned the topic to meeting you. It's a tossup whether they'll ambush you or provide an onslaught of embarrassing stories about me. Neither of which is ideal. I wanted to warn you in case you wanted to cut and run." Madison watched him cautiously.

Rhett wrapped both arms around her waist and pulled her up against his chest. "I'd gladly face an inquisition for you, but I'm rather intrigued by the second option. I would love some great Madison Lyn stories. Will incriminating pictures be involved?"

She chuckled, "Oh, I hope not." Her arms snaked up and over his shoulders to wrap around his neck. Madison surprised them both by pulling him into a deep and intimate kiss. When they finally parted, Madison's chocolate eyes glimmered. Her cheeks colored the barest shade of blush and her smile melted him. "Are you ready?"

Rhett reluctantly released her as he held out his hand. "Lead the way."

The townhouse walls showcased expensive artwork. Decorated, no doubt, by a professional hired to present a specific persona to guests. Together, they walked down the corridor to the sounds of laughter and the television singing in the background. At the end of the hall, a kitchen counter was covered with bottles, glasses, and catered food trays. The space opened into a living room where friends chatted away while simultaneously watching the screen. It looked exactly like Rhett expected it to, a barely used bachelor pad decorated by someone other than said bachelors. Rhett knew Madison had the entire third floor to herself. She called it her oasis from the man cave that was the rest of the house.

Just as Madison told him, there were about twenty other guests. Some family, some friends, but all trusted members of the inner circle. Rhett knew this was more than just meeting the boyfriend. This was Madison, welcoming him into the secret society the three of them had cultivated for years. Rhett did not take this knowledge lightly. He squeezed her hand as she looked up at him with a nervous smile.

Rhett broke the seal and jumped in with both feet as he exclaimed to the party, "At least you're watching the right network! That could have been awkward."

Rhett knew how to win over an audience. The room erupted with laughter and a shout, "Mads, he's going to fit in just fine."

Within seconds, people offering drinks, food, and handshakes surrounded Rhett. Madison stood right by his side the entire time. He wasn't sure if she was more nervous for herself or him. Rhett had been introduced to everyone in the room and given their connection to the group. They had all been around forever. The newest addition was Jackson's fiancé. After only six months of dating, Vanessa and Jackson were engaged right before he announced his candidacy. Vanessa was a model slash wannabe actress. Jackson was smitten with Vanessa. Rich and Madison, not so much.

Rhett was prepared for the protective older brother approach from Jackson and Rich, but to his surprise, they seemed more curious than threatening. Madison didn't fit into either stereotype of younger sister or mother hen. She was their contemporary sage. The fixer of problems and the voice of reason. Jackson and Rich didn't view her as weak or pushy. She was something different to everyone in that room. Rhett soon realized Madison had no idea how valuable she was to every person in their circle. She saw herself as a team player. Her friends saw her as the captain. She reminded him of Jake in that regard. Rhett saw firsthand how much Madison touched the lives and hearts of those she cared about, and that's when he realized his heart was a goner.

Voices bounced around the room. Side conversations naturally intermingled with the main topics. Rhett learned so much from this tight-knit group of friends. They were loyal and supportive, but they dished out plenty of good natured jabs. The one major take away from tonight was that Jackson Cashe chose his friends well. Growing up as sole heir to the Cashe kingdom, Rhett guessed that discernment was a necessity for survival.

Jackson was not the off-the-rails-celebrity-rich-kid that he could have been. Madison said he attributed it to his mother, who made sure Jackson lived like a normal kid, even down to doing chores. After Jackson's mother died, responsibility was engrained in him by the prep school he attended. One thing was for sure, everyone in this room had sworn an oath to protect his secrets. Rhett admired any man who inspired that kind of unadulterated loyalty.

Rhett also had Rich pegged wrong. The political machine they lived in called him the "Spin Master Extraordinaire." On camera, Rich came across as all flash and charm. He could make the coldest cynic melt with the flash of a dimple. Classic gentleman infused with a school boy playfulness. He still was all those things in this room, but Rhett observed the many layers of Rich's conversations. Rich's goal was to make people see things from another perspective, whether or not he agreed with it. Acting as the consummate devil's advocate. Not in a malevolent way, more of a party game in which he helped people see both sides. Rich wasn't "spinning" so much as trying to get people to find the truth through a series of questions. Rhett respected that.

Madison humanized them both while adding her own gifts to the mix. Together, these three were unstoppable. Rhett was in awe of how they complimented one another. This was a rare friendship indeed.

As the party thinned out and the hour drew long, Rhett found himself on the couch with Madison flanked by Rich in a recliner and Jackson sitting on the coffee table. Vanessa had vanished upstairs shortly after Rhett arrived. She was flying to Milan in the morning to film her first movie role. Rhett made a mental note not to watch that movie. Madison changed the channel as Jackson and Rich simultaneously groaned. Rhett looked between them questioningly.

"Mads, why do you insist on doing this to us?" Rich tossed a throw pillow at her, which Rhett caught before it hit her.

"Isn't it rude to watch your boyfriend's competitor while he's in the room?" Jackson slid from the coffee table onto the couch next to Madison.

Boyfriend. Rhett liked the sound of that. "Hey now, let's not forget that I have the highest ratings in my time slot. I don't think calling this guy a competitor is fair." Rhett cocked his head and smiled.

"Check out this guy. He can definitely hold his own around here, Mads." Rich took a swig from his bottle.

"You know why. It's important to hear both sides. How else can we know how you truly did tonight if we don't listen to the counterarguments?" Madison, the definitive voice of logic. Rhett was sunk. He pulled her closer to his side.

"As always, you are correct, but I don't want to listen to Jackson second guessing himself for the rest of the night. I've had too much to drink for that and we're out of aspirin."

"What does that mean? Is there something I should be second guessing? You said I was flawless." Jackson attempted to remain relaxed, but the tension in his voice was unmistakable.

Madison patted his knee. "You did great, sweetheart."

"Madsi," Jackson's tone warned her not to joke about this, "tell me the truth."

"Jackson, you were great! We all know my dad will call me in the morning and ask for counterarguments. I want to be prepared."

That comment struck Rhett as peculiar. Before he could answer, Madison offered him a quick explanation. "My grandparents escaped China during the Cultural Revolution with my father, who was a child. Daniel Lyn does not trust the government, so he taught me to question everything." Madison shrugged. "I drive these two crazy with it, but I can't help myself."

Rhett strained his neck to stare down at Madison. "Wait. Did you just say that your dad doesn't trust the government?" Rich and Jackson both stifled a laugh as Madison squirmed.

"I did."

"He does know what you do for a living, right? That you are leading the team to elect your roommate as the most powerful political figure in the government and the entire world?"

"He does. That is precisely why he drills me on both sides of every issue. Plus, he likes Jackson." Madison tilted her head.

"Daniel doesn't like Jackson. He likes the baseball tickets Jackson Senior sends his way now and then." Rich laughed, Jackson glared. "He, on the other hand, loves me."

"The tickets don't hurt," Madison chuckled.

"Stop. Daniel Lyn loves me." Jackson sounded wounded.

"Wow, I like your dad already. Do you think he'll like me?"

Rich choked on his beer, and Jackson made a strange face, indicating an awkward answer.

"Oh, he's gonna hate you. He calls WBN the barnyard wall from Orwell's *Animal Farm*. Plus, you're dating his Little Button." Rich finished his drink.

Now it was Madison's turn to choke out a response, "You're right. Let's stop and move on to another topic. It's supposed to rain tomorrow."

All three men were laughing now at the unflappable Madison Lyn flapping. "Little Button? That is so cute. Is there a backstory?" Rhett loved this night.

"When I was born, he said I had a button nose."

"Why Madison, are you blushing?" Rhett watched her face light up as her cheeks pinked.

"All right, all right. Let's watch the show." Madison held up the remote and pointed it towards the TV to increase the volume.

The four-person panel bantered back and forth, covering all aspects of the debate. Rhett should have been listening to the commentators, but instead, he watched the three of them. Madison, Jackson, and Rich all picked up on different points of reference. It was fascinating. It seemed the three of them shared one processing center with different spreadsheets. A wave of tension that swept through the space broke his thoughts. It was a rare state of unrest, as they were obviously uncomfortable.

The odd silence morphed into Jackson glancing from Rich to Madison. His eyes were asking a question. Rhett understood immediately and raised his hands in the air. "Hey, I'm completely off the clock, but if you guys need me to leave or go to the bathroom or take a walk around the block, I understand." He really hoped Madison didn't want him to leave. He wasn't ready to part with her yet.

Madison placed her hand on Rhett's leg. "No, it's fine. You watched the debate so you already know the issue."

Rhett racked his brain for what issue they referred to. The only options were immigration and education.

"Since we have an expert here to ask, I'd like to pick his brain." Rich straightened in the recliner. Jackson sighed. Madison stiffened.

For the first time since entering the brownstone, Rhett felt nervous.

"Here's my question. Why didn't WBN make any comments about the immigration stance changing from all four candidates? We watched your show for two hours, and not one person on your panel mentioned immigration other than to applaud the individual statements. Which, if we're honest, were the exact opposite of their stances two years ago. The other three legacy networks didn't touch the topic at all either. I'm wondering why?"

"Rich." The clear warning came from Jackson.

"I'm just curious. These guys can't seem to stop talking about it." Rich waved at the TV screen.

Rhett squared himself to answer, "Honestly, I'm not sure. Nick Branson texted to ask me the same question on the way here tonight. I was more shocked that all four candidates agreed on something." Rhett awkwardly laughed, trying to ease the tension.

Madison leaned into Rhett, attempting to explain the confusion. "Rich was an Army brat. He spent a lot of time in Texas where his mom's family lives. He has a very strong opinion on immigration."

"An opinion which I thought the campaign supported until two days ago," Rich grumbled to no one in particular.

Jackson closed his eyes, rested his head on the back of the couch, and pinched the bridge of his nose. "Rich, do we need to do this again?"

"No, we don't." Madison changed the channel back to WBN. Rhett got the feeling that Madison regularly acted as referee between these two. "We're all tired. We can debrief about this tomorrow, okay? Okay. Now, let's talk about Charlotte Harmon. She comes across to me as a diva. She looks like she wants to eat Rich for dinner every time he's on her show."

Shocked, Rhett laughed out loud. "Charlotte wants to eat every man for dinner." He shivered at the thought.

Like a light switch, they all flipped back to normal. Rich got up and walked into the kitchen, grabbing two beers. Rich went right over to Jackson and handed him a bottle, then clapped his shoulder. Jackson took the remote and changed the channel to baseball.

Rhett felt like he'd intruded on a personal moment, but no one seemed to want him to leave. Madison was still curled up under his arm. She yawned and Rhett watched her eyes flutter. He knew he should offer to leave, but her warmth felt so comforting he selfishly wanted to prolong the feeling. He leaned down and kissed the top of her head.

"West Virginia, right?" Jackson looked at Rhett.

Rhett nodded.

"Pirates fan?"

"Painfully so, yes."

Rich cackled. "Yep, Mads's dad is going to hate you."

And so it became just three guys talking sports. The conversation morphed into a safer arena until they started talking post season play.

Chapter Sixteen

The strange vibration against Rhett's leg caused his thick eyelids to open slowly. His neck was on fire as he tried to turn it. It took him a minute to take in his surroundings. He was slumped on Madison's couch, with her still curled up under his arm. They must have fallen asleep watching television. Someone had draped a blanket over them.

Rhett was still trying to process what woke him when the vibration started over again. His phone. He tried to shift positions so as not to wake Madison. She looked so peaceful. She had this dainty snore that was, well, just downright adorable. Rhett smiled into the early morning light. He shimmied his phone from his pocket. Madison cooed and squirmed, pulling the blanket tighter around her shoulder.

Rhett's screen came to life. Four missed calls and ten texts from Rahemia telling him to call her. Four texts from Oliver asking why Rahemia was blowing up his phone. One text from Jake telling him to call Rahemia. One text from Alexis asking if he was dead. Rhett rolled his eyes. This better be life or death for Rahemia to track him down like that. He held his phone with one hand and struggled to text.

Rhett: *Can't talk. What's so dire?*

Rahemia: *WHAT DID YOU GET ME INTO????? We have a meeting at nine with Jerry! The head of the FDA wants to know how you found out about the symposium.*

Rhett: *Be at the office by 8. We'll talk then.*

Rahemia: RHETT!!! You better have a great explana-
tion for this!
Rhett: I always do. See you soon.

Rhett sent a quick text to Jake and Oliver.
Rhett: Texted Rahemia. Not dead yet. Sorry.

He silenced his phone and sat still for a few minutes, extending this moment for as long as possible. When he couldn't wait any longer, Rhett leaned down and kissed the top of Madison's head while stroking her arm. She stirred, but snuggled closer. This warmed Rhett to the core. She groggily opened her eyes and yawned. Even her yawns were dainty. Rhett loved seeing her so vulnerable with him. He felt honored that she felt safe enough to let down her guard. The familiarity moved him.

"Good morning, sleeping beauty."

Madison stretched. "Oh my goodness. I didn't mean to fall asleep. What time is it?"

"Almost six. Sorry I woke you. Well, my producer woke us both." Rhett held up his phone as evidence.

"Wow, your producer sounds worse than Hayman. He at least waits until after seven to begin his harassment. I guess Hayman needs more beauty sleep." Madison rubbed her eyes.

"This is definitely not the norm for Rahemia. I think I may have gotten us into a pickle, as Grammy would say. We've been called into Jerry's office for an early meeting. As much as I hate to do this, I actually need to leave. My original plan was to take you to breakfast."

"Uh oh, getting called into the principal's office. That sounds ominous." Madison stood up to fold the blanket. "I'll take a rain check on breakfast. I need to leave soon too. Every morning is early for us. I'm actually surprised Rich didn't get up to run."

Curiosity got the best of him. "How do you know he didn't?"

"Trust me, if Rich caught us still sleeping, he would have slammed doors or blown an air horn. Anything to make us jump."

"I'm not sure if you live in a frat house or a townhouse."

Madison laughed at that one. "I've become immune to their pranks. That, and I've learned a few of my own. They fear me enough to think twice before zinging me now."

Rhett stood up and pulled her into his arms. "I have mad respect for you, Madison Lyn. I'm also a little terrified."

"Good." She leaned up and kissed him quickly.

"I hate leaving you this morning, but I need to run." He kissed her forehead.

Madison took his hand and walked him to the door. "We're leaving this evening on the tour bus. Hayman changed the schedule yesterday, but I haven't memorized it yet. I probably won't be back in town for a couple of weeks."

"Now I really wish I wasn't leaving in a hurry this morning. I might be traveling when you get back. The plans are still up in the air."

"We'll have to settle for witty texts and random video chats." She turned to him as they reached the door.

"I'll take what I can get." Rhett wrapped her tightly against himself. The last thing he wanted to do was leave. Her smile undid him.

***

After a few lingering kisses, one cold shower, and two shots of expresso later, Rhett walked into WBN.

Rahemia waited for him in the lobby. "Talk. Leave out nothing. Not one detail."

Rahemia was hand picked by Rhett to produce *Rhett's Take*. Her reputation rose with his ratings. She was dedicated to Rhett and the show, but Rhett had never tested the depth of her loyalty, until now.

"Good morning to you too, Rahemia." Rhett strolled to the elevator bank. Once they were alone, he dragged her down the rabbit hole he was in with Jake.

Once Rhett caught Rahemia up to speed, she sat on his couch like a deer frozen in headlights. He waited while it all sunk in and was washed through her producer's brain. Rahemia shook her head. "Let me get this straight. You are currently entrenched in a 'deep throat' situation in which a group of anti-government-pro-secession-lunatics are feeding you conspiracy theories with so-called undisputable evidence that neither you nor Jake can disprove? And they're doing this through an advanced texting system that our top IT guy can't crack? And you were almost killed retrieving a jump drive the FBI doesn't know you have, but this group knows when you opened it?"

Rhett nodded.

"This is some crazy stuff, Paulson, even for you. You know how insane this is, right?"

Rhett nodded.

Rahemia stood on wobbly legs, then paced. Rhett remained silent as he watched her wheels turn. He waited and watched while she paced and processed, certain steam would be released from her ears at any moment. Finally, she turned with a purpose, eyes laser focused on Rhett.

"This explains Jerry's questions about the symposium. He said the FDA planned to keep this under wraps and wanted to know how you found out about it and why you wanted to attend in person. Jerry sounded cagey when I proposed the live show, but I thought he was being cheap. Remember when he thought the network had a rat during the midterms? How nervous and paranoid he acted? That's how the summons sounded this morning. He acted as if the request was no big deal, but he lacked his usual calm arrogance. He assured me he already had a crew covering the symposium, but I couldn't find it listed on the main board. Do you think he didn't know about it, but doesn't want us to know he doesn't know about it?"

Rhett's curiosity began working out puzzle pieces. "It's hard to tell what Jerry knows at any given time. I find it hard to believe that Jerry had dinner with the head of the FDA the same week he insisted we interview the guy's mistress on our show. During which she talked about the very thing the symposium is based on, yet she didn't mention the actual symposium. Our show would have been prime publicity for the event, but she only covered a food scarcity crisis, not what they're doing to prepare for one. Why would that be a secret? And why would Jerry be so interested in how we found out about it?"

"I don't know, but I don't like it. Something's fishy." Rahemia leaned back on Rhett's desk. "I don't enjoy feeling as if I'm walking into a trap, and that's what Jerry's summons felt like."

They both stared in silence. Minutes ticked between them as their meeting deadline loomed closer. Rhett grabbed his phone. "I have an idea. We need to keep you in Jerry's good graces while making me look like I fell into this innocently. Hopefully, we'll put him at ease so he'll talk. He loves to talk."

"That he does." Rahemia followed Rhett out of his office and up to the top floor of WBN.

Marble floors and golden accessories greeted them as they emerged from the elevator. The executive level of WBN Tower could be described as overloaded extravagance. Jerry's artwork alone reminded Rhett of the most renowned museums. The décor, intended to inspire reverence, worked on most people. Rhett learned in life that forced importance shouted weakness. Jerry's office screamed it.

"He's waiting for you." Jerry's secretary had vacant eyes, but a full bosom. Her plastic smile made Rhett uncomfortable.

Rahemia had no patience for this woman. "Thank you." She looked past the gatekeeper and strode through the floor-to-ceiling doors. They opened with ease at the touch of her hands. "Good morning, Jerry."

"Rahemia. Rhett. Thank you for joining me this morning. I'm terribly sorry for the late notice, but my schedule is booked solid today." Forced bravado gave away Jerry's intent. "Please, sit. Did Valentina offer you something to drink? Valentina!"

"Yes, Mr. Powell?"

Rhett watched Rahemia slightly sneer at Valentina's presence. Jerry looked expectantly between his two guests. "I'll have some water," Rahemia spoke to no one. Rhett hid his smirk as he held up his coffee cup as an answer. Valentina scurried over to the bar and grabbed a sparkling water for Rahemia.

"Good, good. Valentina, please close the door." Jerry preened himself behind his mahogany desk, leaned back, and rested his hands behind his head. The relaxed posture did not mask the restrained questions in Jerry's eyes. "So, Rhett, tell me about this symposium? I reached out to my connections and apparently the symposium is by invitation only, and you were not invited. This isn't something you normally would sink your teeth into. How on earth did you hear about the event?" Rhett wondered who Jerry was protecting.

Rhett turned up the charm. "Actually, a guest we had on last week, Mallory Wiggins, mentioned it to me off-air and it fascinated me. She seemed so passionate about global food preservation."

Rahemia didn't let on that Rhett was lying through his teeth. She just sat and watched, drinking water to cover her apprehension.

"Remember Jerry, I grew up on a small farm. This topic is near and dear to my heart, especially after hearing Mallory's warnings last week. Our viewers need to be educated on the possibility of a large-scale food shortage. I thought you'd love the idea. I'm sorry if I overstepped. I had no idea it was an invitation only event. Is there a problem getting us an official invite?" Rhett knew how to use Jerry's ego to his advantage.

Jerry visibly relaxed. "No, no. On the contrary, I love the idea. I was going to send Ronald to cover it, but if you're interested, I'd much rather highlight it during your time slot. The symposium is more of a mock simulation of how to handle a potential crisis. However, I'm not sure the hosts want all of this leaked haphazardly. That's the reason for the curated invitation list. We want to control the situation and response, not cause widespread panic when it happens."

Jerry slipped. He knew it. Rhett and Rahemia knew it. "I mean to say, the hosts have a vested interest in how the information is presented to the public. Not that there *will* be a food shortage. This is just a scenario for *if* there is one. They want to educate, not incite another toilet paper and milk shortage, if you know what I mean." Jerry laughed at his own joke.

Rhett understood why Jerry made the big bucks. He could sell turnips to a turnip farmer. "Jerry, I couldn't agree more. I understand if you want Ronald to cover it, but I'd love the chance to shine a light on such a noble cause. If I'm not mistaken, I think Mallory said that the Global Alliance is a sponsor. I'm a big fan of their mission. Is that true?"

"Well, yes, they are. In fact, let me make some calls. I can request an interview with one of their board members while you are there. Maybe Adam Ford or Johan Philipsen."

"That would be great for ratings." Rhett knew exactly how to work Jerry. "A huge feather in our cap right before they release the next quarter's ratings."

"Yes, it would. All right, let's make this happen. Rahemia, get a plan together for logistics and what you need. I'll secure invitations for the symposium and work on that interview." Jerry pushed the button to summon Valentina, alerting them that the meeting was finished.

Rahemia and Rhett stood. He was relieved he didn't have to admit he already had an invitation. Now Jake could attend under the radar, tucked discreetly into their entourage. They said their goodbyes and passed Valentina with her notebook. They waited in silence for the elevator. The two of them gracefully entered the gold-plated cube. As the doors smoothly closed, Rahemia whispered, "What are we getting into?"

"I'm not sure, but we're about to find out."

Chapter Seventeen

Rhett breathed in the salty air and rested his head backward, catching some much needed sun on his face. Alexis had commandeered the radio as soon as they hit the D.C. city limits on their way to Massachusetts. They cruised along as many back roads as they could find up the coast. All three of them were raised on two-lane curvy roads. The further they got away from the traffic, the lighter they all felt.

Blue skies and billowy clouds spread out as far as the eye could see. Wind whipped through their hair as they embarked from the ferry station. Jake and his brother converted their grandfather's vintage pickup truck the summer after he passed. They sawed off the top and replaced it with roll bars and a second row. Jake loved this truck. Alexis loved Jake. Rhett loved getting out of the city.

Alexis reached her arm backward with an ice-cold water bottle. Rhett jumped as she placed it against his knee while she laughed.

"Thanks?" Rhett took it from her as he exaggeratedly wiped the cold condensation from his leg.

Rhett watched as Alexis placed her hand on Jake's neck, twirling his hair in her fingers. The two of them were sickeningly happy. Rhett had gladly been their third wheel since freshman year of high school. Alexis had been a team mascot of sorts. She went to every home and away game. During practices, Alexis waited in Jake's truck reading books. She could never be confused for one of those baseball groupies that followed the team. On the rare occasion someone made that mistake, they didn't make it again. Alexis had been devoted to Jake, the guy, not the college bound catcher destined for the major leagues. Jake was just as enamored. Alexis was drop-dead gorgeous, wicked smart, and giving to a fault, but she could also be meaner than a rattlesnake if you crossed someone she loved.

Alexis and Madison could not be more different, but somehow, Rhett knew they would get along just fine. Having Alexis's seal of approval held a weight to it. The level of harassment Alexis dished out daily for the past few weeks to meet Madison was working. Next time Madison was back in town, he'd agreed to their first double date. According to Madison, Rhett had passed the Jackson and Rich test. Now it would be her turn. Alexis would be just as protective as those two, if not worse.

Jake coasted his way through town, avoiding bicycles, locals, and the tourists who were pretending not to look for celebrities. Miriam called Alexis last week and invited them to spend a few days at Branson Villa on Martha's Vineyard. The two of them desperately wanted to move out of D.C., so this trip was a no-brainer for them. Alexis's new pastime was searching for land back in West Virginia.

As Jake steered the truck into the private driveway, the gates opened wide for them. Nick and Miriam walked down the porch stairs to greet their guests. They were both beaming. Alexis was out of the truck the second Jake shut off the engine. Miriam wrapped her in a hug and the women headed for the house, Miriam's hand resting on Alexis's barely there baby bump.

"Hi Miriam, great to see you too," Rhett cheekily called after the women.

"Oh Rhett, you know I love you, but I've got to get this woman inside for a lemonade and a poolside chair. It mustn't have been an easy journey with the two of you as traveling companions." Miriam never missed a beat.

Rhett loved being here with them. Suddenly, he wished Madison was being escorted inside with Miriam and Alexis. He'd never felt that way about a woman before now.

"Never fear. I promise she has lemonade for you boys, too. Now, let's get that truck unloaded." Nick's welcoming grin took another pound of stress off of Rhett's shoulders. This weekend, he would tell Nick everything. Nick would know what to do.

They spent the afternoon in a splendid dream of outdoor bliss. A charcuterie spread fit for a king filled the kitchen island. The sounds of the ocean lulled them into a near meditative state. A shroud of trees provided Nick an impressively secluded lot. Beyond the magnificent tree line, their property opened up to unfettered beachfront access. It was exactly what you would expect on the Vineyard. Rhett relished this time with his closest friends. It surprised him how much he longed for Madison to experience this with him. They spoke every night and were texting partners all day. It was amazing how well you could get to know someone when your only option was long-distance communication not mixed with physical touch. Even from a distance, he felt close to her.

As the lazy day turned into evening, Miriam suggested they all get ready for dinner, as Nick had invited a friend to join them. Nick was not one for surprises, so the guest must be a doozie. By the time Rhett made it back down to the kitchen, Alexis and Miriam were working hard, while Nick and Jake were filling drink orders by the bar. A blender was involved. Rhett hoped he could remain in the kitchen as a taste tester, but that didn't last long. The doorbell summoned him to the front of the house. Finally, the mystery guest.

"Senator Marchio?" Rhett quirked his brow and cocked his head.

"Rhett Paulson. Based on your expression, you look as confused as I am about this dinner invitation." John Marchio was a stoic looking gentleman. He was the old guard in politics, but seemed to be one of the few who stayed out of the political theater fray. He was honest and calm, a rarity in either house. Well beloved by everyone for his call-it-like-he-saw-it candor. Senator Marchio's euphemisms were legendary. "May I come in or was I supposed to bring the pizza?"

Rhett shook his head. "Yes, please. I'm sorry. I was expecting a surprise dinner guest, not the highest-ranking member of congress. Normally, I have to schedule these meetings well in advance, and I usually get turned down like a nice guy on prom night."

John Marchio's throaty laugh broke the ice. "I guess we're even then. I usually avoid meeting with the press like a dad cleaning his gun in front of nice guys on prom night." He held out his hand. Rhett liked this man.

Behind them, they turned at the sound of Nick's voice. "Tonight is a completely off-the-record dinner among friends. John, come on in and meet everyone."

Rhett's mind swirled with questions. How did Nick become such good friends with John Marchio over the past year, so much so, the senator would come to an intimate dinner such as this? Why would John trust Rhett to not use this dinner as an opportunity? *Would* he use it as an opportunity? What was Nick up to? Each question brought a slew of even more questions.

Apparently, the entrance of their dinner guest only confused Rhett. Everyone else seemed to think this was a completely normal occurrence. John regaled Jake and Alexis with stories of his grandchildren and encouraged their decision to move back to West Virginia. Rhett did not like that line of discussion. They skirted the edge of politics as friends would. It took a while, but Rhett began to see Senator Marchio as John, a friend of Nick's who stopped over for dinner.

As Miriam scooped a healthy dollop of homemade whipped cream onto everyone's strawberry shortcake, John broached the elephant in the room. "Well Rhett, I'm not sure what Nick is trying to convince us to do, but I think he gets an 'A' for effort."

"I was wondering the same thing." Rhett speared Nick with a look. "Let's have it, Branson."

"What? I can't invite friends to dinner without asking for a favor?" Nick held up his hands, but he couldn't hold back the grin. "All right, well, I'm hoping Rhett will moderate the secession series with me. He hasn't given me an answer yet, and I'd like John to agree to be interviewed. Getting you both here together is two birds with one stone."

"Both birds die in that scenario, Nick." Rhett felt pressured for the first time since leaving the city.

"Come on now. It's not that farfetched of an idea." Nick took his first bite of shortcake. One would have thought Nick Branson had dropped the most hilarious of punchlines. They were all laughing and eating and shaking their heads. "What? It's not."

"I'm not laughing at the request, dear. I'm laughing because everyone at this table knows that neither man will say no to you. Except maybe John and Rhett." Miriam looked at the three of them. "More strawberries, anyone?"

"Oh, me. Definitely me. And load up that whipped cream, please." Alexis looked around the table. "What? I'm eating for two."

More laughter.

"Now, Miriam, they are both free to say no. They will just be doing a disservice to their country and to their respective crafts. I'm simply asking two giants in their fields to sit down together and show the world what civil discourse should look like while honoring the first amendment." Nick placed his elbows on the table and watched the men.

"Just as I said, neither of them can say no to you, dear. You do that to our girls all the time, and they're grown women with their own families." Miriam offered him a loving tsk-tsk.

"I'd say yes, but he didn't ask me anything. At least I don't think he did. Nick?" Jake, feeling left out, and a little ornery, looked to the head of the table.

"Thank you, Jake. I will need you for a portion of the series. Some subjects don't trust the mainstream media and won't allow my regular crew to film. I can get you vetted by them. Can I count on you?"

"Anything for you, Nick. Gentleman, that's how it's done. Not painful at all."

Nick laughed as Jake swatted Alexis's hand from his dessert.

Rhett waved his hand between himself and Jake. "John, I know how Nick has the two of us tied to him, but what does he have on you?"

John looked at Nick first before he answered, "Nick and I found ourselves in the same D.C. Bible study. He called it coincidence at first, but now he recognizes it as divine intervention. Either way, let's just say that Nick and I have a shared commission. We want to spread the same message. I trust Nick with the medium. So, if he wants me to be interviewed, and he thinks you should be the one to do it, then I agree."

"Another one bites the dust," Alexis choked down a laugh. "Rhett, looks like it's just you."

"He's in, aren't you, dear?" Miriam patted Rhett's hand.

"That's not fair. I could never say no to Miriam. So, I guess I'm in too." Rhett warily smiled and took a long swig of his drink.

"Excellent!" Nick clapped his hands together. "I feel fantastic about this! Great idea, men."

A new eruption of laughter and groans filled the room.

Chapter Eighteen

adison could feel the bus cruising along the Interstate. Which Interstate, she couldn't say, but she knew they were moving at a steady pace. Six states in four days tended to leave one a little discombobulated. After overhearing the boys talk about their wake-up times last night, she purposefully set the alarm on her phone thirty minutes earlier. Madison's two sisters combined didn't take as long in the bathroom as Rich.

Madison's sisters were girly girls. Madison was not. Daniel Lyn was adamant that his girls be on par with their brothers at everything. The one child policy in China sickened him. He wanted to show that his daughters were as valuable as his sons. Daniel and Vivian also valued having children, lots of them. Madison grew up knowing she was loved. She also grew up hearing how lucky she was to be in America. Her grandfather made sure they heard the story of their great escape from the Cultural Revolution at least once a year.

With two parents, two grandparents, and five kids living under one roof, Madison was a pro at getting into bathrooms first and fast. Quick showers were always hot because she was first. Many times she wondered what took Rich so long, but she was never brave enough to ask him. Some things were better left as mysteries. Madison shook her head and stretched out as best she could in her little cubby space.

When Hayman suggested the three of them travel on a tour bus, Madison thought he was joking. By the time she realized he wasn't, she was picking out features she wanted in her tiny room, which she persistently argued needed to be far away from the bathroom. She landed across from the boys' stacked cubbies.

Historically, a bachelor traveling with his two college roommates, one being a woman, would be a huge no-no for a campaign. According to the modern world, the three of them were the new American family. Hayman said their lasting friendship screamed commitment and dedication. It wasn't hard to believe, considering the three of them fared better than most twelve-year-old marriages. Jackson, Rich, and Madison appealed to the largest demographic, everyone under forty. The traditional family structure was out, and this trio was an easy sell.

Madison loved Jackson and Rich, but tour bus life was getting old, fast. She groaned and attempted to stretch her aching muscles. Grabbing her water bottle, she downed what remained in it from last night. Making a mental note to drink more water today, she carried it with her to the bathroom.

As far as tour buses went, not that Madison had been on a tour bus before, this one was top-notch. Hayman assured them the donors would provide the best of everything, and he was right. Although the bathroom wasn't huge, it definitely wasn't as small as she imagined. Madison had envisioned the worst, but ended up pleasantly surprised. A full sink, roomy shower, enclosed toilet, and a linen closet were definitely not in her original vision.

The vibration under her feet became more erratic. That normally indicated traffic, which meant they must be getting close to a city. Madison stepped out of the shower to Rich's knocking. She rolled her eyes and continued her routine. Moisturizer, lip balm, lotion, then the blow dryer, which she knew would drive Rich crazy. That made her feel inwardly triumphant.

Twenty-five minutes start to finish, not too bad. Rich was waiting at the door with his arms crossed as she opened it. "Finally. If I peed my pants, it would have been your fault." He brushed past her and closed the door.

"Said the man I've seen pee into bushes," Madison yelled at the door.

"I told him the same thing when he complained to me," Jackson laughed.

"Where are we? I feel like I'm losing track of states." Madison maneuvered her bottle under the filtered water dispenser.

"I'm not sure. I think Jackson, Mississippi."

Madison actually snorted. "Hey everyone! Come see Jackson in Jackson!"

"That was your worst dad joke attempt ever." Jackson offered her a sad chuckle.

"Rich already said it?"

"Yep. As soon as he woke up," Jackson shrugged. "We have a plant tour, then a rally, and then we're driving to New Orleans for another private donor dinner."

"Two in two weeks. Interesting." Madison began working on her quest to drink more water. She didn't realize how dehydrating travel could be.

"Yes, but this time, Hayman said you two could come. Apparently, I impressed them at the last dinner, so they all pledged to host a private dinner in their respective states. I guess they're some type of gateway collective for the party. The dinner is a big deal." Jackson distractedly texted on his phone, "Someone is getting us coffee. Do you want your regular order?"

"Yes, please." Madison leaned against the counter, smirking, "There were some heavy hitters at your last dinner. Do you trust us not to embarrass you? Well, at least me. Rich is always a toss-up."

"Again with the funny jokes this morning. I have no doubt you will impress them with your witty conversation, and Rich will dazzle them speechless." Jackson rubbed his chin. "Or hit on someone's wife and get us knocked back down to the minor leagues."

"I'm not sure if you're being serious or facetious, but either way, valid point." Madison pulled out a yogurt from the fridge and hunted for a spoon in the drawer. "So, who is the big shot donor hosting tonight?"

"Horatio Theopolis. He backs political elections around the world. Hayman said this guy's candidates never lose. His Foundation is working toward a unified coalition of countries that work together for the good of all. He's a fascinating man. Worked his way up from poverty and dedicated his life to philanthropy. I think you'll really like him. His son Alex is engaged to President Blythe's Chief of Staff."

"Anyone else I should know about?" Madison sat down across from Jackson as the bus jerked to a stop.

"Jeremy Hutton is providing the entertainment." Jackson leaned back and waited for her reaction.

"I love that guy! His is by far my favorite late-night show host." Madison did not fangirl often, but when she did, it was over an odd person. "Now that's exciting!"

"Hayman wants to get me on his show and this dinner should open that door. Hayman said the road to inauguration is paved through late-night."

"Hayman says a lot of things, but on this, I agree with him." Madison licked her spoon clean, then tossed the plastic container in the trash. "So, how much time do we have before the parade of cars begins today?"

"I think an hour. I'm going to get Rich out of the bathroom. Hayman is sending someone over with today's talking points for the communication team. If I'm not out, open the door and get it, please." Jackson scooted out from behind the table and headed directly to the bathroom door. He pounded. The singing inside only grew louder. Jackson groaned.

Madison switched on the wall of communication, as they called it. Six televisions each programmed to a major news network. Madison scanned every ticker. The sound became ambient at some point to them. Instinctively, they could pull out information they needed while making the rest white noise. Madison wasn't sure if it was a super skill they'd all developed or more about self-preservation. Five of the six tickers scrolled the same information. The sixth had completely different headlines. Her parents, of course, watched the sixth network, which explained their concern over her current job.

Madison drank more water. She found a banana and her tablet and got to work. While Rich focused on messaging and PR, Madison had to know everything and how that connected to everything else in order to do her job effectively. She did that by watching. Madison was a studier. She studied people, books, trends, theories. If there was anything she didn't understand, she found something or someone to teach her. Her favorite law professor called her a sponge in class. Madison was proud of that until Dr. Angus warned her that sponges are prone to bacteria unless cared for properly. Rich almost cracked a rib laughing at that one.

Madison sat up straight, breathed deep and slow while pressing two fingers against her wrist, connecting with her heartbeat. She performed this same ritual every time she needed to focus. Her mother worked at a teaching hospital and explained the importance of the pulse to anyone who would listen. The pulse was the foundation for everything one needed to know about a patient. How fast they needed help, if they were calm or nervous, or if they were dead. Dr. Lyn always got a chuckle at that one, but Madison understood her mother's meaning.

She treated the news as her mom treated a triage unit. Madison held still. *Thrum. Thrum. Thrum.* She listened for the keywords. *Thrum. Thrum. Thrum.* She read each word on the ticker and compared them to the words she heard. Were there abnormalities? Were there any emergent issues? Each day on the campaign brought its own pulse signature. It was her job to catch things first and to react. She prided herself on being an astute student of this campaign.

Madison didn't hear the knock on the door, but Rich did. She also didn't hear him get out of the bathroom. He swaggered over and winked at the intern. As he crossed the bus again, he dropped the manilla envelope in front of Madison. "I'm guessing this is for you or Jackson."

"Why would you assume that?" Madison flippantly replied, while keeping her eyes on the screens in front of her.

"Anything in a sealed envelope is above my pay grade. My people work on napkins and ripped up notepads." He plopped down next to her on the couch, drinking his special protein shake smoothie thing he drank every morning.

"That sounded so dramatic. Am I to assume speech writers and PR spinners live the artistic life of paupers? Slaves to your craft with little pay?" Madison squished her nose between her thumb and pointer finger. "And get away from me with that. It smells like spinach. How are on earth do you drink that? Yuck!"

"Spinach doesn't smell." Rich sucked louder on his straw while raising his eyebrows. "Your assessment sounded pretty poetic. Maybe you should be on my team. You have a way with words."

"You're incorrigible, but you already know that."

"See, you even use big words. Great job, Mads." Rich knocked her knee with his.

Madison slid the envelope over to Rich. "This is actually for you, smarty pants. Hayman's office wants us to work off of these talking points. Apparently, these are the new buzzwords the cool kids are using."

"I'm already a cool kid. I don't need a list." Rich pouted. Or maybe it was something else.

"I'm sure you're already ahead of the curb there buddy, but just in case, Hayman wants us to use his special buzzwords." Madison watched Rich pick up the envelope and open it like a snake might pop out of it. "If it makes you feel better, you can write them down on a napkin."

Rich's chin lowered, his head cocked, and his eyes looked over at Madison with the most spot-on "are you serious" look she'd ever seen from him. She couldn't help but laugh.

"What did I miss? It looks like Madison-one, Rich-zero." Jackson walked out of the bathroom, drying his hair with a towel. Jackson also took longer than Madison in the bathroom.

"Oh, nothing. Rich was just regaling me with his writing styles and the tools of his craft."

Rich waved the envelope in the air. "More like Madison doubts my skills."

Jackson snatched the envelope from Rich and peeked inside. "This must be the list from Hayman. Any concerns or additions to share with him?"

Madison and Rich looked at Jackson, then each other, before they erupted in laughter. "Yeah. I have some notes for Hayman on campaign strategy. I'm sure he'd love to hear them from me, a mere woman of modest thought." Madison purred and smiled, which made both Jackson and Rich laugh harder.

After they calmed down, Jackson perused the list of talking points. "These all align with our campaign points. I don't see anything out of left field."

"It's more about the overall messaging, and that everyone is using the same highlighted words that bothers me. Why can't we make our own arguments? If you look, you'll see an approved list of adjectives on each topic that are all in bold. I'll need to incorporate them into the current messaging." Rich stood and walked to the sink to rinse out his special shake cup. "What did you call these, Mads? Buzz words? I think we should call it our buzzy-wuzzy word list. That way, instead of punching Hayman for his arrogance, I'll laugh internally at him instead. Hayman is a buzz-buzz-buzzy-bee."

Madison spit out her water while Jackson tried hard not to laugh. Rich grinned in satisfaction.

Jackson started his normal defense of Hayman, but Rich held up his hand to stop him. "We know. Hayman is very connected and we would not have gotten this far without him. The man knows what he's doing, I'll give him that, but *you* have to give Mads and I a few jokes at his expense. He can be a real ass."

Madison crossed her arms and saw the exact moment Jackson conceded. He attempted but failed to make a good buzzing sound, which sent them into fits of laughter.

"That was terrible, man. Mads, I hope your buzzing is better than that."

Madison chuckled and went back to work. Jackson walked through the bus to hang up his towel, and Rich scanned Hayman's notes. This time with purpose.

The sixth screen caught Madison's attention. "That can't be right." She grabbed the remote and began muting the other televisions while she increased the volume on America's News Channel.

The three of them watched attentively as the morning hosts listed the names of each state that had signed a letter of intent, authorizing their attorney general to investigate a vote of secession. The ticker flashed a news alert that the vote could happen by the end of the month.

Jackson shook the worry from his face. "Wait, only ANC is reporting that. There's nothing on any of the other channels. No way that story is accurate. They shouldn't be allowed to do that. It's dangerous." He walked to his cubby to grab his blazer.

Rich and Madison stayed glued to the screens. Jackson was partially right. There was nothing about it on any other channel, but ANC had footage from different state houses. It was Madison's job to assess the situation, or if there was even a situation to assess.

Hayman broke their silence, banging open the tour bus door. "Good morning! We have a job to do, and you three are late. Let's move out, now." His voice sounded more bark than buzz.

Chapter Nineteen

Sunshine reflected off of white walls, lighting up the inside of Rhett's eye-lids. He rolled away from the illumination and buried his face into the pillow, but he couldn't hide from it. Daybreak was inevitable, and Rhett had to reconcile with the light at some point.

Bones cracked as he stretched out across the bed. Miriam handpicked the guestroom on the northeast corner of the house for Rhett. Now he understood why. There would be no sleeping in on the island for Rhett. Bright sunshine overpowered exhaustion. Even though his payment came due this morning, he would never regret talking to Madison into the wee hours of the night.

Rhett dragged himself from bed and rubbed his face with both hands. After a quick trip to the bathroom to freshen up, he pulled on board shorts, a fresh polo shirt, and flip-flops. Beach attire, check. Rhett meandered down the hall as he made his way downstairs to the kitchen.

Miriam had left a note by a fresh batch of blueberry muffins. Rhett filled a cup with coffee, grabbed a muffin, and headed to the deck. He heard voices, which meant Jake and Nick were already eating and enjoying the day. The warm sea air hit his face and filled his lungs as he reached the opened sliding doors and walked out into the sunshine that greeted him this morning.

"Well, good morning, sleeping beauty. Nice of you to join us." Jake lowered his face as if bowing to royalty.

"It's only ten. My beauty sleep needs longer to keep all this going strong." Rhett made a waving gesture around his head and face.

Nick pulled out the chair next to him for Rhett to sit. "The girls left for the farmer's market and to go baby shopping. I see you found the muffins."

"You can buy babies on Martha's Vineyard? That's odd." Rhett laughed at his own joke.

"And here I thought Jake was going to be the dad, but you're the one trying to make dad jokes. And poorly at that." Nick and Jake both laughed at that one.

"Ha-ha." Rhett took a bite of his muffin and moaned. "This is so amazing. Miriam should open a bakery."

"Wait until you taste her fruit salad." Nick spooned some into a bowl and placed it before Rhett. Jake held out his own bowl for a refill. "Eat up boys, we have places to be today."

Rhett's eyes veered over to Nick just before a spoonful of fruit entered his mouth. "I thought you invited us for a lazy weekend. I'm only prepared for laziness today. Why do I get the feeling there's a catch?"

"I lied. You can choose to stay here for a lazy day on the beach, or you can come with me for an interview on the other side of the island. My favorite oyster bar has allowed me the use of their deck for filming, so we can have lunch there afterwards."

Rhett slowly chewed. The tangy and sweet burst of flavor from the fruit salad made it very difficult to be angry with Nick, but Rhett still tried. He stared at Nick with one eye squinted. He smelled a good-ole-fashion dose of trickery. Rhett recognized the ploy immediately because Grammy was also a pro at it.

"Who are we interviewing?" Jake sat up in his seat, ready to learn everything he could.

"Slow down there, fella. *We* aren't interviewing anyone. *He* is. *We* are on vacation." Rhett smirked at Jake.

Nick chuckled. "I'm glad you asked, Jake. We're interviewing a formerly renowned rabbinical scholar and a pastor with a doctorate in church history. They're going to give us historical accounts of the church in America. Specifically, during times of political upheaval."

Choking on his coffee, "I'm sorry," Rhett offered a hearty laugh before continuing, "but that sounds like the beginning of a bad joke. A rabbi, a priest, and a reporter walk into a bar. You can't be serious. And how on earth does one become a 'formerly renowned' rabbinical scholar?"

"You become a Christian convert while writing a book declaring the falsehoods of Christianity," Nick stated plainly.

Rhett whistled between his teeth. "That'll do it."

Jake followed up with, "I'm in, even if he's out."

"Thanks, man." Rhett grumbled under his breath.

"Now Rhett, I won't force you to come. However, I'm not beyond bribing you with a free lunch at the best oyster bar on the island. Or guilt. Or even calling Grammy Paulson if I have to, but I won't force you to come. It's completely your decision." Nick lazily reclined in his chair and sipped orange juice, as if they were chatting about the weather. "Wouldn't a Pulitzer look great on his mantle, Jake?"

Rhett growled and lowered his head. "Thanks for your concern, but I'm perfectly content with my Emmys. I've been a little preoccupied with my own investigative project lately. Remind me of the premise of this interview series of yours I only officially agreed to last night."

Rhett and Jake listened as Nick explained. "I guess you could say my goal is to show a patchwork of ideas and opinions and what that looks like in today's America. Instead of polarizing opinions, I want to showcase the art of discourse and learning about opposing views. Listening instead of shouting, if you will, in order to find the truth. Truth telling used to be your primary motivation, I thought you would love this opportunity."

Rhett rubbed his chin in contemplation. He'd been doing that a lot lately. Rhett owed Nick everything. They all knew he would say yes, but he wished Nick would have sweated a little in wonder. "That sounds noble. I guess we're going to see a guy about some oysters."

Nick grinned, Jake rolled his eyes, and Rhett finished eating his muffin.

Two hours later, Jake worked with the sound team Nick had hired. They strategically positioned mics and cameras to best cover the two subjects. Rhett realized he'd been scammed as he watched Jake set up his own camera equipment.

Nick explained to former rabbi Isaac Appelbaum and Pastor Jacob Tomlinson how the interview would proceed. He answered the few questions they had and introduced the men to Rhett and Jake. They all exchanged pleasantries before Rhett shared his "a rabbi, a pastor, and a reporter walked into a bar joke" with them. He was relieved they had a sense of humor.

Pastor Jacob shared his own corny joke about how the two men had met. "Unironically, Isaac and I were both taking part in a panel discussion at an ecumenical men's conference with an Abraham and a Joseph. We ended up taking a family picture afterward." Nick and Jake laughed with the two men. Rhett didn't get the joke.

Isaac chuckled and pointed to Rhett, "I take it you're not a reader of the Bible?"

"No." Rhett was annoyed. He didn't enjoy missing jokes, and he definitely didn't enjoy being the butt of them.

Nick must have worried the conversation would take a wrong turn with Rhett, so he quickly directed everyone to their spots before Rhett could bail. "Gentlemen, let's get started. I will quickly introduce you both and highlight your credentials and achievements. Then we'll go straight into our discussion. Questions?"

Both men agreed and took their seats. Jake sat in front of a monitor and keyboard that controlled four different cameras. Rhett watched as Nick launched the interview. Nick, ever the gifted journalist, built up excitement and intrigue with every word. Rhett understood why Nick chose these two men. They were obviously well respected experts.

It was their field of expertise Rhett had a problem with, not the men themselves. As they spoke, it transported Rhett back to a day when Grammy grabbed his hand and pulled him down a long aisle, then straight out the front doors of a white church building. People whispered and turned their heads away from her. Rhett remembered as Grammy turned back just before the doors closed behind her and said loudly, "Lord, forgive them, because right now I see a bunch of people living in glass houses with big ole stones in their hands. And help me forgive them too, because I'm not feeling very charitable."

That was the last time they stepped foot in that church, and the last time Rhett ever willingly stepped foot into one altogether. Grammy read the Bible to him every night until his mother died. Forcing him to attend her new church or making him listen to the Bible became a battle even she couldn't win after that.

Grammy still prayed every day for Rhett, but he'd long given up on her religion. Rhett had no intention of listening to these two men spout off about how important religion was to the building of the country. Founding fathers, yada yada. Judicial and legal systems based off of the Bible, yada yada. Churches doing more for communities than government regulations, that got his attention. What a joke. The church didn't help his mother. It killed her.

Rhett listened as Jacob talked about all the organizations fighting human trafficking. They talked about the billions of dollars in humanitarian aid Christian groups provided around the globe. The one that really caught his attention was the City Healing Network. They described it as a network of over one hundred organizations across the country fighting poverty, hunger, and drug addiction, by helping at-risk youth, training and educating residents, meeting their basic needs, and teaching them about Christ. Rhett worked hard to keep from laughing out loud at that one. His mother died in one of their centers.

As they boasted about churches helping their communities, Rhett made mental notes to verify every one of their statistics. There was no way these organizations were making such an impact. If they were, why weren't people reporting on it? Nope, these were just more church scams by sanctimonious frauds.

Rhett noticed Nick watching him. He offered the man a smirk, then shrugged his shoulders. Nick should have known better than to think this would work to convert Rhett. Nick and Jake might believe this garbage, but not Rhett. He crossed his arms and listened as the two men driveled on with their numbers, examples, delusions, and fake narrative about loving Christians helping others.

The conversation took a turn when Jacob redirected it to "Christian Nationalism," which was a topic Rhett had been covering for years. He regularly highlighted acts of Christian Nationalism on his show. Rhett wanted the world to see these hypocrites in all their false glory with their flags and prayer services. He loved exposing the pious and self-righteous.

"In Jeremiah twenty-nine God told the Israelites, while they were in captivity, they were to participate in city life. They were to behave as citizens and to pray for peace and prosperity. As they followed God and prospered, so would their communities. He also warned them specifically to beware of deceivers who prophesied in lies. As Christians, we have a responsibility to participate in our communities and government based on our Biblical values, not based on personalities or candidates. Believers should always put Kingdom work over country work." Jacob explained that in a way Rhett hadn't heard before, and it threw him for a loop. More *believers* should listen to Jacob, Rhett thought to himself.

Isaac leaned forward in his seat. It was obvious the gentleman was zealous about this topic. "Millions of immigrants risk their lives fleeing oppressive systems for America. Yet, socialist politicians and professors convince our youth that America is a terrible place." Isaac offered a sinister laugh. "The empty promises of socialism, communism, Marxism, I call them the 'isms,' always lead to death and totalitarianism, not equity. Obviously, we aren't teaching history anymore in schools or else people would know they're romanticizing starvation and murder. We have kids wearing Che Guevara t-shirts, yet they do not know what the Maduro Diet is or how many hundreds of millions of people the 'isms' have murdered."

Jacob gently patted his friend's shoulder. "Obviously, we are passionate about this topic. We both could sit here and educate you on statistical and historical accounts of governments throughout history. The truth is, we live in a sinful world. The Bible is filled with accounts of war and strife. We believe God is in control, just as He has been from the very beginning of creation. The Bible tells us that the thief comes to steal and destroy. Satan is the father of lies. He's a fear dealer, and people fall for fear every time. There will be times of Harrods, Caesars, Hitlers, and Stalins, but there is no one greater than God, and that is where our hope holds fast."

"I would like to add one thing more about this global citizen nonsense while you're giving me a soapbox." Isaac looked more relaxed, but still determined to make his point. "Globalism is its own god. Globalists create new religions out of causes, each with its own idols and rituals."

Isaac continued, sadness laced into every word, "Satan preys on the marginalized and the weak. Those who need so desperately to belong to the pack. People are terrified of being left out or excluded. The goal is to breakdown every marker that gives us pride and connection to something bigger than ourselves.

Your faith and your identity are first. The family unit is the strongest bond and the hardest to break in most cases, but we saw it happen with the Red Guard, the Young Pioneers, and the Hitler Youth. Each organization aimed to separate young children from their parents, and it worked. Families were encouraged and rewarded for reporting one another to the government for the smallest of crimes."

Jacob jumped in, "Think back to the original sitcoms when television was in her youth. Lessons learned and wisdom gleaned from the parents. Watch anything now aimed at children. Parents are the butt of every joke and we reward the children for pulling one over on them. Our society has been eroding the family and faith structure for decades in the name of entertainment and the guise that those patriarchal systems were oppressive. Now that we've dismantled and shamed the family structure, has the world gotten better or worse? Depression and anxiety are at record levels. Instability is all around us and we keep chipping away at important anchors like family values. I can promise you that big government and their friends will never be a better replacement for mom and pop stores and neighbors who care."

Rhett was ready to walk out at this point. This crap about nuclear families and new world orders was out of control. What was Nick thinking? Christian nationalism was a cult, and apparently, Nick had fallen for it hook, line, and sinker. Rhett looked over at Nick who was engrossed in the interview.

Back to Isaac, "People wonder how the Germans allowed such atrocities under Hitler. They followed like sheep, believing the lies without accounting for the cost. They hid in the fear and clung to the lies. Less and less people spoke out, and when they did, they were silenced. America allowed a fox into the henhouse and now we're confused because we don't have any chickens or eggs left. Figuratively and literally."

Jacob tagged in once again, "The global world view turns us into individual super consumers. Think about the messaging we hear these days. 'Do what makes you happy.' 'You can have it all.' 'Self-love is paramount.' 'That is *my* truth.' The list goes on and on, but the point is to only think about oneself. Meanwhile, most people have an innate desire to help others. Humans are charitable with their time and treasures. If the enemy pits us against one another, that giving nature will be broken. It's easy to only think about yourself when you've lost faith in those around you. In the end, they have created a fertile ground of anger, fear, and severed relationships. That is happening today in America."

"We are citizens of Heaven, not of Earth, but as humans, we are prone to want to keep one foot in both worlds. We can only be salt and light if we're careful not to water down our salt and put a shade on our light. Jeremiah warned us to let the world turn to us, but we must not turn to them. This new global worldview that is taking over governments across the world is actually prophesied about in the Bible. As a Christian, I will obey the rules of the government as God told me to do in Romans thirteen and First Peter chapter two, but I will only bow to the Lord my God, not a government. At some point, believers must choose between the Word of God or the favor of the world. When the earthquakes come, a man can't span the divide. Eventually, he must choose between the shifting sands of earth or the solid rock of Christ. Sadly, those watered-down Christians I mentioned before are so in love with the world, they wouldn't recognize the Word if it bit them on the bottom. Satan and the demons know the Word better than most so-called Christians."

Isaac shifted forward in his chair and looked directly into the camera. "Let me leave you with this quote from C.S. Lewis, 'Christianity, if false, is of no importance, and if true, of infinite importance.' Basically, if I'm wrong and there is no God and the Bible really is just a work of literature, I'm a hopeful fool who lived a life with good intentions that called me to love and serve others. But what if I'm right? What if the Bible is the Word of God and the only path to Heaven is the narrow one that only Jesus Christ can open for us? The man in Luke sixteen begged from hell to warn his brothers so they could repent. What if hell is real and everything the Bible tells us about it is real? Isn't that worth looking into?"

Jacob sighed as he offered one last summary. "The Bible has not been disproven in over three thousand years, and many, many people have tried. Isaac here tried harder than anyone I know. In fact, the more people try, the more they prove and validate that the Bible is historically accurate. Creationism has yet to be proven wrong, yet evolution has holes and loops that are constantly contradicting itself, but people would rather ignore the discrepancies than go against the grain. Humans tend to mimic herd animals, the choice is ours as to which shepherd we choose to follow. We can follow the dealer of fear and lies or we can follow the shepherd of truth and peace. My prayer for this country is not about the government, or national stability, or for a certain political party to reign. My prayer is that God exposes the lies of Satan and that revival will spread across the nation faster than a wildfire."

"Amen, brother," Isaac lowered his gaze.

Silence filled the room as both men, who had been talking for over an hour non-stop, finished. They had said what they needed to say. Rhett marveled at Nick's idea for the format. Isaac and Jacob gave Nick more meaningful material than any interview questions he would have asked them.

Nick stood and crossed over the wires to shake their hands. "Thank you both."

Rhett watched as Jake fangirled over Isaac and Jacob. His mind spun. Rhett vehemently disagreed with their message, but he couldn't deny their presence. Something about these two shone. They had a fragrance of wisdom that Rhett couldn't ignore. They spoke with an authority and passion that solidified their entire interview. It was unnerving. Rhett stood off to the side as the small crew tore down their makeshift set. Nick suggested they all head inside for a pleasant lunch.

Rhett trailed behind them as Nick turned to him. "I thought for a minute there you were going to bolt on me."

"Nicholas, for a minute, I thought I would bolt too." Rhett shook his head.

"You know Rhett, you can't judge all people by the same cover. Don't let what happened to your mom, and subsequently to you, color your view of God. Grammy didn't. She leaned into her faith. She didn't fight against it. People are flawed. Don't judge us all based on the actions of some. We are all sinners who fall short of the glory of God. Some are just a little more obnoxious about deflecting their sin." Nick patted Rhett on the shoulder as he led him through the door of the restaurant. "Come on, oysters are on me."

Chapter Twenty

Overcome with exhaustion, Rhett rolled his tense shoulders. Some vacation that turned out to be. He dropped his suitcase on the hardwood floor the second he stepped into his penthouse. He kicked off his shoes and fell face down onto his Italian leather sofa, groaning into the decorative pillow.

Nick's little interview ambush and surprise dinner guest threw Rhett off his game. Rhett hated being off his game. Jake and Alexis had a great weekend and spent the drive home mellowed and relaxed. Rhett felt agitated and prickly. Instead of singing along to bad music, Alexis searched every real estate website she could find. Rhett listened to more property descriptions than any human should have to endure. Jake and Alexis were more determined than ever to move out of D.C. and back home to West Virginia. Apparently, now these two wanted to buy land and start a farm. It sounded more like a commune to Rhett. He attempted to sleep on the drive home, but nothing worked. So much for a relaxing long weekend with friends. They torpedoed him instead.

Beeping from his shorts prevented sleep now. He groaned even louder as he debated whether to read the notification or throw his phone across the room. Shifting his weight, he wiggled the phone out of his pocket. He exhaled in defeat and pulled the phone up to his face. Rhett smiled.

Madison: Just had a conversation with the President's press secretary, Patricia. Apparently, someone from your network told her we were dating. She thought it was hilarious and told me to be careful with the press because you're all rats.

Rhett laughed out loud. He twisted onto his back and started pecking out a response.

Rhett: She would know. She's married to some exec at CBA. I think he's a rat, but that's just my opinion.

Madison: Isn't that a conflict of interest?

Rhett: LOL. D.C. is one enormous pile of conflicts. Everyone is tied to someone else in this place . BTW, are we?

Madison: Are we what?

Rhett: Dating?

Madison: We have gone on dates.

Rhett: That's not what I'm asking.

Madison: Well, if you're not scared off by my roommates, my job, or my couch snoring (which I still deny), then I guess I could consider it.

Rhett warmed inside as he read her text. Over time, he had figured out that Madison wasn't afraid of dipping her toe in the water, but she wasn't going to be the first one jumping into the lake. She was skilled at hedging her bets. He fixed the pillow behind his head, then pushed the call button. She answered on the first ring.

Her voice sounded like home, which was odd and comforting all at once. "Are you calling to talk smack on the press secretary's husband or to verify our dating status?"

Rhett laughed into the phone. "Can I do both?"

"I'd rather talk about your beach trip. I'm jealous you had a weekend of fun in the sun."

Rhett sighed. "I definitely don't want to talk about that. My vacation turned into a work ambush. I'll tell you about it later. I'm too tired tonight."

"Now I really want to hear about it, but I'll take a rain check if you insist."

"Thanks," Rhett smiled into the phone, "So where in the country is Madison Lyn tonight? Wait, are you in D.C. since you talked to Patricia?" Rhett sat up in anticipation. Adrenaline pumped through him. "And, if so, can I come over?"

Madison giggled. She hated giggling. That made him smile more. "No. I'm in Wisconsin, I think. I'm not sure if we've crossed state lines yet. The President came to a rally for Jackson. She won in the rust belt states, so the party chair suggested she hit a few stops with us."

Rhett laid back down and stifled a yawn. "How did you guys manage that one? Last I checked, only one candidate dropped after the debate. How did you score an endorsement that big before the convention?"

Madison was silent for a moment.

"Madison? I thought we moved past this."

"Sorry, habit. The only real contender left is a stodgy lifer. I think he started in politics with Abraham Lincoln. The party knows he'll carry the nomination with the senior demographic, but never win the country. They're swinging weight towards Jackson, who will get votes from both the left and the moderates. The convention is coming up soon, so we need to amp up the pressure on this guy. Rich said we need to put on our rally caps. I have no idea what that means, but everyone else did."

Rhett laughed. "Note to self, our next date will be to a baseball game. I can't date a girl who doesn't know what a rally cap is."

"I'm not sure which is funnier, your qualifications for dating, or the thought that either one of us has three hours to watch a game."

"Three hours? That tells me you know something about baseball, so I won't have to break up with you."

"Rhett Paulson, you are such a sweet talker," she laughed. "My dad is a huge baseball fan. He made us all watch at least one baseball game a season because it was America's pastime. I usually brought a book."

"A book! What? I feel like I don't even know you. How do you not like baseball? Baseball is my life." Rhett clutched his chest.

Madison laughed into the phone. "I never said I don't like baseball. I do find it interesting. I just don't understand it, so I never got into it. All that standing around and waiting for someone to, maybe, hit a ball in your direction."

"Well, now you just made this a challenge for me. There is so much strategy that goes into the sport. Teaching you about baseball has just become my number one priority."

"Now I'm nervous." Madison's mirthful tone gave her away.

"You should be. I've been told I'm intense when it comes to baseball. Ask Jake. Well, maybe don't ask Jake, or Alexis for that matter. Either way, we need to nail down a time in our schedules for a game. I'll even fly to you if I have to."

That one statement held weight, and they both felt it. Madison broke the silence, "We'll probably only be able to watch a few innings, but I'm *game* if you are."

"You're so punny, Miss Lyn."

"Why thank you. I like to *swing* for the stars."

"That one was questionable." Rhett still laughed.

"I should stop while I'm ahead before I *strike out.*"

"Wow, that was definitely a *foul ball.*"

"I'm not sure yours are much better." Madison became more relaxed when she talked with Rhett. Her voice was his telltale sign.

"Speaking of calendars, what does yours look like? Do you have any breaks in the near future?" Rhett quickly realized how much hope hung on this one question.

"Not in the foreseeable future. We're non-stop for the next three weeks. The bus is headed to a private air hangar now. We received a last-minute invitation to a symposium about food shortages that our biggest donors are hosting. So we're flying to California tonight. Then backtracking across the country on our tour bus, hitting as many college campuses as we can in two weeks."

"Well, that is incredibly fortuitous, Miss Lyn. I too have received a last-minute invite for the same symposium. My travel packet should arrive tonight. Maybe we can sneak in a dinner or breakfast, or at the very least, a few quick coffee runs." Rhett could feel his luck changing.

"If you tell me next you're also visiting college campuses, I may have to reconsider my stalker theory."

"Oh, how I love your wit. No, I'm not planning on a college tour, although you did just give me a story idea. Although stalking you sounds intriguing." Rhett's deep chuckle rumbled through him.

"If you can behave yourself, I might be able to snag another ticket for the GreEnergy fundraising gala the night before the conference. I think Hayman said we could have a plus one."

"GreEnergy? That's clever."

"*Anyway*, we have to attend the gala because the Philipsen Foundation hosts it. Their support would easily swing the election our way."

Shivers ran down Rhett's spine. "The Philipsen Foundation? I thought they didn't endorse candidates."

"They don't, but their board of directors and most of the gala attendees share our environmental concerns. If they throw their support behind our climate initiatives as private citizens, the election will be ours. Jackson had a meeting with their board before the last debate. That was the private donor dinner Rich and I weren't invited to. Apparently, we're cool enough for a gala, but not an exclusive dinner." Madison's soft laugh caught Rhett off guard and pulled him back into the moment.

"It seems Jackson is privy to information the public is not. I've been trying to locate the names of their board members for a story I'm researching. Each search takes me down new rabbit holes of their subsidiary organizations. They're an elusive group. Is Jackson at liberty to share those names?" Rhett didn't notice that his tone had become tighter, but Madison did.

"Are you asking as Rhett Paulson from WBN or as Madison's boyfriend Rhett?" Rhett heard the slight waver in her voice and he felt terrible.

Idiot. Closing his eyes and taking a deep breath, he attempted to remedy the situation. "Sorry, habit. I blame it on my vacation turned work trip weekend. Moving on to another important topic, I finally know the answer to how long it takes a politician to answer a direct question. According to my phone, I asked about our dating status twenty minutes ago. I think that might be a record. You have officially called me your boyfriend. You can't take it back now. Is it too early to change my relationship status on social media?"

Madison's sweet laughter softened his heart. "No status changes. Unless you want my dad and two brothers showing up at the gala, let's just keep this between us for now, buddy."

"Madison, you can't just try on my emotions like a pair of shoes. I'm not a piece of meat. I have feelings, you know." Rhett joined in on her amusement. "Besides, your roommates gave me their seal of approval. I think your dad will love me. We have baseball in common, remember?"

"You definitely don't have self-esteem issues." Her laughter let him know they were back on solid ground. "I think you're overestimating your charm. My dad will not be as easily swayed as Rich and Jackson are after a few beers. He might like you if you're a Republican, but then I'd have to break up with you, so there's that."

"You wound me, Madison. I will refrain from changing my status, but I'm very interested in hearing about your dad being a Republican. I bet family dinners are fun when you're home."

"You'll have to wait for that story. I'm getting the hand signals from Rich that we've arrived at the hangar. I guess I'll see you tomorrow." Madison sounded rushed. "I have to run. Oh, the gala is black tie, so bring a tux."

"Hey, Madison? Will you text me when you land?"

The pause on the other end of the line made his heart flutter a little. Rhett Paulson did not get flutters over women. He waited.

"You are a rare bird, Mr. Paulson. Yes, I will text you."

"I look great in a tux, by the way. Bye, Madison."

"Bye, Rhett."

He dropped the phone on his chest. What a weekend. Nick threw him a massive curveball. His catcher changed the pitch and wanted to move to West Virginia with Rhett's future godchild. Now Rhett was asking a woman to text him when she landed. His world had officially turned upside down.

As Rhett laid on his expensive couch in his overpriced penthouse contemplating his life, the doorbell rang. Wrenching himself to a standing position, he strode to the door.

Jimmy the doorman stood in the hallway proudly. "I brought these up myself, Mr. Paulson. One was delivered five minutes ago by the WBN runner. I asked for identification this time. The other fellow who came after didn't have identification, but he had a logo shirt from a legit delivery service, so he checked out."

Rhett sighed, "Thanks Jimmy. Have a good night."

"You too, Mr. Paulson." Jimmy meandered to the elevator with his shoulders held high. He served as gatekeeper tonight and would relish this accomplishment. Rhett shook his head and smiled before closing the door.

The WBN envelope held Rhett's itinerary and badges for the seminar. He wasn't happy about the early flight, but his schedule was clear for tomorrow evening, so the gala was a definite yes now. As he opened the second envelope, he braced himself. One sheet of paper was enclosed. The bland font gave nothing away, but the information was nuclear.

Globalization: Unite as global citizens to transform economic, educational, healthcare, environmental, and human rights agendas for the equity and good of all humankind. The Global Alliance trains world leaders to work within their own government to encourage calculated change.

Organization: Strategically utilize enhanced AI based technology and science based solutions to aid in the production and distributions of goods and services while monitoring and supporting a unified mission.

Defend: Support initiatives to secure the welfare of all global citizens during times of unprecedented uncertainty. The Global Alliance seeks to stabilize government systems across the globe for the safety of individual humans.

Rhett read the sticky note attached. "A group of the world's richest people announcing their plans to interfere in governments where they were NOT elected as representatives. How is this not treason against every country across the globe? Why isn't WBN covering this? Enjoy your trip."

Rubbing his chin, Rhett mumbled to himself, "That's a great question."

Chapter Twenty-One

Rich's whistle pierced the silence as Madison crossed the threshold. "Wow Mads, you clean up nice."

The sleek magenta silk gown looked better than she imagined. It fit Madison like a glove. When Jackson announced his candidacy, Madison's little sister Gabby started designing gowns for all the fancy parties Madison would be attending. Gabby got her first sewing machine at eight, and at twenty-one, was in her last year of design school. Madison called her yesterday to request an overnight shipment. Gabby's scream almost broke the sound barrier, but she had the perfect one in mind.

"Rhett is one lucky guy."

"Wow, two compliments in a row from Rich Miller. Gabby will be so excited." Madison curtsied.

"Your sister does have a crush on me."

"Yes, and we've always questioned her judgment."

"Ouch!"

"You do know you have to actually tie your bowtie, correct? The tussled tie look only works at the end of the evening." Madison glided across the floor with her heels in hand.

"I'll tie this dog collar when you lace up those torture contraptions for your feet. How do you wear those, anyway? Don't get me wrong, I enjoy seeing women wearing heels, I just don't understand how it's physically possible to stay upright in them. It's like an anomaly of both balance and gravity."

"Yet another reason women are superior to men. We defy the laws of physics, and we can work while doing it." Madison smirked at Rich. "Not to mention they add three inches to my height, which we both know I need."

"What are you two talking about?" Jackson stopped in his tracks and whistled. "Wow! Madsi, you look amazing!"

"I'm wavering between feeling complimented or offended. You both don't have to sound so shocked."

"What? You broke out a hottie dress tonight." Rich shrugged.

"Thank you?"

"Rich meant to say we're just used to you wearing dark suits every day, and sweats at night. You look very becoming in that color."

Madison gave them both a look. She loved it when they were awkward. These were her goofballs. "Thank you."

Jackson held out his bowtie in a pleading motion. "Madsi, I need you."

Madison stood and took the black fabric from Jackson. "Rich and I were discussing the inferiority of men to women before you walked in."

Not missing a beat, "No. We were talking about high heels and Madison's height complex. I tried to explain that we still love her even though she's shorter than a hobbit."

Madison glared at Rich as she pulled Jackson's bowtie tight and straightened it.

"I'm glad I missed that conversation. I'm also glad I interrupted before she went Lord of the Rings on you. Thanks, Madsi."

"Do me next. I hate these things." Rich rose and hesitantly drew closer to Madison, "Truce?"

Jackson chuckled, "You're brave."

The three friends enjoyed a moment of companionable silence before an evening of schmoozing. Noises from the doorway shattered their moment of peace. Within seconds, team members and activity filled the space as Madison worked on Rich's bowtie, maybe a little tighter than she had to. "There, finished."

"Thanks, Mads." Rich patted her head. Madison poked him in the stomach, making him clutch his core and bend over.

"Oops, sorry," she smiled sweetly.

"If you two could put on your adult hats for a moment and join us, that would be great." Hayman's voice sent shivers up her spine. A low growl escaped Madison's lips before she turned around to where Hayman sat.

Rich snorted then held out his arm for her, "Shall we adult today, Ms. Lyn?"

Madison tucked her arm into Rich's, "We shall, Mr. Miller."

Jackson laughed. Hayman scowled.

Hayman's assistant placed binders around the dining table. Madison couldn't remember the guy's name, but in her defense, this was Hayman's third assistant on the campaign. Madison felt bad for him. Hayman wasn't the most pleasant of bosses.

"Sit," Hayman instructed.

Madison bit her tongue. Hayman rubbed her the wrong way, but they needed him. He had the backing and the connections. Not to mention, Jackson trusted Hayman as much as he trusted them. It was evident Hayman tolerated Rich and Madison as much as they tolerated him. Sighing, she pulled out a chair and sat.

"Each binder outlines the VIP attendees of tonight's gala. There will be handlers present to separate the general guests from the exclusive guests. Be sure to stay in the corralled areas closest to the podium. Jackson, you'll stay with me at all times. You two," Hayman pointed to Rich and Madison as if they were wayward children, "are on your own if you get beyond the handlers."

"We certainly wouldn't want to mingle with the riff-raff. I'd hate to slum it with the general population, at fifty grand a seat."

Hayman ignored Rich's unwanted commentary. "As I was saying, these binders contain info on the must-know people. Attendees are listed alphabetically and color coded by level of importance to the organization they represent. The top tier in red includes the silent backers of the symposium. Unless you live under a rock, you will know each of these individuals. The other two tiers are an eclectic group of international donors and investment partners. It is imperative that you study these binders." Hayman pointed to his assistant. "Phillip will stand behind us all evening to ensure we hit every VIP."

Madison piped in, "Will any of the other candidates be present at the gala?"

Hayman's dismissive chuckle maddened her. "No, Madison. Jackson is the only candidate that matters. The people in the room tonight are the decision makers, and they've chosen Jackson. The presidency is ours for the taking."

Madison and Rich exchanged side eye looks.

"Jackson and I will mingle with tier one, obviously. The rest of our team will target tiers two and three. Madison, it surprised me to learn that you are using your plus one. It goes without saying that this is a work function."

Madison, caught off guard, sat up in her chair. Jackson must have noticed her sudden pang of defensiveness, because he jumped in to answer Hayman.

"Madison's date is Rhett Paulson. He's a great guy and will only help with our branding. It never hurts to remind people that the media loves us."

Hayman glanced between Madison and Jackson before continuing, "As long as he knows that tonight is *not* a work function for him. It is crucial that this gala remain a quiet affair and is not part of water cooler talk. Do I need to speak with Mr. Paulson?"

Madison was livid. Hayman was the most arrogant man she'd ever met. "That won't be necessary, Hayman. I know this may surprise you, but I have managed to build a successful career in my own right. I know how to handle myself and my date. All while keeping these two yahoos in check. You should move on to your next topic." Her gaze never left his. Hayman held her stare before moving on to the rest of his instructions.

Rich's fist tapped Madison's leg under the table. The smile at the corner of his mouth made her smile in return. They weren't doing this for Hayman. They believed in Jackson. She flipped through the binder and began memorizing. Jackson would have Hayman and Phillip. Rich didn't need a binder. He could sweet talk a street sign. Madison was grateful for her photographic memory.

An hour later, they emerged from a cavalcade of cars in front of the palatial estate. Tech giant of the world, Adam Ford, hosted the gala. He was the father of modern AI innovation and the creator of SurfIn, the world's largest search engine, hosting platform, and hub for all social media. Basically, Ford controlled the tech industry. You couldn't build, sell, or use an app without Adam Ford's technology, platforms, money, or blessing.

Rich whistled quietly between his teeth, "Dorothy, we're not in Kansas anymore."

"I'd say," Madison shook her head. "This is insane."

As their team climbed out of the SUVs and approached the grand staircase leading to the massive front doors, Madison noticed Rhett standing off to the side. His expression of admiration warmed her to the core. Rhett carried himself with an old-school swagger that reminded her of the black and white movies her grandparents loved. He was Cary Grant and Jimmy Stewart wrapped up in one.

He met them on the stairs and shook hands with Rich, but his eyes remained glued to Madison. Rich chuckled at Rhett before skipping up the stairs ahead of them.

"You look stunning. I mean, I knew you were going to look amazing tonight, but you are truly breathtaking." Rhett leaned down and kissed her cheek, lingering a minute longer than was socially acceptable for a greeting.

Madison blushed. "You don't look so bad yourself. Shall we?"

Rhett held out his arm for her and they ascended the stairs together. Madison relaxed for the first time in days.

"Anything I need to know about tonight? Other than making sure I use the correct silverware and chew with my mouth closed?" Rhett leaned in and whispered.

"We're supposed to stay between the potted ferns and the front stage."

"Wait, I can't tell if you're joking or serious. Potted ferns?" Rhett watched her as a grin slowly spread across her face.

"I know it sounds like I'm messing with you, but I'm really not. The heavy hitting donors will be in the front, protected by some handlers stationed by the tall ferns. Hayman instructed us to mingle within that section."

"Now I'm picturing an invisible fence and dog collar system for the B and C-listers. Do we get zapped if we cross the status line? Should I listen for a soft buzzing?"

Madison laughed at him. "Maybe. It would be entertaining to watch you try to figure out the system."

Rhett was on a roll now. He had them both laughing as they entered the massive white marble foyer. "I should have asked Jake to give me a hidden camera. I'm sure many people would enjoy watching B-list celebrities get zapped trying to improve their status. Now that I think about it, this would make great reality TV."

Madison stiffened beside him. Slowing her gait, she shuffled them into a corner and turned to look him directly in the eye. "Rhett, it is imperative that you not share anything you see tonight. You are here as my date, not as a reporter. Hayman made that very clear. These people are essential for Jackson's campaign. There is a reason this is an exclusive gala."

Rhett seemed to study her face for an eternity. She felt rattled. She never felt rattled. He reached up and stroked his thumb across her cheek, staring directly into her eyes. "Tonight, my role is that of the supportive boyfriend, and for the first time in my life, that means something. I promise I won't screw this up for you."

Her heart fluttered, then did a back flip. She believed him, and for the first time in her life, that meant something.

Rhett, ever the charmer, winked before flashing his lopsided grin. "I can totally get behind being eye candy tonight. I've been told I do handsome and debonair very well."

She shook her head and swatted his arm playfully. "I'm serious, Rhett. Tonight is important."

He kissed her cheek and winked. "I know. I promise to be on my best behavior. I'm here for you and you alone. I'll stay between the ferns and keep my reporter hat buried."

"Thank you." Madison tugged him back toward the ballroom. "You do make pretty good eye candy, Paulson."

The next hour was a swirl of networking, fangirling, and politicking. Madison conversed with people she had read about in articles. These were the rainmakers. The people who really ran the world. Industry experts and innovative collaborators all together in one room. Collectively, the foundations these people represented poured billions of dollars every year into philanthropies around the globe. These people were changing the world for the better, and they invited Madison to their table.

She was glowing. This must be what Cinderella felt like at the ball. Everything came together for the perfect night. She was not one of those girls who bought into the fairytale princess dream. Madison was much too practical for that. But tonight, tonight she relished the magic. She even had a prince charming, and he didn't leave her side once. He watched her and smiled at her all night with a look of adoration. Madison's heart overflowed.

As they sat for dinner, Rhett pulled out Madison's chair. He leaned in close as he found his own seat next to hers. "You are the most astounding woman I have ever met. You owned this room. You're way out of my league, you know that, right?"

Chills ran up her spine, and goosebumps covered her arms. Rhett whisked a discrete kiss on her cheek. He reached over and squeezed her hand. Madison took a deep breath and waited for the clock to strike midnight. It didn't.

Rich leaned across Madison to ask Rhett about some athlete in attendance. They both joked about wanting a selfie, but they were afraid to cross the fern-line.

"I mean, the guy won the Super Bowl, and he couldn't even score tickets beyond the ferns." Rich shook out his napkin and placed it on his lap in dramatic fashion. "Does this mean that I made it? My parents will be so proud."

"I'm wondering how we scored seats up here over a handful of Oscar winners."

"Hold up there, 'plus one.' *We* scored tickets. *You* scored a VIP date." Rich waved his finger between himself and Madison.

"I won't argue with that one. I definitely won in the date department." Rhett flashed a smile at Madison.

They settled into their seats as servers converged with the salad course. Dinner conversation centered on the weather, the primaries, and baseball. Madison couldn't escape baseball. Hilda Vanderfeld monopolized Rhett. The well-endowed, dripping in diamonds, ignored wife of Reginald Vanderfeld IV couldn't keep her hands off of Rhett's arm. Rhett squirmed throughout dinner. He kicked Madison at one point while trying to move as far away from the socialite as possible. Reginald Vanderfeld, Chairman of BioGreen Eco Laboratories, didn't seem to mind. Either that or his fifth scotch and water blinded him from his wife's flirtatious behavior.

Rhett's pained expression had Madison lightly coughing to cover her laughter. She leaned into him as Hilda excused herself for the ladies room. "That was highly entertaining."

Chocolate truffle cupcakes wrapped in gold sheets were served, and the lights dimmed. "I didn't realize you had a mean streak, Miss Lyn," Rhett whispered. Without skipping a beat, he butted his chair up to Madison's and draped his arm around her shoulders.

"Afraid of cougars?"

"Very."

"Don't worry, I'll protect you."

"You did a lousy job during dinner," Rhett smirked.

"I promise I'll do better next time." Madison's mouth lifted in the corner, stifling more laughter.

"Uh-huh. You don't sound very convincing." Rhett squeezed her shoulder as the speaker rose to the podium and began introducing VIPs. Madison sat in awe of how far she'd come. Here she was, sitting amongst global leaders on this side of the ferns. She breathed in the moment and committed it to memory.

Madison took in the room, her date, and her friends. She couldn't wait to call her parents tomorrow. They would be so proud of her and Gabby's dress design. This moment epitomized everything they had sacrificed to give her and her siblings.

Adam Ford paused at the podium, allowing for applause. "Before I introduce Johan Philipsen, I have another honor this evening. As you all know, the Ford Collaborative has joined forces with the Philipsen Foundation to educate and mobilize leaders through our Accelerate Project. This elite program guides and supports emerging leaders across the world, working to enact change as they encourage inclusive and equitable policies in governments around the globe. Each year, we invite a new class of twenty to join the ranks of the greatest minds across the globe. Together, they cross the divides of borders and ideologies. This leadership team tackles the most pressing issues facing humanity and the planet today. The Accelerate Project builds a global leadership base that will mobilize change for a more sustainable world. These future leaders are called to shape a new global society that stands for equity, peace, and prosperity for all.”

Rich quietly snickered, “The description of the Accelerate Project sounds like every answer given during the Q&A of a beauty pageant. ‘If I win, I’ll strive for world peace and to end hunger’.”

Madison elbowed him while concealing her own chuckle. “Shh.”

“In attendance tonight, we have two members of this year’s Accelerate Project class. Phoebe Evans, the Deputy Chief Financial Officer of Bluesky Multi-national Investment Firm.” More applause. “And Senator Jackson Cashe, who, with our help, will be the next President of the United States of America.”

Madison could feel Rhett and Rich both look at her. She smiled and clapped along with everyone else as she watched Jackson, sitting in between Hayman and Johan Philipsen, stand and wave to the crowd.

“You two didn’t know?” Rhett was quiet and discreet when he asked, but Madison felt exposed.

“No.”

Chapter Twenty-Two

West Coast sunshine was brutal on Rhett's jet lagged eyes. Plus, he couldn't sleep after the gala, and was paying for it this morning. He promised Madison he would leave his reporter hat at home, but too many things rubbed him the wrong way last night. His investigative senses tingled making it hard to sleep. Oliver handed Rhett a pair of sunglasses and some aspirin. Rhett groaned his appreciation as they climbed into the SUV with Jake, Rahemia, and her assistant, Keira.

"How was your fancy dinner party last night?" Jake's obnoxious, snooty impersonation felt flat and annoying this morning.

"Fine, thanks for asking." Rhett growled in response.

"While I'm sure we'd all love to hear about your date and exclusive invite last night, that will have to wait. We have a lot to discuss and only six blocks to get it done. Keira has sent your schedules and checklists for the day. The hosts will record the entire symposium, then distribute the recording to participants. Thanks to Jerry, we have a private interview with Johan Philipsen this evening. Jake, will you be ready? This is a once-in-a-lifetime meeting. We can't afford to screw this up. He rarely gives live interviews."

"Rahemia, you wound me. Of course I'm ready," Jake countered.

Rahemia rolled past the slight and continued her orders. "Tweedledee and Tweedledum here will not have access to the symposium, but will have access to a lounge for assistants and other low-level attendees."

"Ouch." Oliver's retort had Jake and Rhett laughing. Not so much Rahemia.

"Welcome to the table, kiddies. You two get the scraps. I want you both digging for anything scary we can use for click bait. I want links to any doomsday studies they use. If they have end of the world prediction models, I want them. I want anything and everything to pull in viewers. You two are shiny. Find the unfortunate ones and flirt. They love to talk."

Keira looked mortified. Oliver glanced at Rhett in disbelief. Jake shook his head. Rahemia, unphased, went on with her list until they arrived at the symposium. Keira raced ahead of the group to secure their press packets. Rhett encouraged Oliver to assist her.

"I think you scared poor Keira." Rhett watched Rahemia gather items into her bag.

"Rhett, my dear, coddling her in this field won't help her at all. If she wants to make it, she needs a tough skin and clear eyes to find the angles."

"Does that follow the fodder about making it in a man's world?"

Rahemia stopped packing up her things and looked directly at him. "No Rhett. I don't do it for her to compete with men. As a woman in the workplace, I'd take an obtuse man any day. I mentor women so they know how to survive other women in the workplace. Powerful women eat each other alive. When Keira is ready to move on, she'll be fierce and prepared. She'll be able to face a man, a woman, or a bear, but she will damn sure get the story. Now, if you two ladies are finished, it's time to go."

"Aye aye, captain." Jake hopped out and headed to the door.

As they entered, Keira handed out the press packets. Oliver stood to the side and watched her.

"You okay?" Jake patted Oliver on the shoulder.

"Yeah. I think I'm in love. She marched up to the table, pushed me out of the way, and had two staff members darting around collecting our stuff like they were her assistants. She's a force."

Rhett actually snorted. Jake guided Oliver into the building with his arm around his shoulder. "Our little Oliver is growing up. I think we need to get a drink later and have the talk."

As they separated, Rhett and Jake watched Oliver trip over himself to follow Keira. They both laughed as they followed Rahemia into the domed auditorium. The hosts had divided the room into three tiers: participants, spectators, and press. Rhett spotted Madison and Rich in the spectator seats, deep in conversation, with their heads bowed together. He had a pretty good idea of their current topic. After dinner, Rhett got to briefly kiss her goodnight near the motorcade before they whisked her away with Jackson and Hayman. Her morning was overscheduled with meetings and a campaign appearance before eight. This was probably the first time she and Rich got to talk about the big announcement.

Jake followed Rhett's gaze, then nudged his arm. "Come on lover boy, we're back here in the cheap seats. Let's go."

They found their chairs and opened the packet of information Keira had procured. After a few minutes studying the booklet, Rhett could feel Jake staring at him. "Don't say it."

"So, you see it too?"

"I don't know what I see, Jake. There isn't enough information to make an assessment."

Jake snorted, "There is plenty to make an assessment and you know it. This outline parallels the jump drive to a tee."

"*If* you're right, we need concrete connections, not conjecture and circumstantial evidence. We have to tie it all together."

"Speaking of evidence," Jake pulled out a pair of glasses and a lapel pin. He handed the pin to Rhett. "Here, I know the glasses don't match your outfit."

Rhett grabbed the pin with slightly too much force. "Thanks."

"Oliver has a Jackson Cashe campaign pin." Jake laughed at his own cleverness. "Everything we record will feed directly to a private server. Nothing will be stored within WBN's reach."

"I don't want to know how you pulled that off, but good job. All right, let's figure out this configuration." Rhett pointed to the map in the booklet and the corresponding seating chart. "According to this map, there are ten regional stations just like the jump drive said. It looks like each station will be managed by a czar and three chancellors. They will be overseeing global operations, but no names or nations are mentioned specifically."

"Is there a reason this map omits the sovereign borders of each country? Typically we would see the borders with the key outlining the regions, but this has no borders. No references at all."

Rhett could hear the wheels in Jake's mind turning. "Don't read too much into it. I'm sure there's a logical explanation. It probably has to do with population and transportation data." Rhett scanned the map and pointed. "See, they center each regional station near an Agriculture Development Center location where they're growing crops. The boundary lines probably coincide with their distribution capacity."

"Uh-huh, sure. If you believe independent nations aren't going to take command of these 'centers,' or be subdued attempting to do so during a global food crisis, I have some beachfront property in West Virginia for you. Something doesn't add up with this map. I don't think it's a coincidence they omitted national boundary lines." Jake scanned the room with his glasses, catching everything. "Look, there are ten global areas mapped out here, and ten global leaders on that stage." Jake quickly pulled up his phone and searched for something. His harrumph made Rhett nervous. "Well, that's another interesting twist. Each one of those leaders on stage is, or will be, an alumnus of the Accelerate Project."

Rhett blew Jake off, "That's not interesting. The hosting foundations also run that program. Of course they would use their own people. Don't go off the deep end on me. If we didn't have that stupid jump drive, none of this would have registered to you."

"But we do have the jump drive."

"And nothing else but coincidence. If you want me to listen, find me something concrete." Rhett sounded as annoyed as he felt.

Jake responded in kind, "Sure thing, boss man."

Returning to the information packet, Rhett skimmed over the introduction, written by Marchanka Rostinolova, the head of the Global Environmental Protection Network. According to her welcome article, unless radical changes were made in global food production and carbon emission levels, along with green energy systems being solidified, we would inevitably face a global food crisis of epic proportions. It would only take one act of nature to destroy the food supply. Oddly enough, she specifically warned against errant weather systems or an insect infestation. Rostinolova praised the "global alliance" being formed by the Philipsen Foundation, the SurfIn Collaboration, and the Adam Ford Foundation. Together, they would partner with nations around the world to research and grow alternative food sources to feed humankind during such a catastrophic time. She really nailed the point down in the summary, as she thanked the hosts for ushering global citizens into an era of peace, equity, and stability.

Jake's low whistle and shake of the head alerted Rhett that Jake had also read Rostinolova's gushing letter of reverence to this random alliance of philanthropists. "Yep, you're right. Nothing to see here. This is all normal." Jake settled into his seat as the lights flickered, then dimmed. "We were given a jump drive tying all of these recent 'acts of nature' to the 'GA' right before a symposium warning us of a food shortage that these people have the only solution to solve."

A hush settled over the auditorium as a single spotlight shone on a tall, broad-shouldered man. Johan Philipsen oozed authority. He commanded attention without saying a word. The profound silence in the room was a sign of reverence for his very presence.

"Good morning, friends. On behalf of the Philipsen Foundation and our partners in pursuit of a better global citizenship, welcome. Thank you for participating in this exercise. Our goal in this endeavor is to predict, prepare, and execute life-sustaining methods in the event of a global crisis. The symposium allows us to facilitate real time cooperation and problem solving tactics as one global family. This global alliance will support borderless solutions that will benefit and promote the welfare of all."

Jake made some type of clearing-his-throat-growl while the audience heartily applauded their statuesque emcee.

"As we begin our exercise today, you will notice members associated with out Accelerate Project will serve as czars and chancellors. We pride ourselves in that all of our members derive from nations across the world, permitting us to offer an extensive melting pot of experiences and knowledge to solve complex issues. The exercise will begin with a weather anomaly that would topple an already fragile food ecosystem. Imagine a series of weather patterns with the power to kill livestock, destroy crops, decimate grocery stores, and contaminate water systems across the globe in the span of days, possibly even hours. This will follow a rare beetle infestation such as our African neighbors are currently facing. The Global Alliance has been preparing for such a crisis. Your packets will enlighten you on how our ten Agricultural Development Centers have been working with scientists, botanists, entomologists, and nutritionists to design food sources that will sustain life during such a crisis. These culinary solutions are intended to nourish the body while aligning human food needs with a net zero balance for the environment."

"Did he just say *design* food? What does that mean?"

Rhett shushed Jake.

"We are very proud of our work engineering food and lifestyle changes that will promote a green ecosystem for future generations. We will streamline all communication and information efforts through our newly created Babel Communications. This elaborate system will allow the alliance to provide instructions for obtaining life sustaining food. In addition to aiding coordination efforts between regions, it will also offer protection from disinformation strategies aimed at keeping individuals from vital supplies and nutrients.

"Babel? Are you seriously not getting chills? You do know the Tower of Babel was a bad thing, right?"

"That's a bedtime story. A myth. Shh, it's starting," Rhett elbowed Jake.

"Without further ado, we shall begin on a cloudless summer day in June." Johan Philipsen faded out of sight as the room went dark. A panoramic screen came to life, flashing idyllic scenes of people enjoying a beautiful sunny day.

Chapter Twenty-Three

R hett ducked his head so no one could see him shamelessly knocking on the door. He inspected his shoes, the parking lot, his phone. Finally, the door swung open, almost smacking him in the face.

"Welcome to our humble abode!" Rich's voice boomed from the threshold.

Rhett climbed the stairs and took in the space. "I feel like a groupie trying to sneak on the bus after a concert."

"Do you feel cheap and unappreciated? I didn't realize Madison was so cold and callous." Rich's mock look of pity was entertaining.

"Don't you have somewhere to be, Rich?" Madison crooned from the hallway beyond Rhett's angle of sight.

"Trying to get some alone time. I get it, I get it. You two kids have fun." Rich grabbed his messenger bag and hopped out of the bus.

"I'm back here. I needed to change shoes." Madison sounded distracted as her voice went in and out of focus.

Rhett walked down the narrow hallway, following the beautiful sound. As far as tour buses went, this one definitely dripped swag with leather upholstery and a wall of tech. "Is that a walk-in closet?" Rhett could not believe his eyes.

"We have a lot of events that require frequent wardrobe changes."

Rhett looked around to find where the voice was coming from. "There you are." He looked up and came face to face with a pair of legs swinging down in front of him.

"Well, I have to say, these bunks are much larger than I expected." Rhett examined the roomy cubby. Madison's bed was surrounded by shelves, a lamp, wall outlets, and a television.

"That was the only way they could talk me into this crazy idea. If I have to share a moving apartment with those two, I needed my space to be big and private. The boys have that side. I got the space beside the closet, so I have more headroom." She waved her arms like Vanna White.

"Would you like some company?" Rhett grinned up at her with a devilish smile.

"Ha-ha. It's not that big, buddy. I came up here to find a Band-Aid. I have a blister." She was moving things around, searching. "Found one."

Rhett took the Band-Aid from her hand and inspected her foot.

Madison covered her face. "Gross. My feet probably smell."

"I played baseball with Jake. I've smelled a lot worse." Rhett opened the package, found the blister, and secured the bandage. He cradled her foot. The only thing missing was the glass slipper. "Besides, your feet smell like roses."

"Help me down?"

Rhett reached both hands up and caught Madison's waist as she shimmied down from the loft. He held her tight, then pulled her close as she landed.

Her hands wrapped up around his neck as she stared into his eyes. "Hi."

"Hi." Rhett leaned down and melted his lips into hers. He could feel her body relax the longer they kissed. His own stress lifted as he settled into her embrace. "You smell good."

"Like roses, apparently," Madison chuckled in his ear.

"I only have a minute. I have an exclusive interview with Johan Philipsen tonight and we have to prep." Rhett was bragging a little. For some nagging reason, he wanted her to be proud of him.

"Ooh, exciting. You might pass Jackson along the way. Philipsen invited him to a dinner for the AP leaders. Rich and I will be strategizing with the campaign team over pizza and beer."

"Ah, yes, the Accelerate Project. What's the deal with that? Did you guys really not know?" Rhett felt her stiffen. "Boyfriend asking, not reporter. I'm just asking because, if Jake had something huge happen to him and didn't tell me first, I'd be pretty ticked." Rhett shrugged. It hurt a little that he still had to preface questions with an 'off the record' promise, but in her defense, he struggled to turn off his inquisitive mind lately.

She relaxed. "*He* didn't know. Hayman had mentioned something about the program, but nothing was concrete. Next thing we knew, they announced Jackson's name. We were all surprised, especially Jackson. It's a tremendous boost for the campaign, but now I have to rework the schedule for meetings and Rich has to tweak speeches. On top of that, Jackson has to attend a three-day summit this month. It would have been nice to know ahead of time, but I guess that's just life on the campaign trail. We dodge balls and trip wires all day."

Madison looked tired. Her eyes weren't as alert and her cheeks had lost their rosy color. Rhett so badly wanted to breathe some life back into her. "Do you get a break while Jackson is at the summit? Maybe we could take a few days off together?" The thought of this made his heart race.

"I doubt it, but I'll know more after our strategy session tonight. What about you? What's your calendar look like over the next two weeks?"

"We fly out tomorrow, then I'm back on set for a few days. Jake and I head to Indiana this weekend for that project we're doing with Nick. Sunday, I'm back home."

Madison looked disbelievingly at him. "What part of Indiana?"

"We're meeting members of the Cooperative Farmer's Association in Indianapolis. Why?"

"We have three stops around the Great Lakes, then we're making a two-day stop for the Indiana State Fair and a donor reception. My dad has a speaking engagement in South Bend so my parents are renting a car and meeting us in Indianapolis."

Rhett's smile slowly stretched across his face. "Well, well, well. If that isn't a coincidence, I don't know what is. Does this mean I get to meet the parents?"

Madison closed her eyes and shook her head. "I'm not saying yes, but that is definitely a coincidence worth considering. I'm just not sure you're up to meeting Daniel and Vivian Lyn."

"I've interviewed world leaders, celebrities, and one time a baby panda. I think I can hold my own with your parents."

The door rattled open and Rich popped his head inside with a hand over his eyes. "Are you two decent? I hate to interrupt, but I have the new talking points and I need Madison."

Madison unwound herself from Rhett's arms while taking his hand in hers. She led them to the front room, where she held out her other hand for the paper. "Rhett will be in Indiana at the same time as the campaign and wants to meet my parents."

Rich busted out laughing. "Oh, please let me be there for that."

Rhett leaned against the counter, pulling Madison close to him. "Parents love me."

"Oh, I'm not worried about them liking you. I want to watch Vivian negotiate an engagement so she can start planning a wedding while Daniel sizes you up like a cheap suit he donated decades ago." Rich was still laughing as he sat and opened his laptop.

Rhett looked down at Madison.

"He's right. My parents were married by a justice of the peace. My mom has been dying to plan a wedding since before I was even a gleam in her eye."

"Interesting." Rhett watched Madison study the paper in her hands. He couldn't help but glance at it. The document was even more interesting than the wedding story. He shook his head and refocused. "Now I really want to meet them. I've never seen Madison rattled."

Madison elbowed him.

"Ouch," Rhett moaned. "All right, that's my cue." He leaned down and kissed Madison's head. "I have to prep for the show tonight. Text me details for Indy."

Rhett walked by Rich and patted him on the back. "Enjoy your pizza and beer."

"See you, brother." Rich scooted over for Madison to sit.

***

An hour later, Rhett scooped out another portion of pork lo mein as Jake grabbed the last fried cheese wonton. Oliver and Keira were taking bites in between completing tasks from Rahemia.

"I had Keira check the teleprompter three times. It's ready. Jake, did you review the angle requirements?" Rahemia was leaving nothing to chance. She read through her notes while holding out her plate. Keira quickly cleared Rahemia's plate, while she simultaneously chugged her water, and handed something to Jake, all while avoiding Oliver carrying wonton soup. Oliver was correct, this girl was a force.

"Yes, Ma'am. The cameras are ready and coordinated with sound, and I've adjusted each camera to hit Philipsen at the requested height. This guy has more demands than all the crazy divas I've filmed combined."

"Well, he's arguably the most powerful man in the world, so he gets what he wants. I don't care how obnoxious his demands sound." Rahemia held out her empty cup. Keira replaced it with a fresh coffee. "I cannot express this enough, Rhett. Do not go off script! Only the approved questions, in the exact order. I need you to tell me you understand and will obey."

"Obey? Come on, Rahemia. I'll be on my best behavior and make you proud." Rhett flashed his best PR smile.

"You better. Jerry pulled a lot of strings for this interview. This is award-winning material, Rhett. I need this."

Rhett reached out and touched her hand. "We've got this, relax."

Rahemia waved her other hand in Keira's direction. Keira handed her a paper. Rahemia glanced at it, then quickly passed the document to Rhett. "Read this list of talking points. You need to integrate these into your opening monologue."

Rhett's joviality stopped, and his grip tightened as he scanned the words. A calm voice masked his increased heart rate. "Where did we get this?"

Rahemia was too distracted to notice the edge in Rhett's voice. "Jerry's office sent it over right before the food arrived. This is the list we get before every show. I just usually get it early enough to plug everything into my edits before we feed the teleprompter."

"The talking points we review before each show come from Jerry?" Rhett was boiling.

Rahemia looked up at him, concern spreading. "Yes. Is that a problem? I assumed you knew. Didn't your last producer share these with you?"

"No."

"Rhett, you're making me nervous. We can discuss the premise of the talking points tonight after the show, tomorrow, or on the flight home. I don't care when, as long as we get through *this* show with *these* talking points. Are we good?" Rahemia was on high alert. Rhett could feel her studying his every move.

"The show will be perfect. I'll cover what needs covered, but I definitely want to talk about the origin of these talking points with Jerry. I'm a journalist, not a trained monkey towing the company line."

Jake grabbed Rhett's shoulder and squeezed. Jake had Rhett's back before Rhett even knew it needed covered. "Rahemia, relax. Rhett has always delivered. He'll do it again tonight. Come on, Rhett. Let's take a walk around the block and get some air."

Jake stood, Rhett followed. Rhett glanced between his producer and the two assistants who looked too afraid to breathe. "Really, I'll be fine. I just need a minute."

Jake turned as soon as Rhett closed the door behind them. "What was that all about?"

Rhett shook his head. "Something Nick said to me about towing the company line." Rhett paced, Jake watched. "That list was the exact, I mean the *exact* same document that Madison and Rich were given this afternoon. They had to work the talking points into Jackson's campaign strategies and speeches."

Jake started to say something, but he was cut off by Rhett's hand. "Don't. Don't say it. I need more information. Let's just get through this interview."

Rhett started down the hallway with Jake at his side. His cell phone alerted him to a text. His pain-in-the-rear informant picked today to restart communication. Rhett growled. The informant sent a single question.

***

That one singular question, sent by his unknown informant, stuck in Rhett's craw during the entire hour-long interview. As they neared the end, Rahemia beamed. She clutched her headphones, tablet, and coffee as she stood behind

Jake, glancing between his screen and Rhett. She flashed the five-minute warning to Rhett. He was in the home stretch and he knew Rahemia smelled another ratings sweep.

Johan Philipsen was an exemplary guest. He was charismatic, personable, and he exuded authority. He answered every question with aplomb. The entire interview felt like a free advertisement for the Philipsen Foundation and SurfIn Collaboration. Rhett was unnerved.

They covered the Accelerate Project, the Youth Mobilization program, and other efforts to address global issues affecting people worldwide. Rhett listened to every word. On the surface, this was a remarkable collaboration between numerous foundations and industry leaders. Everything about this global alliance of minds sounded inspiring and critical for global survival. It all made sense and allowed people to feel good about themselves and the future of the world, but something didn't sit right with Rhett.

At Rahemia's signal, it was time for the final question. "How do you propose countries tackle these problems?"

"Rhett, I am very glad you asked this question of me. We have been training and mobilizing the next generation of global innovators through our many youth-led initiatives. Our alumni community spans the public, private, and government sectors around the world. These leaders transcend the constraints of borders and work collectively for the global good. As we continue down this united direction as global citizens, we will ensure the sustainability of our planet and the health and safety of humankind. For example, our Global Organization and Defense initiative is currently Beta launching under a team of Accelerate Project alumni."

The G.O.D. logo flashed through Rhett's mind. One czar referenced it during the simulation this morning, but it was not in the packet material provided.

"These global influencers are collaborating to create three models of our Self-Sustaining Pod Sectors, SSPs, as we call them. Each pod can house seven to ten million global citizens. Self-sustaining means that pod citizens will have everything they need within walking distance. They will work from home on our strategic intelligence platforms. AIs designed to provide physical labor for the pods will build, shop, and deliver everything citizens need systematically to reduce carbon emissions. We will provide education and healthcare equitably to all. Personal, health, and financial information will be stored and scored in an implanted chip in the wrist. People won't need to take purses, wallets, insurance cards, or phones with them. Everything will be on their person. Think of it as a 'smart house' but on your body. Our net-zero-vertical housing towers substantially decrease the environmental footprint of these pods. Geo-engineered food and super-powered vitamin supplements, in addition to nutrient rich culinary entomophagy and recycled wastewater will provide protein and hydration when food sources are unavailable. These advances will end food scarcity, and protect the earth from dangerous farming practices currently destroying the planet. It truly is a thing of beauty. Every human being will be cared for sustainably without the carbon footprint they are selfishly making now."

Rhett couldn't help himself, "I'm sorry. Did you say engineered food, supplements, culinary entomophagy, and recycled wastewater? As in, they'll be eating fake food and bugs while drinking their own sewage as water?"

Rahemia's face went ashen. Jake tried to cover his smile. Johan, visibly annoyed, looked like a gnat had flown into his perfectly angled shot.

"Mr. Paulson, you make it sound so crude. Entomophagy has been a culinary wonder since the beginning of time. I hear your Hollywood celebrities are eating insects in movies now. As for the others, science and technology in the private sector are light years ahead. Humans adapt and evolve. These scientific and culinary advances can meet our nutrient needs. SSPs are the pinnacle of innovation, equity, and sustainability. They cross governmental borders, which historically only spark instability and war. The Global Alliance seeks to transcend the traditional institutional framework of borders and nation states to allow one united global geo-economy that will protect and preserve humankind."

There it was, and the text Rhett had read earlier that had been niggling at him throughout the interview came out of his mouth. Rahemia looked like she was on the verge of a stroke. "By 'traditional institutional framework' you mean existing sovereign governments elected or appointed by their citizens? Sir, who will govern this new 'united global geo-economy' if there are no borders or governments? Adam Ford? You?"

Johan Philipsen remained composed, but Rhett saw the icy stare underneath the bright smile. "Mr. Paulson, the Philipsen Foundation and SurfIn Collaboration, along with many other non-profit organizations, are fighting the good fight. We want businesses to be held accountable, people to be treated fairly and equitably, children to be educated, and the planet to thrive. Everything we do is to improve life for all humankind. Change for some is scary, especially for those who think they hold all the power, but we will not stop until the Global Rebirth is complete. Most government leaders are working in tandem with us on this noble quest."

Rhett could hear Rahemia quietly screaming in his earpiece. Livid was an understatement. He was sure steam was shooting out of both ears.

"Mr. Philipsen, our time is almost up, but if you'll indulge me a follow-up question?"

Johan Philipsen nodded his acknowledgement, knowing he had no choice.

"No members from any of these numerous foundations and organizations you have mentioned are elected officials, correct? You weren't elected by any country or nation to make these initiatives actual policies, correct?"

Philipsen didn't skip a beat. He listed off every alumnus of their Accelerate Project, every board member, and every partner of the GA who was an elected leader of any nation. Rhett saw it clearly now. This was the greatest long con in history. They had already infiltrated every government.

There was the crux. A series of loopholes and internal connections. People with power and resources who felt they could control others. This was organized crime at its finest and highest levels. The difference was that the Global Alliance held all the strings and all the money. They were the pigs from *Animal Farm*. They wielded fear, promised salvation, silenced the truth, and pillaged the storehouses. Rhett was positive that Johan Philipsen, Adam Ford, Horatio Theopolis, and all the other global elite would not be living in self-sustained pods while eating bugs and drinking their own pee. No, they would live in their mansions, eat actual food, and fly around in their super-fueled jets while locking the farm animals up in their SSP barns.

Rhett didn't remember signing off from the show. He didn't remember tossing it to Francine in the studio for headlines. He didn't remember Rahemia throwing her headphones at Keira's face or Jake's worried expression, but he remembered Johan's last words.

As the crew tore down and turned off lights, Johan Philipsen removed his own mic, leaned in very close to Rhett, and grinned. "Mr. Paulson, you amuse me. I admire your bravery, but I will not be so cordial in the future. Let me tell you something my father used to tell me after his days in Nazi Germany. He said, 'Johan, those who control the food, the money, and the fear rule the world.' Mr. Paulson, I assure you, I control all three. Good evening."

Rhett sat there and watched the statuesque man walk toward his private dining room. "Mr. Philipsen?" Philipsen turned to face Rhett, clearly entertained by the reporter's bravado. "Out of curiosity, what is on the menu tonight for your Accelerate Project dinner? Surely not bugs and recycled wastewater." Rhett eyed the man curiously.

Johan's lips turned up into a mischievous grin. "Albino beluga caviar, artichoke soup with black truffles, Kobe filets, fresh steamed vegetables, crème brûlée, and imported scotch."

Chapter Twenty-Four

"What were you thinking?" Rahemia paced and yelled. Yelled and paced. "Well, clearly, you weren't thinking. Or worse, you were thinking, and you purposely sabotaged us both. I mean, what else could that have been but intentional sabotage?"

Rhett facetiously glanced at Jake. "Am I supposed to answer her? Or are these rhetorical?"

"Oh no, Rhett. You don't get to charm and joke your way out of this one. I'm currently plotting ways to kill you in my mind. This is bad, Rhett. Really, really bad." Rahemia plopped down into the leather chair, dropping her head onto her folded arms.

Rhett looked to Jake for backup, to which Jake shook his head and pointed directly back to Rhett. Oliver and Keira both diverted their gazes to the floor and out the window, respectively.

Rhett swiveled his own leather chair to the aisle that separated him from Rahemia. Patting her shoulder, "I know I threw you a curve ball tonight, but you have to know I had a reason. When Jerry calls again, I will take the blame. You have witnesses. I ignored you and went off on my own."

Rahemia raised her head and glared at him. "We both know how this works. Talent never gets fired. Talent only gets shifted. I, on the other hand, will be sent to some remote local affiliate for the graveyard shift." Her head reverted to its prostrated position. "How could you do this to me?"

"Come on now. I have always had your back and you know it. I don't turn on my friends, ask Jake." Rhett pleaded for back up and received an annoyed smirk from Jake.

"He's right. He's a total jackass, but he is a loyal one."

"Thanks." Rhett snarled. "Back to what I was saying. I'm sorry for going off on my own. I was following my gut. Something I used to do all the time, but somehow lost my way. In all honesty, I had every intention of following the prompter to the letter. I planned to be on my best behavior, just like you asked. I broke your trust, and for that, I truly am sorry."

Rahemia's head popped up again, "Why? Can you at least tell me why you went rogue?"

Rhett turned and stared out of the airplane's window. They were close to landing. D.C.'s lights were sparkling, but the looming sunrise called the night to morning life. Staring out at the skyline before him, he pondered the same question. Whatever happened last night, it was right. He felt like himself. It felt good to break away from the mold he'd been willingly cast into at the network. There was a taste of freedom in that moment of decision, and he wanted more of it. He rubbed his chin and turned to survey the room.

"There was something so smug about that guy. Think about it. These people aren't elected officials. They are the richest, most influential people in the world. They aren't restricted by borders, or resources, or connections. And they have decided, based on their own personal opinions, how the world should run, and then they finance it. Their resources and connections make it impossible for them to be questioned or held accountable. We're nothing more than lab rats to them. No one is asking them questions. Including me. Take that nutritionist from the other night. I didn't connect any of the dots. I didn't question her authority or experience. I just took everything she said at face value. Meanwhile, she's on the payroll of her boyfriend and spouting out what she's paid to say. Did she conduct any of that research? Did she search for counter research? Does she actually believe any of it, or is she just repeating what they tell her to say? Hell, does she even have a medical or science-based degree? Why didn't I ask her any of those questions? There is more to this story. I feel it."

Rahemia sat back in her seat and rubbed her temples. "Rhett, just how far are we going with this? Do you have anything to back up your *feelings*? I need something more to give Jerry, especially after you embarrassed him and WBN on prime time television, other than you don't trust rich people. Which, I might add, you are one of these days."

Rhett looked at Jake, who shrugged. Rhett knew it was his call. Jake would support him, no matter what.

"What? What are you two hiding? Does this have anything to do with that crazy jump drive? Out with it," Rahemia practically snarled.

"Oh boy." Oliver tightened his seatbelt and his grip on the bag housing the secret laptop.

Rhett nodded to Oliver, holding out his hand. Oliver reluctantly handed over the bag. Rhett settled in next to Rahemia and brought the laptop to life. Rahemia watched silently as Rhett opened files uploaded from the jump drive and those he scanned from envelopes that appeared under his door by invisible delivery men. Next, Rhett pulled out the G.O.D. Initiative diagram that was briefly referenced during the symposium and explained how he had it days earlier. Finally, Rhett shared the leads he and Jake had been working on trying to unmask the group they now referred to as the "Patriot Spies."

Rhett, Jake, and Oliver watched as Rahemia absorbed all of this information. Keira looked sea sick. The pilot announced the final descent. Everyone held their breath.

"This suggests that someone has actually been sabotaging the global food supply while, at the same time, a goodwill-global-alliance-of-do-good philan-thropists is prepared to save the day?" Rahemia looked between Rhett and Jake. "Almost as if this whole thing was planned by the very people who will profit from the only solution?"

Rhett nodded. Hearing it out loud sounded crazier than it did in his head all this time.

Rahemia took a deep breath. She closed her eyes and clutched her stomach. When she finally leveled her gaze at Rhett, it pressurized the cabin with more than air. "You are either crazy or brilliant, but either way, you're asking everyone on this flight to risk our careers on cloaks and daggers. You know this, right?"

Rhett nodded.

"Have you corroborated any of this information?"

Oliver quickly leaned over Rhett's shoulder and opened another file. "Each folder has a tab on this spreadsheet with multiple sources that back up every claim we've verified."

"How did we not know any of this about the food catastrophes and pollution of water sources? We're a news organization! How has all of this been kept quiet? These are major events, yet I don't remember even hearing about them." Rahemia was arguing with herself.

"I've been asking myself the same questions." Rhett was exhausted.

"We need to show this to Jerry. This is the story of a lifetime. Has your source leaked this to any other network? Is this exclusive? Can we trust him? Will he agree to be interviewed?" Rahemia's mind raced with angles and ideas.

Rhett closed the laptop. "We have to be careful. Remember, a man was killed getting this jump drive to us, and the other information has been delivered to me in an even more clandestine manner. We need to be careful. Let's also not forget that these companies are major advertisers. If we expose Bluesky and Vandergrift, we alienate essentially every company on the stock exchange."

The passengers were so caught up in the plot before them, no one realized the plane was landing until they jolted when the wheels hit the runway. They sat in silence as the airplane taxied towards the private hangar. The weight of it all hovering over them.

"All right, I'm going to call Jerry on my drive home and give him a brief summary. I'm sure he'll want to meet us first thing in the morning, so be ready when I call," Rahemia leveled her gaze at Rhett.

"I'll be ready." Rhett carefully loaded the laptop into his shoulder bag Oliver had been clutching like a life preserver for the past twenty minutes.

"Not a word to anyone about this." Rahemia pointedly looked each person in the eye. "Not your mom, not your dad, not your grocer, not your cat. Does everyone understand?"

Heads nodded. As they all disembarked, they went their separate ways. They had four hours before they would return to WBN's headquarters. Oliver offered to share a cab with Keira. Rahemia's driver was waiting. Jake and Rhett climbed into Jake's truck and headed to their favorite diner. Rhett clutched the laptop tightly.

The two friends sat in silence until their food arrived. Exhaustion battled with a plethora of questions that needed answered, but they didn't even know where to search. Crispy bacon, a plate of sausage and gravy biscuits, grits, and omelets were placed before them.

They just stared at the table for a minute before Jake finally broke the silence. "Has your guy responded to your text?"

"Nope. Nothing. Radio silence as usual. He only sends cryptic messages, never responses." Rhett shoved a piece of bacon in his mouth. Shaking his head, "We need a power shift. I can't keep jumping when they say jump. This is a very lopsided arrangement, if they're going to shut me out when I need answers. And I know they saw the show. They monitor my every move, which is very disturbing, by the way."

Jake and Rhett questioned everything that had happened to them since the secretive parking lot meeting. One dead source with a successor who obviously hated Rhett. Instead of peeling back layers to reveal the story, they were leading Rhett in circles. Something had to give. What did they want from him?

"For what it's worth, I think you made the right call tonight with Philipsen. That guy was nothing more than word salad. He threw out shiny words with no substance. The whole symposium was a dog and pony show. It was scripted and creepy. I got cold chills when they talked about food disbursement centers and pharmaceutical supplement programs." Jake shivered.

"I just can't see the bigger picture. I can always see the picture. This whole thing has my head all fuzzy and spinning." Rhett tapped his fork on his plate.

"Seriously. Bugs and recycled sewage water? The scariest part was the flock of celebrities who made PSAs about bugs and pee water. I thought it was a joke at first. I guarantee you they won't be serving that crap at their parties and award shows." Jake offered a grunt in agreement. "I just don't understand how they're going to get eight billion people to buy what they're selling."

"Fear and propaganda. Their entire doomsday scenario yesterday was all about food shortages and mass starvation. The daily death tally by country on their mock tickers was chilling, but the solution reeked of savior complex. I just can't tell who the good guys are in the whole thing." Rhett twisted his coffee mug in his hands.

Jake shivered. "Sitting there watching them playact a world catastrophe like it was happening in real time, was creepier than I thought it would be. It was too realistic, you know? A series of natural disasters combined with a Biblical level pest infestation and weather events?"

"I know." Rhett rubbed his chin. "Based on what we've seen on the jump drive, it begs the question, if those were predictions or inside information."

Silence engulfed them again. The past twenty-four hours had been rattling. They paid their tab and headed to Rhett's building. Rahemia confirmed a meeting with Jerry and texted Rhett a reminder. He needed a shower. Rhett left the laptop with Jake. His gut told him not to bring it to the meeting with Jerry. Besides, Jake wanted to upload the videos from the symposium and create a backup before going home to crash.

Rhett nodded a hello to his new buddy, Jimmy the doorman, as he headed for the elevator. Tension wrecked his body. Leaning against the railing as it rose to the penthouse, his cell phone came to life. The elevator doors opened, as Rhett glanced down at the screen and grunted in frustration, "Now he answers me."

Roe: Adam Ford received a patent for weather manipulation and offered grants to three universities to implement a program last year. They are in the initial testing phase now. It's called the Rainmaker Program.

"What the? That can't be right." Rhett mumbled to himself. He began typing a response when he looked into his ransacked living room and froze. Chills ran up his spine just as pain exploded in his head. The phone slid across his porcelain floors as he dropped to the ground with a thud.

Chapter Twenty-Five

"What? Oh my goodness, what happened?" Madison squeezed her phone tightly in her hand. "Is he going to be okay?"

Jackson and Rich watched closely as she paced the length of the bus. It took a lot to worry Madison, so they knew something was wrong.

"Mm, hmm. Okay. Okay. Who? How long?" The pattern of speaking, then pausing for answers, continued. "Can I talk to him? Okay. Thanks. Let me know. Okay. Thanks, Jake."

"Well?" Jackson hated being in the dark. "What was that about, Madsi?"

Madison plopped down next to Rich at their kitchenette table. She took a fortifying breath. "That was Rhett's friend, Jake. Apparently, someone broke into Rhett's apartment. They were still there when he got back into town. They knocked him out when he walked into the room. Rhett left something in Jake's car. Jake went inside to give it to him and found Rhett lying on the floor outside of the elevator. They're running tests now."

"Wow. That's crazy. Was he hurt badly?" Jackson reached across the table to hold Madison's hand.

"They don't know. He was unconscious when Jake got there. He started coming to when the ambulance arrived, but was woozy and incoherent. The hospital is running tests and getting imaging on his brain and spinal cord."

"Mads, I'm so sorry. Is there anything we can do?" Rich wrapped an arm around her shoulders and squeezed her into his side.

"Do you want to head back to Washington? We can handle the next few stops without you. I can call Hayman and get you a flight." Jackson looked worried enough for the both of them.

"No," Madison shook her head, "No. Jake said to wait until they know something. He's going to keep me posted. I'd rather stay busy than wait around a hospital feeling helpless."

Rich kissed the top of her head, "Mads, you're shaking, darling."

She wrapped her arms around her stomach. "To be honest, I'm not sure what to do. I think I'm in shock. They almost killed him. Again."

"Do the police have any leads? Surely his building has cameras. Do they think it was tied to the shooting?" Jackson, ever the rational thinker, tried to process the facts of the case.

"Whoever did it took the stairs and knew where the cameras were located. The police are still at Rhett's place investigating." Madison didn't realize she was still shaking.

Rich squeezed her tighter. Jackson went to get her a juice box from their compact refrigerator. "Here, drink this."

Madison finished it in one swig. The boys, feeling helpless, watched her. Madison checked her phone in vain for an update or something to hold on to as she waited. She jumped when Rich's phone vibrated.

"Great. Hayman just sent me another round of talking points for your speeches tomorrow. Nothing like waiting until the last minute. Where is he getting these from and why can't we get them earlier?" Rich removed his arm from around Madison's shoulder and shifted his laptop closer. "Sorry, Mads, no rest for the weary."

"No, this is good. I need to do something productive. I hate sitting around thinking the worst. Send me the list and I'll cross reference it with our stops. Maybe you can make general changes so we can streamline his remarks." Madison reached across the table for her own device. It took her a minute to focus her eyesight. She kept glancing between her phone and the screen.

Jackson and Rich watched her closely as she transformed back into their strong and steady Madison Lyn. She was always the voice of reason. They weren't sure how to comfort her, so they just followed her lead.

It was times like this when Madison was grateful for their special bond. They knew each other so well. The three of them were symbiotic in their efforts. They knew when to push, when to comfort, and when to joke. She could feel their concern, and it made her feel secure and loved. They all worked quietly as one.

"Mads, aren't we visiting Detroit on our way back? Jackson is speaking at a car plant, right?" Rich rifled through his trusty legal pad sitting next to him.

"Mm hmm, after Indiana, before Ohio and Pennsylvania. Why?"

"I'm not sure this new strategy about wind and solar is going to fly in, well, any of the four states you just mentioned. Especially when we announce that we're pushing for the elimination of all gas powered vehicles over the next six years." Rich looked up at Jackson. "When exactly did we decide that? My GZ75 disagrees with this policy, FYI."

"What? That's not on our platform." Jackson's baffled response had Rich and Madison looking at each other, even more confused than before.

"According to this memo from Hayman, it is now," Rich turned his laptop around so Jackson could read it for himself.

"I'm great at spin, but even I can't spin asking people to support you when you're eliminating their jobs." Rich leaned back and watched Jackson.

Madison chimed in, "Jackson, Hayman has been drastically altering the platform lately. Is he not discussing these with you? Or are you not discussing them with us?"

Jackson looked between Madison and Rich. "Come on, guys. You know I wouldn't keep you in the dark. To be honest, I've been preoccupied with the Accelerate Project. My talks with Hayman are blurring together with Philipsen's seminars. We'll ask Hayman about this later."

"Since we're making these changes, I have to 'tweak' every one of your speeches to align with your new platform that you don't seem to know anything about." Rich's sarcasm didn't go unnoticed, but was mercifully ignored.

"I think it would be a good idea for us to look at the details of the Accelerate Project to compare their platform to ours. It's too late in the game to be changing course on major issues." Madison's look called Jackson to action.

"I can do that. Let me call my contact at Accelerate. Until then, hold off on the edits." Jackson picked up his phone and walked to the back of the bus to make the call.

"Don't say it," Madison warned.

"What? Don't say that Jackson needs a wake-up call? Or that the Accelerate Project gives me the heeby jeebies? Or maybe that Hayman has hijacked our campaign?" Rich flipped to a clean paper on his legal pad.

"I agree, but you know how the game works. Jackson just needs a reset. I don't think Accelerate was the best idea right now, but how was he going to turn it down without turning down Philipsen's endorsement? It was a necessary evil. We need to make sure he maintains a separate, yet complimentary agenda because Hayman and the party are in too deep with Philipsen and Ford." Madison checked her phone again and sighed in relief. "The CT scan came back clear. They're going to wake Rhett up within the hour."

Rich squeezed her shoulder. "He'll be fine."

Madison reluctantly smiled. She believed in cautious optimism.

"Accelerate is sending their press release material to you both. Check your inboxes." Jackson sat back down. "What I'd miss?"

"CT scan was clear. They're waking Rhett up soon," Rich explained.

"He'll be fine."

Rich laughed. "Apparently, we need to work on our supportive roommate efforts. We're parroting each other now."

Jackson shrugged. Madison smiled. She knew they were both trying to help.

The door slammed open as all three of their heads swiveled at the sound. "Madison, we need to talk!" Hayman's voice pierced the morning.

"Great, just what I need this morning." Madison spoke under her breath.

Rich chuckled while he nudged her shoulder with his. Madison knew without a doubt that these two had her back, always.

Jackson jumped to his feet. "Hayman, Madison is dealing with a personal issue this morning. Can whatever this is wait?"

Madison inwardly groaned. She worked hard to keep her personal life locked up and away from her work life. Men could interchange the two at any moment, but it was seen as weakness when women did it. It was one thing for Jackson and Rich to know her personal business, but an entirely different animal when Hayman sunk his teeth into her.

"I don't care if her hair is on fire or she broke a nail. When you are asked to serve on a presidential campaign, that is your first, last, and only priority.

Ms. Lyn, do you agree?" Hayman's sneer gave her shivers every time. He was so condescending.

"Absolutely, Hayman," she refused to let him rattle her, "what's the problem?"

"Your boyfriend is the problem, Madison."

Madison was rattled. "I'm sorry, what?"

"You heard me. Rhett Paulson, whom we invited as Jackson's personal guest to Adam Ford's home, attempted, during his number one time slot, to discredit Johan Philipsen. Philipsen, Ford, and Theopolis, are untouchables, and he touched!" Hayman nearly spat at Madison.

Rich chimed in, as only Rich could, "I thought the interview was brilliant. Rhett asked all the right questions. It may have ruffled feathers, but Philipsen came across as the pinnacle of philanthropy and humanitarian efforts. If anything, Rhett gave the guy some leverage. I guarantee you the Philipsen Foundation and the SurfIn Collaboration have been sitting at the number one search spot since Rhett's show aired."

Hayman snarled, but listened with increased curiosity. "Can we get those numbers? We need to spin this to them as positive."

"I doubt they need our help. Philipsen's PR team could teach a master class, but yes, I can pull something together." Rich typed furiously on the keyboard.

"For the time being, Madison, you need to distance yourself from Paulson until after the election. At least in public. His opinions could sway voters either way and we don't want Jackson tied to him or his guests. We can't have anything tainting this election."

"Hayman," Jackson interjected.

"No, Jackson, he's right. Publicly, at least, it's best." Madison steeled herself. As much as she hated to admit it, Hayman was right. He was misogynistic and patronizing, but he knew what he was talking about. They had learned more from Hayman during Jackson's congressional and senate runs than they learned from their years of under and post grad combined. She hated him, but they needed Hayman, and they all knew it. He knew what the textbooks and lectures could never teach. He was the chess master, and he was teaching them how to play the game.

Hayman smiled approvingly at Madison. "See, Jackson. Madison gets it. All right, now that we have that settled, let's move on to the schedule next week."

Hayman sat on their couch, crossed his legs, and held court. He rambled off dates and names. Madison grabbed a pen and started writing. Jackson gave her an apologetic shrug before sitting across from Hayman to listen and learn.

"Madison, block off next Friday completely. President Blythe has invited Jackson and I to the White House. She wants Jackson to sit in on her Unified Strategies Group meeting. It will be only the two of us, so the two of you will remain at campaign headquarters to plan for convention."

"Why are we planning for convention already? Don't we need to prep for the final debate in three weeks?" Madison was writing and speaking, trying to keep up with Hayman's changes to the schedule.

The man actually laughed out loud. The sound was so odd that Jackson and Madison looked at him in shock. "No need to worry about the debates. That has all been taken care of. The nomination is ours. Now, back to Blythe. She will offer her endorsement this week. Rich, we need to craft a response that thanks and praises the stepping stones, I mean the other candidates." Hayman chuckled again.

Rich strode to the front of the bus, effectively diverting their attention away from Hayman's oddly cheerful behavior. "Did you see the news?" He picked up the remote and raised the volume. "Finley and Gates have both officially just pulled out of the remaining primaries."

"Told you," Hayman laughed maniacally.

Chapter Twenty-Six

Rhett woke to splitting pain rippling through his neck, shoulders, and head. Bright overhead lights burned his eyelids. Turning his neck to block the whiteness wasn't an option. He learned that the hard way. Wincing in pain, he heard voices and bodies shuffling. Someone must have turned off the lights. Rhett slowly peeled open his eyelids and waited for the blur to subside. Silence filled the room as two faces slowly appeared.

"I hope I don't look as bad as you two," Rhett's voice sounded gravelly. His throat raw and jagged with pain.

Low chuckles followed relieved sighs. Jake spoke first. "Well, his bad jokes are still intact. That's got to be a good sign."

"What happened this time? I didn't get shot again, did I?" Rhett attempted a laugh, but it got caught in his throat. "Can I have some water or bourbon?"

Jake pulled a flask from his bag and handed it to Rhett.

"Jake, that will not help his head."

"It's certainly not going to make it worse. He's been hooked up to IVs all day." Jake shrugged his shoulder in a resigned defense.

"Well, if Jake has a flask in a hospital, and you're here, this must be serious. I'm a dead? I thought death would feel better."

"You're not dead. This time." Nick walked over to Rhett's hospital bed and handed him a pink plastic cup with ice chips. "Here, start slow, then finish with whatever Jake has in that thing after we talk."

"That sounds ominous." Rhett used all of his strength to unsuccessfully sit up, mumbling obscenities the whole time. "Why are hospital beds the most inhospitable place to be when you're in an actual hospital?"

"Here, let me help." Nick reached over and leveraged a pillow behind Rhett's head while holding the up-arrow button on the bed.

Jake held onto the flask and sat in the chair next to Rhett's bed. By the look of it, it was obviously the same place he'd slept at some point.

"How long have I been out? This isn't one of those stories where the guy wakes up from a five-year coma, is it? No, you two don't look old. Close, but not bad enough." Rhett's attempt at humor fell short again.

"Twenty-four hours. You've been in and out the whole time." Nick sat across from Jake.

"The good news is that your head didn't actually hit the floor. The bad news is that your arm and your ribs broke your head's fall." Jake rolled his neck as he spoke. He looked un-Jake-like.

Rhett peeked down at his arm for the first time and saw the cast. "That explains the concrete block on my bed." Luckily, or maybe unluckily, it was the opposite arm where he had been shot.

"Whoever attacked you knew how to drop a man quick and easy. The doctor said you were lucky. The police said you were lucky. The neurosurgeon on call said you were lucky, but man, this doesn't seem lucky to me." Jake picked up his phone. "I need to text Alexis. She's been worried sick."

"I'm surprised she's not here yelling at me for getting attacked." Rhett deadpanned, but stopped short when he saw the look on Jake's face.

"An intruder also broke into Jake's house around the same time as Jake found you. Alexis is fine," Nick quickly added.

Whatever color was left drained from Rhett's face. Not Alexis. "Is she okay? You need to go home. I'm fine. Go."

"It turns out Alexis really is tougher than you. The alarm for our outside gate went off when she got up for work. She went straight to the gun case, then to the window and yelled that she had an AR-15 and enough ammunition to take out a small army. She watched the camera as the guy busted through the fence and ran." Jake shook his head and laughed softly.

"And you left her home alone?" Rhett's shocked face was louder than his shocked voice.

Jake rolled his eyes in annoyed disbelief. "No, idiot. My brother drove up and took her back home. She's staying with her parents until we figure out what the hell is happening." Jake held up the phone for Rhett to see, "She is mad at you, though, here."

Alexis: YOU BETTER NOT DIE RHETT PAULSON BECAUSE I'M GOING TO KILL YOU!

"Yeah, she's fine." Rhett grumbled as he tried to piece things together. "Does Madison know? I don't want her to worry."

"Jake has been keeping Madison updated. She's having quite a busy day on the campaign trail, but she manages to text every hour to check on you. I think this one's a keeper, Rhett."

Nick and Jake filled Rhett in on what had happened since the attack. The police still had no leads. Alexis was safe in West Virginia. Madison pulled an all-nighter since Jackson's campaign was the last one standing. Jerry had cooled off after speaking with Philipsen's team. Rahemia was still mad at Rhett for keeping this from her. Oliver and Keira were following research leads Jake fed them. Jake told Nick everything.

Rhett listened and tried to take it all in as the two tag-teamed information. His arm throbbed, but he refused to take any more pain medication. He needed a clear mind to process everything.

The journalist in Rhett was on fire. His mind connected and cross-checked, questioned, and pinpointed. Each question led them down new rabbit holes. The back and forth between the three minds invigorated Rhett. Hooked on his own story, he needed to find sources and informants. Maddeningly enough, the attacker took his phone. Not that his source ever responded when Rhett texted, but now he was really at the mercy of an elusive shadow. Just as Rhett was about to express this very concern, a voice coming from the hallway froze him in his tracks.

Rhett growled at Jake, "You didn't."

Jake laughed, "Of course I did."

"No. I know my best friend wouldn't do that to me because he knows I would cause him bodily harm."

Still laughing, Jake replied, "She's way more terrifying than you."

Rhett looked at Nick for backup until he realized Nick was laughing, too. The voice got closer and louder.

"Susie, honey, I got your favorite coffee. Tell Mary Beth I got her one too, when she's back from her break. You were right about the potato soup. It was delicious. Okay, honey, I'll see you in Rhett's room. Jake texted me that he's awake, but I still expect vitals on the hour."

Rhett sunk down into his bed, groaning in pain, as the door to his room swung open.

"How's my baby?" Peggy Paulson flipped on the overhead lights and entered the room with a bang. "Susie's on her way down to take your vitals, honey." She walked right up to Rhett's bed and plopped a kiss on his forehead. She tried her best whisper voice, but failed. "I know all nurses are overworked and underpaid, but you're not just a regular patient. They should check on you more frequently than they have. That's all I'm saying."

When the woman finally took a breath, Rhett squeezed in a, "Hi Grammy."

"Hey Sweetheart. How are you feeling?" She touched Rhett's forehead and determined he still wasn't fevered.

"Grammy, I'm fine, really. You didn't have to come. Jake shouldn't have worried you." Rhett squeezed her hand. She looked older. Rhett had been begging her to retire, but she didn't want to sit around her house and be bored all day, as she said.

Grammy turned to touch Jake's cheek. "Of course he did. He knows I would have skinned him alive if he didn't. In fact, Jake had his sweet brother Judah give me a lift. That way, I can stay with you while you recuperate. You wouldn't let me come after the shooting. Fool me once, shame on you. Fool me twice, shame on me. Something's going on, and I'm staying until you tell me all about it and you're out of danger."

Rhett ground out, "Isn't Jake so thoughtful?"

Grammy gently poked Rhett's leg. "Oh, stop. Having your grandmother's home cooking isn't torture. You'll survive a visit with me."

"I'm excited about your home cooking, Grammy." Jake smiled like a kid at Christmas.

Grammy laughed as she straightened up the room. Rhett mouthed, "Kiss up," to Jake, who kept laughing.

"I'm hoping I get to meet this Madison who has been texting Jake about you. According to these two, she's a real keeper."

"She's out of town for work," Rhett grumbled.

"Then I guess I'll have to extend my stay." Grammy winked at Rhett.

Jake held a bag towards Rhett. "Grammy brought pepperoni rolls."

"I'll make some cookies as soon as they release you. Speaking of which, they should be in here already." Grammy walked to the door, and peaked into the hallway and called, "Susie. Oh, sorry honey, there you are. That is so darling. Is that for Rhett? Here, I'll take it."

Grammy popped her head back into the room. She carried a stuffed elephant holding a box of chocolates. Grammy read the card as she walked. "Susie's coming. Look what someone brought for you. What a darling gift. Who is Austin Roe?"

Rhett winced in pain as he sat ramrod straight. Jake lunged for the elephant and tore open the chocolate box. Grammy watched as Jake and Rhett rifled through the items recently ripped from her hands.

"And why did he hide a flip phone in a chocolate box? More importantly, where is the chocolate?" Grammy was confused by the gift and frustrated by the lack of candy.

Chapter Twenty-Seven

Rhett had owned his penthouse for the past two years. His real estate agent and decorator worked tirelessly in tandem to find the perfect spot they said he needed. Rhett signed the lease one day after the ink was dry on his latest WBN contract. As far as the industry was concerned, he was on top. He took over his mentor's slot and boasted the highest ratings for not only WBN, but for all other cable news shows combined. This penthouse was the cherry on top. Everyone who mattered knew where Rhett lived. The real estate agent called it his exclamation point.

It was roomy, decadent, and had the amenities of a five-star resort. His decorator even arranged for a magazine photo shoot to highlight her work and his fame. Floor to ceiling windows allowed Rhett to look over his kingdom. This was the perfect showcase. Except he never showcased it. He never really felt at home. The penthouse was more like a vacation rental. A place to stay, but he didn't live life in it.

Grammy picked up on that as soon as she arrived at Casa Paulson. Rhett sent her a copy of the design magazine spread before they released it, but she had never stepped foot inside until last week. Another point of contention she had with Rhett. Grammy laid on the guilt thick this week. She perfected it like an art form. Rhett's flyby holidays would not cut it anymore. He vowed to himself to make Grammy a priority. She also apparently made her own vow to make his penthouse a home. Each day of his recovery, Rhett awakened to a new blanket, throw pillow, or picture frame. He could only imagine how many bags she packed to come. Grammy even brought his home run ball from the state championship. The additions would appall his decorator. Rhett loved it.

Another upgrade was a freezer filled with Grammy's food. That was Rhett's favorite part. He could dine at five-star restaurants every night if he wanted to, but nothing tasted as rich as Grammy's chili and beer biscuits. Rhett gained at least five pounds since Grammy brought him home from the hospital. He wouldn't be surprised if Jake's freezer had also been filled to capacity.

Grammy was leaving tomorrow. It surprised Rhett how much he wanted her to stay, but he was a grown man and needed his regularly scheduled life. Gym, work, show, dinner, bed, repeat. He took off last week so that the bruises on his face could heal, but it felt good this week to be back on set. The loyal fans of *Rhett's Take* were distraught by his attack. Rhett usually avoided sharing his personal life on air, but he couldn't avoid it this time. Every news outlet exaggerated a story about him almost being killed by domestic terrorists. So, sporting his cast, Rhett went live on Monday with a heartfelt thank you to his fans and a quick update on his recovery. He was exhausted, but grateful to be back at work.

Video dates with Madison were the highlights of his week. She offered to fly back to see him in the hospital, but he insisted he was fine. No self-respecting man wanted his girlfriend to see him in a hospital gown. Rhett was disappointed he couldn't meet Madison's parents, but not as disappointed as they were about it. Daniel and Vivian Lyn insisted on continuing east with the campaign trail and followed Madison back to D.C. Hence, the smell of Grammy's spaghetti sauce wafting through his apartment. Grammy also insisted on meeting Madison before she left. Grammy said it was Divine intervention. Rhett laughed at that one.

Madison called earlier in the day to make sure it was still okay for them to come. She sounded more nervous than he did. Madison wanted a buffer, so Jake and Rich were both invited, too. Rhett gave Jake strict instructions to talk up their baseball careers, but not to embarrass him. Grammy laughed at that one.

Rhett finished setting the table. Jake tossed Grammy's salad. Grammy pulled the baked ziti from the oven, then put in the garlic bread to broil. She sang hymns. Jake hummed along. Rhett shook his head, annoyed by both of them.

"Jake, sweetie, what time are we leaving tomorrow?" Grammy patted Jake on the back.

"If you don't mind, I'd like to get on the road by eight. Without stops and a little speeding, I can make it home in time for Sunday dinner at the Marchio farm."

"I'll be ready by seven if you take me with you to dinner!" Grammy had a standing invitation at Mary Marchio's table and they all knew it. Mary was Grammy's best friend and neighbor. In fact, Grammy is the only person outside of the Marchio family who knew Mary's tomato sauce recipe. She would take it to her grave. "Mary had the prayer team on the phone as soon as Jake called me," Grammy's voice trembled.

Rhett walked around the island and wrapped his arms around his grandmother. "Hey, I'm okay. You're still stuck with me. No tears, remember? We're Paulsons. We're salt of the earth."

She swatted his back as she hugged him tightly. "Rhett Christian Paulson, don't you dare use my own words against me."

Rhett smiled and squeezed her closer. "I learned from the best."

Just as the oven beeped, the doorbell rang. Rhett sucked in a deep breath as Grammy quickly wiped her eyes. She reached up and touched his cheek with a wink. "All right boys, best behavior. Let's show them some mountaineer hospitality."

"Don't mess up, Rhett." Jake laughed. Rhett glared. Grammy smiled at them both.

Rhett headed toward the entryway. He shivered when he crossed the spot where Jake found his body, but he quickly recovered and put on his parents-love-me-smile. Grammy was on his tail. That lady was fast.

Grammy's arms opened faster than the door. "You must be Madison."

Madison's head popped up on Grammy's shoulder. Her expression was one of shock and awe. "Based on Rhett's description of your hugs, you must be Grammy." Rhett fell in love on the spot, as if he wasn't already.

Rhett scooted around the ladies with his hand extended to Madison's father. "Dr. Lyn, I'm so glad to finally meet you."

Dr. Vivian Lyn intercepted Rhett and gave him a quick once over with her eyes. Rhett felt like a pig at the county fair, hoping for a blue ribbon. She wrapped her arm around his and squeezed him tightly against her side. "Yes, it is very nice to meet you, Rhett." He could have sworn he heard her whisper to herself, "Yes, you will do just fine indeed."

Grammy, Jake, Rich, and Dr. Daniel Lyn, if Rhett wasn't mistaken, all laughed as he turned his head back for help.

Dinner was a roaring success. Grammy and Jake balanced boasting and roasting. Even the embarrassing stories from Rhett's childhood managed to highlight some noble character trait. After listening to Jake, Rhett was waiting for their invitations to the baseball hall of fame. It didn't take long for Vivian Lyn to catch on to the theme. She was hyping Madison like an auctioneer, raffling off rare antiques. Madison was mortified, but her father beamed with pride.

According to Madison, Rich and Jackson already gave Daniel Lyn their seal of approval in Indiana and reassured him today that Rhett was a good guy. That didn't mean Daniel gave Rhett a pass. Madison's dad would have made Perry Mason nervous on the stand. The conversation began with Daniel asking Rhett to consent to a background check. He was pretty sure the man was joking. Rhett barely stopped sweating bullets halfway through their meal, convinced Dr. Lyn secretly worked as an interrogator for the CIA.

Rhett finally breathed a sigh of relief after he showed Dr. Lyn his collection of autographed baseball memorabilia. Daniel decided then and there that Rhett couldn't be that bad. That's when Rhett received permission to call Dr. Lyn, Daniel. At least for now. Madison's relief was as evident as Rhett's.

After supper, they all moved over to the couches and settled in for Grammy's famous basil-ginger iced tea and snickerdoodles. Madison sat near Rhett, but left enough room to discourage any touching. She'd reminded him repeatedly today to keep his hands to himself. Rich plopped down right in between them. Rhett groaned while Madison attempted to hide her chuckle. Daniel cackled with humorous approval.

Talk turned to the campaign trail and their busy schedule. Jackson missed dinner tonight for another private strategy session with President Blythe, Hayman, and Adam Ford. Jackson had been to the White House three times this week. Rich and Madison stayed busy correlating campaign messaging with the Accelerate Project. Rich complained about the uptick in talking points they received each day. The more Rich endeavored to spice up the verbiage, the more

Hayman redirected the communication team to stick to the script. It left Rich annoyed, and Madison frustrated.

"Well, you two must be so proud of Madison. What an honor to work on a presidential campaign." Grammy broke her own rule to never talk politics. "Were political issues a topic discussed around your table?"

Madison squirmed in her seat, and Rich cleared his throat. The investigator in Rhett paid attention.

"Oh, we frequently discussed it in our home. My parents barely escaped China during the Cultural Revolution. They made sure their grandchildren knew how blessed they were and how easily freedom can be taken away if not respected and protected."

"Oh my. What a rich heritage you have to share. You would love my dear friend Mary Marchio. Her family immigrated from Italy in the early nineteen hundreds. She always says the best way to honor her heritage is to protect the country her parents risked everything to come to." Grammy saw everything through the silver lining. Rhett loved that about her, even if it drove him crazy sometimes.

"I think I would like her very much. My children were raised to value freedom. To my chagrin, my daughter chose to support the party with pro-big-government roots while attending an American university. Although, I shouldn't have been surprised. The very government my parents fled has bankrolled the higher education system in this country. An entire generation lost to the lies of fascism. The irony is that they truly believe they are the ones fighting fascism, when, in actuality, they are merely the pawns. The serpent snuck in under the dark of night and released a slow poison into the veins of America."

"Daddy, please. Not tonight." Madison looked at her mother for help.

"Don't worry, Little Button, I won't wear out my welcome." Daniel smiled warmly at his daughter. "Madison and Rich have heard my musings for years. I am passionate about teaching history and not repeating it. With that said, I trust my daughter and her friends. I believe Jackson and his team have their hearts in the right place. I can get behind that."

"Well said," Grammy, always the peacemaker.

Rich piped in, "Daniel and my dad are very entertaining when they get together. We obviously don't invite them to campaign headquarters."

Laughter broke any leftover tension. Rhett had come to appreciate Rich's gift for assessing a situation and putting everyone at ease.

Grammy looked at Rhett, revelation on her face, "You should interview Daniel for the project you're doing with Nick. His family's story sounds exactly like what Nick is trying to show in the docuseries."

All eyes turned to Rhett. He nervously twisted in his seat. Not wanting to rock the boat with his girlfriend or her father, "Grammy, they may not want their story shared on national television."

Grammy ignored Rhett, "Nonsense. Nick Branson, that's Rhett's mentor, asked Rhett to help with a docuseries about the American dream and how it relates to the secession talks. It's really timely."

"That sounds very intriguing indeed. I would love to take part in a project like that. These younger people need to understand the lies they are being fed. You know, I used to teach a course called The Marxism Classroom: How Communists Manipulate Youth to do their Bidding."

Rhett butted in, "Used to?"

Daniel's lip raised at the corner. If Rhett wasn't mistaken, the man was warming up to him. "Ah, very astute listener. You picked out the key word. Yes, the dean canceled the course. He claimed it was because of attendance issues, but his secretary secretly assured me that my class was the only upper level course with a waiting list. That it how I began piecing together the sinister agenda we are facing with our education system. Over the past twenty years, I have taught the truth, but it is getting harder and harder. Students began reporting me for 'triggering' them and for fostering an 'unsafe' learning environment. Apparently, teaching historical facts is considered bullying now. I am ready for retirement, so I will continue teaching the truth until they force me not to because my parents almost died for this freedom. I don't take it lightly."

Rhett, in reporter mode, tuned out the rest of the room. "That is fascinating. We did a show in the spring about the rise of student demonstrations. My guests were two university students who founded a non-profit that helps campuses mobilize and protest hate speech. They were very impressive."

Daniel sadly laughed. "Are you referring to Students Fighting Misinformation or Campuses Against Fascism? Not that it matters. I'm sure you did your research on these so-called 'student' groups?" Daniel stared at Rhett, assessing him, no doubt.

"My producer ran the background and research for that one." Rhett offered. For the first time, he felt some shame for that answer. He was at the top. Surely they could understand he was too busy to do the legwork for every story. That was for interns. He started the same way under Nick.

"Well, had you done your research, you would have found out that these student groups are all funded by Horatio Theopolis and his Equity Foundation. The organizers aren't students at all, rather members of Fascism Fighters. They use SurfIn to mobilize protestors. I believe their websites list the names of speakers their national group will help students protest."

"Well, something smells fishy there." Apparently, that didn't sit right with Grammy.

"That's only the half of it. Campuses can host any speaker who supports Equity Foundation causes, while blacklisted speakers are met with violence, bomb threats, physical attacks, and projectiles. We once had a young lady held hostage for six hours before a private security team hired by her husband extricated her. The university actually apologized to the mob and blamed the woman. They don't hide their tactics. They brag about it on social media."

Grammy was confused. "That can't be right. I never heard a word about that. Rhett, did you know about it?"

"I did." Jake piped in while eating a cookie. "Patriot News covered it."

Rhett actually snarled at Jake, who was smirking.

"How awful for her. I don't care what she was talking about. She shouldn't be terrorized for it." Grammy was outraged for this woman and she didn't even know her name.

"It's textbook, really. You see, throughout history, weaker regimes target the youth. They fill their minds with a moral outcry of injustice. There has to be a victim to protect and a villain to fight. Youth today are intrinsically very empathetic. With technology, they are exposed to global injustices at a young age and more frequently than any generation in history. Their compassion and strong desire to make the world a better place is very noble and inspiring. The injustice is not the speakers themselves nor the protests. The real injustice is when institutions of higher learning fail to train individuals in how to think and civilly debate. We should teach our youth how to see the world from different angles so they can hear, process, and make informed decisions. Instead, we have raised a generation of humans to be weak minded and one sided. My daughter and I don't agree on politics, but I respect her ability to listen and formulate a counter argument. The same goes with Rich and Jackson."

Daniel's history lecture obviously caused Madison stress based on how she squeezed the throw pillow beside her. "Daddy, while I appreciate the compliment, can we please move on to lighter subjects?"

The room was electric with silence. Daniel Lyn must be phenomenal in a classroom. Rhett understood why the man's course had a waitlist.

"Forget Nick's project. I want you on my show. I had no idea multi-billion-dollar foundations backed the protest groups. They made it sound like a grassroots movement for students." Rhett rubbed his chin and sat back in his seat. His mind rolling.

"Most people find it interesting to hear that university donors are usually on the beneficial end when speakers are banned. I have found that when one follows the money, they usually find a fat cat funding the rat."

"Okay, let's not get him started on student loan debt, or we'll be here all day." Madison's voice cracked a bit. Rhett liked seeing this jittery side of her. It made her seem human.

"Now that's a topic for your friend Nick. Higher education is a money-laundering machine. Professions that once were apprentice or training professions now require degrees and tests you can only pass by getting degrees. Universities increase tuition each year, all while sitting on billion dollar trusts. They don't even need the tuition money!"

"All right, Daddy. I think that might be our cue to leave. You've given Rhett enough show ideas for one night." Madison rose to start the goodbye process.

"On the contrary. I want your dad to work with my crew scouting leads." Rhett laughed. "I feel like I've been missing the boat on these things."

"There is a reason you don't know things are happening. Those in charge don't want you to. An enemy seeks to devour in silence, while the truth triumphs in song."

"I agree with Madison, Dear," Vivian patted her husband's knee. "When he waxes on poetically, we're all in trouble."

As everyone made their way into the kitchen to deposit glasses and mugs, Daniel's final words left their mark on Rhett. Hugs and handshakes made the rounds. Daniel added a shoulder pat which Rhett took as a good sign, especially when he noticed Rich's surprised, yet impressed, nod.

Madison whispered in his ear during their brief hug, "That went better than I expected."

He replied, "I expected nothing less," before sneaking a quick kiss on her cheek.

After everyone left, Rhett joined Grammy at the sink. She washed. He attempted to dry one-handed. Their old routine comforted him more than he realized. He was going to miss her. A sadness he hadn't felt for a long time crept in like a vise around his heart.

"I'm glad you came. I know I haven't been the easiest patient."

"Where else would I be? We're a team, you and me. We tackle things together. You know that." Grammy winked at him.

Rhett leaned over and kissed her temple. "I know, but I wanted you to know that I appreciate it."

"I know, baby." Grammy smiled then looked at him, "Are you sure you're okay drying? I can handle this if you need to rest."

"No, I'm fine. I've rested enough. I need to learn to live with this cast."

She studied him before casting a line with bait. "The Lyns seem like a wonderful family. I love that Madison. She's special."

Rhett knowingly grinned back at her. "I agree on both counts."

"But that's not what's bothering you." It technically wasn't a question, but Rhett knew better. Grammy kept scrubbing bubbles on dinnerware.

"Nothing is bothering me, per se. It's just something stuck in my craw, as Gramps would say."

Grammy chuckled at the memory, but remained silent. She had mastered the art of letting silence loosen Rhett's tongue. He knew he didn't stand a chance. She waited him out for two hours junior year when Rachael Cox turned him down for prom. Rhett shook his head.

Grammy hummed and waited and waited.

Rhett inwardly groaned. "Daniel made a comment about those in charge not wanting us to know things, or something like that."

"Mm-hmm."

"Well, that seems to be a theme I keep getting hit with lately. Nick won't drop it, but won't give me specifics. He keeps changing the subject. This source I have harps on it. Worse, the guy sends me evidence that has been hidden in plain sight, so to speak. Then, Daniel Lyn's information drop tonight followed by his parting words."

"Mm-hmm."

Rhett looked at Grammy with his "come on, not you too" look. She innocently shrugged in return.

"Nick told me he retired because he realized he wasn't asking the right questions anymore. I didn't think anything of it then, but the deeper I'm getting with this source and Nick's docuseries, the more irksome this feeling I have is becoming."

"What feeling?"

"I don't know." Rhett paused and attempted to compile his thoughts. "I'm the top journalist in my time slot. I worked my way up from the bottom doing research for the network. I made my name doing hard hitting investigations. I helped solve cold cases, for God's sake."

"Rhett Paulson, don't you dare use the Lord's name in vain, or I will knock you upside the head!" Grammy's warning scared him as much as it did when he was five.

"Now she talks."

Grammy flashed her don't-sass-me-look. Rhett laughed.

"I'm sorry, Gram."

"Continue."

Rhett took a deep breath. "My point is, I pride myself on presenting the facts to the people. I want people to know the truth so they can make informed decisions. I don't want people fooled. I want them educated. Now, I keep getting this sickening feeling that I've been playing for the wrong team, but didn't know it. Does that make sense?"

Grammy emptied the sink and rinsed the suds down the drain. She slowly dried her hands and turned to lean back on the counter.

"I know that look. I'm in for a doozie." Rhett leaned beside her.

"Did you ever stop to think about *why* you worked so hard to expose the truth?"

He shook his head.

"Well, I did. In fact, I've been praying for you since you started writing for the high school newspaper. When your Mama died, you became hell bent on punishing everyone you blamed for her death. You wanted to expose her old teachers and principals and Sunday school teachers and our neighbors and everyone under the sun who should have helped her but didn't. Your first year on air, fifty percent of your investigations were based on the opioid crisis. You have been working off of some hit list for years. At some point, you're going to reach the end and realize it didn't help. You will still miss her, and the anger will continue to fester. That mission became your life."

Rhett listened to Grammy's words of wisdom. They hit closer than he wanted, but the anger outweighed them. "Gram, she was getting better. She stopped and they wouldn't let her forget. They treated her like a leper. She needed help, and they turned their backs on her. Your church made her feel unwelcomed. Honestly, I don't know how you can keep going back to any church."

"Rhett, sweetie, you can't blame a bunch of flawed humans for not knowing how to act. Churches are filled with sinners. That's why we're all there in the first place. I won't lie and tell you that some are harder to forgive than others, but at some point, you have to forgive. Jesus forgave me, so I have to offer forgiveness to others. Some days, it's uttered between gritted teeth, but I still offer it. I can tell you this, forgiveness feels a lot sweeter than revenge and anger. Your mom made her peace with Jesus, and that is the only thing that matters to me because

I know I'll have eternity in heaven with her." Grammy wiped her tears that came harder than she wanted.

"Come here, Grammy," Rhett pulled her into his arms into a tight hug.

"I'm just saying, Rhett, you've made punishing people your religion. Not everything is black and white. Choosing one side's 'truth' over the other side's isn't any better than what those church ninnies did to us. There is only one source of truth, and it's found in the Bible. So yes, until you're living for Jesus, you are one hundred percent on the wrong team."

Rhett held his grandmother, the woman who raised him while his own mother lived in her cyclical world of benders and rehab. The woman who held him when the nightmares enveloped him. The woman who got him through high school and college. The strongest, most patient, most faith-filled woman he knew.

Grammy didn't say anything else. There was nothing left for her to say.

Chapter Twenty-Eight

"**G**ood morning! I was just about to call you."

"I beat you to it." Madison's laughter lifted Rhett's spirits instantly.

"Grammy made a pecan pie for you last night since you mentioned you love them but can't find a good pie place. I think she likes you."

"Oh my goodness! She didn't have to do that. That was so sweet of her. She must have been up for hours."

"I'm not so sure Grammy sleeps. I've often wondered if she's a robot. Besides, she used the opportunity to lecture me about frequent ER trips. I almost hid the pecans so she'd have to stop and go to bed. I don't even know where she got the pecans. Anyway, she backed off when I reminded her I met you in an ER."

More laughter. Rhett savored the sound. "Well, my dad was pretty smitten with you, too. He didn't bake you a pie, of course, but he mentioned baseball tickets the next time he's in town. Vivian is a different story."

"What? Your mom loved me!"

"That's my point. She already has our grandchildren named. It doubled rich over in laughter, telling Jackson about her behavior. For a hot minute, I thought for sure she was going to measure you for a tux or offer to take you ring shopping. I was mortified." Rhett pictured Madison with her head lowered in her hands.

"I thought your mother was lovely."

Madison moaned, "Lovely is not a word I've ever heard used for Vivian Lyn, but thank you."

"Seriously, I think it was a great evening. No one got hurt or offended. We made good impressions on each other's people. And, shockingly enough, Jake and Rich both behaved and didn't embarrass us."

"Is it weird that we've already met each other's people? Are we moving too fast?"

"Nope. I've been wading in the dating pool, and it's not pretty. Might as well jump in the deep end with all of our crazy to make sure it's worth it. Why? Do you think we're moving too fast?" Rhett attempted to push the worried knot back into his stomach.

Her pause didn't help matters. "Considering I've only dipped my toes in the baby pool and have never made it beyond date three, I'm relying on your experience."

Relief. "Well, I'm honored to make it to the next level. Instead of worrying about whether we should have done it, how about we focus on how much fun everyone had?"

"That's very true. It was a great night," Madison sighed. Rhett could feel her relief over the phone. "What are you up to today?"

"Right now, I'm sitting in my office waiting on Rahemia. We have a strategy session for a project we're investigating. I haven't had time to work on it between my recovery and Grammy baking late night pies for my girlfriend." He earned the giggle he wanted.

"Did Grammy get off okay this morning?" Peggy insisted Madison call her Grammy. Hearing her say it now warmed his heart.

"Yeppers. Jake picked her up at the crack of dawn. He has been antsy to get back to Alexis. I underestimated how quiet and lonely my place would feel this morning." Rhett surprised himself with his honesty.

"You never cease to amaze me, Rhett Paulson."

"Why? Because I'm a sap and miss my Grammy?" Rhett let out an embarrassed chortle.

"Something like that. Your news jock slash baseball star slash Grammy's boy is a unique combination. I find it very attractive." Rhett felt her blush all the way across town.

"Why, Miss Lyn, if I didn't know better, I'd think you just complimented me." He began chanting, "I think you like me."

"Well, now you've gone and ruined the moment."

"I'm sorry." Rhett tried to contain his laugher. "No, I'm not, but I'll stop while I'm ahead."

"You are impossible."

"Good thing you think I'm attractive."

"Ugh," Madison groaned. "On that note, I need to run before your ego breaks a window. My mother keeps calling for me to eat breakfast. The last time, she used my full name."

"Wait, before you go, what's your schedule this week? Last night was great, but I'd like to see you without family assessing our every move. Dare I ask a date without your roommates?"

Madison sighed, "I don't foresee that in our future, sadly. I'm taking my parents to the airport this evening. I need to catch up on my laundry now. The bus pulls out tonight for our next round of events."

"Any chance you'll be in Kansas for the Secession Convention next week?"

"Not a chance. Hayman doesn't want us anywhere near it. In fact, we're literally driving in the opposite direction. We're headed down the coast, hitting every state until we reach Florida. We stay there a few days for photo ops and to secure some endorsements. Are you going? I'm surprised WBN is covering it, since it's a political stunt. Hayman said the media was planning a blackout as far as it was concerned. Not give them the attention."

Rhett felt the hair on the back of his neck rise. "How would Hayman know that? Regardless of whether it is a political stunt, it bears being covered."

He could tell Madison became distracted with voices in the background. "I'm not sure. I think they heard it at the president's strategy meeting. I really need to run, or else Vivian is going to come in here and take my phone. Then you'll really be sorry."

Rhett didn't want their call to end on a bad note, so he dropped it, but now his tingles were definitely on alert. "I would love to talk to your mom, but I don't want you to get grounded, so I'll let you go. Call me when you're on the road tonight."

"I will. Good luck with your investigation, and try to stay out of ERs this week."

"Miss Lyn with the jokes. I will give it my best shot."

"I'm coming, Mother! She's here. I'm hanging up now for your benefit. Goodbye, Rhett."

"Goodbye, Madison."

Rhett lengthened his stretch on the leather couch. He tossed the baseball above him, then caught it. Tossed, then caught. The familiar rhythm did little to calm him. Rhett could feel a momentum shift, but didn't know where it was coming from or where it would lead. He felt a stirring inside him. The weight of the information sitting on his chest. Rhett had a box of puzzle pieces without a picture to go off of, so he was piecing it together blind.

Austin Roe had been silent since sending his gift in the hospital. A "Get Well" text was the only communication for two weeks. Nick rescheduled their next interview. Jake, Alexis, and Grammy were four hours away. Oliver and Keira conducted background research based on the information from the jump drive, but Rhett hadn't seen it yet. Rahemia drafted a proposal for Jerry about story leads that potentially could result in a weeklong special. Everyone had been working under the shroud of secrecy. The story lacked a singular bad guy to hone in on and catch. It was more like a group of bad guys working in tandem. They had no idea who they were dealing with and to what lengths those people would go to silence the opposition. And he still had no clue who was trying to kill him. Catch. Toss. Catch. Toss. Catch. The rhythm became the only thing Rhett could depend on.

A knock on the door caught Rhett's attention. "Well, don't you look like the picture of ease and relaxation?" Rahemia walked over and placed a coffee in front of him on the table.

Rhett gingerly sat up, the pain still lingering. "I wouldn't use either word to characterize my feelings right now. How about you? Do you feel relaxed?"

"Not in the least bit, and it is only going to get worse." Rahemia dropped her bag and sat across from him.

"That sounds ominous. Do you have information for me? Have the research rats found anything good?" Rhett removed the lid from his cup to release the steam. The smell hit him in all the right places.

"They didn't find anything."

"What? How is that possible? Jake and I found plenty of leads with just a quick internet search. We may need to teach an investigation 101 class." Rhett chuckled at himself.

Rahemia took a deep breath. "Rhett, they haven't found anything because Jerry killed the story."

Rhett looked up. Surely he hadn't heard her right. "I'm sorry. Did you say Jerry killed the story of a lifetime? An exclusive story that would blow up the ratings? A story that could expose corruption at the highest levels? A story that was plopped into our laps? A story I almost died for, twice?"

Rahemia nodded. "I'm sorry, Rhett. I know you were interested in following this thing out, but even with the laptop, we really couldn't verify any of the leads. It was too risky to cover."

Ice went through Rhett's veins. "That's okay. I remember most of the data sources. We can start our research from scratch." His glare pierced Rahemia.

"Jerry nixed the series, Rhett. We need to move forward. It's out of our control. Let's focus on next week."

Rhett studied his producer closely. He needed to find the words she wouldn't say. Rahemia instantly went from producer to interview subject. Her eyes told him she understood. The tiniest nod gave him the approval he needed.

"Did Jerry say why?"

"The White House's Unified Strategies Commission declared all information pertaining to the food shortages or the secession off limits because of homeland security. They have banned any news agencies, websites, and social media platforms from covering any information and/or data sources other than government sanctioned agencies in order to prevent the spread of dangerous misinformation. It's a matter of national, well, global really, security."

"The White House is censoring the press?"

Rhett could tell Rahemia was straddling the company line. Not knowing which side to trust. A profession she loved or her friend who was following some crazy super spy ring of conspiracy theories.

"No," she spoke slowly. Clearly annoyed. "The President of the United States is protecting the people from dangerous lies to prevent a civil war or mass panic over food shortages during a time of national instability. Can you imagine how terrifying it will be if normal people can't grocery shop because some crazy extremists were stockpiling food?" Her voice told him where her allegiance had finally landed. "Sometimes we protect the people with silence."

"An enemy seeks to devour in silence, while the truth triumphs in song." Rhett's voice was barely over a whisper.

"What?" Rahemia, clearly annoyed, looked at Rhett like he had lost his mind.

"Nothing, just something a wise man told me recently. I would like to speak to Jerry," Rhett flatly responded.

"He figured. He should be upstairs in his office now. I told him we were meeting this morning, and he assumed you would want an appeal." She looked conciliatory. "Rhett, be reasonable. We can't run with a story from a renegade group of citizens while a global food crisis looms and this secession convention nonsense is on the line. Did you ever stop to think that, maybe, they are attempting to use our platform to spread their extremist rhetoric? These people want to start a civil war, Rhett. Maybe they are the ones trying to kill you?"

"Did you stop to think that it's weird the press is taking direction from the government? Aren't we supposed to be doing the exact opposite and making sure they're held accountable? Presenting the information to the public and allowing them to make their own decisions?" He could feel his voice getting tighter.

"Rhett, I'm not going to sit here and argue with you. Jerry is the boss. The board shut down the story. We need to move on." Rahemia rose and lifted her bag onto her shoulders. "I'm sure if you go upstairs, Jerry will be waiting. I have a mountain of emails to return before prep this week. Promise me you'll calm down before you head up to see Jerry. I don't need to be sidelined with you. We have an entire crew to consider. This isn't just about you, Rhett. Other people are depending on you and this show." Rahemia left Rhett holding his ball.

This whole fiasco filled Rhett with disgust on many levels. He grabbed his phone from the table and texted Jerry. Instantly, Jerry's secretary responded, granting Rhett an audience with the king. Rhett attempted to cool his ruffled feathers as he made his way to the elevator. A few deep breaths did nothing to quell his frustration. As the elevator doors opened, Valentina was waiting with her plastic smile.

"Jerry is waiting for you."

Rhett didn't utter a word. He was on a mission. Jerry reclined in his Italian leather chair, staring out the window with a glass of amber liquid in his hand. He looked like a fat cat ruling over his kingdom. "I thought I'd see you today. Rahemia broke the news, I take it? And you are angry I vetoed your story."

"Bingo."

Jerry's obnoxious chuckle felt like ice down Rhett's back. "Rhett, my boy. You see a headline. I see the entire network family. Do you understand?"

"Not really. Can you explain to me why I'm sitting on a nuclear bomb that will expose some of the richest and most powerful men in the world? I thought as the World Broadcasting Network, it was our responsibility to hold these people accountable? Or at the very least, report the news?"

"Rhett, I know you are not naïve to how this all works. Spare me your lecture on ethics and the news. Honestly, you're acting like a child. The revenue stream for your show is funded entirely by Bluesky investors. The very men who fund your salary and lifestyle are the same men you want to drop a 'nuclear bomb on.' Aren't those your words? Who is going to pay for your show if you insult and accuse our advertisers with only a secret cell phone and an intriguing tale of espionage? If you're so passionate about it, write a suspense novel. We will market the hell out of it and give you another revenue stream."

Rhett's skin was on fire. "I'm not doing this for more money."

"No? Tell me, Rhett, do you honestly believe the crazy stories these people are feeding you? Are you willing to risk you job for them? Your life? Or can you trust Uncle Jerry, who plucked you out of obscurity and placed you on the highest pedestal of all network news?"

"What happened to journalistic integrity? At the very least, transparency."

Jerry pointed to the bar on the other side of his enormous glass office. "Rhett, get a drink, have a seat. Surely, we can talk this through and you will see reason." Jerry took a sip as he eyed Rhett closely.

A million thoughts ran through Rhett's mind at once. His childhood. Sunday school. His mother. Grammy. Madison. The campaign. The jump drive. Nick. Jake and Alexis. Their baby. The company. His show. His crew. His platform. The truth. What was the truth? Rhett did what he did best.

Rhett sat across from Jerry. "Okay, what if we make a compromise? Let me go remote for the succession vote. I think I can get an exclusive with Senator Marchio. I can cover it from whatever angle you want. I'll drop the story leads from the jump drive, but I need to understand the players so I know what is off limits. Based on what you've shared today, I'm assuming Rahemia broke down for you the limited information we have connected?" Rhett waited for Jerry's nod.

"She has."

"Are there any leads I can follow at all? Can I at least report on non-advertisers?"

Jerry grunted, "You are like a dog with a bone. No, Rhett. I will say this as plainly as possible. You can follow none of the leads from your source. I do not care if you have concrete proof. I do not care if you have witnesses willing to go on air. I do not care if you find the smoking gun of all smoking guns. You will not run with this story. Do you understand?"

"Yes, but why?"

Jerry actually growled this time. He pushed a button beside his chair and held up his glass. Valentina walked in, took the glass, refilled it, then placed it in Jerry's outstretched hand. He took a long drink before answering. "Because everyone is connected, Rhett. We live in a cyclical world. Everyone is scratching everyone else's back. We are backed entirely by Bluesky and Vandergrift Investment clients. Hell, boy, our own parent company is a client. You want to attack the very system that runs the world. To what end, Rhett? These people, our people, rule the world. And you want to, what, create anarchy and dissonance? Humans are sheep. They buy what we tell them to buy. They eat what we tell them tastes good. We tell them what to wear and where to buy it. They believe what we tell them to believe. They follow our rules and hide in cowardice from being exiled. They will jump off cliffs to follow the crowd. People are happy, blissfully following the status quo. You want to upset the apple cart? Right now, everyone graciously receives the apples we give them. If you have your way, those same people you want to 'enlighten' will end up with dirty, squashed apples from the ground. Leave it alone, Rhett. Let the people be happy, while we make money selling them our friends' apples."

Rhett collapsed into the back of the couch. He couldn't believe what he was hearing. Jerry spoke like some generous benefactor helping the masses. "Cyclical? More like incestual."

"Label it what you want. It is a well-oiled, lucrative, multibillion dollar machine. I, for one, enjoy getting my back scratched."

"The talking points my writers get, who compiles the list?"

"One World Democracy. They are a think tank utilizing real-time polling on buzz words and current events. All the networks use their services for market research. Why?"

"I just didn't realize I was a puppet being fed lines by my own writers. I used to write my own material."

The robust man sighed, clearly exasperated with his star. "Rhett, I understand that your near-death experiences of late might have caused you to question life, but this is not the hill for you to die on."

"I actually agree with you on that."

Misunderstanding Rhett, Jerry relaxed. "Good, good. I'm glad you understand. I'll tell you what. As long as you agree to no more crazy talk, I will check with the Unified Strategies Commission and One World Democracy about a remote show for the secession vote. I can't promise you anything, but I will ask. Maybe you will see their flawed narrative for what it is and expose this stunt as dangerous and counterproductive. Now, would you like that drink?"

Rhett stood with purpose. He felt an odd quivering ripple throughout his body. Somehow, his knees didn't buckle and his stomach didn't hurl. "No, thanks. There is someone I have to meet. Thanks, Jerry. Let me know about the remote show."

Jerry pushed another button and his double doors swung open next to his assistant's desk. "All right, my boy. Have a good afternoon." Valentina scurried by Rhett as he left Jerry's office.

Muscle memory carried him to the elevators, then to his office, and finally out through the elaborate glass-walled lobby. The WBN logo screamed at him from every direction. He took the nearest door to the back alley. Drawing in a deep breath, Rhett watched as a red robin landed right in front of him. The bird seemed to watch him, too. Just then a siren wailed, and the robin floated away from Rhett. He pulled the flip-phone from his bag and feverishly typed.

RP: One World Democracy. Who are they and how are they connected?

Austin Roe: Now you're asking the right questions.

RP: We need to meet.

Austin Roe: I tend to agree. I'll make arrangements.

Chapter Twenty-Nine

"You aren't going to believe this!"

"Well, hello to you too." Rhett's spirits instantly lifted upon seeing Madison's face on his phone. They hadn't seen each other in person for over a week. Between her schedule and his show, they carved out time at night to talk, but they were both usually exhausted by then. Rhett fought off the fatigue every morning, but it was worth it to get Madison's undivided attention.

"Hayman just told us about a schedule change. We're headed to the Secession Convention. We will be there in two days." The excitement in her voice matched his own.

"Are you serious? We will both be in the same state and the same city at the same time?" Rhett couldn't believe his luck.

"Yes! Jackson and Rich are already teasing me, so it better be worth it," Madison laughed.

"I'm sure they would find something to tease you about regardless, but I will definitely make it worth your while." Rhett smiled at her shining face that filled the screen. "Wait, I thought the party line was to avoid the secession at all costs to not give it weight?"

"We did too, but a delegation of senators is attending to protest it, and Jackson will be the spokesperson. It is the only non-partisan action since the last election."

"Are they all from blue states?"

"No, they are from red and blue states."

"Interesting."

"Rhett, you are missing the point. Take off your reporter hat. I will be there for a campaign stop and you will be there for work. Does it matter why? We'll both be in the same place at the same time."

Rhett shook his head. "I'm sorry. You're right. That's the best news I've heard all week."

"I have to run. Jackson is going on stage. I just had to tell you. I'll text the details when I know more. Love you."

Everything froze. Time. Reality. Silence. Her face looked like a deer caught in headlights. "Did I say that out loud?"

Rhett slowly smiled. He had never told anyone he loved them except for Grammy. He never even felt the urge to. Until now. He thought this moment would feel scary. It didn't. "I love you too, Madison. Go. We can talk later."

Her voice was quiet, but she was smiling. "Okay. Bye, Rhett."

The screen went dark.

"Did that just happen?"

Rhett turned in the passenger seat to face Jake's cheesy grin, expecting a comment. "Yes, Jake. It did. Asking you to drop it would be futile, correct?"

"Duh." Jake laughed, "I can't wait to tell Alexis!"

Rhett dropped his head to his chest and groaned. "Can we at least table this discussion until after the meeting? We're almost there."

"It's like you don't even know me at all. You are so lucky Alexis is four hours away or else there would be no tabling." Jake's laughter was unnerving to Rhett.

By the time they made their way back to Adam's Ale & Steakhouse, Rhett was downright aggravated with Jake. Rhett gave the hostess his name, anticipating another seat at the bar. She confirmed his reservation at a table near the kitchen. Jake pulled out his phone as they followed the black-clad woman to their seats. "Mr. Buckley, Mr. Paulson, here is your table."

Rhett and Jake exchanged glances. Obviously, the hostess was given some instructions. Was she in on the meeting? So far, Rhett added more questions to his list instead of getting answers. Rhett sat with his back to the room so Jake could have a clear view of the door, the bar, and the back room where they had witnessed a clandestine meeting a few months ago. Rhett didn't care for the intrigue.

"Either this is the best steakhouse in Washington, D.C. or they keep inviting us to the inner lair of someone's den."

"I just hope we're not on the menu." Jake was on high alert. He scanned the room, tapped his ear, then checked his phone. Rhett watched him closely. "I hope the steak is worth it, because our coms are completely out. Our ears, your lapel cam, and my glasses are all fried."

Rhett watched as Jake texted his brother, a retired Navy SEAL. He helped them out on cases in the past. Rhett said he wasn't worried, but wanted someone to know their location. His brother didn't ask questions, only responded with their signature "BCB" for "Be Careful Brother." Jake left Alexis with his brother's family this week. He might have returned to D.C. yesterday, but his heart did not.

While they waited, Mike, their bartender from before, came over and welcomed them back to Adam's. He brought over two glasses of water and let them know their orders would be out soon. The two exchanged glances again. Rhett needed answers. This was maddening.

Jake gritted. "Well, I hope I like what they ordered."

"Okay, first the hostess, now our friendly neighborhood bartender Mike is in on this, too? Are they going to poison us? They could have at least allowed us to order our own last meals."

Jake sniffed his water before taking a sip, attempting humor. Rhett rolled his eyes, then checked the flip phone for instructions or updates. Nothing. Jake began coughing up his water. Rhett's head snapped up, making sure his wingman was still just joking. As Jake recovered his senses, his eyes were wide as he raised a hand. Rhett turned, his eyes popped out as well.

"Rhett! Jake! I can't believe my luck. Great to see you both. What are the odds of this?" Nick patted Rhett on the back as he held out his hand to Jake. Jake shook it. Confusion etched on both of their faces.

"I'm having lunch with my college roommate." Nick held out his hand to introduce the man he walked in with. "Boys, this is John Benson. John, this is Jake Buckley and Rhett Paulson."

"Gentleman, nice to meet you both." The man nodded and sat down at the table beside Jake and Rhett's. Nick pulled out the chair across from John

Benson. Mike delivered water and a bottle of wine to Nick's table. Nick and John unfolded napkins and settled into their seats as Rhett and Jake stared.

"These are your ringers, Nick? Over forty years of friendship, and I still question your judgment." John sipped his wine before picking up his menu.

"Close your mouths, boys. Act like you are having a nice meal with your friend, and we just happened along until we verify you haven't been followed. Now that Jerry knows, we can't be certain that he hasn't run his mouth to anyone." Nick smiled at John and began speaking to his lunch companion as if Rhett and Jake had coincidentally been seated next to their table. "I see that you both are in shock."

John cleared his throat. He directed his words to Nick, but they were clearly meant for the neighboring table. "We don't have time for your shock to subside. Listen carefully as I catch you up to speed. Nick, we call him Tallmadge, over here, decided to bring you into our information sharing group. We are not *spies,* as you like to refer to us. We are patriots who believe in free speech, limited government, and, well, we don't trust any politician regardless of party affiliation. We seek the truth and aim to share it with others who want to actually hear it."

Nick laughed as if responding to something funny John had said, "I knew you would be worried about the meeting, and John still doesn't trust you, so I'm here as the buffer. I wish I could have told you this another way, but things are moving quicker than we expected. We need to give you the information, but don't want to risk another parking lot disaster. So, here we are, in public. This is a safe place for us, but we can never be too careful."

"You fried our coms?" Rhett was angry, but not even sure why anymore.

John smiled, "We just paused them."

"Jake, enjoy your meal. It isn't poisoned. Rhett, try to eat something. I know you have questions, and I will answer them all, but today is for a specific purpose." Nick attempted normalcy in the midst of a mind blowing revelation.

Rhett watched incredulously as Jake settled into his seat and visibly relaxed. Jake waved over Mike and asked for a large draft beer, and placed his napkin across his lap. "If Nick's in, so am I. Lay it on us fellas. Rhett, close your mouth and look at me instead of gaping at them. You look like you just found out about Santa Claus. Focus."

Jake's smile irritated Rhett. He gritted a grin back and began asking questions as if he and Jake were having a private lunch. "So, this whole time, you knew about the jump drive and text messages?"

"Yes."

"Why all this? Why didn't you just tell me all the information? Why the secret source and cloak-and-dagger? You could have just told me." Rhett felt confused and betrayed.

"I wasn't sure you were ready. Besides, it's not my information to share, I'm only one cog in the wheel. There are things you need to hear from John, but setting up a meeting with him would have raised red flags. We have already jeopardized your life twice. Based on your first meeting with a source, it must be obvious how dangerous this is for us. We need to cover all our tracks to protect the mission. The FBI has at least fifty political prisoners sitting in jail, some for two years. We've been told the conditions are atrocious. They're still waiting to be arraigned."

That got Jake's attention. "They can't do that. It's completely unconstitutional."

"They can do what they want." John's icy laugh shook Rhett to the core. "We have documentation that would make your head spin about the FBI. We call them the political police. They make J. Edgar Hoover look like a kid with a decoder ring."

"You call them the PPs?" Jake tried very hard to keep a straight face.

Nick winked at Jake. "I told them that was a bad name."

John grunted. Rhett ignored them.

"If you have the evidence, why don't you take it to the media?" Rhett attempted to keep his focus on Jake and from John, but it was difficult.

Rhett could see Nick's smirk from the side. "How did that work out for you, Rhett? You think Jerry and WBN are the only media company involved in the family business? Even the conservative channels are afraid to air that information. The reporters and owners brave enough to air anything against the machine are silenced, fined into oblivion, or receive visits from the FBI.

Bluesky owns the majority of every single network news agency, magazine, and newspaper."

"Every piece of evidence we have was found in plain sight. They aren't hiding it, they manipulate it until they need it. When we realized the media was compromised, we made videos and podcasts, only to be demonetized and shadow banned. Even if people search for the information, they won't find it. Or worse, they permanently banned the users who were speaking the truth as spreaders of misinformation, regardless of the concrete evidence. So, we started speaking on campuses and at meetings. That's when we realized we were at war. The Fascism Fighters, doxxed families, attacked our homes. You've seen firsthand the lengths they will go to. Hale wasn't the first dead man, and sadly, he won't be the last. They protest everywhere we speak. They are a terrorist militia. Have you ever noticed they have command centers set up with medical grade triage equipment at all of their 'peaceful protests?' The same foundations fund them across the globe. They are militant Marxists. Imagine how powerful Stalin, Hitler, and Che Guevara would have been had they had the backing of the Internet and modern media. Goebbels has nothing on these guys."

Nick tapped the table. "That is a soapbox for another time, John. Let's focus on answering the questions they summoned us to answer."

Rhett thought back to his meeting with Jerry. *Everyone scratches everyone else's back. It's cyclical.* Rhett thought he would be sick. Once he got beyond calling them PPs, Jake started asking questions as Rhett listened and processed. Mike brought them dinner. Rhett pushed food around the plate as he listened to John fill in the blanks while Jake recited song lyrics to make it look like they were having a normal conversation at their own table. Nick and John laughed their way through the information like old friends catching up instead of men passing along secret information to a reporter.

John explained how think tanks like One World Democracy fit into the system. "All global currency is linked to Bluesky Investments. Bluesky funnels the money through shares and a grading system. The more a company obeys the rules laid out by One World Democracy and the Unified Strategies Commission, the higher their stocks rise. Rising inflation and the destruction of independent national currencies is all part of the plan. They're goal is to destabilize the dollar. It will only take one global crisis, like a catastrophic food crisis, to force every nation into a digital global currency that will be based on an arbitrary social credit score. They create the problem that only they can solve. Sound familiar?"

Jake cursed under his breath. Rhett could tell his friend was barely keeping it all in check.

"This new global government they want to usher in is essentially privatized communism. Instead of the traditional tyrannical government model we've seen throughout history, this new world order replaces it with a tiered system within the private sector. The global elite reap the rewards with their insider trading and bastardized version of box-store capitalism. The rich get richer, and the workers are controlled, patrolled, and rationed in their smart cities, eating bugs and earning credits to participate in society."

The more John explained, Rhett found himself impressed by the ingenuity of these people and flabbergasted at how well Democrats and Republicans worked together behind the scenes to line their own pockets. During work hours, these groups threatened and viciously attacked the character of one another. After hours, they went on vacations, barbecued, and shared investment tips with one another. The way John described it, this was much more than "scratching each other's back." Governments around the world had been systematically set up as giant money laundering schemes, and the people reaping the benefits were the very people responsible for stopping it. It was a masterful plan.

"The bigger government gets, the more places to hide money and offer jobs to friends. We will send you an encrypted file connecting the pipeline of government jobs with private and foundation board positions, as well as the money trail tying every non-profit political donation to Bluesky and their lobbyist groups." John asked Nick about dessert as if he hadn't just dropped a bomb of information on Rhett.

Mike dropped off the bill for Rhett and Jake, then took Nick and John's dessert order before walking to the bar. Rhett opened the leather folder to reveal not a check, but a piece of paper with an encrypted web address. He looked at Jake, who had just finished his last swig of an IPA, appropriately called Patriot Powder Keg, Mike suggested.

Nick wiped his mouth with the linen napkin. "I know this is a lot to absorb. We can talk freely on the plane to Kansas. You will have plenty to research before then, so I'm sure you'll have more questions. Don't forget to tip Mike. He's a grad student for John and the universities don't pay their GAs as much as they do their high-priced speakers."

Rhett felt like a zombie. The men all nodded their goodbyes. Jake and Rhett walked to Jake's truck in silence. As soon as they climbed inside the cab, Rhett pulled out the secret laptop from under the seat in the hidden holster Jake's brother had installed last week. He quickly typed in the address. "Son of a...."

"What?" Jake peered over his shoulder. "Well, we have our answer to the *who* question. When they say follow the money, I didn't think it would look like overlapping labyrinths."

Names were flashing in front of Rhett's eyes. Names he had seen for years. Jerry and Nick were both right. Everyone was scratching everyone else's back, and it was the most successful bipartisan act in history.

Chapter Thirty

"Why are you so nervous?" Jackson came up behind Madison and squeezed her shoulders.

She clung to the chair in front of her while simultaneously wringing her hands together. "I don't know Jackson, maybe because I'm minutes away from meeting the first female President of the United States. I'm in the White House, in the room named after President Roosevelt, and we're about to have a strategy session with the most powerful political think tank in the world. Of course, you've been meeting with them for weeks, so it's not a big deal for you. Why, again, are they including me? Not that I'm complaining, I'm just curious."

Jackson smiled at her in that way he smiled at women to put them at ease. Madison tilted her head and glared at him. "Don't you dare give me that look, Jackson Cashe. I'm not one of your admirers."

He laughed, then pulled out a chair to sit. "Madsi, calm down. This is a campaign strategy session with the face of our party. You are my campaign manager. You have worked hard to be in the room. Enjoy it."

Madison couldn't shake the feeling of unease. "I'm surprised Hayman approved this. Let's be honest, he thinks he is the true campaign manager and treats me like his assistant."

"Madsi, Hayman has the connections, but you are the one who connects the dots and makes the magic happen." Jackson pulled out the chair next to him for Madison to sit. "Did you tell Rhett they summoned us back to D.C. for this meeting? I'm sure he's excited for you."

Madison, quick to catch Jackson's attempt at changing the subject, relaxed. "I texted him before we took off this morning. We have a small window after these meetings and his show. We might be able to grab a quick dinner. What about you? Is Vanessa in town?" Madison and Rich weren't fans of Vanessa, but her Jackie O look trapped Jackson in a tight web.

"She's on location filming."

"I thought they were filming in Virginia. Isn't she close to D.C.?"

"She was worried about traffic." Jackson shrugged, then looked off into the distance, thinking and talking like he used to do in college when he processed information. "I really like Rhett, Madsi. He's a good guy. Relationships on the road aren't easy, but he makes you a priority. I know you don't need it, but he has my approval."

Madison slid her hand over Jackson's. He looked at her as they spoke wordlessly. Jackson and Rich were her people. A lot of women went to school to find their husbands or their bridesmaids. Madison walked away with two extra brothers, sometimes more protective than her actual brothers. "You're right, I don't need it, but I value it."

The two of them sat quietly in the Roosevelt room for a few minutes before they heard shuffling from the hallway. Hayman entered with a flourish, as always. He waved his arms like a ringmaster, ushering them in to the carnival.

"Madison, welcome to the big leagues, kid. I hope you brought your A game today. You're going to need it."

Madison rolled her eyes behind his back. Jackson stifled a chuckle. The two of them followed behind Hayman as he talked, mostly to himself, and led them into the Oval Office.

Madison refused to let this moment pass her by in a blur. She took in every inch, every smell, every sound. She savored this moment. She worked hard for this moment. She deserved this moment. She earned it with every weekend spent at the library, every late-night cram session, and every extra credit point. Her parents would be so proud, but, she realized in that moment, so was she. Madison relaxed, squared her shoulders, and acted like she belonged in this room, because she did.

Over the next hour, they crammed in more strategy than their team had done in months. The Oval was a revolving door of party leaders, pollsters, and experts in campaign strategy. Madison and Jackson got a master's level education in one afternoon. President Blythe was a machine. She was the most charismatic and inspiring "girl boss" Madison had ever seen in action. Madison watched in awe as the woman owned the room while receiving and returning information and directives.

By the time they reached the SUV motorcade, Madison was floating, and Madison didn't float. She was levelheaded, but this felt intoxicating, so she went with it. Hayman and Jackson talked donors and dollars while Madison furiously tapped notes into her tablet, summarizing the meetings. As they drove across town to The Babylon Hotel, Madison finished her notes, texted Rhett to find out where they were meeting, then jumped right into Hayman and Jackson's conversation. Today was a great day.

She had no idea how, but the day got even better. Their private lunch was with Adam Ford, Johan Philipsen, and Omar Marduk from ProtoAI. This man held the keys to the business kingdom. Madison had watched every speech the man had given, from climate change to global healthcare to world economic change. Omar Marduk, a trans-humanist, led the charge to embrace the fourth industrial revolution. According to Marduk, AI technology would unite the world under a global economy, healthcare system, and leadership. Not to mention, Madison had a massive intellectual crush on the man. He was a tall, handsome, eloquent, enigmatic genius. Marduk had a plan for global citizenship to ensure human rights and healthcare for all, based on social credits and equity. The man was a god, and today, Madison Lyn sat at his table. She soaked up every word.

Now that Jackson had clinched the party's nomination, the Cashe train rolled full steam ahead, with President Blythe leading the charge. The people Madison met with today understood the crossroads of the country. They weighed what a secession vote would do to the global collective. They believed in Jackson's vision and they had the resources to help him achieve his goals. The quick dinner meeting was productive and promising. By the time Madison, Jackson, and Hayman left the private suite, they were all speechless. Madison created a master list of action steps and Marduk vowed to connect Madison with his Global Strategies Czar for future coordinated efforts. Madison floated on cloud nine.

She couldn't wait to tell Rhett everything and text her family. It would blow them all away. Her grandparents sacrificed everything so that Madison and her siblings could have opportunities just like this. Madison was on a professional high, and it felt amazing.

Then she heard Hayman growl. She looked up and understood why. "Ms. Lyn, I truly hope your boyfriend isn't insulting our close friend, Mr. Philipsen, again."

Jackson processed the scene. "Madsi, did you know he was coming?"

"No. We were supposed to meet later. I didn't tell him we were here."

Madison's stomach dropped. Rhett was not a fan of Philipsen. Worse, Rhett had been antsy since his interview with Philipsen and the attack that happened the very next day. Not with her, but with the "system" as he called it. Madison sped up and crossed the grand lobby to reach Rhett. His look of surprise when he saw her confirmed the randomness of this meeting.

Johan Philipsen was also watching the two of them. Madison noticed the smirk on his face as the confusion grew on both of theirs. "Ms. Lyn, Mr. Paulson and I were discussing our lunch menu this afternoon. He truly enjoys asking all the culinary questions. I hope you regal him with stories of your meal," Philipsen softly laughed as he walked away.

Madison watched Rhett shake his head in confusion before leveling a gaze at her. Madison wrestled with whether she saw a look of disappointment in his eyes, or if she imagined it. Either way, her bubble had burst.

"What are you doing here? I thought we were meeting for dinner at the food trucks?"

"I had a lead on a story, so Jake and I ran over here." Rhett pointed to the bar. Jake waved. Madison responded with her own tentative wave.

"A lead? About Philipsen?" Madison held her breath, waiting for the answer.

"About a meeting between the President and some powerful people being held off site to avoid the White House visitor logs." Rhett's investigative look came out as he spoke. Madison used to think that look was cute. Now it irritated her.

"I didn't realize WBN lowered itself to cover the personal lunch plans of politicians and their friends." Madison regretted the words as soon as they came out of her mouth, but she was hurt. Of all people, she didn't expect Rhett to be her bubble buster today.

"Is that what this was? A lunch among friends? I thought I knew your friends." Rhett was hurt, too. She saw it in his eyes.

Madison smiled and touched Rhett's arm. She needed to break this distance that had formed. "Hey, it's been a crazy afternoon. I was going to tell you all about it tonight. I need to get back to headquarters to brief Rich and the rest of our staff. Do you still want to meet?"

Rhett closed his eyes. She saw him soften before her. "Yeah. I would like that. I can pick you up at your office so we can ride together. Does that sound good?"

Madison nodded. Rhett leaned in and kissed her softly on the cheek. He smelled like home. As he pulled back, they both studied the other's eyes, grasping to understand. She smiled. He winked.

Jackson came up behind her as Rhett reached the door to where Jake was waiting. "Everything okay?"

Madison pressed back her shoulders. "Everything is great. Total random meeting. He was following a lead and wanted to say hello to Philipsen. Let's get back to Rich."

Chapter Thirty-One

Rhett rolled down the window and breathed deeply. The smell of fresh cut grass and country roads flooded his senses. Somehow, the skies were bluer, and the sun shone brighter in West Virginia. He loved his home state. He needed to come home more often. As Jake neared Grammy's driveway, a sign caught Rhett's eye. "God's Apothecary? What's that?"

"Geez, Rhett. You need to call your Grammy more often."

"What's that supposed to mean? Do you know what it's for?"

"Of course I do, and shame on you for not knowing!" Jake shook his head. Rhett mumbled something unkind under his breath.

Jake drove his truck up Grammy's winding gravel-driveway. A feeling of calmness washed over Rhett. The front porch swing brought back memories of rocking with Grammy as a child. Unbidden recollections of his mom stumbling up the front steps were mixed with the sweet ones of her singing him to sleep on the good nights.

Rhett also noticed that the paint was peeling and the gutter on the right side of the house sagged. The old farmhouse probably needed a new roof, too. Rhett sighed. Guilt replaced the calm. His heart beat deeper in his chest and his stomach felt empty. Not hungry-empty, convicted-empty. Mercifully, Jake didn't say a word. He didn't have to. Rhett felt his disappointment.

As if Grammy could sense their presence, the front screen door opened wide. Her shining face was a lighthouse of hope in his darkness, just as she'd always been.

"Man, I love Grammy." Jake parked the truck and hopped out first. Rhett watched his friend skip the steps two at a time to hug Grammy. Rhett smiled.

He grabbed his bag from the backseat and climbed the old farmhouse steps. He remembered doing the same thing as a little boy behind his Mama.

Grammy handed Jake a glass jar, "Give this to Alexis. I already told her what to do with it."

"Thanks, Grammy. Rhett, I'll pick you up at eight." Jake nodded, then left.

"Well, you look much better since the last time I saw you. Now, get inside and let me feed you. You've lost weight."

Rhett couldn't argue with either statement. He followed Grammy across the threshold and dropped his bags. The house hadn't changed one bit. Every photo, piece of furniture, and book was safely in its own place. This comforted Rhett. Grammy's house smelled like pot roast and potatoes. His stomach growled.

"Go on upstairs and get washed up. I'll have dinner ready when you come down." Grammy called from the kitchen. Decades of hearing her say those exact words filled him with love. Rhett carried his bag upstairs. He stopped at the top of the steps to study his mother's senior picture from high school. Her dark, curly hair and bright eyes stared back at him. He didn't know this woman. He knew her eyes. He watched them become trapped inside a body that betrayed her. The black hole he kept hidden inside wanted to open up and swallow him whole, but he couldn't let it. Not today. Not this week.

Rhett quickly washed up and changed into sweats. Grammy placed the rolls on the table as he entered. A glass of whole milk sat at his familiar seat. The old kitchen hadn't changed either, other than the new refrigerator and dishwasher Rhett insisted she let him buy. The stove was the same one Gramp's mom cooked on, so that stove wasn't going anywhere. That was one argument Rhett wouldn't win.

"I know you're only home for one night, but I'll take it." Grammy pulled out her chair and sat. "Let's pray, then you can tell me all about this trip."

Rhett followed her lead, muscle memory taking over. Grammy earnestly prayed to her God, Rhett's hand in hers, his head bowed. He wasn't a fan of her God, didn't trust him one bit, but the tradition of sitting at this table required reverence, so he offered that for Grammy.

Her pot roast melted in his mouth. It was so tender it fell apart at the slightest touch of the knife. Rhett had eaten at restaurants all over the world, but no one's mashed potatoes were as creamy as Grammy's. Don't get him started on her green beans with bacon. Rhett couldn't remember the last time he had seconds. His trainer wouldn't be happy, but Rhett relished every bite as Grammy caught him up on town gossip. Gramps always said that Rhett got his journalism gift from his grandmother because she could get dirt out of a bar of soap.

After dinner, they settled into the familiar act of cleaning up the kitchen. Gramps used to hum while they worked. After his death, Grammy filled the silence with the radio. She rinsed their plates and loaded the dishwasher as Rhett filled containers with leftovers. When they finally finished, Grammy filled glasses with basil sweet tea and they headed to the front porch swing.

The swing rocked back and forth as they listened to the night's symphony. Birds, crickets, and frogs harmonized as the lightning bugs put on their own light show. Grammy sighed. Rhett finally relaxed. The silence felt cathartic. In D.C. noise surrounded him. A dissonance of voices yelling their opinions in a city built on disagreement and unbalanced compromises. This felt much better.

"How is Madison?"

There it was, the question of all questions. Grammy knew it, and Rhett knew it. She wasn't just asking how Madison was doing, she was asking much more.

Rhett blew out the tension he'd been holding. "Madison is great. She's busy, but she's at the height of her career, so she's loving it. Based on the past three election cycles and the polls, Jackson will walk right into the White House with Madison and Rich at his side."

"But?"

"Grammy, who said there was a but?"

Grammy flashed Rhett her give-me-a-break look and waited.

"Madison loves her job and is soaring high, and I couldn't be happier for her. *But*, I am struggling with being her boyfriend and covering stories that involve Jackson."

Grammy stayed silent, waiting for more. Rhett knew her tricks. Her porch swing was more effective than a confessional. "A few days ago, I got a tip about President Blythe taking a private meeting with some pretty powerful players under the radar. These men are pushing for a global society and the dismantling of all borders. The President of the United States meeting with supporters of a borderless society with unelected global leadership is a pretty big story that people need to know about. I went to the location of the meeting and found Jackson and Madison walking out of the so-called secret meeting."

"I take it Madison was just as surprised to see you?"

Rhett nodded. "We met that night for dinner and vowed once again to listen to the other person with our personal hats and not our professional ones."

"No offense, dear, but that's the dumbest thing I've ever heard. I understand the sentiment, but that's impossible to do. You both are human and humans are complex."

"Tell me about it. I listened, and I was so happy for her. She had the best day of her professional life. She was on cloud nine. At the same time, all of my reporter senses were on high alert. I found myself asking questions for information, not for support. I felt guilty and proud of her all at once. She did the same. She was interested in the story lead, but it obviously made her defensive. Since then, things have been normal between us, but we haven't touched the topic of work at all." Rhett took a sip of his tea, trying to cover the catch in his voice.

"You can't have a relationship in compartments, Rhett."

"I know."

"You love her."

"I know."

"What are you going to do about that?"

"I don't know. I do love her. I'm proud of her and I want her to be successful, but my job requires me to find the hidden secrets of her job. It didn't used to be that way. Before the shooting, I saw things differently. Now, I'm questioning everything. I want her to talk to me about her day, but I can't put those conversations in a box and pretend I didn't hear them. A wise woman once told me I can't have a relationship with compartments." Rhett nudged Grammy's arm.

"She sounds like a very smart woman."

"She thinks so."

Grammy elbowed him. "You definitely are in a pickle."

"You can say that again."

"You definitely are in a pickle."

Rhett laughed.

"I wish I had advice for you, but some things in life are too momentous to slide your way through. At those times, a life shift is the only thing that can break the stalemate. Sometimes God brings a life-quake to force you to make a decision. Are you in or out?"

Rhett didn't respond. Pastor Jacob Tomlinson said something similar during his first interview with Nick. He didn't want to have this conversation again.

"God has given me many moments like that. Every time He turned up the fire, I had to answer the question."

Grammy drank some tea and rocked. They sat in silence for a while. Rhett knew Grammy wouldn't last long.

"You never ask about your mom. You never want to hear stories or talk about her. You kept it all inside. Gramps and I didn't know what to do with you. You bottled it all up inside, but you never imploded or exploded, so we just watched and prayed. I never understood how you could investigate everything and anything, but didn't ask one question about her."

Rhett shrugged. "There wasn't anything I needed to know. She had this great life. She blew it when she went to college. Got knocked up by some random guy. Couldn't raise a kid, so she dropped me off here and came back when she needed money. She didn't want me. She wanted drugs. End of story." Rhett shrugged as he stared into the night sky.

"That's not fair, Rhett. She was more than that. So much more."

Rhett's sardonic laugh burned his throat. "Not fair? She chose drugs over her family at every choice and then she died. I learned a lot from her life. I learned to not throw away an opportunity. I worked hard to not be like her. I'm smarter and stronger." Rhett's icy tone didn't fool Grammy, he could feel it.

"You know, I spent years blaming myself for her addiction, and apparently you aren't that great of an investigator because your timeline is way off. Your mom became a drug addict in my house, with my help."

Rhett's foot roughly stopped the gentle swaying. He looked at Grammy in shock, desperately asking questions with his eyes.

"Your mom was a smarty pants. Jenny was a straight-A student, on the honor roll. She was in every club she could join. She was the life of the party. Lit up every room she entered. Her favorite thing in life was cheerleading. She went to gymnastics five days a week. Attending every camp and competition she could. The things she did with her body were amazing feats, but it took a toll. The thing she loved most was causing her pain. Concussions, sprains, and a torn ACL took second place to her determination. She fought through every injury until she couldn't. The summer before her senior year, she was at a camp and her base missed a hold. Jenny crashed to the ground, and she hurt her spine."

Rhett didn't realize the swing had started swaying again. He intently watched Grammy as her gaze watched something he couldn't see. Her memories took her away, far away from the porch.

"She went to therapy and had shots in her back, but nothing worked. Her doctor insisted that she try OxyContin to manage the pain while she healed. I trusted the doctors and filled the prescription. Three doctors, two physical therapists, and two pharmacists knew she was taking it. No one warned us. No one raised any flags or questions. Jenny went back to training and was back on the squad by fall. By the time she turned eighteen, she didn't need me to get more prescriptions filled. They gave her as much as she wanted. She heightened her training so she could cheer her senior year and also try out for college. The harder she worked, the more pain her body was in, the more Oxy she took. I ignored a lot. I buried my head in the sand. I relied too heavily on medical professionals and not enough on my intuition. Jenny was a functioning addict until she wasn't. By the time we figured out what was happening, she was away at college and getting any drug she could get her hands on to numb the pain because the Oxy alone wasn't working. Her grades were non-existent, and she stopped calling home. We took her out of school and found the best treatment center we could. She left in the middle of the night and we didn't see her again for three years. Until she came home with you."

Rhett wiped away a tear. How did he not know any of this?

"She was skin and bones by the time she made it here. Her arms were covered in needle marks. Her face was hollow. She was a shell of her former self. Our vibrant Jenny was decimated in darkness. She had a baby in her arms and a backpack. That's all she had when she came home, but she came and we tried to help. The next seven years were a battle for her every day. It was a cycle of rehab and relapse, but she never stopped trying. She wanted to be a mom to you. She loved you so much. You were the only thing making her fight. She would have given up if it weren't for you."

Memories flooded his brain. All these years he thought the flashbacks of her singing and reading to him were mirages, dreams of what he wanted her to be. Those flashbacks constantly warred with the memories of her strung out and crying. Of Grammy and Gramps begging her to go to the next hospital. Rhett wiped the tears streaming down his face. He remembered his mom running out of church after the pastor spoke a sermon about the demons of drugs and how we needed to rid the city of the half-way centers that were corrupting our youth. Rhett remembered Grammy and Gramps dragging him out of the service behind them. That was the last time they attended that church.

"I didn't know any of that."

"I didn't think you did. If you had, you probably would have been angry at me. I was. For years, I was angry at myself. I was angry at the doctors and the drug companies. But I was mostly angry at God for taking away my baby. For allowing it to happen."

"What happened?"

"I realized being angry didn't take away the pain. Anger only made it worse. I had a friend who walked beside me and reminded me that God isn't a religion. She reminded me that not all *Christians* are followers of Christ. She reminded me that battles could only be won on my knees in prayer. God reminded me that He is good, and that He holds all of my tears. He reminded me that He loved Jenny more than I ever could and that He was working for her good even if the world meant harm for her. I learned to forgive myself. I forgave Jenny. I forgave God. I'm still working on forgiveness for the doctors and medical profession, but my heart wants to forgive. My flesh wants to go scorched earth vigilante on them." Grammy sadly laughed through the tears.

"I remember her leaving and coming. I remember visiting her in different places. I remember her voice. She always sang those songs they taught in Sunday school."

"She had a beautiful voice." Grammy reached over and held Rhett's hand. "My prayers were answered, you know. Not in the way I wanted, but they were answered."

Rhett looked at her strangely. He didn't understand.

"Jenny was getting better. The last facility she went to was Christ centered. After she graduated from the program, they offered her a kitchen job at the City Healing Network. They employed a lot of their former graduates of the program. She was there for six months when she had a heart attack. Her body couldn't take it anymore. It had given up on her."

Rhett was angry now. "How can you sit here and say that your prayers were answered when she died?" He stood and walked to the railing of the porch. He couldn't believe his ears.

Grammy watched him before speaking. "Rhett, I don't expect you to understand because you don't share my faith. You have made that clear your entire life. Jenny gave her life to Jesus at that last rehab center. She was going to Bible study and called me every night to pray with me. Our relationship grew in ways it never would have had we not gone through hell and back together. Rhett, we are all going to die. Every human on earth dies. Whether we're old or young, whether it's expected or unexpected, we are all going to die. The gift is knowing that we will be together again in Heaven. Jenny walked with the Lord, so I know she is walking with Him now. My biggest heartbreak is knowing that if you die, and you have sure tried your hardest these last few months to do so, that you won't. My greatest and most fervent prayer every day is that you learn to walk with Jesus, because the alternative is unbearable for me to fathom."

"Gram, please don't. I can't have this conversation again. This is all too much."

"Rhett, you never want to have this conversation. You see the world in black and white, wrong and right. You follow the rules and do exactly what the world expects of you. All those years of bottling up your feelings, the pressure needs to be released at some point. You hold on to this anger for some church ninnies and a self-righteous pastor, but they aren't God. They are broken people. We are all broken people in need of a savior. You spent your life succeeding in the world so the world wouldn't shun you like it did your mom, but I've got news for you, buddy. The world will always turn on you. One day, it will let you down spectacularly. On that day, I pray you meet the One who will never turn on you. Satan offers you fake apples and lies. Jesus offers you truth and living water. At some point, you're going to have to choose, and I pray you choose life like Jenny did. I just pray that you don't die before it happens."

Grammy got up and left Rhett outside. For the first time in his life, the silence on this porch didn't bring comfort. He tossed and turned all night. Dreams and memories twisted into nightmares.

The next morning, Rhett looked for Grammy all over the house. He found her in the back, working inside a fenced in garden. It wasn't her vegetable garden off the back porch, this was off to the side by her honey bee boxes. Rhett walked over to her. She was holding her basket and clipping flowers with her other hand. They hadn't spoken since last night.

"Good morning, my favorite grandson."

"Morning, Grammy. Are we okay?"

She stared at him with love in her eyes. "We are always okay, sweetheart. I love you more than breathing. I will never stop praying for you. If that makes you mad, then tough cookies. Now, take this basket for me so I can get you breakfast before Jake gets here."

Rhett grasped the handle and helped Grammy close the gate behind her. "What is all this?"

"I'm glad you asked. Your Grammy is an entrepreneur. This is my medicinal herb garden. After everything that happened with your mom, I started doubting the entire medical profession. I remembered Gramps had an aunt that the family called Aunt Healer. Isn't that a great name? Anyway, I called everyone in the family and tracked down her old notebooks. God gave us everything we need to stay healthy, right here on earth. I took some herbal courses online and voila! I have my own medicinal herb company. I started my garden five years ago and only gave teas and tinctures to friends, but word spread, and now everyone in the county wants some. Sometimes, I even set up a booth at craft fairs."

"Grammy, I had no idea." Rhett felt awful. He was so caught up in his own world, he missed this entire life of Grammy's.

"Well, of course you didn't. I wasn't about to tell you. You lecture me every year about getting the flu shot and the shingles vaccine. I knew you wouldn't understand." Grammy took the basket from Rhett and marched him inside for breakfast. "I realized the drug companies have no intention of making us better, because they make all their money keeping us sick. If I could just find a way to make my own vodka for the tinctures, I'd be completely organic!"

"Grammy the moonshiner. Gramps would be so proud." Rhett snorted.

"Oh, stop it. Hey, I have a story lead for you. Did you know that an oil baron and a railroad baron created the modern pharmaceutical companies? They needed something to do with their byproducts. Next thing you know, they're paying every medical school in the country to sell their snake oil medicine and to teach doctors to stop prescribing any natural medicine. Can you imagine? Herbs and plants that have been used successfully for thousands of years, thrown out the window so that people can take synthetic poisons. And it worked! That's the worst part. People threw out what they'd known their whole lives and believed those idiots."

"You don't say." Rhett watched Grammy's impassioned speech as she started pulling out eggs and bacon. Just like that, everything was back to normal. Grammy was Grammy and Rhett was grateful.

Chapter Thirty-Two

The flight to Wichita was bumpy and riddled with turbulence. Rhett hoped the rocky trip wasn't an omen for things to come in Kansas. Dark, rolling clouds followed Jake's truck from Grammy's house all the way to the private airfield where they met Nick. They flew over and through gray skies and ominous weather. Not bad enough to ground their flight. Not mundane enough to evoke confidence. To say there was an eerie chill in the air was an understatement.

Unsurprisingly, Jake slept through the entire flight. Nothing phased Jake. Was it his faith or his fearlessness? Or was his fearlessness because of his faith? Nick listened to a podcast from some pastor in D.C. He conveniently forgot his headphones. Rhett wasn't fooled. He spent the flight tuning out the podcast and Jake's snoring, but he couldn't tune out Grammy's conversation from last night.

Rhett was so angry as a child. Angry at his mom. His grandparents. The rehab centers that never seemed to help. He was angry at the church members who shunned Grammy and the moms who wouldn't let their kids play with Rhett. The parents on the courts and the fields who pretended not to see Grammy and Gramps sitting by themselves on the sidelines. Never welcomed into the precious, pristine façade of their perfect, and fake, lives. Jake's parents didn't care. From the moment Grammy gave Eloise Buckley a quart of her raw honey, Eloise sat on the farthest row of bleachers with Grammy. When Rhett started breaking records and became a local celebrity on the diamond, all the shunning was forgotten and praise abounded. Rhett hated himself for enjoying the praise.

It was nice to see Grammy in the middle of cheering parents instead of on the periphery. Rhett went from the guy parents hid their daughters from to pushing them in his way and arranging house parties in his honor. Rhett accepted the accolades, but he never trusted it. He only trusted himself. He spent hours at the batting cages. He worked hard in college. He earned the scholarships. He got a job working for WBN. He shot to the top of the ratings. He did it all by himself. As a child, life happened to him. He had no control. He spent his entire adult life controlling every detail. Until now.

Now, everything seemed out of his control and out of his reach. The truth eluded him. His eyes were opened, and he didn't like what he saw. He needed to right the ship, like he always did, but he couldn't seem to find the wheel. He had to keep going until he worked it all out in his mind. He would follow the rules, do the work, and make sense of the noise. He had to. He would take one story lead at a time, like he always did.

The farm where Nick had scheduled an impromptu interview was two hours by car. Since the Indiana trip was a bust thanks to Rhett's attack, which still went unsolved, Nick found a backup farmer who was better suited to help them process information on the jump drive. Nick said it was a blessing. Rhett didn't understand how switching subjects was a blessing when substitutions happened every day in their profession.

The three of them spent the drive discussing lighting and interview questions. It felt like old times. Jake was fired up about tying together all the information they had been researching. Nick watched Rhett closely, too closely. It made Rhett feel like a kid walking through a glass shop.

The smell of hay wafted through the SUV. A sunset of pinks, yellows, blues, and purples swirled together like a watercolor painting cut in half by a sea of green crops. The gentle breeze swayed the waves of tall stalks of corn. If this were a painting, it would be titled "Portrait of the American Farm."

Rhett found himself lost in the beauty. The peacefulness of it all calmed his nerves and reminded him of home. Jake interrupted the moment by waving his hand in Rhett's face. "Earth to Rhett."

He shook it off and refocused, "Sorry, what were you saying?"

Jake rolled his eyes. "We're at the farm, genius. Get your tablet off my camera bag."

Rhett gazed out the window again as the white farmhouse came into focus. The two story structure was as tall as the silos in the next field. The silos themselves looked like skyscrapers among the cover of green.

"I thought you said we were interviewing one farmer." Rhett scratched his head. "There are at least ten vehicles. It looks like the overflow lot for a truck dealership."

The red front door slowly opened, spilling a halo of light around a tall man who waved at their approach. "I'm pretty sure that's Big Jim."

Rhett questioned Nick, "Pretty sure? You haven't vetted this guy? Big Jim? What kind of name is that? What are we walking into, Nick?"

"What's gotten into you?" Jake shook his head as he kicked Rhett's foot away from his bag. "Cranky isn't a good look for you."

Nick completely ignored Rhett's caustic tone and moved on. "I've been communicating with Jim's son, Jim Jr., but this is Big Jim's house. According to Jim Jr., the lighting is better and there will be more space for us to film."

Rhett actually laughed out loud. "Big Jim and Jim Jr.? Is there another brother named Little Jim or Jimmy?"

"Jim Jr.'s son is Jimmy." Nick actually leveled a serious gaze at Rhett. He looked like an old, intimidating headmaster. "I agree with Jake. Cranky is not a good look for you. These people are salt of the earth. They are hardworking, educated, and successful. James is a family name going back generations. I'm sure they are proud of it and won't care for you making jokes mocking their rich history because it offends your sense of modernization and original thought. If you can't pull yourself together, stay in the car."

"Yeah, stay in the car, turd." It amazed Rhett how quickly Jake could revert into a thirteen-year-old boy when he got hangry.

Nick and Jake climbed out and began walking towards the front stairs. Rhett grumbled to himself, as everyone had left him alone in the car. "Geez, I just made a comment about the trucks. Apparently, Big Jim has enough space for the whole town to attend. Seriously, the name thing was funny. Maybe they're the cranky ones."

Rhett watched as Jake and Nick were enveloped in the waiting crowd inside the door. Laughter and cheering filled the empty space around Rhett. What was he doing here? He wasn't mentally prepared for this right now. He hoisted the strap of his shoulder bag and trudged up the front porch stairs.

Big Jim was waiting at the door and clapped Rhett on the back. "Welcome!"

"Thank you, Sir."

Rhett couldn't believe his eyes. There had to be over fifty people scattered around the great-room. The kitchen island looked close to twenty feet long and was covered with pots, pans, and platters, each filled to the brim with all kinds of food options.

Rhett felt Big Jim nudging him inside the fray. "The wife thought you all would be hungry, so she organized some food. I think the whole church contributed a dish. Go grab something to eat. Don't miss the cornbread, it's my favorite."

Jake, already holding a plate and ready to start filling it with food, waved over Rhett. Nick was off in a corner dissecting the filming area with someone Rhett could only assume was Jim Jr.

"Did everyone come to watch the interview?" Rhett asked Big Jim.

"Well, not exactly. You see, Jim showed me the questions your friend Nick plans on asking and they covered way more topics than we're experts on, so we brought in some other people to help answer. We don't live in a vacuum. We all help one another out, so it only made sense to get the information straight from the horse's mouth instead of depending on me to relay it all. Mike, over there, works with the state on crop rotation. John teaches regenerative farming practices at the community college a town over. The other Mike, over there in the corner, leads a program with the 4-H kids on how to repair the damaged soil we got hit with last year. Those kids designed a compost tea that has nearly wiped out any traces of contamination in the tampered with soil. We also have a few ladies on hand to help answer the livestock questions. My granddaughter is a vet, so we have her here too. In this room, we have assembled the best of the best from the regions's agricultural community. If we can't answer it, someone else in this room can." Jim was obviously proud of his honored guests and friends.

Between bites of food and a constant stream of introductions, it shocked Rhett they had everything set up and ready for filming. Nick originally planned to interview Big Jim and Jim Jr., but quickly altered his plans after meeting everyone. The farmer interview morphed into a family interview with a panel of 'experts' on the side for follow-up questions. After all the dust settled, Nick and Rhett had ten guests, complete with a studio audience.

Jim Jr. did most of the talking, with his son Jimmy and Big Jim adding to the conversation. Granddaughter, oddly enough named Jamie, added to the banter and conversation. Not only was their interview packed with information that blew Rhett away, their rich history, extensive knowledge, and downright hilarious anecdotes genuinely entertained and impressed him. Beyond Grammy's vegetable garden, Rhett had never paid attention to where his food came from before tonight. The symbiotic nature of farming in America was more valuable than any other system in place, and Rhett had no idea. The men and women in this room literally kept the country running and fed.

Rhett felt as if he were taking a master class. His brain itched to take notes for follow-up show ideas. His head was ready to explode. He learned about the Netherland farmers who were rioting over government outreach and how, if that movement was unsuccessful, it would impact food scarcity and the farming landscape across the globe. Jimmy educated Rhett on regenerative farming and how beneficial it is for the environment, not only for conservation, but mostly to heal damage caused by pollutants and chemicals. While all farmers, especially those with livestock, are getting hit with climate regulations that would decimate the farming industry, family farms are actually designed to heal the earth, not harm it.

"Mr. Paulson, why would we purposefully harm the land that provides for our well-being and livelihood? Farmers are, by nature, nurturers and caretakers of the land. I can't speak for every farmer, but our family believes that we are stewards of the land God created. We feel called to this work. We aren't the ones harming the environment. The CAFOs, sorry, the Concentrated Animal Feeding Operations, are the ones who need regulated, not us. Their version of free range and grass fed is stuffing as many animals as possible in an enclosed pen with a grass carpet. Real farmers want those animals to do their jobs of eating, fertilizing, and roaming. Yet, the big pockets funding those impersonal corporations make sure they are exempt from these new environmental guidelines. The ones actually damaging the land with chemicals and mistreating the animals are the ones who get off unscathed while we are fighting for our lives in this political landscape." Jimmy's passionate montage had the entire gallery clapping, hooting, and hollering, which drove Jake to scan the "backstage" portion of the great-room with the camera.

"Speaking of this new political climate, we spoke off camera about some concerns the industry is facing beyond the regulations and guidelines you are navigating. Is there anything you would like to educate our viewers on concerning these issues?" Nick's question had Rhett turning his head. Where was Nick going with this? Was he trying to tie the information from the jump drive into the docuseries? Wouldn't that put them all at risk?

Jim Jr. sat up straighter on his tall bar stool. Big Jim sat back and crossed his arms, giving the nod to his son to answer. "I'm not sure we have enough time to cover all the issues." Jim Jr. had an ornery smile while the audience chuckled.

"I would encourage everyone to keep their eyes and ears opened so they don't believe everything they hear. Pay attention to where your food comes from and who is growing it. Support family farms who care about their land and their animals. Stop supporting the corporate farming industry. Most importantly, don't ignore headlines that involve farmers. Instead, read them and think critically. If fifteen thousand farmers in the Netherlands are protesting, find out why. If you keep hearing about food processing plants and food distribution centers burning down unexpectedly, follow the story. If tens of thousands of chickens and cows are dying unexpectedly, or if millions of pounds are soil are found to be contaminated, don't just blow it off and think it doesn't affect you. What happens on farms will always affect you at the grocery store. Soon, you are going to wonder why you can't find eggs and vegetables or why they are so expensive. Then maybe you'll wish you had paid more attention to the extremely rare disease the government used as an excuse to kill sixty percent of the chicken population. Some things can't be explained naturally or statistically. Pay attention."

Jimmy followed his dad as Big Jim watched proudly. "Granddad always told us to trust our gut and use a little bit of common sense. Who benefits from destroying the farming industry? Why over regulate the people providing food and closing farms while leaving corporations and factories intact? Or better yet, leave mass transportation systems alone but restricting a few tractors in wide open fields in the name of clean air. Which causes more harm to the environment concrete jungles or green pastureland? I can tell you, it's not us, but to me, that's common sense. Last, get to know the government officials in charge of food and agriculture. You know, the people in charge of making all decisions about your food who have no food experience at all? For example, the new food pyramid came out from the FDA. There are sugary cereals and over-processed foods labeled as healthier for you than an egg. An egg. Let that sink in. Common sense."

Big Jim broke in with a deep laugh. He proudly smacked Jimmy's back.

"I have a feeling there is a wealth of knowledge in Big Jim's laugh." Rhett responded. A chorus of mm-hmms and amens from the background followed. "I know this is a taboo question, but I have to ask. We're sitting here talking to your son, grandson, granddaughter, and a whole new generation of teenagers off to the sides already working the farm. Exactly how old are you, Big Jim, and how do I bottle your youth?"

More laughter followed Rhett's question.

Big Jim's smile owned his entire face. "No need to bottle anything. It's just common sense, like Jimmy said. I eat what God gives me to eat. I love Mama's vegetables. We have fresh cream, butter, and raw milk. Plenty of meat and potatoes. Eggs and bacon every morning, fresh pie for dessert every night. Hard work and sunshine. Friends, family, fresh air, and most importantly, my faith. I pray for rain, sun, and good crops. Some years we get those, some years we don't. In the years we don't, God always provided exactly what we needed. I wouldn't change a thing."

"I think you just described every doctor's worse nightmare. There are high cholesterol, diabetes, and skin cancer warnings on everything you just said. Yet, you look fifty and could probably outrun me on a good day." Rhett truly admired this man and the legacy that he built.

"For over five thousand years, people have been growing or bartering for their own food needs. They have treated their own ailments with herbs from the earth. They have taken care of their own and supported one another. People lived in communities. Nowadays, everything is 'global citizen' this and 'outsource' that. People on the television tell us what to eat, what to wear, and how to heal everything from cancer to headaches. We went from corner stores to box stores and eating from the earth to eating from a box. From what I understand, and I'm just an old man, but it seems to me that the more remote we get from the earth and each other, the more depressed, unhealthy, and dangerous the world gets. Those companies aren't making food, they're making products that are no better than the cardboard it's boxed in. The unhealthier people get, the more medicine they need. People are putting their trust in companies that make money from making and keeping them sick and dependent. Common sense tells me something is up. You want my youth serum? It's easy. Eat what you grow. Do honest work in the sun. Go to church."

"I think my friend Nick here has been following your lead. Apparently, I need to retire."

"Mr. Paulson, my dad won't retire until the good Lord calls him home." Jim Jr. aroused a final round of laughter from the room.

"Nick's wife probably feels the same." Rhett deadpanned.

"May I add one more thing?" Jamie waved her hand like she was waiting to be called on in school.

Nick smiled, "Please."

Jamie sat up straight and tall and looked directly into Jake's camera. "I see these climate change activists on TV destroying priceless works of art in museums, stopping traffic on major interstates, protesting everywhere and anywhere they can to cause a scene. They glue themselves to buildings. They even caused a massive crash during the Tour de France, seriously hurting cyclists, spectators, and first responders. I respect their right to protest and I understand their passion for the earth. My problem is with the knowledge base they are working from. If you ask them why they are protesting, they just shout words back at you they have been fed. They don't know any facts or statistics or even verify if what they hear is true. Spoiler alert, it's not."

Jimmy shook his head, but it was obvious he was proud of his sister. "Here we go."

Jamie nudged his arm. "The younger generation is passionate about the environment and that is a great thing. We all could learn from them. I'm angry because the celebrities, politicians, and so-called-experts are using fear to enrage and distract them from the actual issues. How can they believe those people ranting about carbon emissions while flying their private jets everywhere? Or buy beachfront property that, according to them, will be underwater in five years? I'd like to ask the protestors and experts where they buy their clothes. Do they exclusively shop local or support American-made products to reduce shipping contaminates? No. Does their food come from local farms or from giant grocery stores who pay other countries for their products? Do they realize that vilifying clean fossil fuel innovation only makes us energy dependent on other countries, which is actually way worse for the environment? And don't even get me started on how the batteries for electric vehicles are destroying ecosystems and starting wars around the world. These celebrity hypocrites have their armies of activists fighting the wrong things. They are the guilty ones, not us. So, please stop harassing us and vandalizing our land when we're the ones actually trying to repair the damage caused by the true environmental villains."

Nick nodded away as if he understood and agreed with everything she said. Rhett wasn't sure how far he wanted to go with this narrative. They would get crucified by the environmentalists when the docuseries aired.

"All I'm saying is that as humans, we have done our best to destroy the ecosystem God gave us, but it's not the farmers who have done it. We're the ones protecting it, yet no one, and I mean no one, is protecting us. Talk about biting the hand that feeds you."

After a moment of silence from Jamie's mic-drop, Nick thanked their panel and Big Jim for his hospitality. He also asked for the cornbread recipe, causing everyone to laugh one last time. As he closed the show, Rhett had so many more questions, but didn't even know what to ask.

When filming stopped, Big Jim's wife, Miss Maggie, approached Rhett. She was a tiny woman. Big Jim introduced her by reminding them that dynamite came in small packages. Rhett admired their affection for one another and the strong family legacy they had built together. After watching the group gathered tonight, it was clear how admired and loved Miss Maggie was to this family and the community. Rhett nodded at her, "Ma'am."

"Rhett, dear, Nick mentioned your Grammy is an herbalist, and I have this new tincture I'm testing. I would love her opinion. If you don't mind, would you give her my phone number so we could share remedies? Maybe we can swap some local foraged plants native to our states." Her smile was genuine and warm.

Rhett couldn't help but smile in response. "Grammy would love that, I'm sure. Thank you."

Jimmy walked over and wrapped an arm around his grandmother. The gesture warmed Rhett. "Is she telling you all about her weeds and how they can cure cancer?"

"My grandson teases me, but I'm the first one he calls when he has the sniffles." Miss Maggie poked his ribs, then went back to her guests.

"My Grammy and Miss Maggie have their healing plants in common. It sounds like you believe in it, too. I don't think I could go backwards and give up my medicine cabinet." Rhett softly laughed, not knowing what he believed anymore.

"Mr. Paulson, I read an article one time saying that the average thirty-year-old takes five to ten prescription drugs a day besides their ten over-the-counter drugs, yet the average life expectancy has decreased. My family has not needed an antibiotic, anti-depressant, anti-anything really with my grandmother's tinctures and teas and clean eating. God created us and He created the plants of the earth. Since the beginning of time, those plants have been used to heal us. I'd much rather trust the God who created the body, the cures, and the instruction manual. Food feeds and fuels us. The closer to the source you eat, you healthier you are. It's..."

"Common sense. You guys keep saying that." Rhett finished Jimmy's sentence, then rubbed his jaw.

"You look confused, Mr. Paulson, and a little skeptical about our methods." Jimmy's kind expression bordered on pity. Rhett didn't know if he felt relieved for the opening, or insulted.

"Here's what I tell students who visit the farm. Do you really believe cow farts are more dangerous than private jets? Cows have been farting for thousands of years. I don't remember reading about jets in the Bible. If you think any of this is accidental or coincidental, you are being lied to, not informed, or just plain dumb."

"Honestly, I'm still trying to process all of this information. The theme tonight focused on the attack on the American farmer. I just don't see it. Help me understand."

"I'm not sure what else I can tell you, but let me flip the narrative for you. The federal government can't pass laws against farmers because the politicians know they won't get reelected, so those in charge are backdooring policies through their unelected agencies. The FDA, EPA, and CDC have over-regulated the farming, hunting, and fishing industries to the point of strangulation under the umbrella of climate change. Follow the money. If these people really cared about the earth, their number one priority would be finding out why livestock and soil are being damaged and why tankers and trains are spilling chemicals and releasing toxic gas into the air at record rates. We're talking an increase is these events by over one thousand percent this year. Common sense tells me the only people who would benefit from the farming industry collapsing would be the people who would make money from selling bugs during a food crisis, if you know what I mean."

Rhett felt shivers down his spine. The dots continued to connect. The muddy water Nick talked about, the symposium, the list of daily talking points, Philipsen and Ford and their entwined foundations owning most of the land across the globe. The puzzle was still in pieces, but the complete image began to form, and it looked scary.

"I'm having trouble understanding these numbers that you're telling me when I haven't seen anything about it?"

"Mr. Paulson, that's really more a question for you, isn't it? We're not hiding it and it is definitely happening. I guess you'd need to ask who makes money from keeping it silent. Grandma always had a saying when we used to get in trouble. Jamie and I would both shout our sides of the story at her before she'd shush us. The truth doesn't have to shout because it knows it's right, but lies have to shout louder so it can hide the truth. Truth is always there, you just have to listen. Perhaps you haven't wanted to hear."

Chapter Thirty-Three

"Wake up, Madsi. Hayman is on his way to give us our marching orders for the day." Jackson knocked on the frame of Madison's bus cubby.

"Please tell me the interns are on their way with coffee. Can't handle Hayman without caffeine. Lots of caffeine." Madison croaked behind her wall of heavy curtains.

"They're on the way. Trust me, we all want you to have your coffee." Rich's voice carried from the front of the bus, along with the sound of his blender.

Madison pushed a lavender scented eye mask up to her forehead then rubbed sleep from her eyes. The brightness from her phone coming to life had her squinting at the screen. Forty-three texts, sixty-seven emails, eleven missed calls, and twenty reminders. Slow morning. She opened the only one she could deal with sans coffee, Rhett's. He'd been there for the past two days covering the convention speeches. He and Jake interviewed late into the night. They made it back to their hotel well past two in the morning. His text included a calendar link with his schedule for the day and asked for a "smooch date," eliciting a chuckle from her sleepy brain.

Madison flung open her fabric door and yelled into an empty corridor, "Dibs on the bathroom in two minutes! I mean it. I'm in no mood to fight you two divas this morning."

She tuned out their smart aleck responses and rolled over in the small space, trying to stretch out as much as the coffin would allow.

Madison: I might have actually gotten more sleep than you last night. Good interview?

Rhett: Informative interview.

Madison: Sounds interesting.

Rhett: Daniel Lyn will love it. LOL

Madison: I think that scares me a little.

Rhett: I'll give you the Cliff Notes version later. On my way to meet Rahemia. Breakfast meeting for show logistics, then another interview for Nick's project. Any time to meet today? I'll be inside the convention center all day. I'm guessing you'll be outside the perimeter?

Madison: Some sort of staging area is being set up in the blue parking lot near Gate D. I'll be in the tent all day, but I may have a window for lunch. I heard food trucks are scheduled for the rioters.

Rhett: You mean the supporters?

Madison: Didn't you get the memo? We've been instructed to call them rioters. Get your story straight, Paulson. LOL.

There was a pause. Madison waited for his response, but started to think he was either annoyed or made it to his destination.

Rhett: Right. The memo. The death of journalism and free speech. Gotta run. Just spotted Rahemia and she looks frazzled. See you later. Lunch is a go. Text me a time and place. Love you.

Madison: Love you.

She stared at his picture on her screen. If anyone would have told her she'd be this smitten over a guy she met a few months ago, a reporter, no less, she'd have laughed in their face. Their hectic work and travel schedules forced them to communicate on a level she'd never known was possible. Long phone calls at night when darkness inhibited the pretenses of normal social interactions. Texts and emails that grew raw and honest as their exhaustion deepened each day. She knew Rhett better than she knew most of her family members. She had bared her soul and welcomed the intrusion of his demons as well. The intimacy of their communication was something that equally scared and invigorated her.

Madison texted Hayman's assistant next for an ETA. The response made her groan. Ten minutes meant hair in a bun and a protein bar instead of a mediocre lukewarm shower and bagel. She rolled out of bed and hurried through her routine in record time. The interns arrived right before Hayman, causing Madison to chug half of her iced quad latte.

Hayman, Jackson, Rich, and Madison settled around the small table. Seven assorted assistants and interns crowded along the opposite wall, all armed with tablets and phones at the ready. Hayman walked them through the updated plan. A collection of senators and congressmen would assemble in the staging area. Outside of the tent, with the convention center in the background, would be a platform. Negotiations for standing positions were still ongoing, but that didn't involve Jackson, as he was one of the key speakers and current face of the party. The Capitol Police would form a human barrier from the protestors for effect.

Rich highlighted changes to Jackson's speech and press protocols for the event. His team scheduled Jackson for three interviews before lunch. Hayman added one in the afternoon from the bus, which was odd. Rich was not happy, but assured Hayman they would be ready. Madison needed to coordinate with White House staff on timing, so President Blythe could introduce Jackson and the rest of the delegation. The theme for the day would be patriotism versus treason. Jackson would affirm the talking points used throughout the convention media cycle. He would announce a special committee tasked with charging anyone connected to the convention as conspirators of treason. Followed by a call for decisive action from state legislators against participating state representatives.

"It is imperative we all stay close to the tent. Does everyone understand? There are too many moving parts today for any missteps. I need all of you alert." Hayman locked eyes with everyone on the tour bus.

"Are you worried about the protesters?"

"Madison, lack of preparation warrants worry. I never worry. I simply request that our team follow my preparations and follow accordingly today. Everyone will remain safe if they follow the rules."

Madison steeled her face so as not to betray her deep desire to jump across the table and throw her coffee in Hayman's face, but the coffee was too precious to her. "You normally don't concern yourself with our whereabouts. I didn't know if someone gave you information to warrant the extra preparation. You also don't typically keep half of the support staff back at the hotel and this group, including you, will head back after the interviews. Since only the three of us will remain on site with additional security and a fortified bus, I felt it prudent to inquire about the protestors."

"Madison, you needn't worry about a thing. I have it all under control. You will have plenty of time to meet your boyfriend at the soda shop, or whatever you kids do these days. Now, unless anyone has other questions, we have a packed schedule. Jackson, walk with me to my car." Hayman stood to leave as support staff scattered like startled mice.

As soon as the bus emptied, Rich handed Madison a toasted bagel. "Can you imagine being married to that guy? He grows more pompous every day."

"Thanks." Madison held up the bagel before taking a bite.

"All right, you boy-crazy-unprepared-questioning-irrational woman, let's get to work." Rich opened his laptop and sat next to Madison.

She rolled her eyes, then launched into her notes for the interview schedule. Hayman could sometimes be a great boss and mentor. When the four of them were alone and strategizing, Hayman encouraged and provided useful feedback. Audiences brought out the best in Jackson, the very worst in Hayman. Power was a drug, and Hayman was a junkie.

The morning rushed by in a blur. Madison stood by Rich as Jackson finished the third interview slot. Hayman left with the rest of the staff. Rich and Madison visibly relaxed at his departure. Madison's screen came to life with Rhett's face.

Rhett: Food trucks by Gate C. Is that good?

Madison: I'll meet you there, but can we eat on the bus? I need some quiet.

Rhett: I approve of quiet time with you. I only have press clearance for the convention, so you'll have to get me through the checkpoint perimeter.

Madison: Deal. Be there in five.

Madison leaned into Rich. "I'm going to grab us lunch and head back to the bus."

"You meeting Rhett?"

She nodded.

"Good, the whole protester angle is giving me the heebie-jeebies. Be careful and stay near the CPs."

"You and me both. Tell Jackson to tone down the campaign smile today. He's too cheery for this vibe."

"That's at the top of my list." Rich shook his head and focused on Jackson.

Madison's phone vibrated as soon as she left the tent. She answered without skipping a beat. "Tell me you aren't canceling our lunch date."

Rhett's deep laughter made her smile inside. "No way. It's getting crowded here and a little frenzied. The number of supporters doubled since this morning. I called to see if you wanted tacos or barbecue."

"Tacos, definitely. Can you get extra for Jackson and Rich? We're on our own today for lunch. The boys have become too accustomed to assistants and interns."

"I actually can appreciate that. Alright, I'll get food and meet you by the barricade near the bus."

"I have never been more excited about tacos in my life."

"I'm going to assume you are excited about seeing me and not just the food."

"Sure, you go with that," but the smile in her voice said otherwise.

"I'm next in line. I knew you would pick tacos. See you soon. Yeah, I would like the taco and burrito box and a bag of chips with queso." The call ended as his voice trailed off into the air.

Madison chatted with Capitol Police officers as she waited for Rhett. They arrived yesterday to set up the barricades, and would follow the buses transporting the representatives back to the airport. She felt more aware of the surroundings than the officers seemed to be.

As Madison watched for her lunch date, she noticed a black tent set up at the far end of the parking lot bordering the perimeter. "What's in that tent? Is it part of our group? It's awfully close to the perimeter." She attempted to not sound worried.

One of the National Guardsmen standing across the sidewalk shouted the answer when the Capitol Police just shrugged in response. "That's a Fascism Fighters triage tent. It's a fully functioning field hospital. Better quality than we had overseas. It follows them wherever they organize a 'peaceful protest'."

Madison didn't miss his sarcastic tone. "Why would they need that? Where are they even protesting? I haven't seen the FFs all morning,"

"You'd need to ask your friends there that question. We've been prepared for them all week. They've been recruiting on SurfIn." The Guardsman nodded towards the police standing beside Madison. They ignored him and her. "I'm guessing they need the tent because of the van that also follows the FF's. We call it the grocery store weapons van, but it's just as deadly as the weapons your buddies are carrying." At that, the soldier walked off to continue patrolling his section of the convention center.

Madison studied the large black tent and the medium-sized box trucks parked beside it. The Capitol Police started chatting about the weather today, like nothing happened. Not too hot and the rain had held off so far. Madison felt chills run up her arms. Something wasn't sitting right with this whole day. If the FFs were here, where was their patented black bloc uniform? Why did the Capitol Police allow them to park so close to the safety perimeter? And why did Hayman remove their entire team while ordering extra security for their tour bus?

"Lunch Delivery!" Rhett approached with two armfuls of food. Madison relaxed and ran out to help him. She placed a lanyard with credentials around his neck and a solid kiss on his lips, surprising them both with an uncharacteristic display of public affection. Rhett Paulson did things to her. He brought out something in her that felt right.

As soon as they made it to the bus, Rhett dropped the food on the table and gathered Madison into his arms. He kissed her like she was water and he was in the dessert. It was long, and it was passionate. She returned everything he gave. When they finally came up for air, all she could say was, "Wow."

Rhett smiled and rested his forehead against hers. "Hi."

"Hi, yourself."

"I missed you."

"I missed you too, Paulson."

"I really needed to see you. I'm glad our schedules cooperated for once."

Madison looked into his eyes. There was something there she hadn't seen before. "You okay?"

"I am, I think."

"That doesn't sound good. Should I be worried?"

"No. I just feel off my game. This project with Nick. Jake leaving the network next month and moving back home. This source that keeps putting me in danger. Grammy's revelations about my mom. Jerry's overreach into my show. This whole convention. I mean, come on, this is crazy, right? What will this mean? Another Civil War? I just feel like I'm walking on quicksand. And then I see you and I feel, I don't know, like I'm on solid ground again. Is that the least romantic thing to say to you? You feel like a solid rock?"

Madison placed her hands on his face. "Actually, that is incredibly romantic to me. I love that I make you feel secure. You make me feel lighter, so I guess we balance each other out."

Rhett sighed and relaxed his shoulders before kissing Madison softly. Wrapped in each other's arms, they stood there enjoying their cocoon of silence and solitude.

Madison didn't want it to end. For a few rare minutes, she was a girl, and he was her boyfriend and everything was possible. There was no election. No warring schedules. No near-death experiences. Just two people in love leaning on each other. It was a magical moment that swirled around them both, in a bus, in the middle of a parking lot in Kansas.

That was all they had. A moment that transported them from where they were to where they wanted to go.

And just like that, the click of a door broke their bliss. "Break it up, kids. Your chaperones have returned." Rich bellowed into the bus before climbing the stairs.

Rhett kissed her forehead and ended their embrace. "I hope everyone likes tacos."

"Paulson, you are my new best friend. I've been dying for a meal that doesn't involve rubber chicken." Rich slapped him on the back and opened the bag for a big whiff. "Oh, that smells so good!"

The four of them woofed down lunch. The only thing remaining were tortilla chip crumbs. They talked sports and complained about D.C. traffic. They teased Madison about her nutritious diet of quad lattes, snickerdoodles, and almond butter. Four friends escaping from work, until they couldn't.

Madison walked Rhett to the door as Jackson and Rich tried to busy themselves in the back of the bus. She draped her arms over his shoulders as he leaned down to kiss her goodbye. "Thank you."

He smiled, "For tacos?"

"Yes. And for more than tacos. Thank you for making me feel special and wanted. That sounded sadder and needier than I expected."

"Sad and needy are two words I would never use to describe you, Madison Lyn. You are strong and powerful and wicked smart. I am honored to be in your world."

"Always the sweet talker."

"Always the truth teller. Besides, I should thank you. You came out of nowhere and made me feel grounded. I haven't felt that since I left home." Rhett tucked a strand of hair behind her ear that had escaped her bun. "I have to go. They are taking the first round of votes in an hour."

"I know." Madison sighed in resignation. "Please, be careful. Something feels off out there."

Rhett flashed his winning smile. "Don't worry, I have nine lives, and I've only used up two this year."

"I'm serious, Rhett."

"I know. I'm sorry. I will be very careful." He stole one last kiss. "I love you."

"I never saw you coming, Rhett Paulson. I love you too."

Chapter Thirty-Four

"**I** hope your lunch date was worth it. You have ten minutes to find us before they lock the inner doors." Jake was obviously on the move, Rhett could hear heaving over the line as Jake lugged his equipment.

"It was. Thanks for asking." Rhett scrambled across the parking lot toward the convention center.

Jake grunted, "I'm serious. Ten minutes. Don't stop at the media booth, head straight to the door. Here's Nick."

Rahemia waved frantically as Rhett ran through the outer doors and past the bank of news crews. He shrugged and pointed to his phone. Rahemia's face told him exactly how she felt. She pointed to her left wrist, even though she wasn't wearing a watch. Rhett got the message. "Why am I passing Rahemia? She doesn't seem to approve."

"She will when she finds out Senator Marchio procured us passes for the inner chamber vote. Well, Jake and I have passes. You're still not here, Rhett."

Rhett grunted at Nick, "I'm coming. I'm coming. I see the door now. How will they know I have a pass?"

"Your name is on the list. Hurry." Nick hung up.

"Hurry," Rhett muttered to himself. As if he could run any faster right now. Did they expect him to slide through the doorway like it was home base? He hadn't made an entrance like that in years.

The state troopers who were guarding the entrance held up their hands and blocked the doorway as Rhett skidded to a stop and almost slid into them. "Hold up there, buddy. You got a pass?" It did not impress the tall one that Rhett was fighting to keep his balance.

"Rhett Paulson. I'm on the list."

The female trooper checked her phone, then nodded to affirm Rhett's statement. "Didn't your Mama teach you no running indoors?" She smiled. The tall trooper chuckled.

Rhett gave them a half-amused smile as he squeezed between the officers and headed inside the inner sanctum of this convention. Jake texted their location as Rhett weaved his way through the delegates walking to their assigned seats. Nick caught his eye, allowing Rhett to relax. He'd made it. Jake was helping another camera guy in the front of the room. They seemed to be coordinating efforts. That was an unforeseen development.

"What's going on up there? I thought they banned cameras. And why did I just blow off my producer?" Rhett dropped into the seat next to Nick.

"They're only allowing their own cameras in the room for the final votes. They want to control the information so that nothing gets leaked. Senator Marchio's request to include footage in our docuseries was approved by the Secession Committee at the last minute. Their crew is working with Jake to tie in his equipment."

"They banned all press from this, but you managed to get us inside the vote of the century." Rhett shook his head in awe. "Nick the magician at work again. Even Jerry will approve of this development."

"No, Rhett, *I* got invited. I had to sign, on my life no less, that *you* wouldn't do anything stupid as my guest. Don't make me regret that."

"I promise to be on my best behavior." Rhett laughed at Nick, who wearily shook his head.

The lights flickered over the grand ballroom as representatives from twenty-six states sat in front of the assembly. It was hard to believe that only six months ago, Attorney Generals from these states drafted a no-confidence statement to the United States government for not upholding the Constitution. The weight of what was about to happen fell heavy on the room. No one was asked to be silent. No one needed to be. No one called the room to order. They were present and aware as to the task before them. This was a solemn affair. The men and women in this room were balancing a political tightrope, with the entire world watching. Some believed they were committing treason. They wanted to defend the Constitution from the treasonous politicians currently in charge.

The world ate popcorn and watched it unfold. The greatest republic in the world had torn herself apart. When united, the country was a force for freedom and liberty. Divided, they crumbled. It didn't take a war or foreign attack on our soil. It was a slow weakening caused by cracks in the seams. The weight of which she couldn't bear any longer. America was far removed from her founding. Scars and bruises marred Lady Liberty beyond recognition. The representatives in this room felt every ounce of weight on their shoulders. And the aftershocks would cause momentous shifts throughout the world.

Jake returned to his seat and exhaled. He looked at Rhett and Nick with solemnity. He pulled out his laptop to control and monitor his equipment. Nick patted him on the back as the clerk began taking the roll call. This would be a slow process.

"Why did they push out the press for the vote? Doesn't that sound shady to you? They let us cover the speeches, but not the votes." Rhett leaned into Nick's shoulder.

"The vote is being livestreamed. Marchio said they didn't want a three-ringed circus marring the gravity of the occasion. They wanted the vote treated with the reverence it deserved." Nick turned to Rhett. "Contrary to your jaded beliefs, these delegates understand the somberness of this event. This is not some political stunt."

Rhett didn't respond. He wasn't about to get into yet another political debate with Nick. How did it come to this? Nick was his mentor. Everything Rhett did in his professional life was shaped and molded by Nick's example and guidance. Nick seemed to grow more frustrated with Rhett each day. It was reminding him of Grammy's arguments. They both knew how Rhett felt about God, yet they both were adamant that Rhett needed to make a one-eighty on his opinion of God and faith. It was getting ridiculous.

The three of them watched as the roll call continued with each Attorney General and Governor affirming their presence and authority to vote on behalf of their respective state. Thirty minutes later, the clerk announced a brief recess, but reminded everyone the doors would remain locked. After a pounding of the gavel, the time had finally come. One by one, each group of state representatives stood together as the governor called out a 'yay' or 'nay' vote of no-confidence in the current government. The electricity in the air crackled with each response. When the last vote was spoken into the air, an eerie hush enveloped the room. A weighted silence swirled around everyone like the wind that preceded a hurricane.

The gavel struck the podium, and they moved into the next segment of the convention, the vote to form a new government. It too passed. The Allied States of America was formed in a Kansas convention center. A lone whistle and cheer was quickly drowned out by the reverential stillness and stares of the body.

The third vote was to adopt the document the representatives had been drafting for months. A vote of confidence for the Constitution and a series of resolutions that would disentangle the current structure of big government back to the original intent of a government by the people. The third vote proceeded as the others did. Unified assent verified by each governor's vote of 'Yay' on the respective items.

As the final gavel landed, a piercing alarm followed it. The quietness had been felt so heavily in the room that this new and loud warning jarred their senses. Fear and confusion quickly replaced the somberness. National Guardsmen burst through the doorways and barked orders like they were on a battlefield. The delegates were being directed to follow the soldiers into an enclosed space underground while they secured the building. A tunnel exit would get them safely to buses waiting to extract the assembly when it was safe. Nick ran to help Jake retrieve the equipment, not wanting to lose this piece of history.

Rhett turned to Nick. "I need to cover this. I have to find Rahemia."

The knowing look in Nick's eyes confirmed Rhett's desire to share the truth. Exposing lies is what pushed Rhett into journalism. It was his greatest need, but it never soothed the ache. It was only a band-aid. Now, he didn't know the truth from the lies. They both knew he would keep searching until he found it. "I know. Be careful." Nick's words were laced with concern.

Rhett forced his body through the doors against the fervent protest of the Guardsmen. He scurried back to the press corridor to find the area already evacuated. He checked his phone. Rahemia had texted him thirty minutes ago telling him that the press was being moved outside to a designated area for their safety. They were cordoned off from the action, but were able to get great footage. He ran to her coordinates. Sure enough, they were untouched by the melee, sectioned off from the protestors swarming the building. Rhett watched as every news crew covered the catastrophe. WBN was already live, as were all the rest. He felt everything spinning. Was it his surroundings spinning or his body? The world had flipped upside down in the span of five minutes. The atmosphere felt charged and dangerous. It was the antithesis of the exercise he just left inside the building. The reverential cocoon had popped.

Something wasn't right. All week, the supporters were outside tailgating and chanting. The votes passed. Why would they storm the building now?

In the corner of his eye, a movement caught his attention. The tent and stage from before the vote was rippling in the wind. His brain struggled to piece it together. Madison. Rhett ran towards the barricaded area they quarantined her in today. His legs couldn't work fast enough. He had to find her. He had to find the truth. He ran. As he approached the area, he realized the bus was gone, and they had already evacuated the tent. Of course. Jackson would be the first person secured. Relief flooded Rhett. Madison was safe.

As he turned back to find Jake and Nick, a bright light and loud sound knocked him off his feet. An explosion. Debris from the tent flew in every direction, like shrapnel. Rhett hit the ground hard. Darkness surrounded him. Then silence.

Chapter Thirty-Five

She hummed a lullaby. Something about stolen kiddie cars and busy days. She had a beautiful voice. It was silky and ethereal. He felt her next to him in his bed. She smelled of vanilla and sunshine. Her fingers ran through his hair. Softly letting each strand fall back to his face. Rhett felt warm and happy.

"Mommy."

"I'm here, sweetheart. You're such a big boy now."

A tear splashed on Rhett's sleepy face. He wrapped his arms tightly around her. His own tears barely restrained behind his tiny eyelids.

"Are you staying?"

"No, baby. I'm not. I'm so sorry, but I have to leave again. This will be the last time. I promise. Grammy will take care of you. Be my big, strong boy, okay?" She brushed her lips across the top of his head and pulled him to her. Then she was gone.

Rhett reached out, grasping at the empty air. He tossed and turned. Pictures of his mother flooded his mind. Grammy's front porch came into view next. He was playing on the steps with plastic army men Gramps had found in the attic. Grammy, crying. She sat beside him and held him tight. Mommy wasn't coming home, but she was in Heaven with Jesus, so we would see her again. A closed coffin covered in white roses. The room was fuzzy, and the voices muffled. The same church people who ran her off were there with tears and casseroles. Grammy forgave. Rhett didn't.

A pulpit with a hypocrite behind it. A soft-spoken chaplain came to the house with Mommy's things. Grammy hugged him tightly and thanked God for him. Mommy wore a white robe. She hugged Jesus. She was crying, but they were joyful tears. Rhett could feel it. Rhett was writhing around in pain. He was hot, so hot. He felt drenched and sticky. Mommy disappeared again. He heard a voice. It was calm and peaceful. Quiet, yet filled with all authority, *"I Am the truth, seek Me."*

More silence. Rhett saw nothing but the darkness of his eyelids. Slowly, he opened them. A crack of light burned as he tried to allow in more light. He heard voices. Someone was getting water. Another, Jake maybe, calling Grammy. There was a heavy blanket on him. Too hot.

A cold washcloth on his forehead. He tried harder to open his eyes. A halo narrowed in as his vision adjusted to the light. A familiar face smiled down at him. Miriam.

"You had me worried, Rhett." She squeezed his shoulder as she smiled. "No, don't try to sit up now. Get your bearings first. You were pretty banged up, so it's going to hurt."

Miriam's voice was soothing. Rhett tried to remember. "I needed to see for myself. I needed to know. Madison." Panic raised his voice.

"Oh, Honey. She's fine. Madison is fine. She called Jake when she didn't hear from you. She's safe. They're on the bus surrounded by secret service." Miriam smoothed Rhett's hair. "Does anything hurt?"

"Everything." Rhett didn't recognize the gravelly voice that came from his mouth. His throat felt raw, like he'd swallowed broken glass. "Water?"

"Nick, help me get him up a little." Miriam pushed a pillow behind Rhett's head. She gently placed a glass of water to his lips. "Just a sip."

"What happened?" He drank a little before dropping his head back down. Rhett winced as pain shot through his shoulder and elbow.

"Take it easy. Your body looks like a crash test dummy." Nick's firm hold steadied Rhett as he strained to find any resemblance of comfort.

"How bad is it?" Rhett had so many questions. His brain couldn't keep up with them.

"Someone set off a series of pipe bombs around the staging tent where Jackson and his colleagues spoke. You seemed to be the only one who didn't get the memo. The entire boundary was cleared out in plenty of time. Well, that is, until you ran in. But, in typical charmed Rhett Paulson fashion, you survived an explosion almost unscathed. They rigged the tent to spray shrapnel all over the parking lot. The blast blew you into a pile of garbage bags, instead of concrete. A metal chair landed on your chest and right shoulder. From what we can tell, your arm is fine thanks to the cast, but you may have cracked a rib or two, and they stitched up a gash along your chin." Nick sat on the coffee table next to Rhett.

They were in a hotel suite, not a hospital. It wasn't his room. Where were they?

As usual, Nick read his mind. "We don't know the extent of the attack. It wasn't safe taking you to a hospital. The Guard medics evaluated and treated you as best they could and helped us transport you here. We're in Senator Marchio's suite."

"How?"

Nick shook his head. "You won't like the answer."

Rhett groaned, "Just tell me."

"John felt a stirring. He kept hearing God tell him to come find you. He talked a Guardsman into letting his detail pick us up and swing around to look for you instead of getting on the delegate buses. Out of all the places you could have been, he knew exactly where to find you. It was nothing short of miraculous."

Rhett shivered as he settled back into the cushions. He was silent.

"Wow, you didn't protest. That's a start." Nick rubbed his chin and stared at Rhett.

"Nicholas, leave the boy alone. We have plenty of time to hash out everything. Let him process and rest." Miriam sat on a chair next to his side.

Rhett replayed the broken memories from today, struggling to see clearly. The others paced the room, talking in circles. He fell in and out of sleep, only to be awakened by whoever was on Rhett concussion duty. Jake rotated calling Alexis, Grammy, and Madison. Miriam and Mrs. Marchio sat in a corner on their phones, updating their children. Nick and John sat over a table, mapping out what they saw throughout the day, and fielding intel coming in on their phones. At one point, they left to meet with members of their patriot-spy-team in a makeshift command center in the hotel. Rhett needed to investigate that.

Rhett spoke with Grammy, who yelled at him for his recklessness. Then he spoke with Madison, who yelled at him for his recklessness. He allowed an EMT from the National Guard to check his injuries, who then lectured Rhett for his recklessness. The shower helped erase some of the fog. He refused any more pain medication so he could clear his head. Food made him steadier on his feet, but his chin made it hard to chew. The cracked ribs, broken arm, residual concussion symptoms, and mending gun-shot wound weren't helping matters either.

Rhett moved slow the rest of the day into the evening. He watched and listened to all the conversations, but he didn't speak. He processed information as he heard it and balanced it against what he knew. His journalism professor admired Rhett's ability to be skeptical and analyze information, yet never letting his jovial humor slip. Today, Rhett was only critical. He was a sponge for every puzzle piece he could get. He was determined to solve this puzzle. He had had enough.

"I have the link." Jake carried a laptop to the television and hooked up cables.

"Is this the feed Benson's guy sent?" Nick sat in the closest chair.

"What are we watching? Do I need popcorn?" Rhett held the ribs on his right side.

"A server has been set up online for people with any footage from today to upload it. Every social media platform has already started deleting videos and freezing the accounts of supporters. Some people are also being locked out of their phones. We need to secure any evidence we can before it all goes away. Benson's team has been filtering and storing it all week for prosperity and protection. These are the clips they sent for John to share with the assembly tonight." Nick had a notepad. It reminded Rhett of his early days watching his mentor.

"The assembly is meeting again?" Panic filled Rhett. For the first time since the explosion, he thought about his show. "I need to call Rahemia!"

"Bro, you missed your show hours ago. Jerry and Rahemia made the call today to extend Sally's coverage. They want live footage of the investigation outside the arena. Your accident is all over the news. They're using you as the poster child for this 'terrorist attack.' Jerry loves it. It forced every network news channel to give you air time." Jake looked at Rhett. "It's all taken care of. Let it go for tonight."

Rhett strained to relax on the couch. The thought of Jerry carried bile to Rhett's throat. The man was exactly what Rhett hated his entire life, but he didn't see it until now. Each year at WBN Rhett gave Jerry even more leverage and power, while Rhett retained less and less of both. He spent his life seeking the truth and exposing the lies and hypocrisy he found along the way. He reveled taking down the pious people who looked down on his family. Rhett threw boulders at their glass houses. Now, he realized he was one of them, living and hiding behind his own glass walls. Instead of exposing them, he helped them build new and improved ones with bulletproof glass.

"Wait, stop!" Rhett shot up and flinched, gasping at the pain. "Jake, can you zoom in on the far right corner?"

"I don't have much to work with but I can try." Jake clicked and zoomed, scrolled and isolated.

"Those two guys. The ones in the American flag pants. There is something about them. Can we follow them to find a better angle?" Rhett moved to sit on the arm of Nick's chair.

Jake minimized the video and opened another file. "I have one from another angle. Let me find it." After a few minutes, "Here it is, this is from that reporter who follows the FF's. He has extensive footage of their movements throughout the day. Sidebar, why doesn't anyone talk about the FFs? This guy has enough evidence on their organization throughout the years to have them all tried as terrorists. They are crazy scary." Jake spoke the last part to himself more than the room.

"Because they are on the payroll of the one-world-order-cabal. The very people who want to destabilize governments around the world fund them. They will never be arrested. Believe me, I've tried." John growled, uncharacteristically.

"There! Jake, those two guys are the FBI agents who questioned us after the parking garage. Aren't they? They're the investigators assigned to my case."

"Holy...." Jake's words trailed off. "Who are they talking to?" Jake clicked and switched angles. "I wish I had better equipment for this," he grumbled.

"No way. No freaking way." Jake rubbed his head and sat back in his chair. "Rhett, that guy they're talking to is the guy I saw walking out of your place the night of the attack. The police had their sketch artist sit with me. That's the guy. He evaded all the cameras, but I opened the door for him as he walked out that night."

"Why? Why would any of them be talking to each other? And why are they talking in Kansas two hours before the explosion and riot?" Rhett scanned the room, asking anyone to help him figure out this development.

Nick and John had an entire conversation without speaking a word to the room. John finally explained, but it only opened up more questions. "The man they are talking to is Adam Ford's head of security."

"What? Why would Adam Ford break into my house for a jump drive on farming and food shortage intel? How would he even know I had it?"

Nick began pacing. Rhett had watched him do this for years. Nick was breaking the case, like his favorite TV lawyer he watched as a child. "Did you tell Jerry about the jump drive? Ask him if you could cover the story about the food shortages?"

"Yes, Rahemia called him when we landed. But I wanted to cover the Johan Philipsen angle. This had nothing to do with Adam Ford. Philipsen is tied to the food distribution centers and hosted the symposium. Jerry killed the story and told me to drop it, but I can't drop it. That guy is up to something. The coincidences between him and the food shortages are too much to ignore."

"You have no idea." John Marchio grabbed the notepad from Nick's hand and walked to the dining table. He started making a diagram. In the center circle he wrote "Symposium." "Did you know Adam Ford is the largest landholder per acreage in North America, followed by China? My colleagues in the farmland states have been tracking this for years. We have attempted to bring him before congress to question him, but haven't been able to get enough votes to carry it out."

"I understand why China would want to buy to land, sort of, but why does a tech giant need that much farm land?" Rhett watched as John continued drawing lines and circles on his crazy diagram.

"Why indeed." John continued adding circles, scratching names inside each one, and connecting them with lines.

Nick jumped in and pointed to the Adam Ford circle. "Don't forget the research grants he's shelling out for weather control experiments. I have a source on the ground who confirmed Ford has already executed some unethical experiments in North Dakota with rain clouds."

"Over here we have the 'Big Five Pharmas'. According to their presentation at the symposium, they have patents pending for supplements that will sustain the global population during the projected food crisis. They presented a pamphlet at the symposium about which supplements would pair well with different bugs based on regions and preferences across the globe. Big Food is over here with their entomology and recycled waste patents. Both groups are working with the Philipsen Foundation, Theopolis's Global Society Foundation, and the SurfIn Collaboration."

"Come on, Senator. You can't believe the masses are going to eat bugs paired with pills because some rich guys tell them to?" Rhett laughed at the thought.

"You would be surprised at what the masses will do and believe when people in authority and their favorite celebrity tell them to do it." Nick sighed.

"Besides, they will only hear what *some rich guys* allow them to hear. Bluesky and Vandergrift have riders written into their investment contracts, preventing any company or individual from speaking out against their other investors. When you are the only investment game in town and run ninety-five percent of the market, you can control the narrative. It would be financial suicide to speak out against any of these groups. Don't forget, eighty percent of every network, newspaper, and online market receive billions of dollars from big pharma. What they miss, SurfIn and Adam Form kill on the internet and social media. No one is saying a word. Bluesky and Vandergrift Investors run America. What they can't control, the Unified Strategies Commission is at the ready to silence and spin the messaging. Meet the government's propaganda machine regulated by the Global Media Board of Governors." John drew more lines connecting the circles.

"The rich get richer." Jake looked angry. Jake never got angry. "We're getting off track. The question at hand is why Adam Ford's head of security is meeting with two FBI agents hours before the attack on the convention center and a bombing that targeted United States Representatives. And why they will risk killing Rhett to do it?"

"And why they are wearing those awful pants? Isn't there a 'Men in Black' costume rule for the FBI?" Rhett's attempt at joking fell flat. They all looked at him as if he were crazy. He felt crazy and completely off-kilter. Jake should be making bad jokes while Rhett asked serious questions. His world was upside down.

John ignored Rhett's joke about pants. He continued writing and explaining. "We are fighting a revolution the American people didn't know was waged. We weren't invaded by soldiers on the ground or air raids from wars past. Media outlets and Internet platforms were the battleground. The concept of global egalitarianism sounds like a wonderful utopia. They promise freedom, equity, and protection, and they will use their food provisions to show humanitarianism and global leadership. Meanwhile, their war strategy is the same as every other greedy leader in history. State a problem. In this case, they actually created the problem. Then, they offer solutions to the problem, gaslight the people, silence the enemy, and rule their subjects through fear and intimidation. The endgame is still the same. Amass more land, more power, and more money while limiting the rights and voices of the people. 'The rich *do* get richer,' Jake."

Nick piped in, "Democracy may not be perfect, but its purpose is to give power to the people, not to tyrants."

John finished his diagram. It looked more like a wagon wheel with an inverted triangle inside, instead of the haphazard design Rhett envisioned in the beginning.

John started at the top and circled back to the center spoke. "I think we have our answer. We have tied Ford, Philipsen, and Marduk to the Symposium, food shortages, and projected solutions to the food crisis. Ford is a population control guy. Philipsen has preached for decades that whoever controls the food owns the world. His organization has also trained most of the world's leaders through his Accelerate Project. In the seventies, Marduk's grandfather wrote a mission statement for their endowment, proclaiming Darwinism should help rid the world of unworthy parasitic peoples and nations. Omar Marduk also holds the

AI patents that will control the distribution sites and smart cities. These three have positioned themselves to be in control of the resources needed to save the world from a food crisis they created, while simultaneously preventing people from providing for themselves. They have the ear of governments around the globe who are beholden to them. The cherry on top is having an unending bankroll and an army of militant militia funded by Theopolis at their fingertips. They create the need, they provide the solution, they run the show."

All four men stared at the picture. All the pieces came together. Jake rubbed his chin, then dropped into the nearest chair. Nick walked away and gulped his water.

"Wait. This is absurd! Can we all admit this is crazy-town? What you are hypothesizing is preposterous!" Rhett looked around the room at them, hoping someone would speak reason.

"Am I?" John looked ready for a fight.

"Yes, governments aren't going to give up their power to four men. They especially won't when they realize these people are creating a global food crisis!"

"You'd be surprised at what people will do for a piece of the pie. It was enough to cause the secession vote, wasn't it?" John tapped his pen on the notepad. "You are complicit, Rhett. Every time you push their narrative without the counterargument, you have fired a bullet at the American Constitution. Yes, the secession vote is revolutionary, but I can assure you, it was a defensive move, not an offensive one. If you don't see that now, then you are just as guilty as they are."

"What?" He scanned the room. Neither Nick nor Jake defended him. Rhett felt kicked in the gut.

"Have you stopped and asked yourself why the most patriotic, conservative states in the country would separate from their greatest pride? Most of Washington is on the payroll or a beneficiary of these people and their coffers. Democrats, Republicans, party affiliation is only for the talking points. The government officials who are supposed to protect us are all bought and paid for operatives. Weak men and women sold us down their muddy river. Fake board positions, stock shares, insider tips, family jobs, you name it. The powerful are finding the loopholes and getting paid for it. They fill every government agency with 'civil servants' who either came from one of these companies or will return to them. Our government was founded to prevent the tyranny of a crown, only to be replaced by the tyranny of the purse. We aren't governed by local representatives anymore. Privatized Communism is our master. I'm embarrassed to be a United States Senator. That's why we are doing what we are doing. Not for a political stunt, but to save our country from outside influences."

John was right, Rhett knew it. He had followed along like everyone else. He believed he was on the right side and fighting for truth, but he was duped like the rest. He fell for the lies Daniel Lyn spoke about. "Do you think it will work? How will the Allied States be different?" A strange feeling came over Rhett. He hadn't felt it in years. Hope.

John's face softened, but held all the resolve he'd shown throughout his career. He was a natural leader. "When America entered World War II, they said the Japanese had awakened the sleeping giant. It turns out that America slept while the enemy crept in, bought our land, bought our schools, bought our entertainment, and bought our leaders. We are no longer a feared giant. We are a weak shell of ourselves. We used to be the world's beacon for freedom. Now we are chaff to be swept away by shifting sands to the highest bidder. Today, some brave people stood in the gap and said, no more. Not on my watch. I am proud and saddened by today's events, but I will not back down from bullies, and I will not sit by and watch America fall."

John looked directly at Rhett. "The only unexpected hitch in their plan was you. You ever heard the story of Esther in the Bible?"

Rhett nodded his head. He remembered Grammy telling him all the stories as a child. They were nothing more than fairytales.

"Well, you certainly aren't the prettiest maiden in the land, but you may have a Divine appointment." John tapped the table. "Nick, I'll be in touch. I'm heading to the meeting. We have a new government to form, or rather an old government that needs brought back to the basics."

Chapter Thirty-Six

The tour bus drove through the night. No one slept. Rich and Madison sat around the small table attempting to work, but the melee in Kansas consumed their thoughts. Jackson did a lot of pacing and sitting. It looked like the weight of the world was on his shoulders. Soon it would be. He contemplated the aftermath of both the secession vote and the massacre.

Their frayed nerves began as soon as the Capitol Police cleared the barricaded area directly after the delegate speech. Jackson asked to stay until the voting finished, but his security detail insisted he get on the bus. As the occupants of the tent dispersed, Madison watched as news crews slowly filtered out of the convention center into a roped off area on the sidewalk. She couldn't see Rhett or Jake near the WBN signs.

By the time the bus hit the interstate, calls poured in, checking on them. That's when they turned on the televisions and saw the rioters destroying the convention center. Madison texted and called Rhett non-stop. The silence knotted her stomach, causing her to struggle for breath. When she finally reached Jake, the concern in his voice made it worse. He kept her up to date until Rhett regained consciousness. Relief flooded her when he called her himself. She felt better yelling at him for coming to look for her in the chaos, even if it was sweet.

Around midnight, they stopped at a gas station outside of Columbus, Ohio. A travel soccer team and their parents asked for pictures with Jackson. He flashed his famous campaign smile and encouraged the kids to follow their dreams by working hard and getting involved. Rich flirted with the single moms. A few parents asked about the massacre. That's what the news had been calling it. Jackson shook his head and promised things would be better under his watch. The interaction fueled Jackson, but Madison still observed the strain on his face.

Hayman scheduled strategy meetings first thing in the morning, giving them a few hours to sleep and regroup. The bus delivered the Jackson Cashe Trio to their townhouse as the sun rose over Washington, D.C. Sunrise showcased an otherworldly glow of reds, oranges, pinks, and purples over the city. Daniel Lyn had a saying about red skies in the morning. Madison didn't take the warning lightly, but it was definitely breathtaking. She braced for war today.

By the time the three of them had showered, prepped, and eaten breakfast, they were fortified and ready for the day. Madison felt the nervous jitters of campaign workers as soon as they entered headquarters. Jackson naturally broke the tension with his charm, followed by Rich and his jokes. Madison was all business, but smiled to put everyone at ease. This would be another day to tackle.

Rhett checked in with her throughout the night and morning. He had plenty of jokes about being hit by a bus and trying out his own live action stunt show. Madison was not amused. Jake told her the extent of Rhett's injuries, so she knew he was hurting. Rhett kept telling her he was fine, but she could hear the concern and pain in his voice, no matter how hard he tried to hide it with deflection and humor. She imagined that is how he escaped his inner demons from childhood unscathed. The man had depths he didn't even realize, and Madison wanted to explore them all with him.

Despite every objection, Rhett was determined to head back to the Secession Convention today with Nick and Jake. The meetings remained closed to the public, but Senator Marchio had them on the approved guest list. According to Jackson's Secret Service detail, the rioters were long gone, but Madison was still worried.

An intern delivered coffee just as Hayman erupted through the front door, barking orders. Everyone fell in line, including Jackson and Rich. The four of them sat around the conference table with their assistants.

"New talking points have been emailed to each of you. We need to work on answers for Jackson's media blitz, which will start this afternoon. I have arranged for him to hit shows across the five major networks over the next

48 hours. We have advanced questions, so Rich, your focus will be polishing various responses. Madison, we need your boyfriend for an exclusive interview on Monday night. He still owns the ratings despite his recent absences due to his unfortunate series of accidents. Jerry says he's still in Kansas. We need you to coax him back to D.C. to interview Jackson."

Madison refused to let Hayman ruffle her feathers today. She needed to focus on her job. Rhett was fine and should be back soon. At least she knew she would see him in a few days for the interview. Hayman continued on about the media strategy the party had planned and how the White House would deal with the treason plot. The FBI would be raiding the houses of protesters this week and making arrests. The DOJ opened an investigation of treason charges for the state leaders who took part in the secession vote. Hayman dismissed the assistants and launched into strategy.

"President Blythe requested Jackson for a strategy meeting. The two of us will head over around eleven. Rich, you have plenty to keep you busy with the talking points. Madison, I need you to coordinate with the Philipsen Foundation and Omar Marduk's office. Johan arranged a livestreamed panel discussion for Accelerate Project leaders to address the food distribution centers and how they could help nations during any potential food crisis. The Global Wellness Organization has been monitoring an insect infestation traveling across Europe, wiping out wheat crops and killing bees. Stay on top of that story because we may need to tie it into the scheduled interviews if this secession nonsense can't be contained. Anything else? No? Good. Let's get to work." Hayman left as quickly as he arrived.

Madison spent her morning on the phone with three separate polling companies. Her favorite was this female duo from California. They had the pulse on the public and knew what Madison needed before she did. Annie threw in some questions about the secession that Hayman would flip his lid over, but Madison agreed Jackson should know. Rich offered to go pick up lunch with the flirtier two of the interns. Madison gave him a warning look, but ordered a salad anyway.

Daniel Lyn had been calling every hour on the dot to check on Madison. She looked down at her watch, right on the nose.

"Daddy, at some point, you're going to have to teach class and stop calling me."

"Who said I'm not in class now?"

"Daddy, you wouldn't?" Madison hoped she wasn't on speaker.

"Calm down, Little Button. I'm only teasing you. They have canceled classes today. The faculty was concerned yesterday's events might *trigger* the students." Daniel followed his last statement with muffled grunting, "Weak ninnies."

"Daddy, I think calling your students ninnies might be frowned upon on campus."

"Well, they are. Kids today could never survive a war or a depression. There was mass chaos last week when the froyo machine was being repaired. But I digress. That is not why I am calling you. I have news."

"And here I thought you were still checking on my wellbeing every hour."

"I am. You're just lucky the news coincided with my hourly call, or you would have received two calls this hour."

"Ok Daddy, what is this big news?" Madison opened an email and started scanning while her father cleared his throat.

"Well, I wanted to let you know we are moving."

Madison froze. "I'm sorry. Did you just say you are moving?"

"Yes, Button, I did. Your mother and I negotiated a package deal with a university in Alabama. The good news is that we will be closer to you in D.C., but we will be living in another country." Daniel Lyn laughed at his own joke.

"Daddy, that joke isn't even funny. There is no way that farce of a vote is legitimate. States cannot just separate from the Union. The DOJ is going to charge them all with treason." Madison reclined in her desk chair.

"Sweetheart, I'm not sure where you are getting your information, but the Allied States of America just delivered a Declaration of Independence, well they basically just delivered the same Declaration of Independence from 1776 with a few updates. It was actually quite clever of them to use the same document."

"Daddy! Focus. What are you talking about?"

"The newly appointed president of the Allied States of America just had a document entitled the Declaration of Independence delivered to the President of the United States and the United Nations. Over one hundred delegates signed the Declaration. It included the names of military and government officials who support the new government."

"They can't do that. You can't just declare your independence from the United States. That's insane." Madison walked to the door and waved over interns.

"Honey, they have seventy percent of the military and the lion's share of the money based on the states leaving. Most democrat run states are in the red and dropping in population by the tens of thousands. They can do it because they have all the ammunition and funding. If you want my personal opinion, the US would be crazy to fight it. The only thing they have going for them are a paid-for-militia of rioters and a bunch of self-entitled, over-privileged, weak-minded ninnies who get triggered over froyo."

"Not the time, Daddy."

"Well, they are. I'm assuming you need to get off the phone now? You probably have three interns surrounding you with tablets and notepads."

"Four, actually. I love you, Daddy. Bye."

Madison hung up the phone and started barking her own set of orders as interns scattered. "Someone get Rich back here, now! And I need Hayman's assistant on the phone, pronto."

Madison had so much to do, she didn't even know where to start. Ashleigh, her favorite intern, grabbed all the remotes and began turning on the TVs lining the far wall. Not one station was talking about the Declaration being issued. The screens were covered with video footage from yesterday's massacre. Did they not know? Was this not public knowledge yet? Madison needed a source other than her dad. She knew exactly where to find one.

Madison: Are you still in Kansas?

Rhett: Yes. It is crazy.

Madison: What is the status of everything? My dad just called and told me the convention officially assembled into a government and issued a Declaration of Independence, but none of the media outlets are covering it.

Rhett: As usual, Daniel Lyn is correct. Official couriers delivered the Declaration to Blythe an hour ago, followed by the delivery to the United Nations. They sent out press releases with a copy and included all documentation to every media outlet. WBN won't use any of Jake's footage. I've been summoned back to D.C. by Jerry. I'm heading back tonight.

Madison: The United States won't accept it.

Rhett: I don't think they have a choice. They have no state money to work with and a decimated military. It's brilliant. They actually used the original Declaration of Independence LOL.

Madison: You sound like my dad.

Rhett: Thank you. I take that as a great compliment.

Madison: What does this all mean?

Rhett: You tell me. Jackson will be running it soon. The Republican candidate is from Oklahoma and she just rescinded her candidacy to accept the appointment as President of the Allied States of America. I have to run. I'll forward you the press release and documents. Love you.

Madison: Please be careful. Love you too.

Madison dropped the phone on the table and looked around at the many young faces watching her. They were so impressionable and passionate. She would be the leader they needed. Madison took a deep breath, centered herself, and went into crisis management mode. She started pointing. "You, I need a copy of the Constitution. You get me an expert on Constitutional law. You get more coffee. A lot more coffee. Ashleigh, find me a list of states and their representatives who voted in favor of secession. Ooh, I also need copies of their state constitutions to make sure they didn't violate their own laws. All right, people, move! We have a lot of ground to cover!" Madison clapped her hands together and watched as her team ran off to complete tasks.

The television screens still covered the rioters only. Not one channel covered the secession vote. Madison pounded the table lightly. Confounded by the lack of information she needed. Surely the press knew by now. She had a thought, then shook her head and let out a groan.

Madison yelled into the open office space, "I need every available laptop, tablet, and phone. We need to scour those conspiracy news channels to see what they're saying." Everyone seemed to freeze and look at her as if she had just told them all to jump off the Francis Scott Key Bridge. "I know, I know. But we need to know what is being said about this vote. They might be the only ones covering it right now."

Madison's phone lit up with a notification that Rhett had emailed her an attachment. She pulled up the documents on her laptop and began reading. For a hot minute, it took her back to studying for finals in law school. She read, annotated, jotted research notes, and read again. Slowly but surely, the interns found plenty of the secession coverage on the conservative outlets. None of the major networks even had it on their tickers.

Ashleigh monitored the interns, who monitored the coverage. They fed Ashleigh information. She filtered it and summarized the highlights for Madison, all while farming out Madison's research questions to other interns. Madison made a mental note to pay Ashleigh more money.

By the time Jackson arrived back at headquarters, Madison had an entire report ready to brief him. Rich had a PR response planned for Jackson's approval. Jackson shared the White House response. The Unified Strategies Commission was monitoring all media outlets and personal social media accounts. Any and all secession news would be flagged as disinformation so as not to cause panic during the looming food shortage crisis. President Blythe had teams in place to arrest the Secession Convention participants. She would make a speech tonight calming the country and assuring everyone that the United States of America was stronger than ever and the treasonous coup was under control. Jackson would sit in the front row before making the rounds with the press corp. He gave Rich a memo with updated taglines and talking points.

It comforted Madison how easily the three of them slipped into teamwork mode. It was as if no one else was in the room. They fed off of one another. They bantered and bounced ideas like they always did. They divided and conquered together. As she gazed around the room, the faces of interns all watched with looks of sheer amazement. It reminded Madison how rare a friendship this was with Jackson and Rich.

"Great job today! This was a team effort and everyone went over and above on this one. Congratulations! You were all part of history today. Call your parents and brag on yourselves. Then, grab some food and come back here if you want to watch the President's address as a team." Madison lifted her hands to applaud them.

Jackson stood and followed suit. "Ditto everything Madison said. We couldn't do this without you."

"Ditto? Really" Rich chuckled at Jackson's expense.

Jackson, in his typical way, shrugged and flashed his charming smile. Everyone in the room was under the Jackson Cashe spell. Rich rolled his eyes.

Madison's notification panel reminded her she needed to call her parents back. She picked up her phone to read all the texts she'd ignored. Daniel Lyn sent up to the minute details. The history nerd in him was in seventh heaven. The conservative in him was giddy. The father was worried. Rhett's text brought her back to reality.

Rhett: Hey! Not sure when I'll make it back to town. All roads in and out of Allied States territory are monitored by National Guardsmen. It is crazy! So much to tell you. Jake is getting ready to livestream the President's Inaugural Address from my SurfIn account. We will have front row coverage. The rest of the media is in the back.

Madison: What are you talking about? The media isn't covering any of this! The President of THE UNITED STATES is sending in troops. She's scheduled her own address for tonight. You better get out of there before you get arrested or killed! CALL ME!

Rhett: I can't. Address starting in a minute. This is actually happening. I'm not sure what you guys are being told, but the entire middle of the country is on lockdown and has a serious military presence. Have you not seen the footage of soldiers leaving barracks in droves to head to their respective states for reassignment? Your dad must be like a kid at Christmas! Go watch the livestream!

Madison growled at her phone and pursed her lips so tight they actually hurt.

"Uh oh, who is on your list? I hope it's not me." Rich scooted his chair in the opposite direction of Madison.

"Rhett Paulson is livestreaming some nut job who thinks she is the president of the new 'Allied States'. Apparently, these states have dragged their National Guards into their madness." Madison was frantically searching for Rhett's profile. "Ashleigh!"

Jackson and Rich quickly skirted around the table to watch Madison's screen. Sure enough, Rhett's live feed showed Senator Sally Blackstone addressing a crowd.

Ashleigh nervously peeked her head around the door frame. "Is everything okay? Do you need something?"

"No, and yes. Find anything you can about the military leaving their bases."

Jackson and Rich looked at each other, then back at Madison's face. "What?" they said in unison. It would have been comical under any other circumstances.

Madison filled them in on Rhett's texts. They began scanning the crowd as Jake's camera work zoomed out from the podium.

"What the? Isn't that a Justice?" Rich leaned in and looked closer.

"No. That isn't *A* Justice, that is seven Justices." Jackson ran his hand through his hair. "What on earth is happening?"

All three of their heads snapped up when Ashleigh entered the room, holding her laptop. "I think you guys are going to want to see this. Not only are they showing the Exodus, as they're calling it, but there is a rolling tally of service men and women who are signing up for Allied States duty and the number is, well, it's significant. They are also driving trucks, tanks, and flying planes to their new bases."

Madison, Jackson, and Rich spoke an entire conversation without one word escaping from their mouths. The sudden silence from her laptop made them all redirect their focus. Rhett's video was covered with a black square and a red x. His profile now showed only the twenty-four-hour lock notification for disinformation.

Chapter Thirty-Seven

"Are you kidding me!" It wasn't a question.

"Rhett, calm down." Rahemia sounded much calmer than Rhett wanted her to be right now.

"That's censorship, Rahemia! This is exactly what I'm supposed to be doing as a journalist. First, my livestream was cut off, now Jerry won't run the footage?" Rhett was spitting mad, literally and figuratively.

"The Global Media Board of Governors has placed a ban on any outlet or account covering the Secession Convention, Rhett. This is a matter of national security, coming down from the Department of Defense. Our hands are tied."

"Whose national security? Our coverage area includes the Allied States, and while we're on that subject, since when did the press take orders from the government? This isn't Nazi Germany! This isn't China! We live in the United States of America. Well, I guess technically, I'm still in the Allied States of America, but either way, the First Amendment is still in effect!" Rhett was pacing and waving his free arm as if Rahemia could see any of it. He hoped she could sense his anger through the phone.

She did. "Rhett, I know you are angry. We can talk about this when you get back to the building. Which, by the way, better be in time for your exclusive interview with Jackson Cashe tomorrow night. After your stunt today, Jerry was talking about firing you and telling the world you've gone off the rails. You need to make peace with Jerry and stop jeopardizing the entire show!"

"Now, who needs to calm down?" Rhett smirked at Rahemia's uncharacteristically verbal lecture.

He heard her take a deep, calming breath, "Rhett, get back here ASAP and keep me posted on your ETA. I'm emailing you suggested questions from Jerry that have been approved by Cashe's team. We need to be prepared. This is an important interview."

"See what I'm talking about? Since when do journalists ask pre-approved questions by the interviewee's team? Especially when that person is running for office? What are they trying to hide?" Rhett spat out the question.

Rahemia sounded exasperated, "I don't know, Rhett. Why don't you ask your girlfriend? Get. Back. To. Town." The line went dead.

Rhett stared at the phone in his hands. Rahemia had a point, but that wasn't what he really wanted to know. How had he lost sight of what made him love journalism in the first place? The bigger question he should have asked is when had Paulson the loner become Paulson the sellout? He got caught up in the game. He was Jerry's trained monkey, just as Nick said.

Rhett caught the flying ice pack before it hit his face. Jake didn't seem concerned that Rhett would miss it. They had been in sync for almost thirty years. "Relax. We can't do anything from here. Ice your face. You look terrible."

"Thanks." Rhett gently lowered himself to the couch and winced when the cold ice touched his swollen cheek and chin.

Jake went back to work on the surveillance they were still sifting through from yesterday. They needed evidence to place Ford's guy or the FBI agents at the scene. Guardsmen they interviewed saw the men mingling with the supporters and also lingering around the FF trucks, but cell phone images only showed blurry faces. The American flag pants stood out like sore thumbs, but poor fashion choices wouldn't help a terrorism charge stick.

"Trouble in paradise?" Nick walked over and handed Rhett a bottled water. "I don't think I've ever seen you and Rahemia go at it like that."

Rhett moaned, "It's not her fault. At least I don't think it is. It's Jerry. I sent Jake's footage from yesterday showing that the only danger came from the FFs and not the protestors who had been there the entire time. Heck, the protestors are still outside now tailgating. The violence left with the black trucks and the feds. Jerry told Rahemia to drop it because it was part of a federal investigation. Then I sent the footage from today's press conference, and apparently that's banned disinformation. What does that even mean? Who is banning what and why? And who gave them the power to ban anything?"

"You're getting worked up again." Jake reminded Rhett from across the room.

Rhett threw a pillow. Jake easily deflected. "Good throw. I hope that means your ribs are healing."

"Not so much." Rhett groaned as he moved the ice pack from his face to his side. "I just don't understand."

"What don't you understand?" Nick watched Rhett closely. They had been walking on pins and needles for days. Longer, really.

"I don't understand how it got to this. Unified Strategies and Global Media Whatchamacallits working under the president and DOD. Pre-approved question lists. Only allowing certain commentators to ask those questions. Actual evidence labeled as disinformation. People are literally being banned from speaking. This is groupthink 101. A gaslighting master class. How did it come to this? This isn't the news, it's, I don't know, it's boutique journalism, that's what it is. We're not telling the news anymore. We're selling it."

"I don't know, Rhett. It sounds like you understand perfectly. Businesses need customers. Customers watch the news. Businesses pay the news to help them gain customers. It's a pretty simple equation." Nick drank his coffee as he studied Rhett.

For the first time, Rhett noticed how tired Nick looked. Something burdened him, but Rhett didn't want to open the conversation that Nick really wanted to have. The same one Grammy kept trying to have. Not today.

Nick continued, "Those in power pay for what pushes their narrative. Take that new telescope a few months back. Do you remember it? The one that saw galaxies and black holes farther and longer than the mind ever thought possible. For months, we heard how amazing and mind blowing this new telescope would be for science. It would determine the origins of the world based on stars and gases and what not."

"I forgot about that. We interviewed the project development team. What ever happened to it?"

Nick chuckled, "It narrowed down, within a span of a few years, when the world began."

Rhett waited, "And?"

"And it proved exactly what the Bible stated to a tee. These scientists went out to disprove the Creation story and ended up proving it without a shadow of doubt. They tracked the stars and counted the light years, or whatever they did, and it added up perfectly in line with the Creation story. They killed the narrative. No one talks about that telescope anymore. It was moved somewhere out of the limelight. Businesses don't want to prove the existence of God. They want to be God, and they will pay whatever amount it takes to prove their worthiness. You are right about boutique journalism. Instead of the truth, you're selling shiny golden calves."

Rhett was exhausted. He was in pain. He was frustrated and tired and confused and angry and a lot of other emotions he couldn't manage to summarize even with the help of his favorite trusty thesaurus from the college bookstore. "Nick, you keep leading me down these rabbit holes. You keep finding new people to interview for this project. You and your cronies keep sending me links and hidden files. If all of this is true, why not shout it from the rooftops? Why waste your energy trying to convince me?"

Nick leaned forward, resting his elbows on his knees. "That's the question of the hour. Why am I trying to convince you? Two reasons. First, because the truth is being silenced. We *are* shouting from the rooftops, but the Jerry's and SurfIns of the world are blocking and canceling us. The Fords, Philipsens, Theopolises, and Marduks of the world aren't hiding their agendas. They are giving you exclusive interviews, telling people to eat bugs, live in pods, and believe the sky isn't blue. And they're winning. They're winning because they have the money, the advertising market, and the sensors on their side. This isn't about Democrats versus Republicans. Those divisions only help them fuel their global agenda. They have all the platforms. They are the pigs in Animal Farm writing on the Barnyard wall. Meanwhile, anyone who opposes them is silenced. They are being doxed, threatened, investigated, arrested, their livelihoods are destroyed all because they question the ever-changing barnyard wall."

"That leads me to the second reason. And most important to me. You, Rhett Paulson, the teller of truth, the exposer of corruption and hypocrisy, have become exactly what you began fighting against. You are Squealer in this story. You write the words on the barnyard wall. You write what they tell you to write and you convince others to believe it too. Just like the farm animals who ran off the farmer. They exchanged the farmer for greedy and evil pigs that treated them worse than the farmer. You blocked out the gossiping church ladies who defined you and your mother for the elites of the world who still define you and tell you what to say. I'm taking you down rabbit holes because you have an important and powerful voice, but you're using it on the wrong barnyard wall."

Rhett watched as Nick got up and walked around the room. He didn't know what to say to his mentor. He wasn't sure if he felt called out, called up, or both. Rhett looked back and forth between Nick and Jake. Neither spoke a word, but it was obvious they both had a lot to say.

"Apparently, this is wail on Rhett day. Let's go. Bring it. Jake, you want to unload on me too?" Rhett shook his head in disgust.

Jake waited a minute before sitting back in his chair and crossing his arms. "All right. I just have one question. Since we're on the topic of gossiping church ladies. I've known you practically my whole life. I've always been a believer. Alexis has always been a believer. My entire family. Your grandparents. Nick and Miriam. Heck, most of our coaches and their families were followers of Christ. Yet, instead of basing your opinion of Christians on us, you based it on a group of small-town, small-minded busybodies who no one liked anyway. I just never understood that. Actually, that has always ticked me off. Hurt my feelings a little too."

Rhett's jaw hung open as he listened in disbelief to Jake's diatribe. Jake, the level-headed, cool in the face of danger, Jake.

"Well, that felt good. I'm done. Nick, continue." Jake visibly relaxed in front of Rhett's eyes. He went back to his work like nothing had happened. Rhett turned to Nick, looking for what? He didn't know.

"Do you know why the New Testament is so powerful? Because the authors did nothing more than tell the truth. Paul didn't silence the other side or make up click bait. He simply told the truth. Every time he was questioned or imprisoned, he told his story. He connected the dots and shared his personal testimony with anyone who would listen. God didn't need Paul or anyone else to convince or trick others into believing, and he doesn't need anyone today. Paul simply reported what he saw without embellishments and applied the truth of what he knew about God and Jesus. He reported the truth and shared it with anyone who would listen. Rhett, I was a Pharisee. I put on a show every night with smoke and mirrors. Never fully telling the truth and not really even caring about the truth, only my followers. Numbers, ratings, shares, likes, all empty tokens that were void of substance. I wasn't a reporter, I was a performer. God opened my eyes and I couldn't peddle the lies anymore. My whole being yearned to share the only headline that matters, 'For God so loved the world.'"

Nick came and sat on the coffee table in front of him. "Rhett, the people in your life who have always had your back. Those of us who truly love you want you to have the peace and healing that Jesus died to give you. You fight and fight against God, yet He relentlessly pursues you. Jesus didn't come to condemn or condone. He came to save. He said, 'I am the way, the truth, and the life. No one comes to the Father except through me.' Your mother found mercy and grace freely in His open arms. She lives in peace now. You keep fighting a battle that was never yours to fight. You're like Paul before Damascus Road, wearing the right uniform, but hitting for the wrong team. At some point, you have to make a choice. You can continue living in anger, or you can have 'peace that surpasses all understanding' and live in truth. Let God heal the pain you carry and turn it into something beautiful and real. That is why we keep bringing it up. Because we love you, but God loves you more."

"Yeah, man. We love you. Stop being a jackass." Rhett watched in shock as Jake wiped a tear from his cheek.

Chapter Thirty-Eight

His skin was red from the scolding water that cascaded over him. Even the waterfall couldn't wash away the thoughts running through his mind. Rhett twisted the faucet handle as he rested his head against the cool porcelain tile.

As he pried himself from his walk-in shower oasis, thick steam hung in the air like a weighted blanket. Rhett rubbed a towel over the mirror and groaned at his reflection hiding behind wet streaks. Both fresh and faded bruises and scars covered his body. He looked and felt like he'd been in a war zone. Ironically, he'd escaped unharmed from an actual war zone when he covered a SEAL unit with Jake at the beginning of his career. It took living and working in Washington to almost kill him.

Rhett winced as he attempted to put on his shirt. One arm at a time. Even putting on sweatpants took time. He dressed in silence. WBN, muted in the background. Still no mention of the secession or the Allied States. The only headlines were the riot and the insect infestation taking out crops across the globe. Rhett balanced Nick's words against what he knew to be true. Sadly, the truth seemed upside down. He had no idea about the talking points he had inadvertently been following for years. He definitely didn't know about the strangle hold Jerry had on his programming. Of course, until recently, their intentions were the same, cover what the people wanted to raise the ratings.

Rhett thought about his mom and the revelations Grammy shared about her. What would she think of this, of him? Grammy always taught him to tell the truth and take the high road. Was he on the high road or lurking in the dirt like the snakes he hated from his youth? Wasn't he doing exactly what they did to his mom, to his family? Viewing others based on the cultural norms and passing judgement? Who was right? Who was wrong? Who was he to judge between the two? Who made him the authority on all things? Jerry? His ratings?

Rhett pounded the vanity countertop with his fist, then gasped at the pain. He dropped his head to his chest. Nick's words shook him. He spent his adult life emulating the man. He was a big brother, mentor, and father figure rolled into one. Nick allowed Rhett to see life from the other side for once. A life where Rhett could be on top, make the rules, and set the standards instead of being compared unworthy to them. Now Nick was telling him it was all a lie. Everything was a lie.

The dinging sound from the elevator doors had him running for his closet. Someone was coming. Rhett grabbed his baseball bat and waited around the corner. He attempted to regulate his breathing as the doors slid opened.

"Rhett?"

Relief rushed through his body, along with another feeling that overwhelmed him. Gliding around the corner, the bat lowered to his side. His shoulders relaxed, and he melted into the arms of Madison.

"You okay, slugger?" Madison tried to make light of it, but her voice held the tight realization they both knew. Rhett was someone's target.

"I am now." Rhett nuzzled her neck and relaxed into her. "I didn't know you were coming."

"I don't have much time. The entire party is in crisis mode. We spent all morning working on joint messaging and a counterattack. I had a small window to shower and change before the onslaught of appearances today. I needed to see you with my own eyes."

Madison leaned back and appraised her boyfriend. Her eyes showed what he felt. Bruised and broken all over. He was a shell of himself. Not even the harpies of Community Baptist made him feel this low. This time, he did it to himself.

"Rhett, really, are you okay? You don't look like yourself." Madison ran her fingers through his damp hair, pushing it from his forehead. She gently touched the bruises and cuts covering his face. "My god, you look awful. You could have been killed, Rhett. What were you doing there?"

"Looking for you."

Madison sighed, then pulled him into her arms. "I can take care of myself, you know."

"I know, but I don't think I can handle losing you right now. Everything is upside down. You bring me balance."

"Rhett, you're scaring me."

He untangled himself from her to lead them both to the couch. He sat on the edge while she studied him closely. Taking her hands in his, he took a small leap of faith. "What if I told you that everything we thought we knew was all a mirage? A lie. Like we are living in the Truman Show thinking everything is one way, but it's really not. We are actually like a herd of sheep, thinking we're in charge, but really, we're just following the invisible shepherds."

Madison's eyes, skeptical as ever, tightened as she tried to follow. "Rhett, what are you talking about?"

"What if I told you that the government is really being run by a group of elitists who call themselves philanthropists funded by their investment firms that control ninety-five percent of the global market? That we are really pawns in their game of eugenics and population control?"

Madison shook her head. Concern laced her face as she touched his cheek. "Rhett, do you have a concussion?"

Rhett launched into what he knew about the deep state operations he pieced together with Nick, Jake, and John Marchio. He told her about the jump drive, the text messages, and the clandestine meetings and tips he'd been given. She knew some of it already, but now Rhett finally had all the puzzle pieces. He just needed to put them together and show her the big picture he'd discovered. That wasn't always easy, but he'd built his career on it, so he could do it again.

Madison listened intently to every word he spoke. Every once in a while, she asked questions to clarify a point. When he finally finished, she sank back into the couch cushions and processed the information. Rhett reviewed the conversation in his head, hoping he didn't miss anything. He realized this was the first time he'd actually put it all together into one flowing story. This would be a great run through before his meeting later with Rahemia and Jerry. He watched as she shook her head, staring carefully at him.

"Rhett," Madison placed a hand on his knee, "I'm really worried about you."

He stood, rubbed his hands through his hair, and began pacing. "Madison, look, I know how it sounds. Trust me. I've been trying to wrap my head around this all day. Hell, I have been trying to explain it away for months. Every new puzzle piece, I tried connecting it to a different puzzle. This is insanity, I know it, but it's the only explanation. Honestly, once you see it, you can't unsee it. The scariest part is that they aren't even hiding it. They talk about it in their interviews and speeches. They plaster it all over their websites. They market it to us all and we buy it hook, line, and sinker. We are subjects like in the Asch Conformity studies."

"Are you listening to yourself? 'They, them?' You do realize you're talking about me? And Jackson and Rich, right? Do you really think Jackson is part of this? That I wouldn't know?" Madison's eyes clouded over. He saw it.

Rhett sat down next to her again and grabbed her hands, pleading for her to help him understand. "I don't think Jackson knows, but I'm pretty sure Hayman is on it. Some of your donors are definitely in the inner circle of this."

Now Madison got up to pace.

"Madison, please listen, not as Jackson's friend, but as my girlfriend. I trust you. I need your thoughts. I'm just as blown away by this as you are. I need you to help me process all of this. You know the players. I think you know more than you realize. You can help me stop them."

Madison closed her eyes and lowered her head. She inhaled deeply before leveling him with concerned eyes. "Rhett, I love you. I'm trying to understand what you think you know, but this is asking too much. You were almost killed three times in the past few months. You have a concussion and are under severe stress. Please don't do anything crazy until you have time to process your thoughts and you have time to think about it more. You aren't thinking clearly."

A guttural pain grew from the pit of his stomach to his burning throat. This was the moment he lost her. He lost everything he thought he wanted. Rhett had to choose between the truth or living in the illusion of what he'd built. This was his personal earthquake and he couldn't span the divide.

"Listen, I'll make you a deal. I will sit on this for today if you promise to at least consider everything I've told you. Run it by Jackson and Rich and see what they think." Rhett pleaded with her to hear him out, "Can you come over tonight? I can show you all the evidence and we can talk through it."

"I don't know. I doubt I can even get away before midnight."

"That's fine. We can make coffee and order from that Italian restaurant you love. The one with the tiramisu." Rhett flashed his charming smile at her.

Her pause gave him a glimmer of hope. "I'll have to wait and see. Rich and I are scheduled for interviews too, which is not my favorite, but necessary to make all the rounds. We have every prime time slot covered this week. Starting with your interview." Madison looked up at him, clearly rattled. "You aren't going to ask Jackson any of this on air, are you?"

Rhett hid the hurt with humor, like he always did. "I heard Jackson's crack team created a pre-approved question list for me."

Madison looked tired and concerned. "Rhett, I'm really worried about you. If I can't come tonight, I promise we'll talk tomorrow, but either way, I think you need to consider separating yourself from these people. They are going to get you killed."

"I'll be fine." Rhett rose from the couch and held out his hand. "Come on, we both need to get going."

They walked to the door in silence. As she turned to tell him goodbye, Rhett pulled her into him and held her tight. He kissed the top of her head. "Madison Lyn, you have changed my world. I love you. You know that, right?"

She looked up at him. Her chocolate eyes melting him. "I know, Rhett. I love you too." She cradled his face in her hands. "Please be careful. You're the only news jock I like."

Her smile liquefied his heart. Rhett leaned down and kissed her like it was the first and last time, etching every curve of her lips into his memory. He rested his forehead on hers. "I'll see you tonight."

***

Rhett spent the rest of the afternoon replaying their conversation. He went over every piece of evidence, every name he dropped, and every allegation he made.

He thought about the questions she asked and the faces she'd made. He knew she would come around. She had to. He needed to sit down with Jackson and Rich. They would be as reluctant to hear all of this as she was, but surely he could convince them. That's what he did. He found the truth and told the story. They would listen. They could help him right the ship. The weight of this was too heavy without Madison.

He felt the shift as soon as he entered WBN. The looks, the fake condolences for his latest accident. The younger reporters jockeyed for position, his position. After spending an hour with Jake and Oliver in his office drafting a plan, Rhett was ready to meet with Jerry. As he waited for the green light from Jerry's assistant, he texted Madison and gave her relaxation tips for her interviews and told her she would be great. She replied with heart emojis.

As he paced in his empty office, Rhett ruminated on Nick's words and Jake's. He had spent his life hating Christians based on a few people, while ignoring the people in his life whom he trusted with his life. Jake and Alexis relied on their faith as they battled infertility and miscarriage. Grammy asked God for the strength to forgive herself and others for the death of a child. The death of her only daughter. Nick and Miriam found salvation in the River Jordan. They were happier than he had ever seen them. Miriam called it pure joy. Even his mother found Jesus in a rehab center. Her sponsor told Grammy that she had been reborn and healed.

All of these loved ones had purpose and something to live for now. Rhett needed faith in something because he built his life's foundation on shifting sand, and now everything was crumbling. He needed forgiveness and joy. He needed rebirth and purpose. His whole his purpose was to prove his mother's scoffers wrong. He wanted to punish them. In the end, he only punished himself in the same prison.

Rhett gazed out over the city from his corner office. He wanted what his friends had. It wasn't enough to be near them and play the role he created. He wanted the authentic life they were actually living instead of riding along beside them. He wanted truth. Nick and Grammy told him where to find it, but Rhett fought them. He didn't have any more fight left in him.

"God, I have no idea how to do this. I don't even know what to say, and I always have something to say. Grammy walks around the house talking to you all day. She always told me she was talking to her best friend, so I guess I'll try that. I don't know anything about you other than what I've heard others say about you, and the stories Grammy read me as a kid. But if you're there and you're the real deal, I'm willing to listen. I don't want to run anymore. I want to learn who you are. If you are the truth, like Nick says, I want that. I want to know the truth. If you can hear me, and I haven't blown it with you, show me the truth. Show me what they have. I'm willing if you are." Rhett swiped a tear. "I guess that's it. Thanks."

Rhett was sure he imagined it, but it was hard to ignore the feeling of peace that rushed over him in that moment. He closed his eyes and saw their faces in front of him, Grammy and Gramps, Jake and Alexis, Nick and Miriam, his mom. He needed wisdom. He didn't know what to do with this information. For the first time since the parking garage, he actually was grateful he knew it. He didn't want to pretend it wasn't happening or explain it away. He wanted to expose it. Instead of a burden, Rhett finally saw it as a gift.

Rahemia popped her head into his office and summoned him to Jerry's. As they rode the elevator, Rahemia ran through the details for the show tonight. She gave him the list of questions and asked him if he wanted to add anything. They only had thirty minutes to add or alter any of the questions. Rhett shook his head no. He could see Rahemia watching him closely.

"Rhett, are you okay to do this tonight? This is a huge interview. Our show needs this interview. You need this interview. The country is watching us tonight. They are scared and confused and they need you to tell them that everything is going to be okay and that Jackson Cashe is the answer they need. Can you do that? If you can't, I need to know right now."

"I've got this."

She continued watching him. He could feel the nervousness flowing off of her in waves.

Rhett turned to look at her. "I've got this."

The elevator doors slid open as Jerry's assistant greeted them. Rhett watched everything in slow motion as it happened. He walked in stillness and peace. He felt like he was walking on solid rock instead of the shifting sand he had been fighting.

Cigar smoke permeated the air in the office. Jerry's gregarious voice boomed with excitement. "Rhett, my boy. Tonight is a big night for us." He came over and clapped Rhett on the back. Rhett winced in pain.

"We are ready, Jerry." Rahemia beamed between her boss and Rhett.

"Good, good. That's what I want to hear. We have prelim numbers coming in that are off the charts for tonight. Everyone wants to see this interview." Jerry sat behind his desk and lit a new cigar. He offered one to Rhett, who declined, as always.

Rahemia and Jerry reviewed the plan for the show as Rhett listened. He held up the list of questions when Jerry asked about them, but he remained silent. He would give Jerry one last chance to make this right.

"Paulson, either the cat's got your tongue or you have something big you want to say." Jerry's fat fingers brought the cigar to his lips as he pulled in the toxic vapors.

"You are correct, Jerry. I do have something I want to run by you for next week or the week after. It might ruffle some feathers, but it's an award-winning investigative piece in the making. It could spark congressional hearings which would only add to the amount of coverage. The material is deep and long ranging. We could milk this for all it is worth. And, if we buy the rights to Nick's docuseries and run it alongside, we would own the market on the coverage."

Jerry laughed, "Nick is a has-been. He's turned crazy on us. I'm not airing his nonsense, but I will hear you out if you have something."

Rhett bristled at the assault against Nick, but continued. He handed over his tablet to Rahemia, knowing Jerry couldn't be bothered with the details of swiping slides. Knowing Rahemia would share the slides that Jerry needed to see, Rhett began his proposal. Rhett spoke evenly yet passionately. He highlighted the evidence and connected all the dots. There was not one stone left unturned. One name not unmasked. He laid it all on the table for Jerry.

Rahemia looked sick to her stomach as the slides continued. Rhett wasn't sure if it was outrage over the information or fear that she would lose her job.

The verdict was still out for them both. Jerry contemplated Rhett's story board with an intense gaze as he unveiled the argument he had been building for hours.

Finally, Rhett finished. Rahemia laid the tablet on her lap and waited. Jerry broke the silence with an obnoxiously booming laugh.

"It's not April Fool's Day, but that was a doozy Paulson. I'll give you that."

"Not a joke, Jerry. This is real and verified."

"Oh, I have no doubt it's real. It fascinated me to see the details of how it all came about, and I do applaud your investigative skills on that front, but we won't be running that story."

What? Jerry knew? How?

"Paulson, we live in a global society. The powerful are saddled with regulations and policies unique to each government. They need to be released so that everyone can reap the benefits. Global capitalism helps everyone. Think about it. If the world moves to one global world power, there won't be wars, or dictators, or genocide. Everyone will have equal rights and powers. We can move about the globe as universal citizens, with one currency. We can sell goods and grow markets. We can make more money without the restrictions of government control. Everyone wins. I don't care how they do it, but I'm sure as hell glad they are. That's more money and more reach for WBN, and you, I might add."

Rhett's skin crawled. "A self-appointed global government that isn't elected by anyone? One that controls the people through AI and Pavlovian treats? That's what you support?"

"A global market system ran by people who make money from the success of said global market. Yes. Everyone benefits in that system. The people get their products, we get their money. Seems straightforward to me." Jerry took another puff.

"The farther government gets from the people, the farther the rights of the people get from the government." Rhett argued.

"Paulson, I never figured you for some sentimental, patriotic fool."

"I'm not, but I certainly don't trust politicians or big business. Both have shown repeatedly they will sell the souls of people for profit every time. They don't care if they abuse, kill, or harm their consumers as long as they have more consumers."

"Why do you care so much? You don't like politicians, this solves the problem. We have an over-population crisis, anyway. A few dead consumers won't hurt anyone. This food shortage is going to help with that."

Rahemia even gasped at Jerry's callousness, and Rhett was pretty sure she was taking Jerry's side on this one.

"Thomas Paine said, 'I become irritated at the attempt to govern mankind by force and fraud, as if they were all knaves and fools'."

"Mankind are knaves and fools! They are idiots walking around eating their over-processed garbage and watching mind numbing trash on television. The masses are uneducated, unmotivated, consumers. They want what we're selling. As long as they have their comforts and someone patting them on the head saying everything is fine, they are happy and content little worker bees."

"I'm running with this story. The people have the right to know what is happening under their noses. My contract says I have content independence and final approval."

Jerry chortled. "Your contract says you have content independence as long as you have advertisers. If you run that story, you will have zero advertisers."

Rhett stared unbelievingly at Jerry, "I have the highest ratings and the highest ad market on this network."

"Bluesky represents one hundred percent of our market share and ad revenue. They are funding the global revolution and you think they're going to pay the guy who wants to expose them? Come on Rhett."

"Someone will run with this story. If we don't air it, these people will take it to another outlet."

"They can try. I will tell you what we are going to do. We are going to bury it, just like we do with every other one of their headlines. We have the entire country thinking the secession is a right-wing solo act. By the time they ask questions, or hear differently, we'll already have an explanation waiting for them. If silence doesn't work, we are going to put every researcher we have on staff on this story in order to find, or create if we have to, as many holes as possible. We, along with every other major network, will paint anyone who pushes this narrative as crazy lunatics. They will be the punchline for jokes. They will become a cheap meme by the time I'm finished with them. That includes you, Rhett."

The room went silent. Rahemia sat paralyzed with fear. Rhett couldn't believe his ears. This was madness. He went from the top of the world to an episode of the Twilight Zone.

Jerry walked around to the front of his desk and sat. "Be reasonable Rhett. Think about this logically. I hired you because I saw a driven and over-confident go getter. You had a spark that people reacted to. Use that spark for good."

Rhett's stomach churned inside him. There was nothing good about this situation.

"Now, do we have a problem with tonight's show? Will you be able to pull yourself together for the interview with Cashe, or do I need to pull you? I'm assuming your girlfriend is my insurance policy."

Something inside of Rhett that he had never felt before gave him strength and clarity. "I'll do the show. I can interview Jackson."

"Good, good. I knew we would come to an understanding. Now, let's put this behind us and look to the future. Okay?" Jerry's cigar was dropping ash and singeing the carpet. The smell repulsed Rhett as much as the man causing it. Jerry's arrogance assumed Rhett's compliance. He seemed unflappable, but Rhett knew better now. The once powerful man lived in a glass house, and Rhett had finally seen through it.

As Rhett walked to the door with Rahemia, he silently asked, "All right, God. You gave me answers. What's next?"

Chapter Thirty-Nine

Today started out amazingly. Madison nailed her interviews this afternoon thanks to Rhett's advice and Rich's coaching. Shockingly, Hayman relied on her delegation skills for multiple projects today. President Blythe complimented her ability to coordinate chaos, and Omar Marduk's chief of staff requested a lunch meeting. She should feel on top of the world. However, she was a nervous wreck. At some point, the flip switched, and everything that could go wrong went wrong.

She'd been off her game since arriving at WBN. Nothing went as scheduled tonight. Hayman was stuck in traffic with Jackson. Rich was busy confirming details with Rhett's producer. Madison spilled coffee all over her top while driving to the building. She had Ashleigh running around trying to find something she could wear before her last interview of the day.

Madison thrived on consistency and logic, neither were in abundance tonight. Her parents were sharing posts all over social media about the secession, driving Madison insane. She sent a text asking them to stop until she could talk to them about the madness. She needed to knock sense into them before they quit their jobs and irrationally moved across the country on a farce.

On top of that, Madison's texts to Rhett weren't being answered. Oliver brought her an iced coffee per Rhett's specifications. Apparently, he was working in IT with Lucas, and his service was wonky in the basement. She'd been worried about him all day. Something was different with him this morning. Hopefully tonight she could get to the bottom of his story. He needed to get away from that secretive source, putting him in danger and feeding him lies. Madison also assumed Rhett was dealing with PTSD. She thought about finding Jake to ask his thoughts. He was also MIA tonight.

Rhett walked into the studio just as Ashleigh handed Madison a silk top with black beading around the neckline. It looked adorable. A fleeting moment of excitement over a cute new top, frustrated Madison even more. Today was not about fashion. They were on a mission to save the country.

Rhett's face visibly relaxed when he saw her. That alone made her heart soften. His bruised and cut up face called for her to reach out and gently stroke his cheek. She was head over heels for this man. From the intense burning in his eyes, she knew he felt the same.

"Hey, are you okay?" Madison wanted to say more, but didn't want to at the same time. Her wishy washiness tonight had to stop. She made a mental note to get it together. They were both at work and pushing time.

Rhett looked at her skeptically. "I'm fine. Are you okay? You look uncharacteristically frazzled."

She shrugged and pointed to her stained shirt. "I've had better days. Thank you for the coffee. I needed it. That was very sweet of you."

"I figured." His smiled warmed her all the way to her toes. "Go use my dressing room around the corner. It will be private. Oliver can take you."

Madison relaxed a little. "Thanks."

As she turned to leave, Rhett tugged on her elbow. She saw something different in his face. He had a countenance of peace she hadn't seen before. She studied him as he locked eyes with her. She squeezed his arm. "I'm worried about you."

"Don't be. My entire life, I fought to get to the top. I'm here, and realized it's not what I wanted after all. For the first time in my life, I see clearly. I can't go back to who I was. I want you to come with me, but I understand if you can't."

She felt kicked in the gut. "Rhett, I can't do this right now." He was freaking her out. Jackson and Rich were with the sound guy. Chaos and people were all around them. "You said we could talk tonight. Can this wait? Jackson needs me."

"Yeah. I'm sorry." Rhett smiled at her. His feelings were written all over his face. "Madison, I love you. You believe that, right?"

She cocked her head. "I know. Are you sure everything is all right with you? You've been through so much. Should you be rushing back to work tonight?" Hayman would murder Madison if he heard her put her boyfriend over the campaign, but she was truly concerned for Rhett.

He smiled, "I'm fine. I just needed you to know that. Go change, I have to find Jake."

Madison grabbed Oliver and ran down the hallway to Rhett's dressing room. The scent of him hit her as soon as she entered. It made her smile and warmed her all over. She took in the room and determined that this room was more like him than his own apartment. Sports memorabilia lined the walls and pictures of people he had interviewed were shelved next to his many awards. He had taped pictures on his mirror. A picture of Grammy. One with Jake and Alexis. One with Nick. And two of him with her. This was Rhett's space, and she was now intrinsically part of it. This was his place. Not the fancy penthouse. Not the life-on-display office made of glass walls. This dressing room was simple and honest and showed his heart. Just like him.

Ashleigh knocked on the door to let Madison know Jackson was already mic'd and Rich wanted her. She quickly changed and took a rare opportunity for a potty break. When she exited Rhett's bathroom, she saw a stack of books from his office. Odd. As she grabbed her things and opened the door, she almost ran into Jake and Oliver. They were carrying empty boxes. She looked at the boxes, then back at Jake.

Sadness filled Jake's eyes. He tried to speak, but nothing came out, only a reluctant shrug. Rhett's words came flying back at her. *I understand if you can't. I just needed you to know that. I'm sorry.*

Her voice pleaded with Jake to tell her she was wrong. "No, no, no, no, no. He's not. Jake, please tell me he's not doing it?"

"I'm so sorry, Madison."

She took off running back to the studio. Her legs violently shook with every step. The air sucked out of her lungs and vomit rose to her throat. The red light was on as she swung open the production door. Rich looked on as Rhett interviewed Jackson. A jump drive resting in Rhett's hand.

Poppy's restaurant was packed to capacity. It was pizza and karaoke night on the outside deck. Rhett held a sleeping baby in his left arm, and a green crayon in his right hand. He had just lost his tenth game of tic-tac-toe. Jake and Alexis were butchering a Dolly Parton classic on stage. Rhett pretended to not know them.

As the off-key duo made their way back to the table, Rhett's phone started vibrating. A face from his past flashed onto the screen. He froze. He scanned the table as all eyes watched his reaction to the call. Jake looked over Rhett's shoulder and whistled, "Here, give me the baby. You gotta get that."

Rhett excused himself and weaved his way around the building to the edge of the parking lot. He had been praying for this moment for five years. The phone had stopped ringing by the time he'd made it out of earshot. "God, not my will, but Yours be done." He held his breath as he pressed the redial button. One, two, three rings.

"Still screening calls so you don't have to deal with groupies?"

"I'm surprised you still have my number."

"Not as surprised as I am that I had to use it." The crispness in her voice broke his heart a little.

"Whatever the reason that drove you to it, it's nice to hear your voice."

"Is it?"

Rhett might be mistaken, but he thought he heard a slight tinge of hope buried underneath layers of sarcasm. "Madison, it will always be good to hear your voice."

"I hope I'm not interrupting anything."

"Just enjoying pizza with Jake and the girls. You called on the tail end of a rousing karaoke performance by Jake and Alexis."

"Those two are still torturing people with their duets?"

Rhett couldn't contain his laughter. "Sadly, yes."

"Well, I won't keep you long. I'm in need of some information, and my dad suggested I call you."

Rhett chuckled to himself. "I bet that was a hard pill to swallow."

"Not as hard as listening to my dad tell me every time he's been a guest on your little podcast."

"My little podcast is the most listened to hour in the history of media, thank you very much. Daniel Lyn is an expert in just about every topic I cover and he's a fan favorite." Rhett straightened his spine taller.

"I just think it was ridiculous that my father was your first guest. That was petty. On his part and yours."

"Your dad is brilliant, and I needed someone who could answer my civics and history questions after the Separation." Rhett countered.

"I didn't call to argue, Rhett."

"Then why did you call Madison?"

"This was a mistake. I shouldn't have called. I'm sorry to bother you. Please apologize to Jake, Alexis, and your date."

"Madison, wait. You have me on the phone. I want to help. Please, ask me anything."

He nervously waited to see if her pause would turn into words or the click of disconnection.

"I can't say much over the phone, but I need to know more information about the topic we discussed in your apartment. The last day was saw each other. Do you remember that conversation?"

"That conversation will be etched into my memory for the rest of my life." Rhett couldn't hide the regret.

Madison sighed, "Right, well, do you specifically remember the information you told me? The story you promised to sit on until we could talk, but then you ambushed my best friend on national television over it. That information?"

"Yes, Madison, I remember. I also remember baring my soul and begging you to help me, but you asked me to follow your rules. Rules that I knew were dangerous. I also remember calling you relentlessly for weeks afterwards, begging you to listen to me." Rhett's voice rose in the parking lot, startling a teenage couple walking to their car.

"You are such an ass, Rhett! You broke a promise. You humiliated me. You hurt the campaign."

Rhett interrupted loudly, "He won!"

"That's not the point, and you know it. You betrayed me." Madison lost her composure, obviously not wanting that last line to slip out.

"I know, and I'm sorry. So very sorry."

The silence cut through him like a sharp knife. He couldn't bear knowing that he hurt her. "Madison, I truly am sorry. I wish I could have handled that night differently. I have replayed it in my mind over and over, but that was the only way I could stop the train. Jerry was going to fire me after the interview. I was a liability to him. I had to get out the truth before he destroyed my reputation and silenced the story."

"He destroyed it anyway. Your name was mud, and so was mine for a while. Jackson and Rich stood by me. You left." Madison's voice quivered.

"Hurting you was never part of the plan. It was the worst night of my life, but I wouldn't change what I did. That night gutted me. I'm so sorry. I wish you believed me."

"Thanks."

"I can help you if you still want to talk to me. I remember the conversation. What do you need to know?"

"Everything. I need to know everything, again. Is there any way we can meet? I can't discuss this over the phone."

Rhett was worried about her safety now. "I understand. That's probably best. I've been told by Jackson's Secret Service detail I will be arrested if I cross over into the US border. Can you meet me in Allied States territory?"

Madison chuckled, "Yeah, Jackson has you on a special list. You definitely shouldn't cross the border."

"I can leave right now and be in Martinsburg in three hours. Can you meet tonight? There is an all-night diner I know outside of town."

"Your date might not appreciate you ditching her."

Rhett laughed. "The girls I referred to earlier are my goddaughters. Jake and Alexis's girls. I can buy them off with ice cream. If only ice cream could fix things with you."

Madison was quiet again.

"Madison, please let me help. I can be there by nine if I leave now."

"Okay, text me an address. And, Rhett, thank you."

Rhett kissed his goddaughters goodbye and ignored the relentless teasing from Jake and Alexis. They understood how long he had been waiting for this call. Rhett made it to the diner in record time. He pulled out his Bible to read and pray while he waited for Madison.

"Abba, I need You to take the lead on this one. I don't know where she is or how much she knows, but You do. Please guide our conversation. Please use me to share Your Truth with Madison. I want her to forgive me, but more importantly, I want her to know You. I pray this in Jesus's name. Amen."

Jake ordered two pieces of pecan pie and waited. As his coffee grew cold, he worried Madison changed her mind. When the door opened and she walked in, his heart stopped. She was even more breathtaking than he remembered. And he remembered a lot.

Rhett stood. It took everything in him not to wrap her in his arms, but he knew she would probably punch him. Awkwardly, he waited as Madison walked to the back of the diner, where he snagged a table out of sight.

A baseball hat shielded her eyes from him, but she couldn't hide the tiniest of smiles. "Rhett Paulson, news jock turned podcast pirate."

His smiled was uncontainable. "Podcast pirate? I guess I've been called worse."

"You've definitely been called worse by me." Madison held out her hand. "Thanks for meeting me. I really appreciate it."

Shaking her hand wasn't what he wanted, but Rhett would take what he could get. "That's fair. I'm sure Rich and Jackson had plenty of words for me, too."

"You have no idea. You're lucky Jackson didn't send special forces after you." Madison shrugged as she scooted into the booth. She eyed the pie. "Grammy, ruined all pecan pies for me. No one can measure up to hers."

Madison could still melt him into mush. "She'll be happy to hear that. So, I'm dying to hear what made you so desperate you had to call me."

"Your buddy Governor Marchio and Jackson have been working together on Reunification plans. The first summit went well, the second is being torpedoed by the Allied States. All of which, I'm sure you know. Anyway, in the process, he gave Jackson a list of names and leads to follow. It was my job to verify the intel. As you can imagine, the rabbit hole took many twists and turns, but ended at the same place. The Global Alliance. I called my dad. He told me I had to call you to apologize if I wanted the truth. Go ahead, say I told you so, and let's get on with it."

Rhett loved Daniel Lyn so much at this moment. "Madison, I'm just grateful you called at all. I know it must have been hard. I've spent every day since the interview praying you could forgive me. Saying 'I told you so' implies a winner and a loser. Five years ago, I lost you, so I don't feel like the winner. I feel more like the loser."

"Rhett." Her eyes begged him to stop. "I can't go there. It was too hard. Can we just stick to the topic for now?"

Sadness and regret engulfed him, but he deserved it. He also couldn't help what vomited out next. "I will stick to the topic, but I can't promise to stop praying for you to be back in my life. I still love you, Madison. I never stopped. You are the most extraordinary woman I've ever known. I need you to know that, but I understand you not wanting to talk about it. Now, how far down the rabbit hole are you? And how can I help?"

"Rhett."

He held up his hand to stop her. "No, really. I understand, and I deserve it. You don't have to say anything, especially if it will break my heart or bruise my sensitive ego. You know how fragile news jocks can get. Now, how can I help you solve your puzzle?"

Madison softened a little. He could see it in her eyes, but her guard remained firmly in place. Rhett expected nothing less. He pointed to the plate in front of her as he pulled out a notepad. "Eat your pie and put away your tablet. They're tracking your search history."

Madison and Rhett talked all night. He did his best to fill in the blanks left by John Marchio. He drew diagrams and made lists. He connected every dot between the Ten Rulers, the Bad Three, the End Plan, and the Muddy Water Money Bags. He coined the terms and based most of his podcasts on exposing them. He explained how he, Jake, and Oliver drove a mobile studio around the region to bounce their broadcast signals off a series of towers and satellites to keep them safe and untraceable.

They caught each other up to date on their lives. Rhett had watched her career closely. They both realized what a sneaky match maker Daniel Lyn had been over the years. While their lives kept them separated on the surface, their paths skirted close frequently, but she had no idea just how close. Jackson's personal life brought their team to West Virginia frequently. Rhett, Jake, and Alexis kept their distance whenever Madison was present, out of respect for her.

Madison blew him away with her questions and ability to process everything he threw at her. Pie turned into burgers and fries, then milkshakes and a steady stream of coffee. They didn't discuss their feelings again, but Madison's laughter and teasing gave Rhett a glimmer of hope.

He shared his faith journey with her. It wasn't easy, but following the Truth became his greatest priority after Jerry ran him out of D.C. and he ended up living with Grammy until he got back on his feet. Madison acknowledged he had a countenance of peace about him and told him it looked good on him. That encouraged Rhett.

Nine hours later, Madison left in the morning light with the truth and a job offer. Rhett left with forgiveness and hope.

***

Five Months Later

Rhett flipped through his notes beside his mic stand. "Are you ready for this?"

"I think the better question is if Jackson's ready?" Madison drank the iced tea Grammy made for her while she checked her phone for updates.

"Can you ever be ready for an announcement like this?"

"It's definitely historic. He's en route with Haddie right now. They should be here in five minutes." Maddie gathered her own show notes and placed them beside her mic stand.

"You've made your own history this month. You should be very proud of yourself. Your dad is, and so am I." Rhett reclined in his studio chair to watch her prepare for their show.

"Most news jocks wouldn't offer their ex-girlfriend a co-host spot on their podcast. Then celebrate her spiking his ratings higher than anything he'd experienced since the show's beginning."

Rhett laughed out loud. "You'll never let me live that down, will you?"

"Absolutely not." Madison's smile warmed the entire studio.

"Well, we make a pretty good team, Miss Lyn. I'm honored to be on your show."

Rhett looked up, expecting Madison's comeback. It never came. Instead, he caught her studying him.

"You okay? Did I say something wrong?"

"You mean that, don't you?" Madison watched Rhett.

"What? That I'm honored to be in your presence? Yes. I've felt that way since I heard your voice behind an ER curtain five years ago. You amaze me every day. I've never met anyone like you, Madison Lyn. You make everything better, including me."

She walked over and leaned against the table beside his chair. "I was so angry at you for five years. I'm talking, cursing your name, mad at you because I thought you betrayed me. When really, I betrayed you. I didn't listen when you tried to tell me. Then I had to crawl back to you and ask for your help. You never rubbed it in my face. Never said 'I told you so.' You offered me forgiveness and a job. Why?"

"Madison, I spent my entire life angry at people and God for what happened to me as a kid. I pretended nothing mattered to me but fighting for the truth. Turns out, instead of seeking it, I was actually running from the Truth. God chased me down and offered me forgiveness. I'm not the same person I was then, and I don't want to be. One thing hasn't changed, how I feel about you."

Madison instinctively brushed a wild strand of hair from his forehead before pulling her hand back. Rhett tentatively reached out and placed her hand in his.

"You give everything you have to others. You busted your tail in school to honor the sacrifices of your grandparents and parents. You've spent the last decade of your life protecting and promoting Jackson and Rich. You give and give to everyone else, working and striving and fighting to meet every obstacle and every goal in your path. I just want to be a part of your world. I don't want to be the news jock anymore. I want to be the cheerleader. I want to be your cheerleader, Madison. Please, let me be that for you. I promise I won't screw it up again."

She swiped at a tear peeking out from the corner of her eye. Before he knew what happened, Madison slid onto his lap and took his face in her hands. "You're pretty special yourself, Rhett Paulson. And I promise I won't screw it up again, either."

Rhett pulled Madison close as she lowered her lips to his. They kissed like they needed air and the other person was oxygen. It was mixed with tears, forgiveness, and promise. When they came apart, Rhett wiped the tears from her cheeks.

"I love you, Madison."

"I know. And I love you, too. So very much."

She rested her forehead on his as they caught their breath and relished the moment. Madison felt so right in his arms. He would never let her go.

Jake's voice came through the speaker beside them. "Thank God. I can't wait to text Alexis."

Madison and Rhett started laughing as the door to the studio opened.

Rich's voice, louder than ever, yelled. "You owe me twenty bucks. They're in here making out. I told you they'd get back together."

Rhett kissed Madison again. "I think we need to go on a vacation. Alone."

"Agreed." She kissed his nose, " Now, let's get this show started."

Until next time.....

Author's Notes and Acknowledgements

Dear reader, thank you for sharing your precious time with me, it is an honor I don't take lightly.

Thank you to my editors, beta readers, and cheering section who keep me on track and make me a better writer. I could not do this without you! Thank you to my family who listens to me chatter on about formatting, cover design, and other ins and outs of this business. Thank you for waiting to eat so I could finish "just one more paragraph." Thank you to my faithful readers who asked about this book and pushed me forward. Thank you to my prayer warrior friends who prayed as I wrote Truth Seeker, this was a hard one to write.

All of my books up to this point have been inspired by women from the Bible. I loved watching Haddie (Esther) stand up for Jesus. The love story in Ruthie's Daughter blossomed from the seeds of dedication and loyalty like Boaz and Ruth. Frankie's Confections (Dinah) taught me that forgiveness is sweeter than revenge. When I met Rhett Paulson, I was overwhelmed by how his life resembled that of Paul's. An expert in his field, fighting for what he believed was right, and at complete opposition to the Christian faith. Until. Until God opened his eyes on the road to Damascus. You see, once you meet Jesus and feel His presence, you can't help but give your life to Him. That's what Paul did after three days and that's what Rhett does by the end of Truth Seeker after three near death experiences.

In complete transparency, dear friend, I did not want to write this book. I didn't want to write a book about Paul (talk about intimidating and overwhelming), and I certainly didn't want to write a political book in the midst of current events. I politely asked God to let someone else write it, I was good with my current book leads. But God (whew, how much of my life has been defined by those two words....BUT GOD) wouldn't let me write anything else. I dreamt of Rhett's story at night. I saw it in things around me. Every new story idea I brainstormed circled right back to Rhett and Madison. The words were blocked from every other project I tried to write. When I finally gave in and tried to be obedient (acting like a stubborn toddler, no less), the words poured out of me. I couldn't stop writing about Rhett and Madison. Both with noble ideas and good hearts, perfectly matched in every way, being divided by the political landscape. Sound familiar?

An underlying theme of Truth Seeker is church hurt and modern-day-community-shunning. I could write about Grammy Paulson sitting off to the side in her chair, because I've sat there myself. You've heard the saying, hurt people hurt people? Well, they've got nothing on "perfect" people compelled to help the imperfect. If you've been hurt by the church or "church people" in the past like Rhett, please don't judge the overwhelming love of Christ against flawed humans. Christians are not perfect (even if a few claim to be). Find a new church that teaches the Bible.

The entire premise of Truth Seeker is just that, seeking truth. Where are you getting your information? Are you seeking from a world view or a WORD view? God promises wisdom and discernment, so if you spend your days seeking Him, He will show you the truth. If you're following the world you're getting fed a diet of lies and deception. You see, we can't serve two masters. At some point, we have to choose between the world and the WORD. One will always let us down and tell us we're not enough. It will require more and more sacrifices in order to meet its constantly shifting benchmarks and standards. On the other side, the Bible has withstood the test of time and attack, yet it remains unchanged. It promises truth, joy, peace, comfort, provision, blessing, and everlasting life. God only asks for our hearts in return, but He will treat them as His treasured possession. We must only believe that we are all messy and flawed, but the Man on the middle cross paid for our invitation. We simply have to accept it.

I pray that instead of listening to the commentators and influencers shouting at us every day, we all spend more time in the WORD of God. That we listen to Paul in Philippians 4:8 "Finally brothers, whatever is true, whatever is honorable, whatever is just, whatever is pure, whatever is lovely, whatever is commendable, if there is any excellence, if there is anything worthy of praise, think about these things." Just like Rhett, when God reveals His truth, you can't help but be radically changed by it.

I am grateful for the Bible teachers in my life who lived their lives for Christ based on the Word of God. If you want to know the TRUTH.....go to the source! Compare everything to the Bible! Thank you God for the shepherds, the servants, the warriors, and the fighters for the Truth!

In a world of so-called experts I'd rather be a Truth Seeker!

From the bottom of my heart, thank you and I love you!

Other Books by Amy

Vineyard Seeds Series:
Future FLOTUS?
Ruthie's Daughter
Frankie's Confections

Thank you for reading!
If you enjoyed *Truth Seeker*, please take a minute and write a review. As a new
author, your recommendation means the most to me!
Check out www.amydensonbooks.com for other books and updates!
I am an Indie author. I am human. My beta readers and editors are human. If
you catch a typo, please shoot me an email and let me know (amydensonbook
s@gmail.com).
Thanks, friend!

About the Author

Amy Denson grew up in a big Italian family from West Virginia. She loves hearing and telling stories about her family history. Her Nunnie and mother taught her to love Jesus with all her heart. She loves cooking, reading, writing, and learning. In her spare time (obvious sarcasm), Amy is the mom to four kids, a lovely daughter-in-law, one scrappy dog, and another dog who thinks she's a cat. She is married to her college sweetheart. Together, they ride the unpredictable rollercoaster of life, hanging on by the seats of their pants. Amy loves spending time with her friends and family, usually around a table breaking bread and laughing a lot.

www.ingramcontent.com/pod-product-compliance
Lightning Source LLC
Chambersburg PA
CBHW072056190726
48294CB00005B/1557